Rhys Davies (1901–1978) was one of the most prolific and unusual writers to emerge from the Welsh industrial valleys in the twentieth century. Born in Clydach Vale, a tributary valley of the Rhondda arising from Tonypandy, he was the fourth child of a small grocer and an uncertified schoolteacher. He spurned conventional education and left the valley, which was to be the basis of much of his work, at the age of nineteen, settling in London, which was to remain his base until he died.

Early in his literary career, he travelled to the south of France where he was befriended by D. H. Lawrence, who remained an influence in his writing. Though sex remained, for Davies, the primary determinant of human relations, he differed radically from Lawrence in that he saw the struggle for power rather than love, either sexual or emotional, as the crucial factor.

Though the bulk of his work was in the novel he achieved his greatest distinction in the field of the short story. Having few predecessors, Welsh or English, he drew his inspiration and models from continental European and Russian masters; Chekhov and Maupassant, Tolstoy and Flaubert. His view of humanity was Classical in that he saw people as being identically motivated whether in biblical Israel, Ancient Greece or the Rhondda valley. Much of his output was concerned with women, who would almost invariably emerge triumphant from any conflict.

He was a gay man at a time when it was difficult to live openly with his sexuality. He lived alone for most of his life and avoided relationships which seemed to betoken commitment on his part. His closest friendships were with women. He avoided literary coteries and groups, though he might have joined several, and held no discernible religious or political convictions. He lived, to an intense degree, for his art.

A TIME TO LAUGH

PARTHIAN

LIBRARY OF WALES

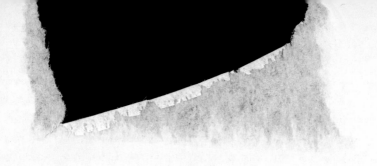

A TIME TO LAUGH

RHYS DAVIES

PARTHIAN

LIBRARY OF WALES

Parthian, Cardigan SA43 1ED
www.parthianbooks.com
The Library of Wales is a Welsh Government initiative which highlights and celebrates
Wales' literary heritage in the English language.
Published with the financial support of the Welsh Books Council.
Series Editor: Dai Smith
First published in 1937
© Rhys Davies Trust
Foreword © 2014 Chris Williams
Library of Wales edition 2014
ISBN 9781910409114
Cover design: Marc Jennings
Typeset by Elaine Sharples
Printed and bound by Gwasg Gomer, Llandysul, Wales

FOREWORD

I live seven miles by road from Rhys Davies's boyhood home – what was once The Royal Stores, Clydach Road — in Clydach Vale. It's a steep climb on a bike, even when you start in Pontypridd. Thirty-five minutes there, but only twenty minutes back, so that gives you some idea of the gradient. But when you arrive, heart pounding and out of breath, you're in the world of *A Time to Laugh*. The mines have gone, there are some incongruous new buildings – not many – there are some derelict old buildings – too many – but this is recognisably the built landscape Rhys Davies described when he wrote about it in the 1930s.

A Time to Laugh itself is set in the 1890s: its closing pages herald the beginning of the new century. So Rhys Davies (born 1901) did not enjoy eye-witness knowledge of the years about which he wrote here, but that matters little. The events which are packed into its seven chapters stand for the period between the introduction of the Sliding Scale system for determining miners' wages by the sale price of coal in 1875 and the outbreak of the First World War in 1914. The fact that the author could recall the Cambrian Combine strike of 1910-11 and the Tonypandy Riots of November 1910 allowed him to draw on these episodes for his vivid opening scenes.

The novel is almost entirely set in Clydach Vale and mid Rhondda, with the occasional sortie into neighbouring valleys, and one section set in Bristol. It's almost what Davies described (in his 1969 autobiography *Print of a Hare's Foot*) as a 'sealed valley' – what sociologists would later refer to as an 'isolated mass' or an 'occupational community'.

A Time to Laugh is clearly, defiantly, a Welsh novel: one episode has the miners noting that 'still the mountains were theirs' after

i

turning back 'the interfering invaders' (the cavalry). But Rhys Davies was not writing predominantly for a Welsh audience. My second-hand copy spent many years (from 1939 to 1981) on the shelves of Fulham Central Library (and in the homes of its borrowers). Davies once used the phrase 'Down with passports to Art!' to deny that he was 'an Anglo-Welsh writer' (his preferred term was simply 'a writer'). But with *A Time to Laugh* he provided his readers, few of whom could have shared his intimate knowledge of his 'truly democratic valley', with a passport to Wales's own El Dorado of the Rhondda.

Yet Davies does not write from the epicentre of that community. He is the boy in the upstairs window above his father's grocery stores, gazing out, looking down on the miners and their families as they go about their epic struggle for humanity. Neither he nor the novel's central character Tudor Morris are 'of' the workers, and although Davies defined his family's position as 'neutral but threatened', for many others of the mid Rhondda shopocracy the strikers' verdict as to their 'neutrality' was delivered in the form of a volley of flints shattering plate glass windows. Perhaps Davies's semi-detachment allows him to lay bare what he evidently felt was the scarcely suppressed violence ('bitter ferocity', 'savage beliefs') lurking beneath the surface of mining communities. He is not unsympathetic to the rioters, but he does not shy away from suggesting that the rioting (and looting) was not always guided by motives which social historians would later be able to explain as the 'moral economy' of the crowd: 'private enmities broke into lawless behaviour'. Elsewhere in 1937 (in *My Wales*) he would write of the Rhondda's strikes and riots that 'probably in times to come those ugly chapters will acquire a significance pertaining to a religious crusade', but for him, at that time, it was 'a sombre past'.

A Time to Laugh is the middle volume in what has become known as Davies's 'Rhondda trilogy', the others being *Honey and Bread* (1935), set in the early decades of the nineteenth century, and *Jubilee Blues* (1938), which begins in 1925. *Honey and Bread* ended with the character of Bronwen about to give birth to Tudor's father Elwyn, with 'shouts and noise and movement ... all about them – the clamour of new, changing life surging everywhere all through the valley.' By the time of *Jubilee Blues* Tudor is in his fifties and 'still a socialist' although 'his idealism had almost gone'. But one need not have read *Honey and Bread* to understand *A Time to Laugh*, nor should knowledge of *Jubilee Blues* be permitted to clarify or confuse the messages one takes from its immediate predecessor.

In his trilogy Rhys Davies came to terms with the narrative arc of 'the rise, decline, and fall of an industrial civilization' – 'a struggle which is the very breath of modern life' (*My Wales*). It was this 'strangely exhilarating' 'vital chronicle', containing 'elements of nobility, passion, determination, and bravery' which, for Davies, connected Wales to the rest of the world. And it is in *A Time to Laugh* that we see these qualities at their starkest and most glorious in the depiction of a society that 'stank with abundant life'. For it was in that late Victorian / Edwardian moment that that society was burgeoning, prosperous, undefeated, pregnant with possibilities.

Tudor Morris is attracted by that life, vital, unrestrained and vivid. He wants real and honest passion, heedless of puritanical ethics and inhibitions. Tudor's father Elwyn has a reproduction of the late Victorian favourite George Frederick Watts's 'Hope' hanging above his 'collection of oppressive books' in his study. His son's more radical tastes in art encompass the satirical cartoonist Thomas Rowlandson, the visionary William Blake and the controversial Aubrey Beardsley. In renouncing the privileged opportunities into which he had been born, in following the democratic instinct he senses in the spirit of the colliers and their families Tudor comes to socialism. His socialism is not an abstract, arid creed but one put into practice through guiding and advising the miners and by providing them and their families with medical care. The ideological core to the novel is provided by the 'subversive' Melville Walters, who brokers Tudor's engagement with the colliers and who bears the autodidact's awareness of the coalfield's working-class heritage. Rhys Davies knew revolutionaries: Clydach Vale's Marxian Club (the legacy of a rare Welsh interest in the Social Democratic Federation) was on Court Street, within a pebble's lob of the Royal Stores.

The idea that a doctor such as Morris would have had the opportunity to exert such influence in the 1890s as is suggested here stretches credulity: they had their own Member of Parliament by this time in the substantial form of William Abraham ('Mabon'). Yet, redressing the balance of historical fidelity, one can identify elements of the characters of the coalowners D. A. Thomas and W. T. Lewis and the colliery manager Leonard Llewelyn mixed up in the fictional creations of C. P. Meredith, John Johns and Sir Rufus Morgan. We get a strong sense of the associational flavour of Rhondda life – the cricket club, the ambulance brigade, the naturalist society. And the novel is full of period detail: Osborne biscuits, phonographs, fried fish shops, 'imperial moustaches' in the plural, shag tobacco, brake-rides, life preservers and 'striped blancmange shape'. The scarred landscape is powerfully conveyed: this is a society experienced not just on the streets but on the hillsides above the terraces, in the rocky clefts, in the man-made quarries and amidst the industrial spoil heaps, the tips.

And the human society itself? This is no collective monolith. *A Time to Laugh* is full of people. Over a hundred characters are named – colliers, patients, husbands, wives, shopkeepers, mine officials, revivalists and marble-swallowing adolescents. There's a Noah and a Nellie, a Bertha and a Beriah, a Melville and a Myfanwy; there are Beynons, Bowens, Clarkes and Pratts, and behind them, implicitly, hundreds more – individuals and families together constituting a 'raucous, teeming valley'.

Perhaps the novel's greatest achievement is in the laying bare of the diverse social gradations of this community. There are so many strata, such fine grained distinctions: Max Weber would have been impressed. It is a society with two main languages, even if one is clearly already dominant. Notwithstanding the 'thin brotherhood of the mines' it remains aware of ethnic markers: Welsh, English ('Bristols'), 'raw' Irish. There are the religious and the agnostic, the church-goers and the chapel-goers, the Baptists and the Congregationalists (the blanket anonymity of 'Nonconformity' is explicitly refused). The young men swear, sit in their pit clothes in the pub and don't attend chapel. Bay windows, lace curtains, fine furniture, 'corpulent umbrellas' and 'frisky aspidistras' are markers of respectability and elevated status, semi-detached houses and villas clear expressions of income differentials. Few works of fiction focused on the South Wales coalfield have captured so convincingly that society's multiple layering.

A Time to Laugh is also a novel about love, sex and power between men and women. The closest the inaccessible and inhibited solicitor's daughter Mildred comes to animal passion is the squirrel's fur she wears around her neck, but Tudor still treats her with an unbecoming brutality, manhandling her more than once ('he suddenly … touched her sexually') and deliberately offending her (' "bugger off to the kitchen" '). Tudor's behaviour towards Melville's sister Daisy's 'athletic glowing body' is assumptive and proprietorial ('he put out his hand and touched her breast'), but where the 'fastidious' Mildred shrinks from physical love the 'elemental' Daisy revels in it. Their first bout of passion in a bed as 'high and substantial as a boxing-ring' is profoundly rewarding for them both – 'she was luxuriously roused', he 'aware … of a most satisfying sense of excellency in the world'. Their accidental post-coital discovery in a police raid on the house Daisy shares with her brother prompts a crisis in the Morris family: Tudor's father suggests he finds a job in Pembrokeshire, his mother has 'a slight stroke'. Tudor worries Daisy might become 'a cosy slattern', but a bout of love-making al fresco carries him beyond doubt. Daisy is a force of nature, she 'smells like a young tree after rain', and Tudor is free to treat 'her superb body as though it were put on the earth merely to illustrate technical accomplishments of love'.

This is not an enlightened novel in terms of gender relations and sexual politics. Tudor Morris is ill-at-ease with the working-class abortionist Violet Fox, unlike the Promethean colliery manager C. P. Meredith, and admits he 'had never devoted any thought to the female aspect of socialism'. 'Women are best for staying at home' affirms Daisy, whose ambition is instead to go to bed with Tudor every night and bear him a dozen children. 'Cantankerous wives' are a brake on collective action, the forty-year-old 'day-woman' Hannah 'liked being pulled about schoolgirl fashion', and it is said that one character 'was a wife-beater *without reason*' (my emphasis). Should we accept this simply as an accurate depiction of the undoubted imbalance of power in mining communities in the 1890s? Or could it reveal an author striving for a heterosexual persona, generating a smokescreen of machismo in the process?

Does Tudor Morris succeed in his quest to 'wrest something remarkable out of the world, something that was granted very seldom'? When we leave him and Daisy in the early hours of New Year's Day, on the cusp of a new century, it was still possible he might. Whatever, his future is that of the people of his valley: 'They were the world with its beauty, mystery and pain; they fought and yielded, they were garlanded and they were battered. They had the full tarnished brilliance of life in them.' They would need it in the century that was about to break over them.

Chris Williams

A TIME TO LAUGH

RHYS DAVIES

CHAPTER I

I

SUDDENLY there was a huge sound of smashed glass and the window of the shop at the corner dropped in fragments to the road. The stiff double row of policemen ranked in the street, headed by a sergeant with tense reddish moustaches, received a growled order: the rank jumped into movement and, batons drawn, went careering round the corner opposite the shop, where the rioters had advanced from one of the lanes backing the main street.

The gang of rioters was already at the far end of the lane, a mass of crouched figures ragged in the early evening light. But the policemen were young athletic chaps whose stomachs had been receiving proper nourishment: they pursued like eagles. In two minutes they were among the scuffled rioters and distributing cracks successfully.

Yells, oaths and groans filled the bleak January air. Policemen roared, kicked on their fed bellies and swiped vengefully across jaws; rioters yelled with the scratched hysteria of men fed for days on rage—but they were laid low, red-flecked foam at their lips. They tumbled like dummies to the ground. But half of the gang got away, plunging round the end of the lane; they were allowed to escape. A good catch remained, some already recovering from a brief knock-out and promptly handcuffed.

The policemen trundled their captives back into the main street; some had to be carried. The mounted sergeant, left with half a dozen protectors in this dangerous thoroughfare, nodded approvingly. The upstairs windows above the closed and

1

threatened shops were full of watching faces—the tradespeople and their families, neutral but threatened, owning goods needed for empty insides and shivering bodies.

But suddenly from the corner at the other end of this shopping-centre, a new swelled horde appeared, flints in hands and loaded in pockets. The sergeant's swift order cracked the air: the policemen abandoned their captives and advanced again with their bristling batons. A voice cried out with harsh power among the rioters:

"Smash, boys, smash! Them or us. At them! Keep it up."

They met. Flints whirled and truncheons crashed. The sergeant, a reared dark bulk stiff upon his horse, trampled into the midst of the roaring fray. Flints met shop windows and the sound of smashed glass cracked the air. Children were hastily withdrawn from the upper windows, and now only pale, helpless women's faces peered forth watchfully: the men-folk had gone below to guard their property as well they could.

"Kill the bastards!" screamed the powerful voice, now scarcely human.

The sergeant, riding bulkily above the writhing dark mass of the battle, was soon wrecked. Struck, he shuddered, drooped, slid down and sagged among arms that were raised like spears all about the amazed mare.... A fist crashed with a sickening thud among the imperial moustaches, and the fine body was chucked into the door space of a house wedged among the shops.

Triumphant, the rioters stared round. Some slavered with blood, others could scarcely see. Dark blue uniformed bodies sprawled on the road. The great gang of rioters, cunningly peering round in that moment of respite when a strange silence fell through the street, tested their bitter success with a sensual exaltation. Then immediately rose the cry:

"At the windows!"

Used flints were again picked up. The riderless mare fled at a gallop, but leaping with delicacy over the sprawled uniforms on the road. A series of splintering noises sprang along the streets:

window after window fell in, fell out, and boots ground among the glass on the pavement. Doorways were smashed in. From the upper floor, shopkeeping wives saw the rioters infest the wares in opposite gaping windows like swarms of rats.

The two food-stuff shops were the most favoured. In one window a display of tinned foods—tomatoes, salmon, plums and such-like—disappeared in a twinkling. They did not stop at the windows, but crammed into the shops, and thereafter a rioter emerged with a ham under his arm, another with a mass of butter hastily wrapped, another with tins of biscuits.... Happy cries filled the darkening street.

Butcher, draper, tobacconist, hosier, baker—each shop spurted goods out into the road. The burly draper, William Matthews, appeared on the half-way landing of the staircase in his shop and brandished a rifle at the rioters, purple of face. They roared laughter at him; he flung the empty rifle at them, screamed, "Swine of thieves", and sprang, headlong with helpless rage, back up the stairs. For his insult he paid dearly; they needlessly wrecked his shop and tore up those women's costumes and blouses which they could not take away. The tobacconist, Eddie Curl, who had at one time worked in the mines, attempted a deprecating appeal: "Now, boys, you know I'm with you. Go and steal off Shenkin next door. Very rich he is and I'm only a beginner...." Perhaps if he had not been a tobacconist they would have been lenient with him. Weeping, he was hustled back into the living-room behind his shop.

The more discreet rioters had laden themselves quickly and disappeared; the successful coup might be a short-lived one. Policemen were recovering in the roadway and slinking off.... But no relieving force arrived in the bleak vale. For an hour the rioters plundered, some enjoying themselves on the spot off cheese, bread and the newly discovered taste of butter.... They smoked, and fitted themselves with caps at the hosier's mirror; one man succeeded in donning the jackets of three women's costumes and, carrying the skirts and a great pile of nondescript

3

towelling, underwear and odd blouses, staggered out of the draper's like a clown in a sinister pantomime.

At last they were gone. The street, strewn with broken glass and goods from the shops, stood struck in a desolate silence. It was almost dark now. None of the policemen remained; those who had not recovered had been borne off by their more fortunate mates: the meagre police station, that had not been built in preparation for such a business as these riots, was not far off down the road. The sergeant was one of the last to gain consciousness.

And nearly all the gas-lamps in the street had been smashed. The lighter came along in trepidation with his long pole, muttering personal little threats before him in case any rioter still lurked in the dark doorways. At last he found a lamp which functioned. It shed a wan gleam across the hacked street. Splintered glass and oddments thrown out of the shops were strewn everywhere: women's stockings, men's pants, dummy packets of cocoa, cigarettes and, abandoned for some reason, a large dirty leg of mutton. Joshua Jones, the lamplighter, stared at the joint desirously, but shook his head. The pallid face of Andrews the baker peered out of his splintered doorway.

"They are gone?" he asked hoarsely, "the...the..." But he curbed himself. It was dangerous to express abuse.

"Aye," muttered Joshua, "apes and demons as they are." He was a strict chapel-man of law and order.

"S'sh," warned Andrews, "you never know where they're hiding."

"The lamps all smashed!" cried Joshua indignantly, as if he owned them.

"Ha," whined Andrews, "and where's my bread and cakes gone!" Angrily he peered up and down the street. Two or three shopkeepers were venturing forth to examine the damage. None of them appeared excited now; there was the calm after the passing of the whirlwind. They bemoaned and swore a little, but accepted the calamity with that strange perverse indifference that people feel after a wholesale destruction of property—providing their own flesh and bones are left intact.

Then high on a low slope of the mountain far down the vale crimson and yellow flames began to shoot, a livid mass of fire that made the mountains around shine in a green splendour.

"Jesus!" somebody shouted, "they've got hold of C.P.'s house."

The mansion of C. P. Meredith, the general manager of one of the collieries, stood isolated on that slope, an ugly mongrel of a dwelling that sprawled offensively amid one of the few little woods still left on the valley sides. It was raw and new and sham-impressive with its beetling gables and Gothic windows. Meredith's family had moved out of it since the strike began, but C.P. himself still lived in the house, obstinate and wrathful and contemptuous of the strikers.

People now ran in hordes out of the long rows of dwellings to watch the conflagration. Which of the gangs had dared this! Most of the watchers exclaimed in horror at this new outrage. But they watched the massed nasturtium-coloured flames with thrilled and excited faces. How the high new house burned! Large dragons of flames sprang to the heavens. The roar and hiss of the falling roof could be heard up and down the valley. The first week of the strike a wonderful new grand piano had been delivered at the house. It created a scandal: grand pianos and starving miners! But where was the piano now?

"It's the Irish gang that's done this," some said. Opinion was that the Welsh gangs stole for food and clothing, but did not wantonly destroy. The Irish revelled in destruction for its own sake, but the Welsh rioted in the sacred cause of belly and pocket. The sprinkling of raw Irish who had arrived in the coalfields from dark barbarous bogs and isolate pre-Christian villages often shocked the Welsh, though they were accepted with a deeper sense of familiarity than the quiet English, who had settled in sprinklings also. The English seemed not to riot or agitate at all: they were able to ignore their empty stomachs and ill-clad backs, causing a sniffing wonder.

A rumour passed round that C. P. Meredith had been burnt to death in his mansion. As yet the reign of terror, begun three days ago after only two weeks of strike, had proceeded without loss of life. C.P. the first! Nervous women ran back into their dwellings and locked and bolted their doors. Surely the military would arrive soon with guns and swords. The fire had died down to a brooding gold glow. Police were now patrolling the streets with stern faces, many of which bore the marks of mutilation.

Men advancing from the big main valley to their homes up the vale were closely scanned by these police. Any parcels or bulging pockets? Rioting and thieving had been proceeding elsewhere that fierce day. The various attacks had, apparently, been well organised; probably they had been planned in secret meetings of strikers well up among the mountains. Wherever there was a group of shops there had been an attack, either big or petty. In some cases the strikers had been routed by the extra police already drafted into the district, and numbers of arrests had been made.

And at many a bleak hearth that January night a fire was somehow raised and a meat meal prepared. Those men who had been fortunate enough to secure a ham, a lump of bacon or a joint, shared it with neighbours. The taste of meat was again wedded to back-yard grown potatoes: a golden dab of butter shone like treasure on the table. Young children were withdrawn from bed and older children hung round the table with brilliant and gluttonous eyes.... The sacred odour of cooking meat was enough to make one swoon.

Tradespeople nailed boards across their gaping windows; some sat up all night, suspecting odd marauders and further nocturnal attacks from the demented rioters. But more police were arriving already from the outlying districts. Tomorrow, it was whispered, a battalion of soldiers would camp on a hill-side. Meredith's house continued to smoulder all through the night, now and again spluttering and coughing out sparks.

But the general manager himself had not been burnt; he was

not even scorched. He was sitting quietly, but grinding the end of a burnt-out cigar, in a room of the Glan Ystrad colliery offices. He sat alone, in that long big room that had once been the drawing-room when, in the old days, the place had been the manor-house of the valley. A heavy figure, with the grey motionless face of a man who has struggled with a large intricate industry and governed masses of workmen, he did not feel the coldness of the bleak room—for there was no fire under the old carved marble mantelpiece. And he had not set a light to the gas brackets inserted round the walls: he sat in the darkness, chewing his cigar, now and again glancing with an uncommenting eye through one of the tall windows from where he could see his smouldering mansion. But the arson had given to him too a certain detached satisfaction. From the day he had entered the house he had disliked its barn-rooms and draughty corridors. He had been reared in a thatched cottage in the country, simple and pleasant as a square loaf of bread, and almost as small.

II

On the bank of the stream was an oblong of dwellings, dirty-looking and squalid, that seemed even in the daytime to have always a damp shrouded look. Long ago the oblong, divided into eight dwellings, had been plastered white, but now the wash was peeling and caked with coal-dust. At the end of the strips of garden bony bushes spread out writhing arms above the stream, black branches that were barren or sometimes productive of a grey shrivelled bud or two. The stream was slimy with dust, washing like some desolate stream of the underworld, under a grey mountain-heavy landscape.

One would have thought that the human beings who lived in such a corner, among garbage and foul water, would be of melancholy disposition. But the interiors of the dwellings were far from desolate; in each, except number six, breathed a large family given to non-chapel habits—drinking, quarrelling in the open and suchlike. The poorest of colliery labourers settled here, and in the early evening, after school hours, many children squealed and yelled round the sore oblong, finding delight in the odourful earth and the mournful stream.

Number six contained, however, only adults. Normally, it was occupied by a brother and sister, Melville and Daisy Walters, and their lodger, Billy Saunders. Tonight they sat in the kitchen, where an oil-lit globe, perched on the head of a china owl, gave a shallow light, and also sitting on the sofa and odd chairs were five or six youngish men. The curtains of the window were closely drawn, and when one of the men in his anger raised his voice, Daisy warned him to be quiet. Now and again she would lift a corner of the curtain and peer out.

It was about two a.m., and some of the men had been sitting there for three or four hours. One or two had come in since midnight with what reports they had been able to gather.

"What about some tea, Daisy?" said Melville at last, wearily.

"There's no sugar or milk," she said, looking at the men.

"Never mind. Anything to wet our whistles."

Daisy sank the kettle deep amid the dying fire. She thrust a few sticks in the grate and blew up a blaze. She was in the middle twenties and seemed uncommonly tall, in a land of short women. She behaved with a familiar confidence among the men; there was no putting forth of her sex. She had just accepted from one of them half of his cigarette, for she had a passion for smoking, and all day she had been without a fag. While waiting for the kettle to boil she pushed her athletic glowing body between two of the men on the sofa, easing herself down and narrowing her eyes, emitting a cloud of smoke through her nose.

"Someone," she said, looking round the men, "might have brought a tin of salmon or a bit of bacon."

Everyone in the room was unmarried and though all of them except Daisy and Melville had been out among the rioters, no one had obtained even a packet of fags or a penny cake.

"We done our share," said Billy, the lodger, "urging them to it."

"And got nothing for it," one man with a blackening eye-socket was disposed to complain.

"The glory!" another said ironically, and passed his tongue again over a swollen blue lip.

Daisy's brother, Melville, sat at the table drumming his fingers against it. He was tall, like Daisy, but more worn and nervous. His face was haggard and alive with a keen fierce light: he was good-looking in a remote non-physical way, as if his features were transcended by some glowing spirit looking out from them, fierce with some inner half-tragic strength. A mat of black hair was shoved forward untidily over his high forehead, his long lips were of a thin pure curve. The quality of his voice was harsh, but his words, as he spoke them seemed to be torn out of his mind in a weary agony, so that he was listened to with wonder and attention.

"You know," he said, "you can steal if you want to. I'm against it personally, but that might be a limitation peculiar to myself."

"A gammon of meat was staring at me out of Price's window," said a rioter woefully, "and just as was turning it over in my mind, someone nabbed it like a cat a mouse."

"Oh," cried Daisy ecstatically, pushing up her face, "oh, the smell of frying ham!"

Melville looked at his sister with strained, remote amusement. Daisy! When she was flushed with thick colour like a dahlia, high-springing as a sunflower.

"Did you hear what time the soldiers are arriving?" he asked the man who had entered last, with the news.

"No."

"They can't interfere with our meeting up the mountain" Billy Saunders said. "Free speech's allowed anyhow."

Melville shook his head. "There'll be warrants out by tomorrow afternoon," he said. "If the police discover about the meeting they'll be there searching. Soldiers with them, probably."

"Why," someone said, "that battalion's nearly made up of chaps from places like this."

"Soldiers," said Melville, "never stop to think. Military training eats into a man's brain like a disease. They're good at two things, are soliders—killing and copulating, both of which functions brainless animals perform with equal success."

Daisy rose to brew the tea. As she passed her brother she smoothed her hand over his mat of hair. The bitterness that gnawed at him so constantly hurt her too. But as she set out the cracked thick cups she hummed a gay tune to herself. No one in the room had had a decent meal all day. A dejected evil atmosphere could so easily fall on them.... She had kept back in the pantry half a loaf of bread and a thick slice of cheese— breakfast for Melville, the lodger and herself. But now she brought the food out and divided it.

"Sure it can be spared?" one of the men asked anxiously.

"Oh yes," said Daisy.

An injured foot, earned in the first minor skirmish of three days ago, had kept Melville indoors. But it was he who had organised the battle with the police of that evening, the men in the room leading the different gangs that had attacked from the lanes. But the pillaging of the shops had not been included, officially, in his campaign. All he had wanted was a demonstration of physical power and solidarity... a warning.

Billy Saunders, who had gone to an upstairs window to look out, returned and said:

"C.P.'s castle still showing a bit of flame."

A short cocky young man of tenacious flesh and sudden jumping movements like a frog's, he drank up the cup of hot amber tea at once, and swallowed the bread and cheese in one gulp. Everyone supposed that he was Daisy's lover.

"They are saying that the Irish did it," a man said, "but if it wasn't Ianto Game Leg's doing I'll eat my boot, nails and all."

"You mustn't say that outside this house," Melville said.

Ianto was a very angry agitator with a strictly personal

10

grievance. For four years, since his left leg had begun to betray signs of being a shoddy limb, he had blamed the colliery for its decay—because of a slight wound he had sustained in the mine years before. Not a penny of compensation had been granted him, and he was unable to work owing to the cancerous limb. He had gone so far as to insult C.P. in the street and had never ceased to promise vengeance.

"He wouldn't be able to hop out of the house in time," someone else said, "poor Ianto. Nowadays his old leg's thick as a barrel with stuffing and wadding."

"He has plenty of mates."

"All of them got game legs or arms or broken down insides. Too sick they are to hide in a house and set fire to it. They sit about and grumble, but they do nothing."

"Ianto's old woman, perhaps, was the one. Hot as hell she is about his leg."

"Indeed now," agreed another, "that's likely enough. Old Gwyneth's got rare blood in her."

There was a light tap, repeated twice, on the kitchen door, which led to the backyard and a lane. Daisy unbolted the door and opened. A young man, wearing a good but shabby tweed overcoat buttoned up to the chin, stepped into the room with an unsmiling greeting, pulling off a cap.

"You're late," Daisy said. She peered into the teapot. "Have a cup of half-stale tea? With no sugar or milk."

"Please."

With his entrance the atmosphere of the room changed. Two or three of the men looked dimly hostile; the others, except Melville, eyed him inscrutably. As he unbuttoned his coat he said:

"Well, they've made pretty messes of the shops."

"I was one that helped," said a man on the sofa, aggressively.

"No one's brought loot here," Melville said quietly.

"Our pantry's still bare."

"You've heard the soldiers are coming tomorrow?" asked the newcomer, sitting down and beginning to sip his tea.

11

Melville nodded. He was looking at the newcomer with a glimmer of an ironical smile. But a certain softness had entered into his manner as he spoke. The young man laid down his teacup and looked round vaguely and hesitatingly at the men on and grouped near the sofa.

"Infantry arriving in the morning and cavalry in the afternoon," he said.

"The bastards won't frighten us at all," a man growled.

"No," said Melville, "but they'll suppress you. Cavalry too!" he said. "How many brigades of artillery?"

The newcomer shook his head. "It seems we can't riot and plunder," he said. "It does no good."

"That's for them who's starving to decide," exclaimed the growler on the sofa. "I bet you don't know the feel of an empty belly, Tudor Morris."

"No," said Tudor, "I don't."

"Well then—"

"Doctor Morris," interrupted Daisy, "couldn't help being born where there's no shortage."

The men subsided into an unwilling silence. They could not quite accept Tudor Morris into their workmen's sacred revolutionary circle. Ringleaders of that day's riots, they were inclined to suspect that he was quite capable of being a spy. His family belonged to the order of those in authority, with connections among the managers of the collieries. They found it difficult to believe that a man belonging to that set could be honestly sympathetic.

"Are you coming to our meeting on the mountain tomorrow?" Melville asked him.

"They'll rout that, after today's business, you know…. Still, I'll be there."

Daisy sat looking at Tudor with her shrewd good humour still evident. She asked him if he had a cigarette. He threw her a packet across the room; she caught it accurately. Tudor was blond and restless looking, with curly hair and a fine curved aristocratic nose: his body seemed strung up to a quivering pitch, slim, finely-tempered, and long of limb. He and Melville were oddly alike in their personalities, the makeup of their characters, except that Tudor's restlessness did not break forth in such weary fierceness: It was more curbed. And Melville belonged to the real working-class, the slum variety, except that he had studied and read and become the leader of a particularly subversive group of men, dragging along his amiable but quite intelligent sister with him.

"If there'll be a row," Daisy said to Tudor, "you'll be best out of it."

"Yes," put in one of the men, still distrustful, "nothing to gain has Doctor Tudor Morris." He spoke the full name with a jeering obsequiousness.

Tudor turned his blue restless eyes upon the speaker. "No?" he said. "Why do you imagine that only strikers can learn something at the meetings? Your intolerance is as silly as the capitalist's." He smiled. "Come now, you mustn't be snobs, you're no more blue-blood than I am."

"Us workers," said the other stubbornly, a man with a swarthy bullet-head, "got no use for such as you. What have you done to help us?" he demanded truculently. "Hanging round at our meetings and talking like a book, while us chaps do jobs, jobs with danger in 'em—"

Melville tapped the table as the speaker's voice began to shout.

"Doctor Morris," he told the men, "has been a great help to us. He's helped our funds with money and he has helped us in our discussions." He addressed the man who had just ceased growling. "You mustn't become conceited because you do jobs, as you call it. There are other men who serve the cause by doing other kinds of jobs, if it's only breaking away from the upper-class environment they've been brought up in and sympathising with the workers—"

Tudor broke into a laugh. "Oh, hell, I'm not annoyed with him, Melville," he protested. Then he began to preach himself, turning to the men: "Remember, this movement is still in its

13

infancy. You've got a long way to go yet, a nasty stony way. You workers have plenty of courage and strength among you. But it'll help you a great deal to win into your ranks some of the middle-classes—win them by ideas, by your religion, not by smashing up shops and plundering and arson—"

He was stopped in his turn by Daisy, who began to bustle about the kitchen, clattering up the teacups and declaring:

"It's too late to begin a meeting. Three o'clock!" She turned to Melville remindingly: "What about those blacklegs?"

"Yes," said Melville, "we've got to do something to them." He looked at the men. "Three hauliers went back to work today." He named them, with their addresses. "There's a pail of tar and a brush outside. If you want something to do tonight, I suggest you go and write 'blackleg' on the front walls of their houses."

Two of the men undertook this task. They rose, tightening their belts and answering Melville's grin in a secretive, malign stretching of their lips. Melville added, with a brisk sharpening of his voice, "But no other damage, please, no smashing or robbery."

"Right-o, boss," said one of the men, easily and satirically.

"There'll be a few policemen out tonight," warned Melville.

"There are policemen hidden in the back lanes of the main street," Tudor gave information.

Melville glanced at him. One of the men whistled and muttered desiringly, "Now would be the time to call up the boys—"

"No, no more tonight," Melville said.

"Why, a fresh day it is now—"

"No more, I say. We've done a bit of good this last bout, brought it off all right, and I don't want it spoilt."

As they left, two by two after intervals, they nodded with more liking to Tudor. When they had gone, the brother and sister and their lodger and Tudor gathered round the last glow of the fire.

"They're not getting easier to handle," sighed Melville. "God, if they had had their way, they'd have smashed up the whole place tonight and set fire to any house boasting a bay-window or a set of lace curtains."

14

"All the same," Tudor said, "I like their fury." His voice became casual. "There are times when everyone would like to see the whole damned world go up in flames and be licked clean."

Billy Saunders cocked up his tight-skinned little head at Tudor and demanded suddenly:

"Why don't you leave your home and come among us!"

Tudor smiled under his fine arched nose, the colour of his eyes gleaming. "I'm not fond enough of you," he said.

Billy cocked his head again, glowering a little. "You don't want to be one of us then?" he asked.

"I'm after the same things, perhaps," Tudor answered. "But we're going a different path."

Daisy seemed slightly nettled and disapproving at his reply, glancing at him. But she said nothing. The lodger, sitting next to Daisy and insisting on touching her knee with his, went on turbulently:

"There's only one path in our movement—the road to smashing up the bosses."

"My fight," said Tudor, slowly and as if he hadn't heard the last observation, "is inside myself, yours outside. But the goal seems to be the same—physical and spiritual ease."

"There doesn't seem any use for you to come among us then," Billy said, a little sullenly.

Melville, who was leaning forward as if tensely, his shoulders contracted, gazing into the fire, said in his strange voice of pain:

"He comes among us because I suppose we've chucked away most of the fears and taboos of organised society. He feels a certain amount of freedom among us." He twisted himself round on his hard kitchen chair and looked at Tudor with a sudden bright assumption of intimacy. "Isn't that true, Tudor?" he asked, his voice dragging. "We *do* mean something to you, don't we?"

"You're alive," Tudor said.

"We're alive," repeated Daisy with smile. "And not stuffed up with a lot of dead mess. Even if," she laughed, "there's nothing in the house for breakfast."

15

"I've got some money on me," Tudor said.

"Good," she said, "I'm glad I spoke."

They sat for a couple of hours talking. No one seemed to want to go to bed. They discussed past strikes and disputes between the workers and the coal-owners, and past rioting. Melville, who had a small library, told of the band of terrorist agitators known as the Scotch Cattle, who operated earlier in the century. As a warning to a blackleg, a bull's head was painted in red on his front door, and if he continued working, the gang of cattle, with turned coats and blackened faces and headed by a man blowing a horn, attacked the blackleg's house in the night, destroying the furniture and beating the inmates with thorough brutality. Engine houses of the collieries were wrecked and whole rows of houses destroyed. Imported military and large proffered rewards were useless in bringing these picturesque bulls to justice; they hid in the mountains like the marauding tribes of old; but they were fighting for recognition of the first Union of the Workers, a revolting idea that the mine-owners sat on, as Melville put it, with "behinds quivering like jelly-fish in fright",

The history of the miners was a long tale, dark with squalor, noisy with yells, savage with violence, smelly with sweat—from the beginning of the century, when strike-leaders such as Dick Penderyn and Lewis the Huntsman were sacrificed at the gibbets, to this last year of it when he, Melville, supposed he'd soon be doing stretch of hard labour for his organising ability.

"They'll get you over my dead body," declared Daisy with a laugh that squatted grimly in her throat. She had kept house for him for six years; their parents were dead, the father killed in a particularly gruesome accident in the mine; the mother, one of those many grey wasted women who have not sufficient animal mindlessness to emerge triumphant from the bitter life of those early colliery days, had followed her husband a few months afterwards. The life that the brother and sister had looked upon seemed full of angry mutilations, arid efforts to feed off bones, and worship of a God who kept the honey, walnuts and roast duck

16

of life safe and remote for a meal after death. Their parents were strictly religious. It was Melville, wayward and studious in his adolescence, who detected the insolence of the life that was mapped out for them—and the people all about them—by those in authority. He began to spit venom and fire. Daisy learned to see too.

The house became a secret centre of the insurgent elements in the district. The men who went there were mostly the rawest stuff. Often Melville felt himself helpless before the crude fire of mutiny that shot from them. Perhaps already he had burnt himself out in hopeless visions and could only serve now with proletarian lamentation and canticles of anarchy. He had taken part in the first riots of the present strike and had been in misery, sick with a sense of futility. But consciousness of a sacred duty still gnawed at him, he felt himself driven on to some bitter fulfilment of his being. Daisy watched, and calmed him with her cool, half-sexual laugh, her mixture of domestic solidity and liberated mental warmth. She refused to marry, but had taken a couple of lovers, philosophically and rather drably, as if to spite the rigid puritanism of her upbringing. Billy Saunders was paying court to her now, but she had not yet given way to him.

They always lived in extreme poverty, strike or no strike. Melville had worked at odd jobs about the mine—in the lamp-rooms, the offices, the power-house; but his subversive ideas were always discovered and soon no colliery would employ him. Now, in the front room of the house, he made pieces of simple furniture—plain serviceable chests of drawers, chairs and dressers—and sold them now and again, at a low profit. And there was the lodger, and Daisy occasionally took in the washing of such tradesmen's wives who would employ her. Books were bought, and many wandering young miners of no family ate in the house when there was money, sometimes being provided with a shirt, socks or a cap.

"What's going to be the next move?" Tudor asked, rising in preparation to go. He lifted a corner of the curtain at the window. A grey streak was in the sky.

"These blasted soldiers—" Melville said.

"Looks as if the men will have to sit still."

"By their temper," Daisy said, "I think they're going to hold out this strike, sitting still or no."

"They want to burn down a couple of chapels next," Melville said meditatively. He named the two. Billy flashed him a frowning look; he could not quite get over his mistrust of Tudor.

There was a general move. Daisy vaguely brushed off a smudge of dust on Tudor's jacket. Billy watched her with a scowl now. Tudor laid half a sovereign on the table.

"We'll pay you back sometime," Daisy smiled.

"Sure you can spare as much?"

"Oh yes." And catching her bright companionable smile, he smiled back with a certain hesitation; it was as if something should have been communicated between them, some understanding which had not crystallised in their minds.

When he had gone, Melville went up to bed, taking a book with him; he suffered from insomnia. The kitchen had become cold in the slow January dawn, for the fire had long since gone out. Daisy sat on the sofa to unlace her boots. She yawned and said to Billy:

"Don't expect your breakfast too soon. But if you're up before me, you might go and do some shopping with that money. I suppose there's something left in the shops?"

He made one of his quick, jumping-frog movements across the kitchen, and tumbled against her on the sofa.

"You're after that Tudor Morris, aren't you?" he said, thickly and crudely.

She boxed his ears, annoyed. He pushed her back on the sofa, untidily, but his body alert and tenacious.

"Kiss me, Daisy," he begged in a whisper, "kiss me."

"Kiss you!" she exclaimed stridently. But again there was the short dark laugh in her throat.

Then suddenly he seemed to crumple up against her, his face became oddly contracted and as though he was about to weep.

But his hands still gripped her shoulders. "You've got no pity," he whispered miserably. "You don't know what I'm going through." As suddenly he sat up and said contemptuously, "Teasing bitch that you are."

Now she laughed openly and uproariously. She half lay on the sofa and her healthy, warm, well-shaped body shook with laughter. Fists on knees he sat beside her and took no notice of her amusement, staring with glowering meditation across the kitchen. Then Daisy lifted herself a little and wound her arm about his gruff, sturdy neck.

"We don't get much out of life, do we, Billy?" she gurgled. "Kiss me."

III

Tudor walked away from the oblong of dwellings a little unwillingly. He had wanted to stay, to sleep for an hour or two in the house, and then share the morning with its small family. There was in it a kind of spiritual warmth, an atmosphere of released forces and independent bravado, which was vaguely comforting to him. And exhilarating too—even Billy Saunder's hostility, compounded of jealousy and class contempt. And he liked and respected Melville.

Daisy was attractive, too. She had no sexual limitations, no coyness or conceit, no virtuous locking-up of her treasures, and she wasn't on guard for marauders. There were not any like her among the lot that trod his walk of life. All the same, he suspected she was rather too free game…. His short mouth under the fine arched nose set itself for a moment in a fastidious grimace.

After the turmoil and disorder of the previous day he would have liked to have been roused to belief by Melville's antiseptic idealism, that went cleansingly amid the squalor of the local conflict—brawling warfare over a pitiably small reduction in wages. Melville was working for a firmer consolidation of the miners, an impregnable Union. If a strike failed, the miners, submitting to the owners' decrees and creeping back ignominiously to work, he became ill in a kind of vitriolic nervous storm that was unattractive and yet purifying in its bitter wrath. He was so faithful to his vision of a properly rewarded, healthy, liberated community of workers. But again and again he was shoved back brutally into darkness by the frequent surrender of the men. His dream of a gigantic strike of all workers through the country, prelude to revolution, seemed very remote and unattainable. Such small, infrequent triumphs came of these niggardly local stoppages.

"A kind of nineteenth-century little Jesus, I suppose," murmured Tudor to himself, reaching the main street. "Except that he's working for comfort in this world."

A couple of policemen on the corner greeted him— "Morning, Doctor." He stopped and talked to them for a moment, opening a fresh packet of fags. Hiding the cigarettes in their fists, they took furtive whiffs. They supposed, he thought, that he was out on a case.

He climbed the low slope of a mountain-side to an upper road winding through the valley among a few groups of better-class houses, semi-detached villas and the like, where lived clerks, officials and the middleclass. Dawn was well on the way to full flowering, a burst of clear grey veined faintly with red. The sky had a cold watery stillness; the vale beneath slept in brief forgetfulness of its woes. That gleam of dawn seemed to offer a delicate peace. Quiet slept the jumbled rows of ugly dwellings, the long lines of slate roofs were a shadowy blue, and vague white mists hung within sulky, coal-dusty back gardens. Tudor paused for a few moments to gaze down on the unusual, placid aspect of the place.... Soon doors would open and short two-legged creatures scuttle restlessly up and down raw streets, opening mouths out of which would jump noises of dissatisfaction, warfare, threats. Would it always be so? There had been such a long, long chorus of jangled noises.

The other side of the vale, immediately opposite from where

he paused, and thrust up from a ragged little wood, stood the old beautifully-shaped house about which his grandmother had such tales to tell. It was still a little apart from the drably-climbing rows of dwellings, but even so, on its promontory, it seemed out of place, a fragile relic of forgotten times.

Tudor smiled as he thought of his grandmother and began to move on. Today was her birthday, her eightieth. And she still woke regularly at seven o'clock: he wanted to be the first to greet her. Ten minutes later he was entering the gate of a dark-grey stone villa bulging with many bay-windows and boasting quite a stretch of bushy garden around it—hard stunted bushes they were, which looked as though they had pushed their way with extreme suspicion through the coal-dusty earth. He plucked a sprig of evergreen.

The domestic was busy in the kitchen, clattering on the grate, but no one else was down. He ran upstairs and knocked at his grandmother's door. A wideawake voice bade him go in. She was sitting up in bed, knitting in the half-light, a white shawl across her shoulders. He drew the stem of evergreen through the lace of her night-shift and tickled her chin.

"Eighty!" he said.

"And I don't feel old at all," she complained. "I wish I had aches in my joints or was deaf or daft, so that I could have something to cry about.... But perhaps I am daft, Tudor? An old woman's likely to make mistakes about herself."

Her round crinkled face was buxom with health, a faint flush of pink showing through the tanned skin. Lively full eyes had become fragile but shrewd and her wealth of hair had turned to cloudy silver. Tudor sat beside her on the bed and laughed into her kind face that for all its age and experience still preserved a look of wonder.

"Quite daft. You're not really eighty, you're ageless. You've lived for ever and you're likely to go on doing so. You're a piece of the original world and you saw the sun along with the first buttercup."

Bronwen looked at him vaguely for a few moments. She was looking down into his eyes, far past the iris. Her hands rested limply on the quilt and the shadow of some remote spasm crossed her face.

"What is it ?" he asked tenderly.

"You were talking exactly like someone I used to know. With the same voice."

"Who?" he demanded.

She took up her knitting and began to work industriously. "Someone connected with my past," she murmured with a little prudent sigh.

"When you were a wicked girl—?" he laughed.

"That'll do," she said severely.

The episode in her past was more or less common knowledge. But sometimes Bronwen was disposed to be secretive and touchy about it, though other times she would allude in a veiled, romantic fashion to its details. For a lifetime she had been a faithful member of the Congregational chapel, and in the Sunday School had shepherded hordes of girls through the bumpy meadows of strict virtue.

"Anybody would think you had something dreadful to hide," he teased.

"You've been out all night!" she accused, looking at him again, sharply, in the brightening light.

"Well?"

"You been with patients?" she demanded inquisitively. "A lot of them there must be, with all this rioting."

"I've been with some friends," he answered, getting up from the bed.

He was always rather reticent and mysterious about his private life. Bronwen suspected, with regretful but helpless disapproval, that he was having a love affair with some idle, good-for-nothing girl, who couldn't be produced with any pride.... "Go and have some sleep," she suggested. "I expect your father can go down to the surgery alone this morning."

"There may be a great deal of work with all these bashed heads and cracked jaws."

Bronwen sighed. "The place is going mad," she murmured. "When will it have peace?"

"Not this side of a revolution."

"Oh, go away, you with your revolution," she exclaimed. She shivered a little, in the mellow withdrawn backwash of her eightieth year.

"I shall be up in time for the surgery," he said at the door. "Here's Lily with your tea." He grinned at Bronwen, as the domestic, with a smudged, early-morning face, pushed past him importantly with the tray of tea-things.

"Many happy returns, mum," Lily cried excitedly. "And a very fine morning it is for your birthday. There's a day it will be, with all the soldiers coming to the place and all." She was thrilled as when the big Fair arrived.

"You'd better not go outside the door for the next few weeks, Lily," laughed Tudor, going off. "Call me at ten o'clock."

He went to his room and was soon asleep. After two and a half hours he was called and got downstairs as his father was preparing to go down to the little building in the main street which was the consulting-room, dispensary and general meeting-place for ailing miners and their wives.

"I'll be along after a bit of food," Tudor said.

Elwyn nodded. He was wrapping a muffler round his neck in the hall. He had a gaunt aspect, grey-headed and dignified of feature. Gazing with a long pondering stillness at people and things, he was thought to be aloof and critical, but it was because he required to absorb hungrily and intensely all that his eyes saw.

"You've been out all night, I hear," he said reprovingly. "You had no cases, did you?"

"No, but I hung about to see if I was needed. I treated two or three rioters on the quiet."

"I was out until midnight," his father said. "Up in White

Terrace mostly. A nice lot of bruised heads there. The police got kicked about too, I hear. They had Nicholls in to them." Nicholls was the rival doctor and favoured by the conservative.

"No one in C.P.'s house when it was burned down?"

"No. C.P. walked out quietly and disappeared—they say he didn't mind the place being set on fire. And the domestics got away safely."

Tudor helped his father with his overcoat. Elwyn, hatted and coated, looked imposing now, an upright figure with his strong and didactic face, powerfully moulded. No one would have suspected a streak of unworldly mysticism in him; his look seemed so deliberately matter of fact. But over each local baby that he helped to bring to birth he said a prayer tinged with melancholy, ordering the harassed or stodgy midwife to her knees and impressing the exhausted mother into calm. And he mixed with the local bards and wrote hymns in the Welsh language and occasionally preached a passionate sermon in a chapel pulpit left vacant for a while.

"Do you think you'll be busy this morning?" Tudor asked.

"No," his father answered, gripping his corpulent umbrella, "the wounded men won't show themselves in the street by day— a bruise will mark them rioters. And the women will be too excited to remember they've got bodily complaints. But there's a couple of measles I've to visit. You'd better be down in the surgery by eleven."

Tudor nodded and went into the dining-room. His grandmother sat at the large breakfast-table surrounded by letters and the paraphernalia of opened parcels; his mother stood by the open window reading a letter through a lorgnette—she looked up and asked mildly:

"Why had you to be out all night?"

"Oh," he answered off-handedly, "I wanted to see if there was anything I could do."

"Dying men lying about the streets, I suppose?" she suggested in gentle reproof.

Handsome and fastidious, she was already dressed and arrayed as if she were about to receive important guests. A good singer in her day, she spoke with careful articulation, rounding each word correctly. Her grey streaked hair was piled up massively over her broad low brow. She was so obviously the wife of the dignified looking Elwyn that Tudor often poked fun at the sentimentality of their "Darby and Joan" appearance. Trained for a professional career on the concert platform, she still walked and gestured with the vocalist's half-curbed showing-off. But inside she was tranquil and subdued, a provincial doctor's quiet wife, expecting no more of the world.

"Tudor," said his grandmother, "you wicked boy, to buy me quite a ton of buttered-walnuts! You know they're not good for me." His present, a large box of the sweets which were her favourite, lay on the side-board.

Presents were strewn over the room—shawls, mittens, pieces of lace and silk. After her husband Ben had climbed to a decent position in the colliery, Bronwen had liked to dress up and sally forth into the streets arrayed in colourful but good finery; she had quite a fame for her laces and bonnets.

He sat down and his mother rang for his breakfast; she glanced at him secretly, and with anxiety. He looked well enough, and even alert. She had heard that there were several kinds of disreputable people in the district who met in houses for the performance of unconventional practices. But surely her Tudor was too finely tempered, too scrupulous, to allow himself to be drawn into unkempt behaviour. All the same, she dimly apprehended that his mind churned with ideas unknown to her. Since he had returned a year ago from his studentship in London he had seemed to her less her familiar son than a young man belonging to alien things outside the domestic circle. She sighed over him, she yearned; she had a weak heart and always waited fearfully for disaster, in spite of her placid look.

"Show Tudor my letter from David Llewellyn," said Bronwen, laboriously reading another one—she had never learnt to read English quickly.

His mother handed him the letter she had been reading. On each of her birthdays since she was twenty, Bronwen had received a note and present from the brother of an old lover; she had a boxful of such letters among the treasures of her past life which she kept in her bedroom. The present one bore an address in Llandrindod Wells, and in a sprawling rather schoolboy hand ran:

Dear Bronwen,

Once again I greet you and this time it seems an anniversary indeed. Eighty is such a landmark and a triumph! And here I am catching you up, as I myself will be eighty early next year.

Writing these words this last year of the century makes me pause and I say to myself, "Why, it cannot be sixty years since I saw Bronwen skating on the pool at Clan Ystrad one New Year's Eve with my brother Owen!". That night seems particularly impressed on my memory and I can see the ice gleaming now, and the moonlight on the snow.

Do you know that writing this annual letter to you is an effort for me—but an effort I would not forgo? You will probably realise what I mean. We very old people know that even grief is precious, and must be held to one carefully.

Sometimes I feel, even, that I would like to visit the vale again— but then, when it comes to actually planning it, I draw back. One lives so much in memory now. All the reality of life seems made up of nothing but things that are gone. (I suppose this is really a disaster, the disaster of age. But to me it is not so, and I thank God I have still my memory left, if not my hearing or my teeth or the energy to walk more than a mile.)

So you will understand why I would rather not accept your last invitation to stay with you for a while. One is merely too old to look at things that are now different.

My best wishes to Elwyn. (How odd to have a nephew of sixty? Indeed, this business of being eighty in the modern world seems odd altogether.)

I keep seeing you, as I close these few lines, walking in one of our old beautiful lanes and you are carrying an ewer of milk and I am on horseback.

Yours affectionately,

David Llewellyn.

"He seems suddenly tired," Tudor remarked. "His last letter was so jovial."

"Not underneath, it wasn't," Bronwen said, sadly. "All his life he never stopped grieving, though he pretended to forget mostly and said that things couldn't be helped." She was lapsing into a sad dream herself.

"What things?" Tudor asked.

Bronwen pulled herself out of the tempting reverie with a sigh. "No good it is to make a long face on my birthday," she said vaguely, and returned to the perusal of her letters.

Tudor, as he ate his breakfast, thought of David Llewellyn. Brother of that mysterious young man who had interfered romantically and obscurely in Grannie Bronwen's early life, he seemed to hover continually in ghostly fashion behind the family. Tudor had never seen him. But he knew it was this David Llewellyn who had paid for his father's education, and sent him a thousand pounds on his twenty-first birthday, to set him up in a practice. The old man had been a middling important name in the Merthyr ironworks; he had sons and daughters of his own and was now a widower. So much Tudor knew. But the exact details of David Llewellyn's connections with Grannie Bronwen had not yet been revealed to him. Bronwen was always about to tell him and then interrupting herself saving "Oh so long ago it all is and perhaps best forgotten." And she would look very virtuous and severe and perhaps begin talking instead of some of the difficulties of teaching modern girls in Sunday school, where she shed such a bright and leading light.

Spruce and comfortably looking, his mother was glancing up and down the newspaper, sitting beside the sparkling fire. At intervals she uttered slight noises of distress, plucking deprecatingly out of the columns those items concerning the local rioting.

"Such a bad name the place will earn," she sighed.

Tudor, glancing across the table for a moment, thought she looked like a plump pigeon. In her nipping, fastidious way she was sympathetic towards the miners. But from a far, far distance. Some of the miners' dwellings horrified her into a loss of appetite when she had undertaken slum visits on behalf of a charitable institution during a previous strike; she had come home and gone to lie down without lunch. Now she sent gifts by messengers to needy families; and in chapel she prayed that succour and success might come to the strikers. Perhaps she was under her husband's influence in this—she was an old-fashioned wife, imitative of beloved Victoria, and believed in the absolute wisdom of the man God had granted her.

"Not in history," her son commented on her regretful remark.

"How do you mean, Tudor?" she asked, swerving her lorgnette round to him.

"When these struggles of the workers become a matter of history, a hundred or so years hence, they will be seen as rather noble, you know. And courageous and justified."

"That depends," she murmured, returning to her newspaper, "whether that Revolution of yours is ever achieved and the result found to be the better way." She treated this leaning of his towards socialism exactly as if it was a pet rabbit he kept in the back garden.

Grannie Bronwen had laid down her letters and was gazing at a daguerreotype portrait which hung, in an important gilt frame, over a small side-table on which was a pot of frisky aspidistras. She had been gazing at it intently for two or three minutes. It was a portrait of her husband Ben taken when he was forty-five. His honest wide-spaced features had settled into a thick-set calm: he had worked hard and earned good money, he possessed a pleasing wife and Elwyn, a strapping son, who had become more or less his own: a dignity was enthroned in his trustful face.

"Ceridwen," asked Bronwen at last of her daughter-in-law—
"what about having it over this mantelshelf again?"

On each of her birthdays since Ben's death Bronwen had moved
his portrait to a different position. It had been all over the house.
She declared it was fresher to her in a new position, she noticed
it more after it had been moved. The deep respectful affection,
amounting almost to passionate love, that she had learnt for Ben
from their wedding-day, lived continuously with her.

But her daughter-in-law had recently bought an overmantel
which now rested, carved mahogany inlaid with three mirrors
and decorated with stars of mother-of pearl, where Bronwen
desired the portrait. The two women began to purr. Tudor, lighting
a cigarette, rose and prepared to go down to the surgery, throwing
his woolly slippers under a horse-hair chair and calling for his
boots.

CHAPTER II

I

AMONG the little knots of people out in the main streets there was a kind of reckless, carnival air. The infantry had arrived already by train, and were now erecting their tents on a lower spur of a hill. Unknown policemen patrolled the streets regularly, officers on horseback and new fresh unmutilated constables pacing sternly. Groups of miners gossiped at street corners, squatting on their heels or lounging against the walls of urinals, careful looks of innocence on their faces as the policemen passed. Left alone, they spat, grinned, and looked their triumph in thus being able to tease the authorities into bringing forth the important military and these strutting police.

Shawled women ventured out of dark doorways, sniffing the sharp January air suspiciously and scurrying to cronies for a gossip or the borrowing of a teacup of sugar or a pinch of tea. Today the mountains seemed cold and they hung forward as if vengefully throttling the vale with wrathful-looking limbs. A short keen wind scampered through the place. The broken shops, with their amateur barricades, were dismally without customers, their owners going up and down the street complaining and exchanging tales of losses.

Up in the stony catacombs of back streets that rose tier upon tier against the lower slopes of the hills the rioters hid, thick as bees in hives, probably scheming crafty plans to overcome the military and police in sly ways only known to native tribes. But no bruised or bandaged men appeared out of doors. Here and there, however, a whiff of cooking bacon escaped a bolted door.

Some, having no bacon, ate tinned peaches or pineapple for breakfast.

Tudor, with his quick stride, took a short cut through these streets that lay between the row of villas on the main road. They had an odd respectable silence this morning. Usually, they were raucous with exclaiming women chucking out refuse and depositing babies for an airing on the pavement. He was late; and there might be many applications for visits to men who needed their wounds dressed privately after last night's battles...

Since returning from his service in a London hospital, he had become assistant to his father, who now talked of retiring, even though he had made scarcely any money. Dr. Elwyn Morris ministered to the bodily ills of the local people as though he were a saint whose reward lay beyond this earth: the bills he sent out were more often than not dropped into a void. The people were quick to perceive his unworldly sympathy with their sufferings while he attended to them professionally, and a long tale of woe could even produce a spare half-crown to purchase some delicacy (such as stout and shag). Tudor was aware of his father's idiosyncrasy and, more suspicious but himself tender to the oppressed local people, mildly protested.

"Tut, tut, my boy, whatever I give or lose, I'm still much better off than they are."

There were only two people in the surgery when he arrived, a woman who clung affectionately to her sciatica, and a very old man who, once a week, used up the morning sitting in the waiting-room—he always arrived first but insisted on being the last to enter the consulting-room.

"Morning, Doctor," said the old man exuberantly. But the dank-looking woman sat staring into a dreamworld of sickness and whining diseased people. She disliked a young doctor and did not intend to acknowledge Tudor's existence.

Tudor beckoned to the old man, who followed him into the dispensary unwillingly—his morning was to be cut short after all. But he made a long business of his bronchial trouble, wheezing

31

and sighing in an accomplished theatrical style. He was a retired old milkman and dated his decline from the day he had fallen into the local stream and wetted his body—he had worn two flannel shirts ever since. He asked for a double lot of medicine. His piggy eyes shifted about with bright cunning. After a while he began to invent a complaint in his knee and suggested that Tudor took a look at the joint. Tudor vaguely began to brandish a scalpel and the old man quickly pulled up his trousers again.

Elwyn, after disposing of the sciatical woman, appeared in the dispensary dressed to make his visits. "Mildred looked in," he told his son, "and is calling later, I think, she said."

Tudor nodded. His father jotted down two or three prescriptions, hesitated, and said, reaching for his umbrella:

"I suppose you were with the socialists last night?"

"Yes," replied Tudor, glancing at the prescriptions.

Elwyn, gazing with his usual absorbed aloofness at a bottle of arsenic, shook his head.

"I don't think you'll get any comfort among them, Tudor," he said. "You're out of the run of their minds."

"I don't expect comfort," said Tudor. "I'm inquisitive about them," he explained. "I know they're rough and raw at present, but they may be the important people of the future."

"Maybe," said his father, "maybe, but I can't see it. The other system has had too long an innings—the world's grown up on it."

"How d'you know the world's grown up yet?" Tudor smiled.

"True, I don't know," agreed Elwyn, smoothing his tidy silver moustaches. "But when we've gone on so long without socialism—"

At which a young woman's head appeared round the door. "Ah, there you are!" it said. "What was that about socialism?"

"We were wondering if socialism was a sign of growing-pains, Mildred," said Elwyn, moving to go. "No rioters about in Bryngarw this morning?" he asked. She had been walking down the valley.

"Ugh," she pulled a face, but delicately, "socialism! The very word's ugly. Why does it always make me think of drain-pipes and the smell of sour beer."

Elwyn laughed quietly, glancing amusedly at Tudor before going out. "Flat beer, Mildred, my dear," he said in the doorway. "Flat and small beer."

The door closed. Mildred lifted her red mouth to be kissed. But Tudor suddenly placed on her lip a dab of zinc ointment out of a pot that happened to meet his hand.

"Oh!" she cried, snatching up some cotton-wool, "Oh!" For a moment or two, darting glances at him, she did not quite know how to treat his action. There was only a shred of a smile on his lips. Then he burst out laughing. But still she was uncertain of its sound....

"You kid!" she exclaimed, sniffingly. "Schoolboy."

"Yes, very stupid," he said. "Quite silly." But seeing her perplexed frown, he slipped his arm round her and attempted to kiss her cheek. She drew away and sat on a tall stool beside the sink. Now she looked at him with a glance of mockery.

"You're looking seedy," she said. "Give yourself a tonic."

For some weeks an air of resentment had sprung up between them, unreasonable and mysterious. She watched him make up the prescriptions; he was deft, quick, his fingers were sensitive, hovering lightly. Yes, she thought, altogether he had a light indefinite touch—he could spring away easily, flash out of one's vision, like a kingfisher. This springing away in him both irritated and stimulated her, secretly. Embraced, his body definite within her arms, she was so sure of her power over him, she tasted a triumph that gave her intense satisfaction, and she would kiss and caress him gratefully. Soon, however, he would lift himself quickly away, look at her sideways, criticism in his eye and say something purposely banal that cooled the air immediately. And she would smile in outward mockery, apparently indifferent, and add something to his commonplace remark.

"Weren't you frightened of going out this morning?" he asked absent-mindedly, measuring some magnesia. Yes, he had gone again; she was anybody sitting there on that stool.

And she still felt resentment, as she could still taste the zinc ointment on her lip. "Bah," she said contemptuously, "these louts' riots! Who'd be afraid of them?"

"Swank!" he said.

"They're bestial," she said, flashing scorn, "these rioters, just bestial."

He shrugged his shoulders. "Have a drop of peppermint?" he asked, holding the bottle.

She buried her chin in the grey fur round her neck, looking down and frowning. One hand clasped a heavy muff of the same squirrel's fur. Her coat was good Scotch tweed and fashionably cut; two gold bangles fell over the wrists of her gloves, and an arrow boasting a diamond was fastened on the lapel of her coat. He noticed she was dressed-up a little more than usual and then suddenly remembered she was coming to lunch at his home: he had forgotten. A little guiltily he approached her and patted her free hand.

"Do I really appear seedy?" he murmured. "Perhaps I am a bit out of sorts."

Lifting her head she smiled brilliantly, and easily, showing excellent teeth. Her apple-rounded cheeks and slim nose gave her a young-girl look. But she was twenty-eight and the fixed, devouring gleam in her eyes, that made men who looked into them feel wary, displayed that she was conscious of the approaching landmark of thirty. She was the only daughter of the local solicitor, who hailed from Carmarthen and was of good family, one-time squires. There was always an element of haughtiness in her demeanour and her behaviour, which sometimes irritated Tudor and sometimes amused him. Otherwise, she possessed good taste and the fastidious character he thought he expected in women.... He leant to her now and kissed her red, well-fed cheek, rounded and smooth and fragrant as a fleshy apple under his desiring lips.

Quickly she jerked her head and gathered his mouth to her own hard lips. She still sat on the stool. His hand fell to her legs. Tearing her mouth away, she jumped off the stool, hesitated, then stepped across to the mirror over the sink and gave a twist to her hat. Tudor smiled ironically and went back to the prescriptions.

"Grannie Bronwen very excited?" she asked, too idly.

"I think she's quite proud of being eighty," he answered, remotely, studying a prescription.

He was gone again. She strolled, very casually, round the dispensary, studying the bottles, taking one or two down and sniffing them.

They had known each other since childhood, their families living in the same line of villas and worshipping at the same chapel. In adolescence they had had a high-souled romantic affair, reading poetry together and exchanging letters dealing with religious and literary topics: Mildred had a habit of writing little fables and allegories and sometimes a poem in bad imitation of Tennyson's *Idylls of the King*—some of them would have been attractive in style if the matter had not been so stuffy. She had a belief in fantasy, and she looked with horror and dismay at the life under her nostrils, down in the raucous, teeming valley. "Maggots," she would say, with the violence of the fantasy-lover smelling reality, "maggots in a piece of stinking meat". Once past twenty she became quieter and ceased writing and entering religious trances. But she was still remote, walking with her chin in the air and snobbish about the sacredness of women. The life below was something ugly far beyond the fringe of the villa garden; it might have been two hundred miles away.

While Tudor was at college they exchanged long letters and somehow a tacit understanding grew up between them that they were lovers. Long companionship with her made Tudor feel ownership of her pretty face, tidy limbs, and oddly attractive voice that always made him think of a wintry sunset. Nothing he liked better than to hear her recite poetry: a poem became a

35

sunset-coloured stream flowing in its own grace and scarcely touched by the human voice. She seemed to became mysterious and inaccessible to him. She was the mystery of perfect Woman, his Beatrice, and quite, quite different from the street-corner shop-girls he and the other students scrambled for.

Hospital work had, however, done something to him. He had begun to think of Mildred's suave inaccessibility a little comic. Sometimes, as if vengefully, he deliberately and perversely achieved damage to his vision of her by thinking of her organs during some dissection at the hospital. On the other hand, he was glad at other times to think of her as an escape.... She was still rather—

> *I touch her, like my beads, with devout care,*
> *And come unto my courtship as my prayer.*

And when he treated her in this manner she was very pleased, very grave, very prepared to devote all her soul and energies to his welfare. Since his final return from London, however, and taking up practice with his father, he had begun to behave in a wilful manner, treating her sometimes as if she was anyone he had picked up at a dance the week before. He had been back a year and still there was no talk of the wedding everybody under stood to be imminent. And everybody felt it was far better for a doctor to be a married man....

Roaming about the dispensary, she became irritated again at his entire absorption in the prescriptions. As he measured a drug he seemed to be putting his whole soul into the act. She knew that to him she might not be present in the poky little room. She reached the sink again, picked up an empty medicine bottle, and dropped it sharply into the porcelain oblong. He gave a slight jump and stared round at her frowningly.

"Clumsy—"

"Oh, your nerves are bad," she exclaimed, her cheeks flushed. He returned to the prescriptions without another word and

36

continued as before. There was a tap on the door of the little aperture through which the medicines were handed; he slid it back and a child's thin face, blue with cold, stared in with extreme gravity.

"Please for the medicine for Mrs. James."

"Hello, Carrie," he called brightly. "Why, you are looking cold."

And he would insist on bringing the little girl, who was accompanied by her smaller brother, into the dispensary, where there was a small oil-stove. The children were ill-clad and slovenly, thin, without coats. Their faces were expressionless with cold, their noses blue and running; they stood near the stove and stared stolidly at Mildred. She had not a word to say to them, she sat back on the stool and waited, very aware of their blue scraggy legs and vacant, unsatisfied faces. She was embarrassed by their presence and almost in misery. Somewhere, deep in her, but ashamedly, she resented their presence, their ill-fed greyness, as they stood there speechless and stupid in the warmth of the stove. But she could do nothing, she could not move to them, speak, or connect herself with them. But her sense of misery grew as they continued to stare at her. They were terrible little menaces out of the unknown.

"Why, Carrie," asked Tudor, "haven't you got any coats?"

Carrie shook her head, mouth hanging open.

Tudor wanted to know if Mildred had an old coat which Carrie's mother could cut up; he knew she was good with the needle, his mother had already given garments to her. Carrie was one of his pets; her mother had been a domestic at his home. Mildred, in relief, said she had some warm clothing which could go to them; and further, she opened her purse and gave Tudor a shilling to hand to the little girl. The children backed out of the dispensary overwhelmed.

"Christ! they're struck stupid with cold and half-feeding, Mildred."

She nodded. "Yes." And with an effort, "Poor darlings."

He noticed the recoil in her voice, and the uneasiness in her face. She was quivering with some strange, deep and

37

unrecognisable emotion. Suddenly she slipped off the stool and went across to him, stood behind him and whispered in his ear:

"Can't we go away from here, Tudor, away... to live, I mean? It's horrible here, and stupid, life's stupid here."

Tudor stood very still. He was astonished. And yet, at the back of his mind, he had been waiting a long time for some such approach from her. He stood still for some moments. Then he turned and said, with difficulty:

"Why, my dear, I don't know... you see, I think I want to stay, somehow I feel I've got to stay here—" They were looking into each other's eyes now, nakedly. And yet they did not stand revealed to each other. Quickly she dropped her eyelids and moved away. There was something helpless and pathetic in the droop of her head, and then he saw tears run down her cheek. He wanted to go and caress her, and he held back; he wanted to make love to her, and he watched those tears abstractedly. Just then there was another tap at the closed aperture.

It was Billy Saunders. Without a word he handed Tudor an envelope and disappeared. Glad of the interruption, Tudor opened the envelope and read:

Comrade,

Our meeting of 3 o'clock this afternoon is to be attacked by the military. We suggest that you join us at 2 sharp at the top of the ravine leading to the meeting place. Brecon.

He turned to Mildred. "I shall have to run away during lunch," he said barely.

"I see." Again she flushed and looked suspicious. They were going to take a walk somewhere in the afternoon. "And not come back?" she asked.

"I don't know."

"Where are you going?" she rapped out suddenly.

"Where am I going?" he repeated aloofly. And there was another tap, someone for their medicine. By the time he had made it up and handed over the bottle, Mildred had returned to her own cold remoteness. She was detached. So that again he slipped an arm round her and licked her fragrant cheek.

At one o'clock they were sitting down at Bronwen's birthday lunch-table. There were three or four other guests, cronies of Bronwen, including the chapel minister and his wife, so that the hilarity of the table remained nicely subdued. Bronwen, wearing, tiara-fashion, a spectacular head-gear of lace and mauve silk, seemed a trifle apprehensive, now and again glancing out of the window which looked over the front garden. The table was laden with good things. She was half ashamed of them. People who had been forced to loot shops were living a hundred yards away. What were others sitting down to? Pieces of stale bread soaked in basins of weak tea. And in front of her, fat and odorous in its golden splendour, lay a goose. The minister was coming to the end of grace, in which he had paid a tribute to God's good humour in allowing His excellent daughter to attain eighty. Bronwen wished he had made some allusion to the troubles outside the house, praying for peace, so that the hungry out there would be filled again.... She pulled herself together to meet the volleys of compliments and tributes levelled at her. What difference could a cooked goose make to the strike! God alone knew her heart ached for the suffering people. And in her day she had protested enough against the ugliness of all the business done in the place.

Surely this was not going to turn out one of her melancholy days after all! One of those days when she kept thinking of all that was gone. She had tried so much not to be a tiresome old woman who kept on producing the past to the disadvantage of the present. She often told herself that she was a peaceful and contented grandmother who had no further performance to make in the light of day; a dream or two, a bit of knitting and her pew in chapel were her portion now. But still there were days when her heart cried out with sick disappointment, when her soul was swamped with gusts of anger, like the swollen, threatening clouds that scudded against the mountains in winter.

A sparkling pale yellow wine was poured. Bronwen was toasted. She appeared to the others to be looking benignly at the wine. But a couple of tears were seen to run down her cheeks. Her eyes seemed suddenly faded and tired.

She had lived so long, she kept on thinking, so long. And her life had been a bustling one, a full and steadily prospering life. Yet all such personal success was petty and of little account. The world was ugly and mean and a place of treachery. Beasts had come to roam and roar where there had been such peace.... Greedy, demented men had attained power. Since her twentieth year, when the valley had been handed over to the merchants, her progress had been a lucky journey amid other lives that were nothing but squalor, filth and endless toil. So shocked and revolted she had been again and again: she could remember the days when girls of seven and eight worked at odd jobs down in the mines, half stripped because of the heat, when women hauled in coal among the men, and boys of six were labourers with their fathers: they worked for fourteen hours a day, and there had grown in the valley a race of stunted underworld creatures, rat-like of face and deformed of body, who were foreign to the sun and offensive in the daylight.

Ah, this was her birthday. She answered the toast with a smile. And was not all the extreme misery past, the real savagery gone! True, still there were strikes and starvation, but the evil period when men were whipped beasts and women were of foul manner, rotted of lung and bone, inhabitants of black slime-dripping corridors where they ate with the rats and consorted in brutal, deformed nakedness, tribe with tribe—that evil period only existed now in the memory of such foolish old women as herself.... Urged, she lifted her glass of shimmering wine. Ach, she had got cold, why had her limbs become cold! Birthdays when one was old made one brood. She regretted the visitors and the feast. Once the excitement of the morning had gone, opening her presents and letters, the day seemed to become one for mourning.

It was because of that letter from David Llewellyn, of course; it was at the back of her mind continually. Tudor was right when he said David sounded tired. Tired and mourning, as if everything had been of no use, as if something important had gone wrong in the beginning of their lives. When one was young and unthinking, accepting life just as it came along, whether purring with smiles or menacing with portents, then one stood up straight and strong and transacted successfully the business it brought. But old, one sat down helpless and alone, seeing beyond the day into a background of twilight that held both the landscapes of the past and the commotion of the future. There was to be no peace; she could hear the barbarous, harsh voices crying; and longingly she turned her eyes to the blue hills and the vales and the green and silver woods that were no more, but could still act as an incantation on her mind.

There was a bright gallop of conversation round the table. Her abstraction seemed unnoticed: she supposed a very old woman was allowed her moods. But Tudor, who was sitting next to her, whispered:

"Come now, Bronwen, have some of these saucy little brussels sprouts." Coaxingly he placed a spoonful on her plate.

Making another effort, she began to paddle amiably into the conversation; they were discussing the new gas-lamps that had been installed in the chapel. The minister thought that the old oil-lamps were troublesome, but he preferred their mellow light for divine worship; gas-light suggested shops and public-houses. Bronwen was asked her opinion, but for the life of her she could think of no illuminating remark on the subject. She was obliged to say that she didn't think it mattered whether there was oil or gas, provided there was light enough to read the hymns and Bible; and so she brought the discussion to an end.

She was sitting at the head of the table, her back to the window. A silence fell over the party for a minute. They ate busily. Then the minister began talking of the Sunday school attendance having dwindled seriously of late; something would have to be done to recapture the young people—a nice Revival in which they all could be little preachers and missionaries among themselves. There was a sharp crash, a thud, and Bronwen swayed forward twice, lifted herself, stared dumbly at the others and then hung over the arm of her chair.

One of the panes of the window was shattered; beside Bronwen's chair lay a flint. In the confusion that followed only Tudor jumped out of the house, ran across the short front garden and out of the gate to the road. No one was to be seen; there was a meal-time silence and emptiness in the road. On the other side of the road were several openings into the honeycomb of miners' dwellings; whoever had thrown the stone could have easily disappeared in a few seconds. Tudor swiftly searched around the few clumps of black bushes, and ran down the most likely back lane. By the time he had returned to the line of villas, neighbours who had heard the crash were already out enquiring.

He dashed back into the house, in a tumult now. That stone had been meant as a warning to him; he was certain of it. He was suspected of being an informer by some of the rioters. His mind jumped instinctively to the reason: the few moments' conversation he had had with the policemen last night, and the authorities' knowledge of this afternoon's meeting had been discovered by the strikers. Melville had sent him the note that morning – Melville believed in him. But those hostile men last night, they had seen him later had waited and followed him when he left Melville's house. The stone was a first warning.

Pale, with glittering eyes, he took Bronwen's hand for a moment. She lay on a sofa, while Elwyn bathed the back of her head, squeezing out the blood-soaked lint into an already crimsoned pan. But she was recovering and looking round dazedly. The guests were caught in horror, whispering beyond the sofa. Tudor's mother continued to murmur a kind of calm encouragement, kneeling beside Bronwen. In silence Tudor helped his father to dress the wound.

"Was it a rioter?" Bronwen whispered.

Elwyn looked at his son sternly but quizzically. All the time he had been the professional man, unmoved, attending to his mother with his usual intent dexterity, that had about it the aloofness his patients did not like.

"I couldn't find anyone," Tudor said. "There wasn't a soul to be seen anywhere."

"They must have made a mistake," Bronwen half cried. Her voice rose in a sudden bitter cry.

"Hush, now, dear, hush," crooned her daughter-in-law. "Of course it was a mistake. No one here has done anything against them."

Across Bronwen's grey face passed a shaken smile.

She was still dazed, and her confused aged eyes seemed frailer. "Anyhow," she whispered, "it was a birthday present.... They didn't forget me." Even as she smiled, she quietly fainted again.

II

He was late. Resentment burning his mind, he sped up the first slope of the range of mountains, going by an inner path winding from a small creek. He had managed to escape the alarmed but puzzled discussion in the house following Bronwen's recovery. His mother had cried indignantly for the police, but finally they came to the conclusion that an untidy error had been made. Probably the stone was meant for Alec Williams's villa three doors away; Williams was an official in the mine and notoriously on the side of the owners. But Tudor saw that his father, at least, was not deceived.

The rioters couldn't accept him. They were in so raw and suspicious a state. To them it was unnatural that he should leave his proper sphere to make excursions into their workers' world. Melville, of course, being freed from personal consciousness of any class and aware only of the economic struggle, accepted and trusted him. But most of the others, still crude in their hostility, looked upon birth in a villa as damnation and productive of a natural enemy for ever.

Speeding up the steep windy slopes, he searched the rocky tops of the range for signs of the strikers: he guessed from the note there was to be some move against the military. There was neither sight nor sound of anyone. But probably they were crouching behind those age-broken boulders that still were like dark defences of the sky.... The air was cold and sweeping on the naked slopes: soon he had to slacken, his heart and mind beating in a discordant tumult.

Why was he interfering in this warfare, in which he had nothing to gain or lose? Why did he feel himself continually driven towards identification with people who, nearly every one of them, were antipathetic to him? He did not know. He only knew that their "cause" was like a religion to him, the rhythm of their lives, the beat of a sombre piece of music, a symphony to whose forceful if noisy power he was compelled to listen. Resting for a few minutes on top of the first hill, to cool the leaping disorder of his blood, he could see the far sinuous reaches of the valley, narrow and far-flung, crowded with human habitations. Ugly, and where brutalities mingled with a strange mystical beauty.

Arriving at last on the edge of an upland, he stood directly over the entrance to the ravine mentioned in the note. It was scarcely more than a crevasse, as though the thick mountain had cracked into a deep fissure. The two slopes leant back, but steeply, and the drop from the rock-bound brows was stark, without bush, hedge or plateau. The whole bed of the ravine was covered with a road, wide enough for two horses abreast and stretching for a quarter of a mile until it wound up to the inner mountains and over to the adjacent valley. The road was loose with stones, uneven with holes; nowadays, since the opening of the big industrial road between the valleys, it was not used much.

They were waiting, he could see them now, squatting in groups behind the boulders that stretched along the brows of both slopes: why, the upland was black with them, there must be hundreds of them! And in a moment he was surrounded by half a dozen men. They pressed close to him in silence, waiting for the word. He looked back at them with a momentary jeer, sardonically tasting their threats and hostility. These were not known to him personally, but he vaguely recognised their faces, a ring of dark, unruly heads scowling at him.

"You got a right here?" one of them barked at last.

"Brecon," he said.

They drew back. "Keep inside," one said shortly.

"Where's Melville?" he asked.

They told him he was somewhere towards the middle of that side of the ravine. He walked across the upland. Some of the smaller boulders which jagged the earth everywhere on the upland had been dug and torn out; they were placed now along the rim of the ravine. Shadowed by the big rocks, the groups waited, dark clots of men that could not be seen from below. They spoke in whispers as they crouched and watched. The place was tense with a sense of coming battle.

He found Melville leaning against a rock, silent, his gaze fixed towards the entrance of the ravine. Billy Saunders and two of the men who had been in Melville's house last night squatted near. The two men looked at Tudor as he approached with a cool stare that was much too deliberate. He strode to them and said:

"You, was it?"

One began picking his teeth, the other snitched up a lip in a grin. Melville turned hastily and greeted Tudor. "Why, what's wrong?" he asked quietly.

Tudor rapidly told him what had happened. Melville glanced with a frown at the two men. Billy looked inscrutable. "It was you?" Tudor threatened. Still they not reply. He advanced to them. He saw them as sub-human, baboons squatting in the shadow of the rock. "D'you want me to open your mouths for you?"

Melville laid a hand on his arm. "Not now, Tudor," he murmured. "We'll settle it later."

One of the two squatting men, suddenly fired jumped up and

snarled. "What was he doing talking to the coppers last night after he left the house?" He turned to Melville. "We watched him. He's a split! A split, d'you hear? You, you trust him like a bloody fool. But I don't, and a lot of the other chaps." He pointed a thick, stubby finger at Tudor. "That's where the leak about the meeting came from. You tell us where else, then. There it is, I say. Heads together with the coppers last night, having fags with 'em—"

The last straining leash fell away from Tudor. He gave the other man a moment, then hit out. There was a smart exchange of blows that found their marks on each. Melville gave an impatient exclamation and signalled to Billy and two or three others who had been attracted by the row. The combatants had fallen to the ground. They were torn apart. Tudor, leaping up with a spring, began to feel round an eye. The other man pushed his fingers through the blood on his mouth and savagely tore away a tooth, chucking it contemptuously on the grass. "I'll get hold of the b— one night," he promised the chaps still holding him.

"You'll heave a stone through our windows first, to warn me, won't you," sneered Tudor, "and run away to the hole where you hid today... son of a bastard."

Melville, meditatively aloof, was staring at Tudor in surprise. He was perceiving a strong quality of coarseness in Tudor's face, which usually appeared so pleasantly austere with a kind of classic purity. Now the eyes and mouth seemed to be thrust out brutally, thickened and coarsened. Something that had not been evident before suddenly jumped into being. He was in the same sphere as his opponent now. And Melville noticed too, how the opponent had recognised that quality and, even among his abusive threats, was less aggressive, cocking glances of surprised acknowledgment at Tudor. A further string of local oaths issuing from Tudor's mouth and the opponent became almost subdued, his eye beginning to glisten with recognition. But he growled obstinately:

"What was he doing with the cops, anyhow, and where'd they find out about our meeting?"

Impatiently, Melville told him to shut up. A subdued little whistle had run along the groups of men from the opening of the ravine: a hand signalled cautiously to Melville from the brim of the opposite slope. The men crouched in readiness, easing themselves on their bellies towards the stones and boulders. There was a smart clatter of hoofs on the road of the ravine.

Tudor, peering between boulders, saw the cavalry trot up, a smart double string slowly reaching through the bed of the ravine: the cavalcade was headed by six mounted policemen. When the cavalry almost filled the stretch of road, the policemen nearing the upper end, the boulders began their hastening journey. Faster and faster they rolled, becoming heavy black wheels as they speeded towards the legs of the horses. There was a sharp order from below, the double line of shiny animal flesh seemed jolted into stark deadness for a moment, then quivered in a sudden electric movement: for a few seconds the double line of horses flashed into gallop.

A second volley of boulders swished down the slope. And suddenly the quick, tidy rhythm of the clattering hoofs became a confused discord. The bed of the ravine was a tumbled mass of heaving flesh, out of which the necks of the horses were stretched in lunging astonishment. Shouts and curses of the soldiers were shrill with a sense of ignominious defeat. Some of the horses trotted up the first easy ascent of the slope, skirting their fallen companions. More boulders were rolled. The defeat was complete.

There was another sharp order, and the dismounted soldiers were foolishly obliged to attempt a scaling of the slopes, brandishing their rifles. They were met with a shower of small flints: they were forced to retire. There was no order to open fire: there was no shot: they could do nothing against this wily move. The ambush was totally unexpected. An easy dispersal of a meeting by force of numbers of skirmishing horses was all that was expected. To attack professional soldiers!

47

At a signal, the silent clots of men darkening the two rims of the ravine abruptly ceased their attack, and in a minute the uplands were deserted. They scurried away as efficiently as blackbeetles familiar with their tracks and the position of the holes that were sanctuaries. In secret clefts and hollows the men gathered, resting and discussing their triumph. A sense of confidence held them. Their success was like a good meal; it fed and warmed them. They had shown that they had strength and power yet; they had struck successfully at the interfering invaders. Still the mountains were theirs.

III

By the time Tudor arrived home, after darkness had clothed the hills and the men had stolen down by roundabout ways, his left eye was half circled by a blue-black bruise. Melville, who was unofficially accepted as the men's leader in these bouts of warfare, had angrily reprimanded the man who had thrown the stone. But really he was helpless in these small personal disputes. Numbers of the men used the riots that were general all over the valley as an excuse for doing damage to people of whom they disapproved. Private enmities broke into lawless behaviour. The man who had attacked Tudor's home, behind his genuine suspicion of Tudor being a spy, had an unappeasable dislike of all the middle-class in the place. The men were still raw and loose from a long heritage of grievances, and their angry movements towards recognition of their plight had not yet solidified into expert union.

His mother happened to be coming downstairs as he entered the gas-lit hall, and she uttered a cry at sight of his bruise.

"My poor boy, what have you been doing?"

"I found the lout," he said gruffly. "How is Bronwen?"

"She pretended to be quite well, but, of course, she was suffering from shock and I've managed to get her to bed." She patted her son's shoulders, glinting with admiration. Now he had seen how barbarous were the strikers and had turned against them at last. "Go up and let her see your black eye," she added proudly. "Or have something hot first—"

"Everybody gone?" he asked shortly.

"Yes. Mildred wants you to go and see her tonight. Perhaps, my dear, you'd better not go down to the surgery this evening with an eye like that."

"It's been seen by plenty already."

"Did you have a public fight?" she exclaimed in horror then. "Oh, Tudor, not in the street!"

"On the mountain," he answered, running upstairs, after pinching her cheek.

But the black eye was certainly an embarrassment. Bronwen, propped among pillows and denied her knitting, wept. The obscurity of his replies to their questions was taken for modesty. He thought it inadvisable to tell them of his dangerous association with the afternoon's attack on the soldiers. He felt he could not deal just then with their horror and shock. His father was reading Donne's sermons in the study, and there was an air of Olympian detachment about him; he looked at his son's bruised eye with a careful scrutiny, but said nothing.

"You've heard about the attack on the military this afternoon?" Tudor asked.

Elwyn nodded, looking at his son, shrewdly but aloofly. "What good it will serve, I don't know."

"A gesture of independence," Tudor answered, troubled, because he, too, was uneasy about these violences. Those injured, bleeding legs of the horses; sharp flints that had found their mark; the destroying of property.... "They have limited means of asserting themselves," he went on. "No money, no powerful voice, no influential representation."

"They've struck work and that should be enough," Elwyn said quietly. "They've chosen to starve themselves and they should do it bravely. I'm with them there, I'm with their strike, as you know."

His sympathy was of a religious and idealistic kind. He loved the men as brothers, they were all children of God, and imperfect here on earth. But it was useless to look for joy and security on the earth. Some day each man would enter into his appointed state of bliss, rid of petty jangling and the iniquitous idiocy of the world. Always, always strife here below, and if one set of troubles died it merely left the spawn of another. Better to sit still and wait—and, while waiting, sing together, listen to sermons, steady the heart in contemplation of the eternal. Elwyn loved the men in mystic brotherhood, he was no better and no worse than they, and he gave to them his talent for healing as freely as he could. But he distrusted their reversion to savagery—this thieving and arson and civil fighting—it was a going-down into the domain of the Evil One, an excuse for the barbarous releasing of the Satan in everyone. He wanted to bring them back to a sense of divine superiority, to worship, to the viewpoint that the scars of this world were the roses of the next. He wanted them to sing in chapel, to be choirs of sweet martyrs, to make the effort of becoming demi-gods almost immune from the petty iniquities of the earth. He gave addresses and lectures in chapels on weeknights, and had a certain following. His son Tudor sometimes thought of him as a fool. But a poetic fool. Moonstruck. But pleasant in an aridly materialistic time.

"Their temper is getting desperate," Tudor said.

"It's difficult to keep calm and detached on an empty stomach."

"Far more difficult to fight mountain battles on one, Tudor. No, their only way is to hold out and play on the natural greed of the pit-owners. Accumulation of more and more profits has become such a vice with the owners, the men can make them ache with a hunger far more desperate than their own. Let them hold out for a year, two years." Elwyn began to smoulder with his own particular kind of fire, the religious power to bleed and go to the stake.

"And how feed and clothe themselves meanwhile?" Tudor asked, beginning to be restless. He stood up and stared broodingly at a print of *Watts's Hope* which hung above part of his father's collection of oppressive books.

"In point of fact," answered Elwyn, "no one actually starves. Soup-kitchens will be opened, cast-off clothes arrive in abundance, funds started. A second-hand kind of existence, of course, but worth while if one's inner belief remains strong and unshaken."

"Belief in what?" asked Tudor, who was beginning to want to be out among the strikers again.

"Belief in having the ability to rise above suffering."

"I don't think they ought to ignore their sufferings," Tudor protested. "Suffering, they'll cry out and give a kick at the backside of their oppressors. A kick is something definite and generally means that the kicked is made to jump, if not move on."

"Ah," sighed Elwyn, looking at his watch, "I suppose it's right that a young man should see only the visible conflict." He got up. "That's how he comes to have the honour of obtaining a black eye.... Well, my boy, it's time we were down in the surgery."

"That stone," said Tudor awkwardly, forcing himself, "was meant for this house. Though, of course, the chap who threw it did not know Grannie was sitting near the window."

"I suppose you'd done something to annoy the strikers?"

"One of them," Tudor answered haltingly. "He thinks I'm an informer against them."

"I see." Elwyn slipped a copy of the *Consolations of Boethius* in his pocket. "You've still got to prove your mettle to them, eh?"

After taking a hasty meal Tudor followed his father to the surgery. There was a crowd of patients that evening, so his father having to pay some visits and leaving him alone in the surgery, it was nine o'clock before he got away. The patients in the surgery had been particularly unkempt and miserable; the evening had seemed like one long dolorous whine. They had asked for medicine and more medicine; he noticed that whenever there was real poverty the patients became greedy for larger bottles of mixtures, bigger boxes of pills. A sudden weariness came to him. The day

51

seemed full of ugliness. He had intended going down to Melville's house for a few minutes before meeting Mildred; earlier in the evening he had felt like seeing Daisy, to be near the simmering liveliness of her voice. But now he turned abruptly away from the descent to the river-bank and made his way up to the villas.

Mildred was sitting alone in the drawing-room before a cosy fire. She was dressed in a soft magenta gown: she looked warm and pensive in the lamplight, with her book and a box of Turkish delight. Leaning against the door the maid had just closed behind him, he looked at her long and slowly. Her expression jumped for a moment at sight of his black eye.

"Pretty," he said, "you look pretty there by the fire."

She flushed a little with pleasure and looked very young. "I've been waiting for you," she said. "You look tired. Why do you stand there? Come and have a warm."

He had felt pleasure at seeing her as he entered the room, sitting in her glinting silks by the fire, her lovely arms bare. She knew how to sit still, holding the quiet of evening within her; she would be the perfect wife, her house would have an ordered peace—life in it would be soft-stepping as a cat. He saw her across the distance of the room, a softly bright temptation, pleasant in her silks.... Daisy would probably be wearing a harsh skirt and a soiled cotton blouse.

"It's very cosy here," he said, advancing. "Got same grub for me?"

She pushed a tiny gilt fork into a fat slice of Turkish delight and held it up to him, enquiringly.

"Ugh, no!"

"Indeed," she laughed, "I ought to have known better, offering it to a tough with a black eye."

"Yes," he answered in a mock growl, watching her, "bugger off to the kitchen and get me a lump of bara-caws."

Mildred's expression became a confusion of surprise and dislike. Then she looked severe. Finally she swept all expression from her face and pulled a knob beside the mantelpiece.

"I'll see what Polly can do for you," she murmured.

When the servant had gone, he took a cushion and squatted beside her chair. Laughing up into her face, he said: "Quite the *grande dame*, aren't you?"

"Not yet."

"You will be," he sighed, "you will be."

"Bad language sounds so discordant," she said, wrinkling her nose.

"Sometimes it's a corrective."

"Tell me about the black eye," she asked.

He gave her a garbled account of his fight with the man who had thrown the stone. And suddenly he was extremely irritated at his inability to tell her the complete truth of his excursions among the rioters. Why should he have to dodge about like this? "As a matter of fact," he said, breaking sharply into his account, "I was with the rioters this afternoon when they attacked the military."

Mildred's knee stiffened under his hand. He saw the recoil in her face: her features seemed to close meanly her red lips shrinking. "You *are* one of them, then?' she exclaimed.

"Almost," he answered, with a slight jeering laugh.

"But why, why?" she asked in confusion. "You don't belong to them, you... you have no *right* to be among them. Their troubles are not yours."

"Aren't they?" he said. They looked at each other, across a gulf. His hand had left her knee, he was sitting back on the cushion.

"Certainly not," she replied. "Of course they're not."

"Yet," he grinned, "I *feel* their troubles are mine."

She shook her head. "I don't understand you. This deliberate going down. I thought that people always wanted to improve the value of their life."

"All depends on what you think constitutes value," he said, sniffing the delicate perfume that came off the skin of her face-skin that suddenly appeared slack and without bloom.

"All sensible people," she answered, rearing herself up a little, "think the same. The value of life is in personal security, comfort, and such wealth as one can best earn."

"All that the workers don't possess," he smiled.

"It can't be helped they were born into the workers' class."

"But it can be helped that as worker they are deprived of security, comfort and wealth."

The gulf widened. She gazed across at him with eyes full of distrust. And a movement of pain passed across her slackened face. Her stiffened neck relaxed, she shifted her gaze away from him and looked about her loosely for a few moments. He felt then that she had cut adrift from him, perhaps finally.... She looked miserable and as if haunted by some grave but secret fear. He remembered all their tender reveries in the old days, their worship of moon, star-cluster, winter in the stark hills, the poems of Wordsworth, the rhetoric and antics of local chapel preachers sweating into the "hwyl"—all the old enchantments that had held them together.... He wanted to go to her and caress her hair. He stood up and remained leaning against the mantelpiece.

Polly brought in a tray. "A long time I've been, indeed," she puffed from out of her enormous stays—they held her stout body rigid from knees to the broad shelf of her bosom. Three black velvet bows were fixed to the piled cables of her hair. "But a piece of meat I tucked into some pastry and popped it in the oven." She beamed over the pasty she had brought for Tudor.

He sat with the tray on his knees. Polly lingered, as was her habit. "And while it was baking," she continued, visibly flooded with horror now, "Temperance Thomas came in from next door and told me about the riots in the mountains this afternoon— you've heard, Miss Mildred?"

Mildred nodded, with a small smile curling back her lips.

"Eh, a lot of blackguards they are," the housekeeper went on, "these rioters. Riff-raff, and I dare say Bristols and Irish for the most part; not many black-blooded people do the Welsh make. I told my nephew Emlyn," she went on, bristling, "Emlyn that went into the pit a year ago, you remember, Miss, I told him that if I found him among those drunkards and jail-birds that make riots, disown him I would and give to the chapel the little pound or two I got put by and was for him. Foreigners it is," she declared powerfully, "that's coming here and doing damage and sowing mischief in peoples that was nice before. Ach y fi, when I go out sometimes smell them I can like a lot of bad cattle."

"I believe there is quite a large number of native Welsh among the rioters, Polly," Mildred murmured, looking pensively into the fire, whilst Tudor hungrily ate the golden pasty.

"Then a shameful scandal it is, Miss Mildred. But born everywhere are blackguards and fools, I dare say.... How is the pasty, sir?" she demanded, wheeling round, her truculence not yet died down. Nodding her head righteously, she made a swishing exit after a moment or two.

"There," said Mildred softly, "is the genuine spirit of the working class, comfortable and contented in its work. It's got its own sense of pride, too."

"A mass of slave-flesh," Tudor said. "But even she's got the spirit of protest in her, misdirected though it is. Another fifty years of better education for her class and there'll be a tremendous amount of good power ready for use...."

After finishing the snack and placing the tray outside, he sat down opposite her at the other end of the hearthrug and felt rather at a loss. Whenever he spent evenings at home with her, the hours were used up in conversation, playing the piano, and an occasional bout of love-making when her father was not at home. This evening he felt that conversation with her was futile, she showed no disposition to go to the piano, and he as withheld from making love to her. Her father was in the dining-room—he could hear a low murmur of voices, and presently she told him that C. P. Meredith was there on business.

"Your enemy, of course," she added, with a peculiar smile. "I expect they'll come in here soon."

They whipped up a small amount of trivial conversation across

55

the length of the hearth-rug. Tudor was relieved when her father and the general manager of the local colliery entered the room. Mr. Richards was a military-looking man, smartly moustached and turned out; he had a softly purring manner, suggesting that all the difficulties of the world could be soothed away by a calm sitting-away from them, as far back as possible: all his features were reasonable and just so. About his temples his drabbish hair was touched suitably with clean silver. Meredith, squat and with a large air of intense industry, gimlet of eye and disillusioned of mouth, moved always as if he was uncomfortable in his ordinary envelope of flesh—something seemed to restrict his movements, which should have been quicker, more violent, more imperial than they were.

"Hello, Tudor," Mr. Richards greeted his supposed son-in-law-to-be encouragingly, the purr louder; "you've been neglecting us lately. Do you know each other?" he added, turning to Meredith; "this is Doctor Elwyn Morris's son; he's just taken up practice with his father."

"I know your father," grunted Meredith, his lips lifted a moment in disapproval. "Good doctor, good doctor. But very foolish with the men: they take advantage of him—told him so myself."

"Yes, he has a reputation of being kind to them, I believe," Tudor said.

"Over-kind, young chap. So that he gets a lot of the shammers. Men who want a day in bed, off work." Prowling his way to a chair, he shook himself into it and looked round with restless discomfort.

"Personally," murmured Tudor, "I've got nothing to say against a day in bed occasionally. It's good for the mind; gives one time to make a stock-taking of life."

"H'm, I don't know that many men want to do that, young chap. Especially our men round here. They want to snore. I know 'em." Fretfully he moved in his chair, his gimlet eyes digging here, there and everywhere. He had brought an element of rude force into the room. Yet, for all his grim and restless

56

strength, he seemed as though he might burst into tears at any moment.

"Well," purred Mr. Richards, "what are you young men thinking of the dispute?" Always fatherly and nice towards his juniors, he was constantly demanding of them their opinions: towards youths and boys he was even motherly, enquiring if they wore enough underwear and whether their boots leaked: he had a Sunday-school class of boys. Now a widower, he yet oddly suggested that the shadow of a wife walked constantly beside him and was indeed very much one with himself.

"I think the Sliding Scale ought to go and the scheme of Regulation of Output adopted," said Tudor.

Meredith said, wearily now: "God knows I'm in favour of Regulation of Output, if such a thing were possible. But the men don't and won't realise that the coal trade is no longer sheltered. Our pits are not such precious things as they were. Continental competition's got its teeth into us." He spoke as if to himself, as if, indeed, he had reiterated his statements thousands of times, an incantation. "When coal prices are high and trade good, the men don't complain of the Sliding Scale rates of wages—they take their luxurious wages then, spend them all, and don't save for the day when prices are low, trade bad, and bang down goes the Scale for both profits and wages. Always wanting the penny and the bun."

"Continental competition arriving is going to keep the coal trade in a low state always then?" Tudor enquired, recognising the divided being in Meredith as, curbed and fretting, the squat general manager grimaced in his chair. "What about the enormously increasing demand for coal and its different qualities? Ours here is of the best."

"So it is, so it is," grunted Meredith, giving him one sharp glance of summing-up and treating him thereafter as among the blacks in the place. "But no coal's good enough to fetch the prices we'd have to get if we listened to the strikers. Diamonds are what they ought to be digging for, sack-loads of diamonds."

Mildred was frowning at Tudor, her father's face was full of uneasy deprecation: Tudor was a black sheep going out from among the white flock of the place. He was disloyal to the set to which he belonged. There were enough criminal agitators in the place already, and everyone knew of their ugly, barbarous disposition, given to drinking and immoralities.

"Yet," said Tudor, feeling himself recede farther and farther from the circle that enclosed the other three, "your Company's profits the first half of this year were staggering, weren't they? However low the coal prices, you can still declare your comfortable dividends by working the pits overtime."

"The men," suddenly roared Meredith in a manner usual to him when cross, "are miners, not bosses. We give them a deal according to the principles of Capital and Labour everywhere. Miners are better paid than any other mass of workmen in this country." Ending his stock phrases, he flung a look of surprised contempt at Tudor. "You, young chap, you'd be better employed minding your own business in your surgery than trying to poke in where you won't be thanked."

"Going among the miners and their families so much," said Tudor slyly, "I can't help becoming a bit like them, I suppose."

"He's one of the socialists, I expect," said Meredith to the solicitor, cocking his thumb at Tudor. "Been reading a few books, got six ideas in his head, and no experience."

"Six ideas, when they're the right kind, are plenty for any man, Mr. Meredith. And as to experience, I've smelt and breathed the air around your pits since I was born: it's in my blood."

"Young men," Mr. Richards endeavoured to soothe the air, "generally get hot-headed about something. If it's not politics, it's religion or gardening or something—" He became arch, "something not so nice. Eventually when they're settled down and have families of their own, they all become good citizens with temperate views." He looked benignly at his daughter, inferring that the medicine was in her hands.

The general manager had not listened to this. He cast another look at Tudor, sulkily now, and more than ever he seemed oppressed by some inner dissatisfaction. Tudor knew that buried deep under Meredith's collection of duties and acquired principles, his ambitions and memories of tremendous personal labours, lay an intrinsic sympathy with the men. He was one of them. And even now he wanted to be a democratic employer, knit into the same texture of thought as his men. The times were against him. Not yet had the powerful hierarchy of industrial barons, with their feudal ideas of master and slave, died out. He had to contend with the great Sir Rufus Morgan, one of his companion employers in the valley, who still would not recognise a Trade Union, except to fight it with bitter and intolerant wrath. Meredith secretly welcomed a Union, despairingly hopeful that it would contain interceding men of reasoned judgment who could sort out the miners' everlasting troubles and express those which were just and genuine. But another part of his being, which contained the urge that had lifted him from next-to-nothing into the ranks of the great employers, kept him loyal to the interests which he served. He had a wide-eyed awe of great wealth and, slowly achieving it, had come to feel its responsibility like a sacred cause within him. The shareholders of his company had given him their trust and he looked upon his duty towards them as something that must on no account be bungled or treated with antics. His life and outlook were intensely serious.

"The men think we can afford to pay them a twenty per cent advance," he almost cried, staring at Tudor. "Why don't they go into my shareholders' homes and steal their carpets and their cutlery and their pocketwallets! That's what they ought to do. Not try to force *me* to do their stealing for them." But he was not really talking to Tudor or anyone else; he was talking to himself. For days he had been wrapped in a brooding misery thick as stone, though now and again he darted out to make denunciations of contempt against the men. They had struck in violation of their agreements, made after the last strike, not to leave work without proper notice of six months. They had not consulted him, who had always given ear to them and talked their language, unlike Sir Rufus Morgan, who had barricades like mountains about him and who tried to imitate God.... He had striven to be a human father to them and they had plotted and schemed behind his back. They had burnt down his house, though last year he had built for them a meeting-hall complete with library and billiard-room. Something had gone seriously wrong with the bond that existed between him and his men: *they* had soured. He blamed the secret teaching of a pernicious doctrine brought to the valley by elusive outsiders. A respectable trade unionism, kept steady by temperate men, was to be welcomed; but there were other anarchical creeds filtering into the place through adventurers: his men were being corrupted. "They can go on striking," he went on obsessively, "they can go on striking again and again and maybe they'll seem to gain a fraction. But in the aggregate their earnings will show a loss. Six weeks' strike in a year and they wipe out the worth of the twenty-per-cent advance if they gained it. And next year they'll be striking for something else—shorter hours, compensation pay or," he added, with sudden bitter humour, "cups of tea and cake at four o'clock or free squirrel muffs for their wives."

"Well, then," Tudor said, "they'll gain most of what they want in time: the strikers of today are being martyrs for the coming generations. *I* think we're just beginning a whole era of strikes and agitation. The men are becoming conscious of a new outlook." He stood up, affected by the obsessive restlessness of Meredith, huddled in stony bitterness in his chair, and thrust out a young, serious face. "I think the new century is going to hear the last gasp of capitalism. Labour is going to be something else beyond purchased muscle and brawn, it's going to be aware of itself as the power that gives life to a country. There have been amateur preparations for it this last part of the nineteenth century. In the twentieth there's going to be professional organisation of the power of labour, and strikes are going to be national and affairs of the State, not local quarrels over a shilling a week more. A master is not going to buy ten stone of human flesh, but a man who realises he's got a tongue and, linked with his fellow-workmen, collective force." At the back of his mind, as he stood alert and cocky on the hearth-rug, was the thought that perhaps he was cutting quite a dash as a speaker, and he began to wish that this was a meeting attended by a few hundred: he continued enthusiastically: "What the workers are becoming conscious of is, of course, that they are entitled to a larger share of profits than has been granted them since the Industrial Revolution decided that workers, being merely lumps of flesh and muscle, were to be considered least in its scheme. Industry has developed, but the masters forget that its workers have developed too. They can now read and write, and their wives have learned that there are other materials besides flannel, and they know there are days to be spent by the seaside, and it is possible to have pancakes for tea on other days beside Sunday. The people are growing up and want recognition of themselves as men and women, not hardy beasts with weals on their unwashed flesh—"

Mr. Richards, who had been sending him deprecating looks, broke in, a breeze ruffling the cat's fur of his voice: "Well, Tudor, this is quite a speech. I must interpose, I'm afraid. Please retain your oratorical powers for where they are necessary and will be welcomed. Really, really—" He spread his long artistic hands and looked appealingly at his daughter, who sat inscrutable in her chair, turning a gold bangle.

"Oh, I don't mind him, Richards," growled Meredith. "I been wanting to know for some time who were the chaps in this place who were preaching. Here's one of 'em. Been reading Robert Owen and that latest Bob in the hot pan, Karl Marx, seems to me. Talk, talk, all talk." He darted a sudden rather school-masterly look of menace at Tudor. "It seems to me, young chap, that your business is to give up doctoring people's bodies in this place and attend to their minds, perhaps. Yes, perhaps."

"If they'll have me," grinned Tudor, still drawn up at the hearth as though on a platform.

"Aye, that's true," replied Meredith, with a squirming grunt. "Chaps of your kidney have come, and gone, afore now."

"Come now, I'm no stranger here." Tudor thought of his grandmother Bronwen's proud declaration that he was a descendant of the family who had ruled the valley for seven or eight hundred years.

Meredith suddenly declared with passion, heaved up in his chair: "The men belong to me! They'll have to listen to me. A year ago they swore to remain faithful to me. I was among them." Again he was wrapped in his own brooding self, talking to himself. "I will go among them again, they know I am with them."

"Give them their twenty per cent!" Tudor urged. "You can afford it."

Meredith came back to him, with his voice of weary contempt. "Aye, I can afford it. I can afford to give 'em all the colliery, all the profits—if there'll be any. They're after running the pits themselves, aren't they?—that's their final demand. And what happened when that was done as an experiment up in the north of England! Bankruptcy in a year. And such a mangy mess made of things that nothing could be done but leave the place to go to ruin. You're after the Kingdom of Heaven on earth. Men'll have to be born different before what you want will come to pass. There'll have to be sixteen ounces of brain given to every man, and one standard character to each, and no lie-abed and sluggard born to Mrs. Harris while Mrs. Jones next door has a boy that wins all the scholarships and works sharp as lightning."

"Men are not so different as all that," Tudor observed. "It's a recognition of the important hardworking mass of men that we want."

The general manager made a gesture of dismissal. "Anyway, young chap, you can tell your agitating friends that we've bolted the door for a long time now. *We're* going to have the say as to time and terms now. I've had a fair sickener this time: I can't abide men with no code of honour. Chucking down tools without a moment's notice. No, young chap, they're not taking them up in a hurry again." His gimlet eyes were full of a hard misery; his mouth hung sulkily. "I'll give 'em soup-kitchens for their youngsters, bread and pea soup every day, but I've got knuckle-dusters on for the men—aye, since they put 'em on first!" And he closed up with a snap of finality, afterwards treating Tudor as though he were not there. Mr Richards took up the reins and purred soothingly of the merits of a young Baptist minister he was favouring for appointment at the chapel of which both men were deacons. The solicitor treated Tudor with marked remoteness now. Ostracism was beginning.

Tudor, with a curious sense of liberation, prepared to go. He did not dislike Meredith—only looked on him as a victim of a scheme so vast and powerful that he was made helpless in it. He suspected that Meredith, secretly and sulkily, worked for the men's benefit as far as was possible. What Tudor did not know was that at the board meeting of the Colliery Company that week the general manager had recommended a fifteen-per-cent advance—which, of course, the men would have accepted. But the Board had indignantly opposed and rejected his plea. And Meredith all the time bitterly complained of the strikers; in his heart sorrowing over them—there, in his heart, was a touch of Jesus Christ which scalded him even while, outwardly, he had to behave according to the scheme of earthly business. And all his sulkiness came from the awareness that implacable forces were turning him to stone. He had no right to feelings, in his position. Sir Rufus Morgan did without them and was very grand—he had the bearing of a duke and the grandeur of a king. Once, it was said, Sir Rufus was down one of his pits and, taken short, had used a five-pound note where other men use newspaper: the story had been a godsend to strike leaders and, when one of them succeeded in approaching him, Sir Rufus had replied to the accusation: "Ah, yes, there was quite a rush afterwards. I am sorry it was not a ten-pound one, which I generally use." There was the grand contemptuous manner which he, Meredith, both itched after and fled from.

Mildred went with Tudor out into the hall. In helpless silence she watched him put on his overcoat. Her look was disturbed, almost tearful. He turned to her, knowing she was waiting for him to make some personal gesture towards her: she was in utter confusion. And he was attracted to her thus, broken open, disturbed, and glowing with a red half angry, half frightened flush.

"Do you think I've ruined myself?" he asked banteringly.

"What do *you* think?" she quivered. Her nervous hand turned up the collar of his overcoat. It hesitated before drawing away. She was so unsure of him now.

"Socially I've ruined myself. Probably professionally too, more or less—Meredith having such power. But inside I feel such curious satisfaction.... Smugness, if you like." His finger stroked her red cheek: it was hot but hard under the gentle touch. "Have patience with me, Mildred. You don't know what I'm going through."

"Why can't we go away?" she exclaimed, with half subdued passion. "This place is not good for you. You could easily find a job in some quiet country town."

"A job!" he repeated vaguely, looking through the open door into the thick valley night.

She laid her arm eagerly then on his arm. Its touch was possessive, loyal, warm. He turned his face to her.

"Tudor, you know I have some money left me by my mother. Let's use it to buy a practice. I don't need the stuff." She burst out a little louder: "We'll go away. While there's still time-"

He swiftly touched her lips. "You mustn't risk your money. I'm so unstable, you know... in myself, I mean."

She swayed back a little. "Yes," she murmured, almost inaudibly, "I think that's true."

He suddenly leaned to her and touched her sexually. "All at sea," he whispered.

She swayed back so that her face was now well in the yellow gleam of the gas-bracket. He saw the fear in her eyes. Her gaze was concentrated on the black bruise about his left eye. Warm in her silks, perfumed and unused, she was attractive and tragic, shrinking against the shiny varnished wall. He pulled his gloves out of his pocket.

"Are you coming to the surgery tomorrow morning?" he asked in the withdrawing, absent-minded way that so perplexed her.

"As usual," she said bitterly. And as he stepped towards the doorway: "But don't get your other eye blacked. I can't bear it."

IV

As soon as he was out of the garden and had closed the iron gate—she stood in the light of the doorway faithfully until his steps had died away—he strode with unconsciously quick steps down the slope to the bed of the vale. Not far away, higher on the slope, was his home, and since he had had very little sleep the night before, he ought to have gone there and to bed. But he felt very awake, deep inside, though his eyelids were heavy and there was a dull ache in his head. But elsewhere that curious sense of power and aliveness. Almost he strutted as he walked.

It would soon be midnight. There was no one about. In the main street the naked boards of the smashed shop-fronts gave him a reminder of the mischief with which he was becoming associated. He shrugged his shoulders. What, after all, were a few broken shop windows compared to the everlastingly barren pantries of the beastly old dwellings reared behind the main street! Uncomfortable, noisy and disreputable to smash up shops, but it was the work of a primitive instinct that was ineradicable... as yet.

At the corner there were six or seven policemen in conference. As Tudor approached in the darkness they turned towards him, suspiciously. They were mostly new policemen, but one, the sergeant, recognised him with what Tudor thought was an ironical note:

"Another case, doctor?" Tudor nodded.

"Hope it's not twins tonight."

"All these riots and excitements," Tudor answered jauntily as he passed, without stopping, "are bringing things forward like the sun in March."

"Aye, and with all these soldiers coming here there'll be out of season blooming again."

He did not take the turning which would have led him quickest to his destination. And he took no short cuts through the back lanes between the rows of houses. These nights one never knew what spies or policemen lurked and patrolled in them. But at another corner of the main street, standing in a deep alcove, he saw three more policemen, who made no movement or sound as he went past. If he hadn't caught the dull glitter of the silver spike on one helmet, he would not have noticed them.

This was probably the last time he would be able to go through the streets late at night unsuspected or unchallenged. After his showing-up of himself to C. P. Meredith he would be a marked man.

Half an hour later he was tapping at the front door of Melville's house. Previously everyone had used the back door in the lane, walking through the black strip of garden down to the kitchen door. But now it was safer to go openly to the front entrance, above the murky river, where the shrivelled, bony bushes swung in the swooping mountain winds like black skeletons.

Daisy opened the door: the passage-way was dark behind her. For a moment or two he stood silently tasting her physical presence, which always seemed to ring through the air. Never shrinking or hesitant or die-away. He grinned, unseen. The darkness was complete.

"I know who it is," she said.

"You were expecting me, of course," he answered as he stepped in.

"No. I could sense you."

He put out his hand and touched her breast. "As sensitive to me as that!" He felt he was touching some warm waxen flower, thick and pulpy.

66

"I could tell *all* the men who come here, just the same," she said, with a short laugh, "blindfolded."

"A wonderful gift," he said. He was wondering if the gift told her what he was thinking then. She did not move away from his touch. There was a silence, while they both stood in the blackness of the passageway. A low murmur of voices came from the kitchen.

"We'd better go in," she remarked carelessly.

Swiftly he asked: "Can I stay here tonight?"

He felt her quiver. Then, after the briefest silence, she said: "Yes."

They went into the kitchen. Tonight he was greeted with more friendliness from the five men seated about the room. The triumphant skirmish of the afternoon, in which he had joined, disposed them to acceptance of him. The black eye was a badge, too, howsoever earned.

"A doctor ought to have got rid of that by now," remarked Billy Saunders, still a little ironical.

"I like it black," Tudor said briefly.

Melville smiled, his worn, half-sour, half-sweet smile. His face showed more pallor tonight; his mat of black hair was unkempt, shoved far down his forehead. But for the steady disillusioned weariness of his eyes, he would have looked the complete fanatic. "That bloody idiot who threw the stone won't give you any more trouble, Tudor," he said. "He's been warned, officially, and the gang he's with."

"They pinched twelve pounds of shag out of Price's in yesterday's riots," one of the young men said indignantly. "Tonight they were going to hide in the cwtch where Pritchard used to keep his pigs, on the mountain-side, and sit chewing until it was all gone."

"God damn them for their stealing," Melville exclaimed fretfully. "They're making things a hundred times more difficult for us."

"Any further news?" asked Tudor, sitting low on a three-legged stool at the fender's end.

"The Federation is weakening," Melville snapped. "There's talk of a five-per-cent offer from the owners."

"On the Sliding Scale basis?"

"Of course. The owners know what they're doing. Foreign competition, you know! Prices coming down every month.... In three months' time that five per cent will be worth nothing at all."

"It's the Sliding Scale's got to go altogether," Tudor said. "Let the men go back and have another ducking under falling prices. They'll get so mad at being taken in that they'll come out all over the valley in a solid bunch and stick out until they're granted the minimum."

"They must stay out now!" Melville cried passionately. "All this disgusting patching up of the shoddy garment—how can they put up with it? And that milk and-water Miners' Federation— oh, hell," he subsided wearily, "they're too busy changing each other's napkins, I suppose, and shaking their little rattles—" After various attempts to be elected to the local Federation committee, he had been turned down.

"I hear they're coming to the end of their funds," one of the young men said, while he dreamily poked about in his ear with a match-stick. "Next week their members are to get two bob less."

Tudor mechanically took out his packet of cigarettes and handed it to Daisy's eager clutch. She took it round the company. There was a sigh of pleasure. Physically aware though everyone was in that room, and strongly muscled—except perhaps Melville—and raw with a kind of fleshy power, there was a look and an air of austerity about them. No one had had a respectable meal for days, except Tudor. The spotless kitchen, bare table and fireless grate suggested a room where there had been no celebrations of domestic life for some time. The brown china owl, with the lamp on its head, squatted on the mantelshelf in desolate brooding. Framed over the sink was a picture of a purelooking young woman gazing heavenwards: it was called *The Soul's Awakening*.

68

For a while there was silence while they contentedly smoked the cigarettes. Daisy's gaze darted once or twice at Tudor with bright curiosity. She accepted him simply and trustingly, but she had never had an intimate to do with any but the rough-and-ready young colliers. Melville went over to the tap and washed his face, wiping it on the "roller"-towel fixed to the back of the door: he still limped from a policeman's kick. From Billy Saunders's broad nostrils shot dense streams of smoke; his short thick body, even in repose looked ready to spring.

"What's the next move to be?" Tudor asked Melville.

"I'm calling a mass meeting tomorrow evening. On the fairground. Dai Lewis is going out with a bell tomorrow morning crying it." He asked suddenly, "Like to speak at it?"

"I don't mind... yes," Tudor said.

They looked at him. Two of the young men on the sofa sniggered quietly. "Could you stand the disgrace?" Billy Saunders asked, jealously.

He told them of his talk with the general manager that evening. Melville sat listening intently, without comment. Only into his eyes there crept a guardedly tender gleam. Daisy sat in high-coloured astonishment, smiling to herself: gradually her face took on a look of pleased preparation.

"So at last you really are one of us," she said, as Tudor, finishing, spun his cigarette into the grate.

"Under our banner," Melville said, "at least."

"You'd better come and *live* with us," Daisy went on, opulently and with a large gather-them-all-in gesture.

"Oh no," said Melville at once, "Tudor will be far more use if he stays where he is. We need some heralds among the socially elevated."

Billy Saunders, who had looked surly at Daisy's invitation, spat with one swift sure aim into the sink. The white whistle of liquid shot through the air past Daisy's nose by six inches.

"Haven't I put that old tin under the window for you?" she remarked evenly, like a lady.

"The sink's easier to find," he jeered.

"It's no place to spit in," Melville said with severity. "Please turn the tap on."

Billy went to the tap, springingly, and turned on the water. Then, whistling, he went outside to the lavatory.

"I find that young man," Daisy said with a sudden stagy grandeur, mincing her voice, "gross, disgusting and common."

The three young men on the sofa took huge delight in her remark, swelling with laughter.

"Why have I to keep lodgers?" she demanded, with the tragic intensity of a Clytemnestra. "I'm made for greater things than lodgers and bending over a washtub."

"In the eighteenth century," Melville said, "you'd have been a great lady kept by some gouty old nobleman. Now you're nothing but the pet cockatoo of a lot of grimy revolutionists."

"The future is so dark for me," she complained. "All I'm preparing for is to be caretakeress of a workhouse." She went on ardently, her beautiful vitality flashing from her. "Sometimes I long for a golden evening dress, and ostrich feathers, and a white young poet to hold my hand in the box of a theatre."

Billy Saunders noisily pulled the chain of the lavatory, which abutted on the kitchen, and returned whistling. Melville was telling his sister.

"You're far happier washing a collier's back, you know you are. Besides, we're all poets here—real ones. Think of that witty limerick Billy wrote about you. Real stuff."

"If you call that real!" she said indignantly.

"There's worse words in the Bible," Billy remarked comfortably, taking the last cigarette.

"I'm not one of those Old Testament women." She arched her graceful neck at him.

Her indignation was quite amiable. And really she did not want to move from out of the circle of her brother's life, his activities and his friends. They had read books together—he the mentor— and together they had become liberated from the old stale rigidity of their nonconformist upbringing. Together they had walked out of the dark stony little bethel of their childhood. Only sometimes she had a spasm of fear that they had not gone the right way after all. She would like a little more hard cash, and a little more obvious beauty in life. She would like to perceive a gentler look on the face of the future. She had her fears.

"One o'clock!" said Billy, winding the cheap tin clock on the mantelshelf. "Seems that there's nothing more to say tonight." He gazed round the company as if expecting them to disperse.

Melville had been glancing shrewdly from Tudor to his sister. He smiled. But a shadow of obscure agony was on that smile. His thin upward slanting eyebrows gave him a faintly satanic look. Everyone, except his sister, felt that he was a mystery, and that inside his soul a bleak struggle was always being waged.

"Are you staying here tonight?" Daisy asked the young men.

They were. They often spread themselves over the house, on sofas or mats, or sharing the lodger's room.

"Well, there's no breakfast for any of you," Daisy said flatly.

"We can go out in the morning for some food," one of them said, looking at Tudor. Tudor said that he had some money. "I'm staying too," he added.

Billy Saunders scowled at Daisy. She looked back at him serenely. In a temper he bounced out of the room and stamped springingly upstairs, slamming his door.

Melville rose and took a book down from some crowded shelves nailed against the wall: it was a volume of the *Yellow Book*. "I'm going to read for an hour,'" he said. He could never get to sleep before four or five in the morning.

"I'll go and share Billy's bed," one of the young men said confidently.

Another was to have a sofa in the kitchen, the third a chair in the middle-room, the fourth the floor rug. Daisy fetched old coats, a rug, and a blanket to cover them. Tudor sat waiting, amused and interested—and calm, now that he had seemed to reach some definite point in his association with this household. He watched

Daisy. She was acting a drama and enjoying it. That abundant vitality of hers—it had to find some outlet. But the stage was so narrow and dark for her in this tiny poky house. No wonder they all felt her presence, were conscious of her strength and her power. She circled like a lioness in a cage. Her strength was too condensed.

She went up to her room at last. Melville held up his book, showing a picture. "I like this man Aubrey Beardsley," he said. "He can see straight. His pictures smell of rotten cabbages, but they're art." The picture was *The Wagnerians*. "He's one of us, though I don't suppose he knows it."

The young man on the sofa was already breathing stoutly under the rug, only his coarse strawberry-coloured hair visible. Tudor examined the picture, nodded, and murmured, "I'm going up to Daisy."

"Look at that stout woman in the foreground," Melville urged excitedly—"she's got all the decay of a civilisation in her face. Gross, perverted and unclean."

Tudor looked, said something, and added good night. Leaving Melville searching the volume for more Beardsley, he stumbled up the dark staircase. There were three rooms. As he reached the landing, the door of the back room opened and Billy Saunders came out in a nightshirt.

"Hi," he whispered angrily, "where you going to?"

"To bed," Tudor answered cheerfully.

"Whose bed?"

"Now you go back to yours, or you'll be catching cold."

"Why don't you keep to your own blasted women," hissed Billy. "Coming here because *they've* got padlocks on 'em, eh!"

"Well," said Tudor temperately, "there's some truth in that."

"Blasted cheek!" Billy glowered. He shifted from one bare foot to the other in helpless anger. "Look here, I'll fight you tomorrow morning for her. On the mountain-side. Game?"

"I don't mind. But first we must ask Daisy if she's willing to favour the man who wins. Otherwise, it won't be much use, will it?" Tudor, going to Daisy, felt that he wanted to placate him.

"But I want to have a smack at you," Billy said, almost earnestly. The heat of his sturdy aggressive body came through the nightshirt.

"Oh, go to bed," Tudor said, pushing past him on the landing. This delay began to make him impatient.

"We'll see tomorrow," Billy muttered darkly. He was afraid to attack now, with Daisy about. More than once she had hit him over the head with some domestic article or utensil.

She was plaiting her hair before the tiny dressing table mirror. In her milky nightgown she looked much younger. She was humming to herself contentedly. The big bed was high and substantial as a boxing-ring, nearly filling the room. He had to edge round it to get to a corner to undress.

"Was that Billy talking to you?" she asked idly.

"Yes... He seemed upset."

"Take no notice of him. He looks on me as though I'm a patch of land he's going to buy and dig over."

"Or win through fighting."

"He's such uncooked stuff," she said, wrinkling her nose like a child. She climbed into bed. "Put the gas out when you're ready, will you?" And she began to sing her pleased little song again.

But for all her composure she was luxuriously roused. He was filled with a grateful delight. Her own amiable pleasure was so downright. When he was a student in London there had been one or two furtive and slovenly affairs. And of course in middle-class Wales he had been reared in the strict understanding that women were as the icebergs floating about in an arctic sea, no thought of men troubling their snowy brows.... But here was no icy desert. A sense of relief flooded his mind. He became aware too of a most satisfying sense of excellency in the world.

They were playfully wrestling when there came the sound of raised voices downstairs. For a moment they remained clenched like stone figures in embrace. Then they heard clumsy footsteps clattering up the stairs, one pair after another, and at once the door was flung open and a burly black shape stood menacingly beside the bed. "Who's here?" barked a voice with a curious undersqueak in it. And the shape lit a match.

By the time the gas was lit another policeman was walking into the bedroom. "No one in the other front room,'" he said. "Two chaps in the back. They're nabbed."

"Hi!" exclaimed Tudor, "what are you doing here?"

Sergeant Roberts was looking at him with stern redfaced reproof. The other policeman, not of the local force, was only mildly interested in the spectacle on the bed. "You'd better be getting your things on," the sergeant said, his odd natural doll-squeak completely swallowing his bark, "you two. You're coming along to the police station for tonight."

"Indeed now!" cried Daisy at once and indignantly. "What right have you to come bursting into my private bedroom? Police station, indeed! Go away."

Roberts had been breathing awkwardly, and the triumph of his squeak, which he always tried to suppress, was evidence of his embarrassment. Tudor Morris in bed with this woman! What a scandal!

"I've a warrant to arrest everyone in this house," he squeaked, almost imploringly. "Come now, no fuss—it'll be best for you."

"Look here, Sergeant," protested Tudor, who was a little pale about the gills, "what's the charge?"

"Offences against Her Majesty's Government, incitement to disorder—to begin with," warned the sergeant. "Come along now."

"Neither of us has anything to do with that," Tudor replied flatly. After the first shock he had become quite cool. "Miss Walters is a friend of mine and I am only a visitor to this house." Now they both sat up in bed a little like wondering primitives.

The sergeant's squeak became ruthless. "Up to yesterday your statement would have been of use to me, Doctor, where you are concerned. Afraid it's no good now. Please be dressed." And he turned his face to the wall, the other policeman doing likewise.

All the time there had come various sounds of clamour from

the back bedroom and downstairs. Evidently there were many policemen in the house. Billy Saunders's voice, cursing and blasphemous, was the loudest. Daisy and Tudor looked at each other for a minute with dismay. Tudor shrugged his shoulders and jumped out of bed: Daisy, more slowly, let herself down from the high and extremely untidy mattress. Two more policemen looked in, stared, and withdrew at a sign from the sergeant. "We've got 'em all handcuffed," one remarked before going out.

Once Daisy was in her clothes—she had taken out from the bottom drawer of the dressing-table her best dress, scarlet and satiny—she began to breathe in, as though it were the most bracing briny air, the drama that had swept into her life.

Impressive in her red, she swung round and declared with flashing bitterness, "A pretty fine pass things have come to when a lady can have no privacy for herself and her young man. *I* don't know what these policemen are up to! What do they want, Tudor, can you tell me?"

He humoured her. "Something about offences against Her Majesty's Government."

"Since when," she asked boldly, "is it an offence to be in bed with someone you're fond of? *They've* offended against all decent laws by bursting in on us like this. We might be in the Dark Ages again."

The sergeant turned back from the wall. His face was a pained beetroot-colour now. The drawn-up woman in scarlet, her face lifted in offended enquiry, beetled over the other side of the bed like holy wrath. He was a chapel man, though not bigoted, and he had never had to do with such a business as this before. He was upset and scandalised, having great respect for Tudor's father. "I'm not arresting you and Doctor Morris for being together here," he squeaked alarmingly. "I tell you I have a warrant for arresting *everyone* in this house on suspicion of inciting to disorder and in connection with the riots of this week."

More astonished wrath sprang out of her face. "Suspicion,

suspicion!" she cried dramatically. "How dare you suspect me and Doctor Morris of such things! I've never been so insulted in my life. You burst into my private room—"

"It's so preposterous," interrupted Tudor curbingly, struggling with his stiff white collar, "that in the light of day we'll be having a good laugh over it. But I suppose the sergeant's got to execute his warrant, odd though it is." He thought her bluff was becoming too blatant.

A gruff voice bawled from the staircase: "Shall we take the prisoners up to the station now, Sergeant?"

"We're coming at once," the sergeant replied through the open door. "They'll all go together."

Arrested! Prisoners! The words were amazing and idiotic, not to be applied to oneself. Tudor mechanically parted his hair with Daisy's comb. There was a cold fist of numbness inside him. He also wanted to burst into loud laughter. If only those ridiculous but matter-of-fact policemen would leave the room, he and Daisy would slip back into the warm adventurous bed again and he would tell her that he had been having rather a queer dream. Daisy, in her red, was also an astonishing vision; he had never seen her dressed up before. She looked handsome and considerable.

When at last he was ready—for Daisy had slipped into her corset-less apparel swiftly—the sergeant and policeman edged their way round the bed, at the same time producing handcuffs. Daisy reared herself up again, violently red; Tudor made a reasoned protest. But it was of no avail. Handcuffed, they were marched ignominiously downstairs.

All the gas-brackets were flaring, and already, in Melville's workroom, a policeman was busy turning out papers from a desk. Policemen cluttered up the passageway; in the kitchen, along with the prisoners, five waited under their silver-spiked helmets. At Daisy's entrance some grinned. Tudor they glanced at curiously.

"Now," barked the sergeant officiously, the squeak scampering out of his voice, "you're all ready?"

Melville gazed from Daisy to Tudor. Perhaps a ghost of his agonised smile crossed his lips at the sight of Daisy's grand scarlet dress. But Tudor he looked at with a burning tenderness, as he leaned waiting against the table. The peculiar austerity of his face had so much in it of the traditional Jesus quality that he cast over the drab proceedings a kind of tragic glamour. Billy Saunders bled slightly at the mouth; he also foamed in impotent rage and seemed to be biting his tongue. The other four young men looked thunderstruck, avenging and worried. "A pretty good clean-up," the sergeant allowed himself to bark, gazing hard at Melville. "A regular nest of 'em."

They were marched out into the night. Some of the neighbours of the oblong, roused by the clamour, peered out of windows. There was quite a procession, including fifteen policemen. With a reproachful manner, the sergeant walked beside Tudor. Tudor was about to launch into protests again, when he caught sight under the light of the first street-lamp—they were kept alight all through the night now, those that were not smashed—of Melville's white-burning but sardonic face. Presently the sergeant, after waiting until they were almost at the station, suggested:

"Shall I send a message to your father, Doctor?"

"No. He's disturbed often enough at night as it is."

There were only five cells in the police station. Up to the day before they had been packed with rioters, now transferred to the main station up the valley. Daisy, resplendent in her vehement dress, stepped up into one like Boadicea into her chariot. Tudor shared a cell with Melville. In it was a wide bench with a couple of smelly rugs. A kind of narrow bier was pushed into the cell after a minute, two further rugs dumped on it, followed by a huge metal chamber-pot. The door was slammed abruptly, but a plank of light slanted down from a ventilator open on to the corridor.

They stood looking at each other for a few moments in silence.

"You see what you've done for yourself!" Melville said. He crouched on the bench, after pushing the rugs to the floor.

"What have all of us done?" Tudor answered, going beside him. He gazed round the grey cell again. Yes, it was undoubtedly there.

"Six months' hard labour, perhaps. Certainly for me—probably more…. It's the wicked waste of time that annoys one." Bitterness began to surge into his voice. "And the men will go back, they're going to give in now." He was quite aware of his power over a large section of the miners, knew the exact value of his hypnotic oratory and his talent for rousing in the natives that burning mysticism which, when it is not lifting the roofs off the chapels, makes strikes into holy crusades.

"Besides," Tudor remarked vexedly, "this sort of thing makes us look so much like silly thwarted idealists."

"One of these days," Melville said gently, "you're going to get out of the personal view."

"Spread my self out entirely in a cause, you mean?"

And, as though they were at home, they settled down to conversation. There was a faint cold blueness in the air: morning was near.

"Stop making efforts to find yourself under a particular name or with a particular theory of values. You must yield yourself up to the dirty world…. You're trying to do it already, I know." Melville touched his arm, the touch of the thin nervously-shaped hand light as a leaf. "You'll probably not be convicted…. we'll be separated." He was silent for a minute, then went on quietly, "Combat evil, and work to suppress greed and other strictly human mischiefs; try and make men more like animals. You'll find yourself all right."

"One breathes in such a lot of dirt from the air of the world," Tudor laughed; "it seems a full-time job cleaning out one's own soul." He gazed round again at the grey cell with a little grin; he was surprised that he was accepting his presence there with so little dismay.

"It'll be cleaned up for you," Melville said. "You needed a revolution in yourself, and you began it. It's the right way."

"You mean the process will be transferred outside one's own individuality?"

"Yes.... and the difference to anyone who has started any kind of revolution, personal or otherwise, is that the world seems less of a dead end, less of a gigantic and disreputable hoax." Melville's voice had lost its bitterness now; it was quiet with confidence and faith. "The religion here is not enough now; it was created and had its power in a simpler, perhaps a better world. The men are beginning to question, and there'll have to be some sort of reply—I mean they're going to question differently; there'll be a new wording to their demands."

"But the same ancient questions really?"

"Perhaps."

"That things shall have a meaning?" Tudor gazed yet again round the grey walls, musingly. There was a heavy subterranean stillness around the stony place.

"Even though there's always death."

"Yes, there's always death.... But death's evil is that it finishes so many people before it actually arrives."

Tudor began to walk slowly up and down the cell: he had begun to be suddenly conscious of its narrowness, its heavy stuffiness, its grey gloom. It irritated him to have to be there; the preposterous and impudent restriction. "Yes, we've got to work for peacefulness, the peacefulness of life." He went on talking; it had become necessary to hear the sound of their voices.

"Even in anger and violence and riot there is peacefulness. But we've got to learn how to use anger and how violence must have the meaning of religion.... People," he went on, "are taught to chalk a circle around their life, and they won't go beyond it, even though they become sick with nausea and mad with boredom—"

"And sometimes," Melville said, watching the other, half amused, half ironical, "they'll heave you a good clod of dirt if you dare try and call them out, and even point at them. And after all," he added, "everybody is inside some kind of circle."

"Are we? I feel that such as you and Daisy, and myself, perhaps, are trotting across some exciting range of hills, and catching glimpses of new strange countries."

"I don't know about the range of hills.... I'd rather say that we've jumped away from the usual drab little circle most people put up with, to one that encloses a patch of green grass, a fruit tree or two, possibly a couple of those ideal women that the poets always shout about, and no policeman's beat."

Tudor sat down laughing beside him. "In spite of us being here?"

"In spite of us being here. This cell is outside the circle, of course." A sniff of thin laughter blew down Melville's nose. "Personally, I haven't been arrested at all. This cell is full of jasmine and this bench a seat on the Acropolis."

There was a small deep window high in the wall; behind its bars a blue-grey sky began to show. And with the showing of the sky, Daisy, obviously becoming bored in the next cell, began to sing like a hoarse lark.

She sang in a rough chirruping way that would not be denied. At six o'clock mugs of tea were given them, containing sugar and milk, and slabs of bread coated with real butter — which was more than they would have got down in the house beside the stream.

CHAPTER III

I

BY Easter the strike was over and the pits working full time in a burst of prosperity. The miners had gained a five-per-cent increase, but the Sliding Scale system of wages remained—if the price of coal dropped, the miners' pay-packet became proportionately lighter. The price occasionally went up, but not often: at the moment it was good, and the five-per-cent increase gave a pleasant look to the pay-packet.

So there were high jinks in the valley again. After the three months of discontent, of starvation, policemen's truncheons and beerless Saturday nights, spring arrived in full frolic. The pubs blossomed with foaming glasses, the deacons going the round of the chapels during the singing of the third hymn had to hold the collection plate with both hands, for copper weighs heavy. In the shops women's hats were piled with fruits and flowers, grocers sold whole cheeses and at the Italian refreshment bars the melodious tongues of the young miners licked away ice-cream piled up in cornets. Young women, becoming plump again from eating toffee and proper Welsh broth with plenty of fat mutton in it, loosened the lacing of their strike-tightened corsets or bought new pink ones. And on Easter Monday nearly everybody went to Barry Island for a day by its muddy sea.

Safely locked up in jail were no less than sixty-three rioters and dangerous agitators, with sentences ranging from three to nine months. Serve them right, most people thought now. Stirring up riots when the strikers could get some of what they wanted by just waiting. Getting caught like that. Everyone deplored the rioting and couldn't understand how it had begun. It just caught on, like the plague or a fashion or a rotten wooden house on fire. But what a bad name it gave the district. No wonder outsiders thought that nothing but savagery went on there.

So once again the rows of houses stank with abundant life. People ate too much, to make up for lost time, and the men who were not particularly of the chapel gangs announced the glory of beer to the new green of the hills. True, the chapels benefited also, many having their insides plastered freshly or a new clock hung on the centre balustrade of the gallery, where only the preacher could see it without turning round. Poultry and pigs were once more kept in the sliced-out back gardens of the rows, and beds of black earth were raked over for the planting of flowers and vegetables: women freely allowed themselves to become pregnant again. Altogether, up and down the narrow valley, where never a cherry-tree or an apple blossomed, a spring with everyone safely in work again declared itself loudly, like the knocking of a bright brass knocker on a mouldy old door.

Already the builders were at work on a new house for C. P. Meredith, on the site of the old burned-out one. But this time it was not to be a house like something out of the Book of Revelations, spectacular as a storm at sea and built for the pacing of a malignant God. C.P. was going to have a square brick house plain as a Church of England sermon and not demonstrative of what his enemies said was uglily-acquired wealth. The one good thing of the recent riots was the burning of his bastard Gothic palace. Any building that aimed at grandeur or the splendiferous looked offensive and ridiculous in this valley of mean rows and dwellings dropped like dung from some hell's beast that had galloped madly over the hill-tops.

The only large house of the district which toned with the scarred hills was the ramshackle old mansion of Clan Ystrad, a floor of which C.P. and his family occupied while his new house was being built. It was on a slope and a small black wood still preceded it. But a minor pit had been sunk at the edge of the wood and for fifteen years had belched sombrely at the graceful shabby old shape. In it had lived the last squire of the district, Tudor Llewellyn, a fool of a man for music, who had wanted life to be one long singing of pretty operas and who had been obliged as a result to sell the estate owned by his family for seven hundred years, to the mine prospectors. It was said that he had died in London clasped in the enormous arms of a *prima donna* who came straight from the last act of *Martha* to his death-bed, his bees-in-her-bonnet wife Nest, who had separated from him, also arriving from a meeting of peculiar women united to make their sex recognised as possessors of brains. The graceful shell of his old manor house still enduring among dust-tattered trees, was all that was left of a quiet country life still remembered by very old people of the district. Colliery offices were on the ground floor.

Now that they were back in work C.P. went among some of his men complaining bitterly of their broken promises when they had struck without giving him the six months' notice to which they had agreed after the strike before. In his dirty old mackintosh and pulledabout cap, thumping his thick stick fretfully on the round he spoke to old colliers whose faces were as familiar to him as the nervously stumpy fingers of his own hands.

"This continual striking has got to stop. Who's monkeying with you? I've recognised your Federation. They seem to have a grain of common sense. But there's other people among you. Why do you listen to them?" Aggrieved and worried, he peered at the five or six old colliers collected in the white-washed stable down in No. 1 pit.

"It's the young chaps, it is," Gronw, hollow-faced and thin as the new pick he carried, said. "All those new ones that's come in from outside. They 'ont marry and they 'ont come to chapel and they sit in their pitclothes in the pub and go to bed in their pit-dirt—yes indeed. Where they come from, I don't know. America perhaps. Meetings they have on their own."

"There's very few bad eggs get past my nose in these pits—I

83

see to that," C.P. said. "No. You're all getting disgruntled, for some reason or other. Your demands are going to choke up everything. The Company was seriously thinking of closing the bally pits altogether, I might tell you, this last strike."

Ag Thomas stared open-mouthed and affrighted. "Then what'll you do, Mr. Meredith bach. Getting on in years you are to find another job." Ag could never understand the constitution of the business side of the pit. C.P. was merely another man earning a few shillings more than himself. "And that stone you got in your bladder that makes you bad so often," he concluded deploringly

"Very worrying things would be for you."

"The stone is gone," C.P. announced dourly.

"First-class thanksgiving you said in chapel on Sunday night, Mr. Meredith," piped up a one-time good tenor singer, Match Lewis. "The wife Gladys and we wass hoping you wouldn't stop at all. Pity the pit took you, Gladys said afterwards, for you would have made all Wales Christian in no time from the pulpit."

"Aye," agreed C.P., thumping his tick in glad appreciation, "I can turn a pretty good prayer when there's a call for it."

They accompanied him to the door of the stable, old cronies that had grown up with him, and knew all about his ailments and his fretting and his hates and likings. The stalled horses turned to look at the departing men and then settled down to the soft warm darkness, after the long day of twists and turns through the holes of the earth. C.P. went with the men to the pit-shaft, where a cage was waiting.

"Gronw here, his wife was confined on Tuesday," one of them was telling the general manager.

"Yes," Gronw, very elderly and self-conscious, stammered, "yes. Well. On Tuesday it was, sure enough." It was his first, but he had married a new wife, a young and less faulty one than the other, who had hated the world and nagged herself across Jordan.

"You have a cradle for the baby?" asked C.P.

"Not yet. Sleeping between me and Blod she is just now. I haven't seen her in daylight yet at all," he declared happily. "But there's a pink face she has in candlelight! Pink and wrinkled like a little old country woman."

"My Bertha looked like a dirty old spud of a tater for the first six months," piped the ex-tenor. "Awful frights I had that black blood there was in me or in Mag. Specially in Mag, for her great grandad went to live in London beginning of the century and brought back four children of funny colours."

"You go down to my eldest daughter's house in Plas Gwyn," C.P. said to Gronw. "She has a nice cradle there. You mustn't sleep with your only child," he warned worriedly. "You might crush it. And don't give it this condensed milk everyone is using hereabouts these days."

"Blod is full herself," Gronw said. "My new wife she is, Mr. Meredith. The old one died two years back."

"Ah, yes, I remember. Marged, daughter of the best fireman I ever had."

"Good she was, too," Gronw said stoutly, "in ways peculiar to understand. She went of the shingles."

In the cage going up to the top of the earth, where things were different, C.P. withdrew his fretful consorting with the men, and began to wear a stern demeanour, haughty about the mouth. As the cage banged to the surface some young colliers were horse playing nearby, chucking at each other handfuls of small coal out of a tub and swearing. They did not notice C.P., who could not abide bad language, especially if it had a sexual connection. He swept up to them grandly and laid about him as if he were the Almighty or Sir Rufus Morgan, thunder in his mouth and his stick cracking the air like lightning. The young colliers scampered away among the sheds like agile black cats.

II

Tudor was obliged to lie low for a while, having escaped prison by the skin of his teeth. The magistrate at the local court had refused to believe that his presence in that bad house was anything but a young man's prank. He had been attending the woman prisoner, Daisy Waiters, of course, and had stayed to debate with the men in the house. No doubt the young doctor had socialistic leanings and in this case they had got him into hot water, staying half the night to talk in a dangerous house. Let this be a lesson to him.

Daisy got away, too, there being nothing material to prove that she had incited men to mutiny. But the magistrate stared at her over crooked pince-nez as if she were a cow that had appeared in the dock. In his remarks he implied that there might be charges against her which would be dealt with in a more eternal court than the limited one over which he presided. Daisy wore in court her scarlet dress, and her black hair sprang about her head emphatically: she stood in the dock with a kind of obstreperous calm, like a lioness in a cage. She was released with Tudor the same day as the arrest. The others, against whom there were definite charges proved, it was said, by the finding of certain papers under the rafters of the house, were sent for trial at the Assizes. Three weeks later Melville was sentenced to nine months' hard labour, and each of the other young men to six.

News of Tudor being arrested in bed with Daisy leaked out, though it had not been mentioned in court. The affair was "hushed up", as they say, which meant that it obtained an underground publicity far more potent than the largest newspaper headings. His father feared action by the Medical Council; his mother had a slight stroke.

He returned from the court with his father. Travelling in the same brake down the valley was Daisy, with a woman friend, Maud Powell, who now kept a sweet shop, but had once woo many prizes for elocution in Eisteddfodau—a respectable woman, though liable at any moment to burst into sickly Welsh poetry of unknown parentage. Tudor had introduced the stately Elwyn outside the court.

Daisy was in a state of indignation for her brother, her face golden red. To be sent to the Assizes meant perhaps two years.

His health would never stand it. Not only that, what was *she* to do? Elwyn and the woman friend thought she meant materially. Tudor felt oddly cold in his bowels.

"You'll have to go into service," the woman said with homely finality. "A very good washer you are, Daisy, you know you are, and you can cook." She turned brightly to Elwyn. "Perhaps Doctor Morris here will know of a place."

Tudor sat in a divided agony. His arms ached to take Daisy there and then, but all the time he felt as though he had had a kick under the stomach, numbing him. The gross stench of the ill-ventilated court was still in his nostrils; he saw the magistrate staring stupidly over his pince-nez. But it was the semi-suppressed squeak of the police sergeant that tore down his body. It was tearing and squeakily ferreting out something that had been about to become precious to him. The squalor of that assault into the room! Now it was safely over, its ugliness revolted him. Though at times his face showed a forced grin. If he could only forget that squeaking bark!

"I'm afraid," his father was saying, polite but aloof, "I know of no such situation at the moment." His kind, other-world eyes were very startled from all this business. He did not mind meeting this shocking Miss Waiters, who was apparently the darling of these agitators, but he had not yet disentangled the proprieties from the shock his erratic son had given him. Fortunately, the brake-ride did not last more than ten minutes. They parted ways at the Square.

"I'll be down to see you soon," Tudor whispered to Daisy.

"God knows where I'll be tomorrow," she said wildly. "I feel like having a jaunt to Bristol." And that is what she did— disappeared for a while, until the day of her brother's trial at the Assizes.

Tudor's mother had had her minor stroke that evening in the dining-room, dragging the tablecloth and many dishes with her to the floor. The spectacle of his well-preserved cosy-looking mother sliding to the floor, her beautifully-coiled white hair falling about, saliva drooling from her mouth, struck further horror into him. How one was at the mercy of the squalid world! His father's half-articulate whimper, before he sternly and dexterously attended to his wife, was also like the stab of a knife.

But he hardened himself, refusing to feel the shame and fear that, he supposed, were expected of him. His mother would have had that stroke in any case later; both he and Elwyn knew she was subject to paralysis. And again he was torn and sick in the sense of conflict rising like a two-headed monster within him. Surely it was not his fault if they were overwhelmed by the social disgrace of his being mixed up in an affair that the conventions only would judge unsavoury. If they were shocked and overwhelmed, it was because of their own limitations and lack of vision. Meanwhile, he supposed that he was beginning to be looked upon as having progressed swiftly from being a turncoat to a depraved ruffian.

Bearing the feet of his mother as he and his father carried her upstairs, he shrank from lamentations over her sagging body, her blue, stiff eyelids, her clenched wet lips. But his soul was sick. Later that afternoon his father came to him. "You'd better not come down to the surgery this evening," he said, from a distance.

"Why not? It'll be better for me to be back as though nothing had happened—" He wanted to get away from this sense of drama in the house.

Elwyn stroked his tidy grey moustaches. He was being deliberately mild, carefully aloof. "You'd better stay here in case you're needed, though I think she'll sleep until about midnight. Bronwen is with her now."

"I shall be back at work tomorrow morning," he said, half enquiringly, half threatening.

"I suppose so," Elwyn murmured. His austere head with its dean expanse of noble brow, lean folds of cheek, and far-away eyes, nodded doubtfully.

"Why *suppose* so? You don't think I'm going to bury my head in shame, do you?"

"Not in shame, perhaps. But in discretion."

"And walk through the streets for a week with a guilty look? Ah—"

"Tudor," Elwyn said, laying a spiritual white hand on his son's restless shoulder, "I do not know what you are after, or what disorderly demon is driving you to these antics of yours. But don't you think that you'd better look for a job elsewhere?"

Tudor looked up swiftly. Was this the sack? His father could really work without him.

"Or," continued Elwyn smoothly, "Wylie in Pembroke wants an assistant. A nice country practice, Tudor, easy, and near the beautiful town of Tenby."

"No," Tudor said sharply, "I prefer to be here, if you don't mind."

"Do you realise," Elwyn asked, after a cool pause, "that if you don't go I shall probably lose what good-paying patients I have?"

"We'll get more of the workpeople, now they know I'm one of them."

"They're interesting to attend," Elwyn said, with an allowance of delicate irony in his voice, "I enjoy them as patients. But, as you know, I've been taught to seek my reward for my services somewhere beyond this world of small wages."

Tudor jerked away restlessly. "You mean it's not merely a question of my political views? People know about me and Daisy?"

Elwyn nodded. Though he was himself like a father in Israel among the workpeople, cherishing them and yearning over them, a shadowy look of repugnance crossed his face now.

"That I was found with her?" Tudor added.

"It was about the place early this morning," Elwyn said, very slowly. "In a way, that was why you were not convicted today…. She was looked upon as a loose woman, you as a… yes, I must say it, a customer."

"I *am* in disgrace!" Tudor cried with sick bitterness.

"You know what this place is," Elwyn remarked, gone very far away again in his abstracted, mystical look—"there may be extreme conduct and licence among a section of the workpeople, but in our class such spotlessness, such sanctity, that God in all confidence has left us to ourselves." His fastidious fingers were caressing the albert hanging from his heavy gold watchchain: it had been given him for courageous services during a pit explosion.

"For your sake I suppose we'll have to separate," Tudor said moodily. He had, however, no intention of leaving the place.

"For the time being, perhaps you'd better take a holiday. Run up to London for a few weeks."

"No," he said.

After his father had gone he took a bath, angrily splashing the water and scrubbing himself. Of course, the proper thing for him to do now was to marry Daisy and try to make a good-class woman of her. Scrubbing his back with a coarse loofah, he remembered Mildred. What was she thinking about it all? Perhaps she, too, had taken to her bed. He dipped and then jumped irritably out of the bath. He could still smell the stuffy odour of that court. He still saw Melville's shadowy, sardonic face, his fleeting gethsemanic smile as he turned to leave. All the disaster had possessed a nightmare but grotesque quality. But it was raw and ugly with life, too. Looking at his legs as he dried himself, he wished for a moment that he had kept to football as a hobby.

He went into his mother's bedroom. She was sleeping peacefully, but her soft, plump face had taken an alienly rigid look. He felt her pulse. His grandmother, Bronwen, laid her hand caressingly on his, whispering:

"Don't take this to heart too much, Tudor."

Bronwen was so much like a piece of the old eternally fragrant earth, battered but calm as an ancient elm, that he felt eased at once in her touch. He bent and lightly kissed the rosy pallor of her cheek.

"Is this my fault?" he asked, glancing at his mother.

"Nobody's fault," she whispered, "except life's, perhaps... can we leave her for a while?"

He nodded. They went downstairs. In grey velvet and lace, Bronwen disposed herself in the plush armchair beside the fire. All her movements had a sure dignity, clearly enunciating a triumph over the battles and pettiness of life. "Sit down, Tudor, and smoke a cigarette."

"Are you going to lecture me, Bronwen?"

"Heaven forbid." She was looking at an agate ring on her finger, next to her wedding-ring. "But I want to say that I understand very well what you've been up to—"

"Up to?" he repeated, beginning to feel refreshed. His grandmother's sweet primness was like dew.

"This young woman you are friendly with," she said—"I was no better than she is in my time."

He waited, eased and his mind already delicately connected with hers. He half knew what she was going to say. At intervals she would reveal semi-cautious details of her romantic past: he had already pieced them into a more or less accurate whole.

"You see, Tudor, you are a descendant of those who owned this vale for seven or eight hundred years—owners who kept it like a nice country part, full of good things, such as orchards and meadows... I made my son Elwyn give you the name of Tudor because that was the name of one of your ancestors—a funny old man of whom I was fond."

"The Squire!" he teased. "Oh, Bronwen, we all know how you were a good girl taken advantage of by the bad Squire."

She shook her head, turning the agate ring tenderly. "No, his young son it was, and indeed he didn't take advantage of anything I didn't choose to give him."

"Bronwen, Bronwen!" he exclaimed again in delight.

All the stuffy smell of the day was going; dirt was being blown off his body. "Were you very wicked?"

"I sinned and sinned again," she answered, with the aged calm of one who sees these things as no more than the drinking of a cup of tea. Then she raised her eyes in grateful adoration to the portrait of her husband which now hung over the what-not. "Ben married me when I was carrying your father, my Elwyn, that was not his child."

"Good old Ben," Tudor said gently. He always thought that Ben, in his portrait, looked like a dignified and sterling sheep-dog. He had risen to some position as a self-taught engineer in the first colliery in he district. And he had died full of sanctity, buried with great pomp by Caersalem chapel, which he had helped to build and where he had been a deacon for forty years. Tudor could dimly remember the enormous funeral.

"He was a good man," she said, sighing, "but of course as different as could be from Owen, who was your rightful grandfather."

"Your young lover, Owen Llewellyn? What was he like?"

"Something like you," she said, a fond compassion in her voice. "It is in you he has been reborn, not his son, though your father in his way is just as odd—only he is a dreamer and is contemptuous of this world."

"Odd ?" Tudor questioned. "You think your son and grandson peculiar, Bronwen?"

She struggled for some moments, her rose-and-silver face puckered. "Yes, odd," she said breathlessly, "because you don't follow the rules and regulations set down by—what is it they call it?—society."

"Well, neither did you," he pointed out, laughing. "You sinned with the Squire's son and made my father a bastard."

"Now, now, Tudor," she warned, "now, that will do. Ben married me before I was confined." She paused and continued, still in grave compassion, "You want to live for the people, like Owen did, and make this world easier for them. That is why you have been going down to this house, isn't it, and mixing with these socialists and being friendly with that young woman."

"Possibly," he said—"but also for personal reasons. Their free way of talking and their free behaviour satisfied something in me."

"Something you inherited," she murmured, far away, dragging at her memories again.

92

"What?" he asked, half idly, not quite believing in this hereditary explanation.

"Love for this land," she answered.

"Ugh," he said, "I think the land is as ugly as hell and full of wickedness."

"All the same, you can't leave it alone."

"No, that's true. But I feel quite a lot of hate for it."

"The same thing," she said, old and wise.

For some minutes they sat silent. The great accumulation of years had fallen from her and a young girl peeped out from her frail eyes. Instinctively, he knew why she was talking to him like this. She had been afraid that he would be overcome by shame and fear and disgrace, cowering before the grim guns of the times, always ready to be levelled against offenders of the social order.

"Owen," she resumed, "used to come out of the Big House in the dead of night and meet me under a certain tree—and where that tree was is now a public-house—and I'd stay half the night with him in a field. He was very romantic," she added pensively, "and talked very well, even though I didn't always understand what he was saying. He wanted me to marry him," she said proudly.

"Why did he die so young?"

"Consumption."

"Ah," Tudor said warily, "consumption, was it?"

"If there were any traces in his child," she said with the certainty of her proud physical health, "*I* destroyed them. So don't be frightened that it's comedown to you."

"No, I don't think I'm T.B."

"But you've got Owen's restlessness and—you know what it's called"—she used the word cautiously, as if she were frightened of it—"idealism."

He had always disliked the word idealism. His nose snuffed at it now. "I don't know about idealism. All I want to do, Bronwen, is to whip the backside of dishonesty."

"Very hard work there is waiting for you," she sighed. "For that backside is as big as the world. There was Owen now," she continued, still preoccupied with the renewed vision of him come to her that day of shocks, "he wanted things kept pure, he wanted this place kept fair—and right fair it was in the old days—but what was the use? Over the mountains the people came and tore up the place, making it as it is now, so that sometimes very difficult it is for me to remember that once it was clean as bread and smelt like a hazelnut. But they had to come: the world belongs to the people and it seems to me that they will tear up and stamp and spoil wherever they choose to go." She paused, pondering deeply in her reverie. "So my Owen had to die. He was like a sacrifice—the old world going in the shape of a young man who was too handsome for the likes of the new world." She sat back, rather surprised at herself: pink spots burned in her cheeks and she gazed at Tudor almost shyly. "That's how I see him now that I am very old and can look back and think slow. And I am telling you all this because sometimes I am afraid that you are wasting yourself, that it is no good, no good at all fighting against these ugly things of life that you can name better than I can.... Now I've finished indeed and will say a welcome Amen." She smiled across at him with a kind of young girl modesty.

"You think I'm destined for an early death, too?"

"No... very healthy you are," she answered.

"But you're thinking there's more than one kind of death."

"Well, Tudor, very true that is," she said quietly.

"But I'm not chucking the struggle, for all your warnings."

"No, of course you won't," she said, approvingly.

He ran upstairs to look at his mother: she still slept heavily. When he returned, Bronwen asked him if he had any plans for the future: she too realised that, for the sake of his practice, Elwyn would have to dissociate himself from his son. Tudor thought he would begin a practice on his own, in the rawest quarter of the valley: it would be hard work with a return of next to nothing: none of the middle class would be likely to consult him, of course. Then Bronwen announced her intention of turning over to him immediately six hundred pounds. The usual affectionate dispute followed, Tudor refusing to accept the money. But it had been willed to him already, and she had no use for it; she spent next to nothing; only half a crown per week for her pew in chapel, and sweets, and flowers every first of the month for Ben's grave. The old had no right to hoard money which the young badly needed. Presently he accepted her offer, since what she said was the truth. Then she said:

"You ought to get married…. most patients don't like bachelor doctors."

"I don't know whether Daisy would want to marry me," he said, grinning a little, wryly.

She refused to be shocked; neither would she ask questions about this extraordinary young woman.

"But what about Mildred—aren't you in love with her any more? All three of us are expecting you to marry Mildred."

"Yes, she's likely to have me, isn't she, after this disgrace. Mildred of all people."

"She will, she will—if you show you want her enough. Though, of course, very good excuse you've given her to set more railings about herself."

"You know she likes railings then," he asked, pleased at her implied sympathy—for most people imagined he was to be blamed that Mildred remained unmarried so long.

"High ones," Bronwen nodded. "But behind them a very good woman there is…. And, after all, Tudor, the fashion of the day is for railings." She allowed herself a faint smile. "Even in our clothes they are. Mrs. Evans, the minister's wife, was telling me the other day that she always makes her two daughters wear five petticoats in the summer and seven in the winter. Subject to colds, she said they were."

When his father returned that evening, Tudor told him that he had decided to start a practice of his own in the very poorest quarter of the valley. Elwyn was deprecating but patient. He warned Tudor that his surgery would become probably a charitable institution: he perceived his own unbusinesslike methods developed tenfold in his son. "You had much better use your grandmother's money buying a partnership of some strictly materialistic doctor," he warned. He for ever regretted that Tudor had not found it in him to enter the Church, since it seemed to him obvious that the boy, like himself—though in a different way—took more count of what is vaguely termed the soul than of the body.

But Tudor, he could see, must go his own way, make his own mistakes. Elwyn that evening read several chapters in old philosophical books that took one far above the behaviour of this world into cloudy regions, where men dropped their garments of flesh and entered into a placid bliss. All is vanity on this earth, and it is no use expecting celestial harmonies therein. One is obliged to walk in the world, but it is a mistake to trail one's soul in its mud. For Elwyn the soul was separate from the body and could at times be liberated into calm regions that were like foothills preceding the snowy mountains of eternity. He sat reading beside his wife, knowing she would wake from her stupor soon. At about two o'clock she woke slowly, struggling to return to faculties that from now would be more difficult for her to exercise. She did not recognise him for some minutes and his heart contracted. But his mind was quite calm. He saw her as a being that must perhaps be racked and bent and broken. But he had taught her that there was a divine residence where one could dwell intact from these slovenly injuries.

She met his calm gaze at last. No word was spoken and he took her hand and stroked it. In his eyes was the gentlest accusation. She must not allow this attack from a ridiculous world to affect her. Had he not in the long years of their peaceful life together taught her escape?

They had loved each other as though the holiness of love was a flower whose roots could never be nourished in the soil of this world. Sensual passion had been a state of slow, unclamorous and wordless dreaming.... He knew this paralysis was not really serious. But she would have to be careful in the future, she would have to be watched and kept from receiving the shocks of the ugly world.

III

Of course Tudor was not allowed to forget his offence. During the next few weeks he was the cause of much neck-turning, vacant staring into the air and rigidly lowered eyelids. Social society was unanimous in its condemnation. Though he was a member of the committee of the Cricket Club, no notice of the first spring meeting was sent him; his name was deleted from the list of voluntary instructors to the Ambulance Brigade; the newly-formed Naturalist Society went on their May jaunt unaccompanied by member Tudor Morris. There was hard criticism of his shamelessness in remaining in the valley. Surely a doctor, who had access to one's private life, must be more than anyone a paragon of virtue. Behaving as though he were still a student in London! Hadn't the man the gumption to see that he was among people who lived clean as the herbs of the field?

At the same time, when news of his intention to begin a practice of his own was received by a shocked community, he obtained by roundabout ways evidence of support from people who were of unkempt reputation in the place, such as unusers of pews in chapel, mongrel persons of no background or property, hard drinkers and hard fighters of both sexes, and other riff-raff who had come to the place from Heaven knew where, squatters and half-gipsies.

At the moment there was need for another doctor—an energetic and a cheap one for popular and elementary complaints. The burst of prosperity which the district was enjoying after the strike included the luxury of consulting doctors. Quite a lot of such consultations were necessary, for over-eating and over-drinking brought the distinction of illness in their train, and the number of people who could boast that the stomach-pump had been used on them made the operation a commonplace at last.

In these rumours of supporters women appeared to be the more solid in their promises. These said that Doctor Morris had a "way with him" and was "broad minded". Tudor understood that many of them meant that, after his disgrace, he would be expected to condone excesses and behaviour which the old-fashioned family doctors took it upon themselves to condemn, harshly and bullyingly.

He was accosted in the open by Mrs. Violet Fox, an English widow once married to a collier who had been killed in the pits in such circumstances that compensation had not been granted her. She had since become a kind of attendant to women suffering from esoteric complaints, and she also practised herb cures for bad legs and suchlike; some said she could be hired to nip in the bud a blessing not desired just then.

She wore when she approached Tudor a bold, impudent face with blue blown-out cheeks and simpering, insecure eyes. A big brisk fur was slung across her shoulders. Her menacing bust and solid hips were tightly encased in a nigger serge jacket. From under it a voluminous skirt billowed out fashionably; with one hand she held up a fold like a lady. She smiled ingratiatingly.

"I hear, Doctor Morris, that you intend starting a practice in the Terraces? You will excuse me asking, won't you?" she appealed with her feminine simper.

She had exercised a certain discretion in speaking to him at a place where no one was about—a division between rows of houses off the main road. He vaguely remembered that he had seen her hurrying towards him in the distance some days before. He was half amused by this interest in him.

"Probably," he said, distantly, "probably."

"I live in that district, Doctor," she went on, quickly now and keeping a wary eye about her—for the sake of both of them— "and many of the women come to me for advice—I was a nurse before I married. I only wished to say that should I be of any use to you professionally I should be very pleased to oblige—"

"In what sense?" he asked abruptly. "How—professionally?"

"Why, as a nurse, Doctor." She looked above her big lumpy cheeks at him.

He shook his head as if puzzled. How far would she go? She made a sudden plunge.

"I can get you many patients," she said, quite boldly then. "Now I mustn't stop long"—he had begun glancing about him too—" but I would like to say that I work hard trying to do good in this place, and the way you are being treated and what is being said about you has made my heart bleed for you—"

He looked into her loose eyes. He recognised that she had forced herself into believing that she was a crusader. But there was a kind of awful perversity in her too, something witch-like.

"Thank you," he said, "but I doubt if I should need you as a nurse."

"The women of the Terraces have great faith in me—" she persisted, almost malignly then.

"Good God, woman," he burst out suddenly, "what are you suggesting—that I enter into partnership with you?" He badly wanted to add, "As an abortionist?"

She retreated a step quickly, staggering into her great swirled skirt. Her voice became a whine:

"It was only a suggestion, I meant no harm." The blue of her big cheeks had become a frightened purple. Her prosperous hat, piled with flowers, shook.

"You take care of that heart of yours," he said sternly, as he began to stride away. "Besides bleeding for me, I shouldn't think it's any too sound."

A pretty contact. All the obvious crooks of the place would be looking to him as friend. He laughed, wryly. What could he expect? No one would be likely to adopt the point of view that he was a little prophet taking lamp down among the outcasts. After being found in bed with the easy-going sister of an inciter to rioting.

99

One of the best preachers of the place, Parch Moses James, had already given to a packed chapel a resounding sermon on certain evil elements prowling about in a place that God meant to be a fair and pleasing example of the sweet bondage between employers and men. The sermon contained veiled references to sad misled characters originally of good family: private prayers would surely be asked for such. Continuing, Moses called the strikers a blasphemous ungrateful lot: had not God created coal and its uses for men, yet what were they doing about it? Fighting and making it an excuse for a lawless going back to a time before Christ. Coal was sacred and the best Welsh steam coal was probably used in Heaven—Moses's sermons were known for a strain of nationalist humour. Why invite Satan to the place to have a look at these collieries, the property originally of God? Parch Moses warned a closely listening congregation that disciples of Satan had already arrived, to prepare a way for their master. Let him have a good hold and Heaven would be sure to withdraw its interest in Welsh coal; prosperity would cease; foreign orders would go elsewhere; there would be no dividends for shareholders, and the colliers themselves would either starve or, if they could, return to the country districts and live on thin broth with no meat in it…. Moses was himself a shareholder of a collier recently involved.

And C. P. Meredith, boss of the place, asked Tudor to come and see him at Glan Ystrad, the old manor which he was using while his new house was being built. So Tudor climbed one late afternoon through the thin, bony wood that still fringed the manor. The hazels were greyly in leaf and there were still a few great oaks. He even saw some violets and a few late windflowers. The sloping lawns before the house were unkempt and knobbly, and the dusty terrace was cluttered with old wheels and other rubbish. This was where Grannie Bronwen went to a New Year party some time in the forties and first met what she called his "rightful grandfather", her lover Owen.

From the terrace there was a good view of slate roofs stretching down the vale, persistent and monotonous rows shoved lengthily almost everywhere on the flat and on the lower slopes of the dusky mountains. According to Bronwen, from this terrace in the old days there could be seen snatches of green fields, hedges of wild rose, pink, white and blue cottages and, in June, floods of bluebells gushing out of the small woods. "A *real* picture it was," she would say. But it was the abundance of trees that she sighed for most. "So naked the place looks now," she complained. "Trees make clothes; these old hills always look as if they're shivering now." What trees remained were ill and emaciated. The little wan wood below him was all that was left of former pastoral abundance.

C.P. received him in the old drawing-room upstairs: its big spaces were furnished temporarily. The ancient chandelier was still there, the property of the Company, hanging like a fall of dirty ice; but the tall Italian mirrors between the sconces had gone—their dim splendour now decorated a London ballroom. C.P. sat grumpily in a horse-hair arm-chair, a strip of thick flannel tied round his head; living in the musty damp old house had given him ear-ache. He disliked consulting doctors and would much rather listen to remedies suggested by old country wives. It was known that he had no objection to the activities of Mrs. Violet Fox.

"What's this I hear of you starting a practice down in those slums?" he demanded in a grizzling manner.

"There's room for one." Tudor still could not help liking the worried general manager, victim of a process that had sucked him under like a whirlpool. C.P.'s mind would not admit any new order of economic justice, but he had bowels of compassion. The rigidity of the one and the yearning of the other made him a pitiable figure.

"Not for one of *your* kind," C.P. grunted, peering out restlessly from between the flannel. "Look here," he went on bluntly, "what's this nonsense you've got in your head about—what's it called?—making people more politically conscious."

"Well, they need to be, I suppose," Tudor said smoothly, "but I had never put it to myself like that."

"What do you want to do then, messing yourself up with people?" C.P.'s voice rose to an anguished note that might have been due to the ear-ache. "You're a doctor, aren't you? People's bodies is your concern. Why do you want to interfere with their *minds*?"

No one could have taken umbrage at C.P.'s intolerant demands: they arose from such a passion of worry.

"It's possible that by making their minds healthy there'll be less hard work for me on their bodies."

"You'll teach them to cut their own throats," snapped C.P. "You're setting yourself against very powerful forces, young chap, and I've got you up here to warn you. I don't like to see a young man walking blindfold to the edge of a cliff, so I want to tell you that you'd better start a practice in another district. I like your father, for all the fly-in-the-air notions that he's got, too—but a good chapel man he is, and knows well enough that the kingdom of heaven can't be moved from above down to a Welsh coal district—" He placed his hand over his ear in pain.

"Have you put some warm oil in it?" Tudor asked. But C.P. went on stubbornly: "What I wanted to say is—go away now, unless you want to starve. My Company has a scheme on foot to provide medical benefits for all employees and their families, deducting some petty bit out of the wages. Now then, you will not expect to be one of the doctors chosen for our use, will you? I want to be fair with you; I'm telling you before you've spent brass setting up."

Tudor, shoving all expression from his face, asked calmly: "But what if the miners won't accept such a scheme?"

"There's a lot of fool independence, true enough. But when they see that for a few bob a year they can get ten pounds' worth of medical attendance, if they want, I can't see that even politically conscious blokes'll be so grand as to say no."

"And the doctors?"

"Ah, we haven't called a meeting of them yet, but the four we've got, not counting you, aren't likely to go haughty about this—not even your father."

It was typical of C.P. to reveal these immature plans like this, bluntly and proudly. In a way, he felt secure in the power of his Company: it was only that nagging mystical streak of bowel-pain that broke up his peace of mind.

"All the same, I shall stay here," Tudor said. He only knew he was the more determined to stay. He could not think just then of the actual bread-and-butter problem. "I don't see," he went on, "that you can be allowed to buy up everybody like this. Someone must stand unpurchased and unowned; you mustn't rule the roost entirely."

"Bluff," growled C.P., "bluff." He ambled over to a cupboard. "Have some whisky, for the love of God. Such chaps as you make my belly sore." He poured two drinks. "All theories, all theories, and no experience of men and things."

"Ah, but I'm fast gaining experience, and it's better to set out with a few theories, not blindly."

"You'll go under, young Morris, you'll go under."

"Perhaps I will, according to an economic scale of values." Tudor drank cheerfully, C.P. gloomily.

"A pity," the general manager sighed, "you didn't become a Church of England parson, like your father wanted you. You'd be able to save men's souls in a proper fashion then—for the only way to save 'em is through religion, my boy."

"I can see the end of that belief coming during the next decade. It's true that Heaven can't be lowered down here in a cloth, but there's going to be a lot of cleaning up of the rubbish-dumps left by this century." Tudor gazed at a picture of some flying swans over the yellow mantelpiece.

"Rubbish-dumps!" exclaimed C.P. indignantly. "The Victorian age has been the most wonderful that ever was. There'll never be another like it." Cross and still troubled by his bladder, inclined to gout and his face wrapped stuffily in the flannel, he sank back

103

in the great ugly horse-hair chair. "It's an age that's produced great men fit to deal with the opportunities that industry's brought. England's fat, England's prosperous—"

"She's well dressed and eats well," murmured Tudor, taking advantage of C.P.'s gulping of his whisky. "But what blemishes on her body, what blemishes!"

"And now chaps like you want to try and scratch at her," C.P. went on heedlessly. "But I tell you, Doctor Morris, that you'll never get more than a few silly scratches in. That old blighter Karl Marx—I've heard of the cranky fool, I know all about him; he's about as suitable for brass-brained British people as a viper is for meat-pie."

"Karl Marx!" said Tudor slowly, finishing his whisky, which he had taken neat. "I haven't read him yet, but he sounds good."

"Well," C.P. concluded the interview, fixing Tudor with a sudden baleful glitter out of his liver-heavy eyes, "get up to your mischief, young man. Perhaps a bit of corruption's necessary to bring people to their senses at last. But remember this—" he beat the arm of his chair excitedly with his fist—"if I find any agitations for strikes coming from your quarter, I'm going to act. Out of my pits the agitators will go, neck and crop. I can replace everybody.... And *you* may not get off so lightly next time," he added, with a knowing nod.

"Agitation!" said Tudor innocently. "I'm only trying to get the love of man for man going as a practical proposition."

"Love of the Devil," snorted C.P. "Well, I've warned you." And he mumbled into his flannel fretfully: "A young man just setting up in life!"

"In a way, we're parallels," Tudor said obscurely, going off. "Never to meet."

For C.P., too, burned with consciousness of the life under him. He did not want his wealth, had no use for it, it was merely a symbol of his earthly success and his use of the talents God had given him. He liked being amongst the men, in his old mackintosh and pulled-about cap, talking about the pits and the social life "on top". He knew that most of them lived in bad houses that had been built by the Company, that their hard and dangerous labour was, judged by impossible idealistic justice, rewarded badly. But such was the world. Man was fundamentally evil and the state of his sojourn on earth was conditioned by the activities of that ineradicable evil in certain selected beings. If that evil were miraculously deleted out of man, then man was no longer man; he was something that the wild dreams of poets and rapt visionaries created for occupation of a land of escape where they did nothing but smell flowers all day, where food was whisked out of magic cupboards and there was no necessity to pay for the music wafted by unseen orchestras to ears that never required the lather of soap. "Dreamers, dreamers," C.P. fretted. But he had to grant that the wiser of them only wanted to keep the inherent evil in check, to trim the green bay tree.

Tudor went down the slope from the house in a pleased state of mind. The ban that was to be placed on him by the Company was, under the circumstances, a good thing. High-handed actions of that kind were never imposed with unanimous agreement; there were perverse people who always took pleasure in trying to thwart them. He laughed, then shrugged his shoulders and dismissed thought of the threatened boycott. He had some work to do. Good of old C.P., though, to warn him.

That same evening he concluded transactions to acquire an ugly black old house left derelict among the crowded terraces of the notorious Nant-Ddu district. Before the building of the Terraces, as they were called, it had been occupied by a retired shareholder who had done well out of the early days of the pits; he had built this house among what were then more or less decent meadows where buttercups appeared each year in diminishing quantities. Then in a trice a new Company acquired all the land around him, and slung down all these cheap dwellings, terrace upon terrace, stern-looking and stony at first, then, as the swarms of low-pay workers took possession in a busy period, becoming ever more sordid and stinking, with their drainless w.c.'s stuck at the ends of the five-yard patches of garden and for ever in use. They stretched up right to garden wall of the share-built villa, whose mistress was a fastidious woman with a liking for pink gowns and the soulful works of Marie Corelli; she and her husband soon went to live on Barry Island. The house was offered cheap.

Within a fortnight he had furnished it, even to a piano, fitted a surgery, put up an unnecessary brassplate merely as a gesture, installed a cheerful daywoman, Hannah, who had been sewn in several places after taking part in the famous riots of '95. The whole lot cost no more than five hundred pounds. The other hundred he took back to his grandmother, who refused to accept the money. She said he would need it.

IV

In the midst of these preparations he received a note from Mildred asking if they might meet "for a talk". She suggested a quiet spot near the brook and at a time when it would be dusky to dark.

During all the disorder of the last few weeks, she had remained at the back of his mind. Ominously at the back, he thought, troubled. He had received no news of her, she had not visited his home, he had not, oddly, met her in the main street, where one saw everyone one knew within a couple of days. And his grandmother had remarked that she had not appeared in chapel. Had she gone into a kind of mourning? Impossible, he told himself uneasily.

He had thought it would be tactful not to visit her. His disgrace would surely be the final blow at their friendship; she would surely not be able to sustain it. He imagined her, with that leashed intensity of hers, shuddering at the vulgarity and forcing herself finally into a state of cold repugnance. He had intended seeing her one day and ask forgiveness for his inability to adjust his kind of life to hers. Now he saw that he ought to have gone to her at once. He had given her no opportunity to show her mind—possibly her courage—about the recent grimy affairs.

The inertia that held him whenever he thought of her now oppressed him. She still haunted him, like a woman of some admired poem read long ago, the lines of which one cannot remember. She had some kind of inner mystery that made her evanescent in the mind, yet left a sense of beauty. It was preposterous that he knew so little about her; they had grown up together; they had, as adolescents, even shared various discoveries of the delights of sex. But all had been achieved in a water-colour fashion, delicately and with frequent withdrawals by her into fastidious coigns of irritating fear. She, too, had wanted him to enter the Church, though when he had shown his vexation at her support of this family wish, she ceased to urge him. In a general sense she was submissive to him.

Why had consideration of her become so erratic in him of late, why was memory of her dwindling into a thin emotion of misty regret? Was it because of Daisy? Daisy's downright plunging into his mind, her direct strong, spreading-out of herself, might well push thought of Mildred away, like a clamorously rising sun chasing out a wan moonlit night from the world.

The thought of Daisy always made him pause now in a kind of shock. Sometimes, laughing half grimly at himself, he saw her as the great female animal of the world, lusty and devouring, the grand whore of biblical lineaments, with crude loins and arms that could crush into annihilation. Of course, for all civilised social purposes Mildred obviously was destined to be his wife. The design of his upbringing had included her presence with all its sensible attractiveness, enough for any man. She it was who possessed the wise process of civilised life, not that wild "other woman" who could surely eat an uncooked swede as though it were an Osborne biscuit.

He went to meet Mildred with a disturbed and hesitant mind. For the last few days he had been longing to see Daisy, who was still in Bristol. The physical need had made him feel raw as the north wind; he felt himself driven into a corner about this. Dare he carry his criminally careless conduct still further and marry Daisy, if she were willing to make the experiment! Or, assuming that Mildred was about to be all-forgiving—she must mean something of the kind since she had asked for this meeting—assuming such martyrdom on her part, should he make amends by marrying her and to attain with her some peaceful meeting-place of quiet love?

Surely he had for her a quiet love! Which she—or they—might kindle into something else. But as he waited for her, sitting on a stone beside the wild brook that sprang and fell in dim leaps among a thin scrub of alders, his sense of oppression threatened to become black woe. Nothing had come to flame between them, surely they had better finish!

And yet she was in the texture of his being. Now that the disturbances of the past few weeks were over, she had emerged mistily from the back of his mind, he recognised her. And she was taking on flesh, form; she was an attractive living woman, whose lips and eyes could speak the poetry of his adolescence.

He looked up through the dusk, and there she was before him; even in the dimness he could see that her face was pale. And immediately her presence called forth the old baffled feeling in him. She was so constricted in herself, even her slightest movement showed her fastidious aloofness and her fear of the world, of people. Perhaps they both were constricted—he in the unresolved disorder of his efforts to plunge into the depravity of things. A sense of chagrin surged in him as they looked at each other in a little silence. He felt that even this meeting would be no good, no good. And all the time he badly wanted to touch her, to put his arms around her, to feel that she still possessed that wavering beauty to which he had written youthful poetry.

"I'm glad you wanted us to meet," he said tentatively. "Look, here's a flat stone, come and sit here."

But she glanced behind her. He heard some distant steps then. Lovers came down that way sometimes.

"I saw two people—" she murmured.

"It's getting dark. They wouldn't know you—" But she did not sit down. He saw that she would prefer more secluded place.

The old social fear, to which she would always refer! He rose with a sigh. "We'll go into Glan Ystrad wood," he said. They could follow the brook into the lean wood, which was more or less private ground. They stumbled along. He took her arm and pressed his hand over hers. There was something unyielding in her, but he saw her lip quivering.

"This was very brave of you," he whispered.

"My father," she answered, "said that you were not to come to the house."

He nodded. "I guessed that." He had begun to feel desperate; he sensed in her that inner weeping which she would not admit. How could he lessen her suffering, which took place in some buried cell of her being, proud and distant and silent? They entered the wood, patched with darkness, though the starry spring night gave a gentle luminance in the clearings where the brook dashed among great stones. He found a mossy bank and spread his raincoat; the night was soft. Not far off was a small old colliery; they could hear the cages clang to the surface and the whirr of the wheel flying over the headstock; the men were going down for the night shift. He took off her gloves and held her fingers.

"Come," he urged, "we won't be tragic."

Then, after a few moments of uncertainty, she said in a falsely steady voice: "I suppose everything is over between us now?"

"It seems that circumstances have forced that conclusion, Mildred."

"That's no answer," she said abruptly, her voice gaining a curious power.

"Well, haven't they—particularly for you?"

"Circumstances!" she said, almost stridently. "They can be ignored."

"*You* can say that!" He began to be aware of what she was

109

about to propose. He could feel a power growing in her, he could feel its forced cruel triumph over the bitter struggle in her soul. He began to be aware of a miserable fear in his own heart.

"Unless," she said, more softly, "you were glad of those circumstances."

"To take advantage of them? Come, Mildred, you can't think I could be so mean."

"You made no effort to see me," she accused, bitterness in her voice.

He felt that she was being erratic. This was the famous feminine inconsistency one had heard about. And again he sensed the great sick joy of martyrdom swelling in her. And there was that dominant urge in her voice, new and unexpected. She had turned her face to him. Her eyes were luminous and hard in the star light, the pure oval of her face had a strange unearthly beauty. Slowly, stealthily, his blood began to glow. The drive, the urge in her voice was like a thin stinging pain that passed from her to him. At last, at last, was she wakening!

"No, I made no effort. I felt I was being tactful. I was so much in disgrace, you know! So sunk in squalor." He could not help the ironical note.

"That woman has gone away, hasn't she?"

"Ah, you know that!"

"This," she said, "this, Tudor, is what they call young men's wild oats, I suppose?"

This effort at a simplification of the affair half amused, half angered him. Was she stupid or was she deliberately deceiving herself? Anyhow, he was weary of being looked upon as a wild young man passing through the period of antics and pranks.

"Hardly as picturesque as that, Mildred."

"Well, I hear you are trying to settle down now and start a practice of your own."

"That's true," he said, uneasily aware of the wash of the brook. Dim shapes of writhing trees, twisted and deformed in their dusty life, were all about them. But he could smell the fresh young leaves, a triumphant putting forth of green life. "It's going to be something of a struggle, perhaps," he added.

"Yes," she said, with the same bitter ring in her voice.

"But won't you need help?"

She sat upright on the bank, leaning against a tree; he was half crouched beside her, looking down towards the rough brook. He heard that bitter pain in her voice, beyond the forced-out words; and he was aware, too, of the dull anguish behind her breasts, terrible and afraid and still leashed. He did not know what to say; he felt hopelessness suddenly threaten to engulf him. He lifted himself and put his arm about her shoulders, instinctively. In their youthful friendship they would sit like that while they discussed subjects which in those days seemed to be as lightly solved and understood as the botanic examination of a clump of loosestrife.

"Help? I suppose so," he said slowly, still feeling a little unsure of her. "But you mustn't worry about me. The penalties I am going to suffer are not really penalties from my point of view, you know. Ostracism, poverty, even perhaps the frown of the police—I don't want to sound brave and cocksure, but I believe in the working of the law of compensation. All one needs, I think, is to preserve a certain amount of vitality and belief in oneself. I'm vain enough to think I've got those qualifications."

"But you'll need *help*," she repeated, and now there was an unmistakable self-goading in her voice, "help. It's not good, it's unnatural, for you to go only into yourself for a sense of preservation and belief."

For some moments he was silent. He could smell the fragrance of her hair. The starlight lit her skin, giving it a sheen of youth. She had mystery; she had a pale removed glamour, like a da Vinci idea of a woman, neither woman nor angel. He had always chased after an elusive melodic note in her, a snatch of harmony darting about undeveloped in a plainly austere symphony. That note had always caught him to her. And she was beautiful and compelling now, uttering her goaded bitter suggestion.

111

"Do you mean you would still like to marry me?" he asked, the words wrung from him. He felt his heart lurch in pain for her: he breathed with difficulty. It seemed that the whole dark wood was filled with suffocating presences. Under his arm, beside him, she was still as one of the trees. But he could feel the buried violence of her soul.

"Yes." The word swung out bitterly from her lips. This tremendous sacrifice of all she held dear—social security, the respect of neighbours, an "unstained" life! A small, hard voice scratched through his mind, telling him that she was devoured with fear, that he was becoming old, that it was fear that drove her soul to this savage martyrdom. He listened for a moment. But a gentle compassion filled him, a tenderness for her. She had waited for him, she had always waited, and he supposed that, superficially, he was to blame for this wilting of her young years. But could anyone be blamed for the disasters of love? They were driven before the compulsion of blind forces that took no count of age, rank or social behaviour.

He was still clasping one of her hands: but it was cold as death. "My dear," he whispered, moving his face to hers, "my dear, that would be a sacrifice, wouldn't it?"

"Do you still want that woman?" she asked.

"Mildred, that's a very melodramatic question. I wish it could be answered as simply as you put it—" Her rigidity seemed to break; she cried: "I know her, I've seen her. In a year or two she would ruin you. She wouldn't do it deliberately, but she couldn't help it. She's crude—"

"She's elemental," he said quietly.

"Could you endure that sort of thing for long? Think what you are doing, Tudor. One can overlook the wildness of your other behaviour—after all, that's only a matter of *ideas*. But with her— to go back a few ages, to go into the mud—" The protests broke from her in relief. But tension was still in her voice. Her further arm lay rigid beside her; but at intervals it shuddered.

"A little mud isn't bad for one." He still wanted to caress her.

But he was afraid. It seemed to him that her mind was occupied with issues too important for caresses.

"You want to cover yourself with it, sink in it." The stridency was creeping back into her voice. Yes, she was still occupied with the disgrace, the social aspect: she still rang with bitterness.

"Mildred, don't let this worry you. Is it all so important?" He did not want any more of this intensity and this drama.

Then she faltered, after a silence: "Yes, Tudor. For me it is."

"I don't want to marry yet," he said slowly, wrung again by the deep constricted lamentation to which she was returning.

"Don't you want me?" she faltered.

"I don't know, Mildred," he whispered. "I don't know."

Her further arm was quivering. Slow inner shudders were passing down her body. "I want to give up everything for you," she said at last. But bitterly.

Again tenderness engulfed him. Such tenderness that the compassion had gone. He wanted to make love to her. It seemed that their nerves would be eased if they embraced, said nothing, ceased to worry. His arm tightened on her shoulder. She quivered suddenly, in shock. It was as if full normal consciousness were returning to her. She lifted her further hand. Something dripped out of the hand, and in the silence he heard liquid fall soft as leaves on the moss. Her hand was torn and bleeding; she had been gripping a sharpedged flint.

A kind of curbed hysteria shook her. She behaved as though she were deeply ashamed, and she would not allow him to touch the hand at first; she wanted to bathe it in the brook and wind her handkerchief round it, but the brook was more often than not murky with dust from the colliery: he said that she must come back with him to his new surgery, which was already almost completely fitted. This she refused to do at first, but he would not listen.

At sight of the injury his tenderness had changed to a passionate and aching awareness of her, deeper than any he had known before. He insisted that his handkerchief should bind the torn

113

hand. In the darkness his fingers became wet with her blood. He drew her out of the wood, hastening.

"It's nothing," she said, "nothing. I can go home and bathe it there." But her voice was half strangled in her throat.

"My surgery is much nearer," he said determinedly. They went through dark deserted lanes between the rows of dwellings. But they had to cut through the main street to reach the hive of Terraces. And she shrank into her coat, she lowered her head, so that she seemed nothing but hat and coat. Under a spluttering gas-lamp on the corner a group of colliers looked at them idly; otherwise there was no one about, and he felt her relief. What a struggle would lie ahead for her! Poor Mildred, she must be in such turmoil. Surely the battle was not worth her while. Still, still.... His fingers caressed her wrist as they walked silently together. She was a warm breathing young woman who had trod with him through many good years.

He led her through the Terraces, which in the night were alleys of gloom, the low, dark houses like barbaric huts with small suspicious windows high up, some lit murkily. They stumbled over uneven, smelly ground stale with thrown-out rubbish. Perched on any available bank in the narrow alleys were boxes containing irritable chickens, even a soiled duck or two, and pigeons of unglossy plumage; during the daytime this livestock wandered over the unnatural ground with a look of perplexed grievance, particularly the ducks, who had grown grey from their dusty imprisonment.

"I've never been in this quarter before," she faltered.

"And only a good stone's throw from your home." A drunk was lurching towards them. He sang a hymn with surprising purity as he lumped across the alley. He peered at them agape as they passed, hesitated, and bawled:

"Oi, how's Jinny Lloyd in number six?"

Tudor turned. "Why, what's wrong with her?"

"She was took to bed 'fore I went down to the Cross Keys. Screeching so much that I was drove out of the Terrace." He leaned snorting against a rickety hencote. "You know her, Jinny Lloyd?"

Tudor thought he did. Mildred had shrunk into the darkness and waited with her back turned.

"She went big as a chapel," declared the drunk in great wonder. Then he exclaimed indignantly: "But what I want to know is, where's her bloke hid himself—Ivor Lewis?" He returned to wonder. "Not much bigger, he was, than one of Dai Pigeons' pigeons there.... But where's he gone, leaving her like that?" He spat, and lurched himself up again. "Screeching like an 'ole pig stuck in the slaughterhouse, poor Jinny. And where's that Ivor Lewis now? Gone to England p'raps—he could get in a train hid under an old woman's petticoat, swinging from her garter. He's gone," he spat, "he's gone. And Jinny don't know it yet." He peered into the darkness vaguely. "Courting are you! Funny place to come courting—" He began to lurch away into the night, that smelt of live stock.

Mildred had wandered on. Drunks filled her with terror. But she had heard the lamentable history of the deserted Jinny Lloyd. She seemed retreated further into her clothes and under her hat, as Tudor took her wrist again and drew her on.

"Not much farther, Mildred.... There's not this odour round my house, though it's got to be passed through before the door's reached, this end of the Terraces."

She asked faintly: "Was it necessary to come here? Aren't there plenty of other houses you could have taken in... in neater districts?"

"Oh, I don't *prefer* this squalor. I'm not so sentimental as that. But it's the only section of the place where I'm likely to find support for a practice."

"Yes," she breathed bitterly, "yes, I suppose that's true."

They zigzagged into another alley, climbing. At the entrance they narrowly missed a pan of water that was chucked suddenly out of an upper window. Then, farther down, a door was banged open, and in the slice of oil-light, a man's figure bounded out with a yell and scuttled up the waste-patch the other side of the alley, among the chicken-sheds. He was followed by a fury of a woman screaming abuse. Other doors were opened, and neighbours crowded out. The woman's curses became obscene. But the man had safely locked himself in a fowl-house: her fists beat against the door.

"It's that young Mrs Beate Bowen," a man on the edge of the scattered crowd told Tudor; "she'll screw his neck one day."

Mildred had stood still; she wanted to retreat. In the bursts of yellow light from the opened doors he saw her daunted face. The woman's yells, as she beat against the fowl-house, were fiendish.

But he pulled her through the little narrow crowd of people. The women squealed excitedly, the men exclaimed; some laughed; they were far too intent on the savage Beate Bowen to take much notice of the strangers. Would Beate succeed in breaking down the door? A cockerel crowed in sudden indignation at this disturbance; others took up the cry, and there were bad-tempered hen-cluckings everywhere.

"One hears of these rows," Mildred shuddered—"but that woman's screams... can one have any *feeling* for these people! Not even disgust—" She panted a little. "They're beyond the consideration one would give to animals.... That woman!" Mrs. Bowen had used certain phrases, and in one of her more passionate flights had made a revelation about her husband.

"This is not a special night for the Terraces," he said calmly. "I believe this is quite commonplace. Saturdays are the gala nights."

She suddenly swerved on him. "You seem to admire them."

"Not admiration particularly, Mildred. But I can go among this kind of sprouting of life without being offended by the *people*."

"You want to gather justification for your socialism."

"Well, knowledge perhaps.... What you've just heard won't do you any harm, either," he said briskly. "Come, there's my house." There was a waste-plot and a gate in a dingy privet-hedge. They could still hear, low and menacing, the shrieking of the row. The ugly villa, dumped aggressively on a stony tongue of the hill-base, loomed dark.

She dragged along at his side as though under some compulsion that she hated. He went to a side porch and took a bunch of keys from his pocket. "This is the surgery," he said. And, mockingly, "you are my first patient. I'm going to be strictly professional with you. So stop trembling. I know you think you ought not to be entering this house alone with me. At night-time, too." He lit a naked gas-jet in a kind of lobby, damp and depressing. "This is my waiting-room. Forbidding, isn't it? But the rabble down below won't mind that."

He strove furiously against the sadistic urge growing in him. But her fears, her recoils and maddening distrust were surely demanding some such cruelty. Her eyes burned, her jaw was hard with tension. That last contact in the Terrace, the brawling woman, the frenzied beating, had, he could see, kindled a strange hard flame in her too. She would not look at him, she stood stiffly in the middle of the lobby. He could see that beyond her submissive following of him to the house she was still coiled tight in herself. He went into the untidy consulting-room and lit the gas there. It was also the dispensary, and he filled a kettle and put it on the gas-ring.

"Come here," he called roughly. He was washing the bloodstains off his hands.

She stood in the doorway. He turned. The haggard beauty of her face was like a blow between his eyes. All his dark irritation at her over-refined middle-class sensitiveness seemed to sink out of him. Youth had gone from her and in its place was a heavy tragic loneliness. Surely they could reach to that place of quiet but passionate love where all these conflicts would drift smokily away....

He bathed her hand, anointed and bound it. The torn jagged flesh roused all his tenderness again. She stood still. He buried his lips and nose in a bunch of violets tucked into her corsage, beneath the coat which she had not removed. Vaguely he noticed the stiff unyielding way in which she stood.

"Violets," he smiled. "Nice, after the hen-coops and the alleys."

He was watching her carefully now, without appearing to look at her. He could feel the heat of his veins glowing outside his flesh.

"This house is damp," she said. Apparently, she was occupied in an unmoved examination of the house.

"Yes, the roof needs repairing," he answered, impatiently. "Come and see the other rooms. Some are furnished already." He went before her, lighting the gas-brackets, none of which had been fitted with mantles yet. The blue flaring naked lights gave a dingy aspect to everything. Mildred followed slowly. She kept on sniffing at the damp.

The sitting-room, or study, was untidily littered with books, and the furniture was merely shoved in; he had not spent a night in the house yet. There was a good walnut table he had picked up cheap; and a new comfortable sofa that had just escaped the horse-hair tradition—it was of crimson plush, but well padded. Mildred stood in the doorway and looked round the room with large eyes which he could not fathom.

"Come in," he said softly, "come in. Shall I light a fire?—there are some sticks and coal."

"It's not worth while," she said. "It's getting late."

"Yes, it's worth while, if you're cold. You're not going yet."

"I must go soon," she said stubbornly.

"Sit down. Look at my beautiful red sofa. Come here, Mildred." He sat on it himself and thrust his fist into one of its stout curves. "See how you sink in it—" And all the time he secretly followed her with his bright watching eyes.

"I should put it in that corner if I were you," she said consideringly, pointing. "But not straight against the wall. And have a pedestal behind it with a fern…. What are these pictures?" She turned over two or three which were leaning against the wall.

"Rowlandson cartoons. I got them at an auction in Chepstow."

After glancing at them she offered a suggestion about wallpaper. Then she asked to see the kitchen, fastening her coat.

"Oh, there's little in the kitchen. Come upstairs."

"Is there time?" she faltered.

"Time!" he answered. And there was a harshly desiring note in his voice, at which she stood still again, at the bottom of the stairs. He was already bounding up. "Who owns your time? Or are you just afraid of night-time, like a child. Come on, Mildred." He called to her from the top of the stairs, insistent, intolerant, ardent. "I've got such a nice large airy bedroom. With a view over the Terraces. But I'll draw my new green curtains. Why are you frightened?"

He leaned over the banisters and called down to her. She stood at the bottom of the bare dingy staircase. He called entreatingly, angrily, passionately. She did not move. He laughed at her at last, jeeringly. But he gazed down with hatred. Why should he plunge back in and coax, pull, entice her up! She offended him, though he could see in the crude blue light of the hall the desperate beauty of her face. A strange violence took possession of him. He shouted down to her:

"Do you think I'm going to murder you? I'm already half a criminal, aren't I? The setting's right for it. A derelict old house in a slum, night-time, and a few surgical knives. I could bury you in the back garden.... Ah, you're all but inviting murder... come on... make the *final* sacrifice."

She turned abruptly, and without great haste walked across the hall and disappeared. He darted to a side window, threw it open and saw her emerging from the lobby door.

"Mildred, where are you going? Come here, you fool, come here. We're both fools. Can't you see, don't you understand? *I will not cringe.* Nor give you worship." He realised how incoherent he was becoming; tried to calm the fever in his veins. She was hesitating in the porch, staring out into the huge mountain night. He added, with something like eagerness, "We're fools because we can't keep our love *clear*. We chuck the filth of the world in it. Are you listening?" Once more his voice rose, passionately, "Come back, stay with me. What does your home matter, your father? He's dead and rotten, the miserable moneygrubbing snob. Save yourself, Mildred, for Christ's sake—"

119

But now she hastened, she ran, down towards the evil Terraces. He saw, in the light of the lobby, her head thrown back, her pale desperate face. Her shoulders shook; he heard her sobs. The cruelty in his veins rose; his heart beat in pain. Yet he broke into silent laughter; he sighed in mad relief. She was gone....

But why had she not stayed, broken through? The night would have been a revelation, a new beginning. He lurched into the bedroom and threw himself on the mattress of the unmade bed. Soon he was calmer. But sick disappointment filled him. He tried to ease himself by saying it was a relief she had gone; the night might not have been a splendid revelation; it might have been a bad beginning. She had been too long a victim; she had surely been corrupted too deep. The young vein of poetry in her, at which he had been warmed years ago, had cooled and hardened in the coarse dour nonconformity from which she would not escape.

But he lay in angry lamentation for the failure of this night. She wanted him to plunge blindly into marriage with her, risk it in the tradition of her class, and in spite of his "disgrace". The important thing was to get married. Never mind what might follow.... And she was willing to bear the bitter struggle of trying to get him back to respectability. Ah, a nice lot of clashes they would have had in the future.

Going downstairs he prepared to leave the house for the night. In the consulting-room the blood-stained handkerchief lay on the floor. He picked it up and threw it in a pail of rubbish. But, touching it, the old baulked feeling filled him again and his anger turned to a grieving tenderness. He remembered the burning of her sunken eyes, the low cry of her voice.

He slammed the door and faced the vast night. The mountains were flung up in great dark barriers, the world below seemed drab and lonely—and a difficult place, where no season of joy could last for long.

CHAPTER IV

I

"TIME for a revival," said Minister Moses James, looking round sinisterly at his deacons, who had gathered for a vestry confab. "Hasn't been one for ages. Place getting sinful again."

That bit of prosperity continuing, people were enjoying themselves too much, sitting in bars, or playing billiards, or wearing feathers, or eating cake. So thought the preachers. The people weren't sure. One mustn't take of the pleasures of this world without feeling guilty, of course, but all the same....

No one knew how the wave of repentance and noisy humility was begun. Sour enemies of it said it was engineered by the colliery owners: there was no one like the Lord for keeping the people safe in a contrite spirit. They said that Sir Rufus Morgan in particular had asked this assistance of his partner the Almighty: everyone knew how these two Bosses were much of a muchness and great friends, though God, of course, was really sweeter of temperament and no swanking snob, Sir Rufus being a badly-cast image of Him.

Anyhow, people, when they become bored with too much good-living and peace, like a good whip-up. No more strikes the last one was enough for a while. A revival was less costly; it fed the soul on next to no expense and brought it out to high activity on other days beside Sunday, unlike ordinary chapel religion. A revival warmed one and made one weep; it caused people to gather together in vast loads of heated flesh, united in a common impulse of pleasure acceptable to the divine nostrils.

And most people took to the revival hungrily: their souls had held no worth-while sustenance since the last revival ten years before. Plenty of food of this earth now, plenty of beer and tea; but how long, how long the divine victuals had been withheld! The Sundays just before the revival began its real activities, one could hear great preparatory pantings coming from the chapels. The long, thin valley began to shudder with closed-in emotion ready to burst at the first fiery thrusts of inspired preachers. But where were the sacred men with the heavenly whips, the tongues of flame, the angry bellows? The people demanded them and they appeared: that was the truth.

The heralds were the three Brothers Beynon, and they came of respectable farming folk in mid-Wales. Two were twins and of serious mien, with emaciated faces, out of which black eyes burned red like coals: Joshua and Merlin. They were the preachers, though only one had been ordained in the conventional way. The third, a couple of years younger, was a round-faced pink darling, who sang hymns like a converted *prima donna,* a kind of contralto: Trevor by name. His endearing ways and sexless voice roped-in the middle aged and old women in shoals. But it was the twins who in their long expressive hands carried the balls of fire from Heaven and threw them like bombs into the valley.

And it was a lovely spring, the June days sultry and charged with a sun that snorted heat like an angry young mare. Just the weather for a revival, for not only would the chapels steam with warmth and be like comfortable ovenswhat with the air and the preaching and the testimonies but meetings could be held in the open, unchilled by unkind mountain winds and the usual local wet. And, what was more, the Lord kept the weather fine for a whole month.

Those few who spoke against the revival said that Sir Rufus had invited the Brothers Beynon to earn these fresh laurels among rough miners; it was known that recently he had been for his bad blood at a mid-Wales spa, where the Brothers were conducting a successful minor revival. One or two even went further and said that cash was passed, in a roundabout way but this was a lie, for anyone could see that the Brothers were poor as chapel-vermin.

And furthermore, they had no need of cash. They said so, shouting it from the pulpits.

And they arrived on asses, simply and uncomfortably, like many people travelled in the Bible. They had no luggage, not even a change of stockings for the ones they were wearing, which were in holes and gone so far that they weren't worth washing. They said God would provide, and indeed an oil-man's widow, one of the earliest converts, gave them pairs of her gone husband's as soon as they were safely down in the valley and had taken cups of tea. The three appeared on the high road that winds over the mountain: the asses with their young men burdens could be seen for a while silhouetted blackly against the clean blue sky.

A shout went up from the valley. They had arrived too early, and the welcome prepared for them hadn't got going properly this was to be a procession which would meet the Brothers half-way up the mountain and, on a shelf, hold the first historic meeting. But a tidy bunch had already assembled and those who were good of leg began to scuttle hastily up the slopes.

There was a disarranged meeting some distance up. The three brothers dismounted from their patient donkeys and did not say anything for some minutes, while the worshippers clustered around them waiting for the first inspired words. The twins stared down menacingly into the teeming valley: the other brother, the singer, sat down with tight-closed eyes. At last Joshua, smelling downwards powerfully, said in English:

"I smell the stink of sties down there. The smell of stale old sins and fresh new ones. It comes up strong and thick phew, what a place! Cured it must be."

Merlin, gazing down piercingly, declared in Welsh:

"I see black bodies running about like frightened black-beetles. The foot of the Lord is stretching out of the sky to tread on them, brimstone on His big boots."

Joshua said, beginning to rock:

"Pah, the smell is stronger than new-dropped dung. The place is like a sewer open under God's sky."

Merlin began to lash:

"Who built this place? It is Satan's courtyard. That river is black pee out of a man whose soul is blacker than a nigger. Satan's throne of ebony, rich with the spoils of evil, stands on stout legs by there."

They had wide, sensitive nostrils; their eyes, dark and penetrating, were alive as minerals. None among the welcomers took umbrage at these insulting references to their native place; all recognised the divine power in the Brothers' sword-like voices, their lean proud bodies, their quivering noses and impassioned pointed hands. For one can say as much damage as one likes, providing it is put in religious shape.

The small Trevor began to sing, smiling to himself in gaiety, a true specimen of the joy that came to youngsters who give themselves to God. The words were of his own making, fitted to an old Welsh chapel tune. In them he compared himself, before he had attained holiness, to a bruised fish that swam in muddy waters, to an expensive copper kettle with a leak in it, to a plum-tree frosted as the bloom put forth, to a ledger with a lot of bad debts on its pages. But now he was without bruise, leak, frost or debts.

And truly anyone could see that he was a youth of good parts and proportions, with inside him a bubbling fountain of sunny waters that would never dry up. The language of his hymn, with its many verses, was choice. The listeners, some of them chapel bards in their own right, smiled with pleasure. What is there more gratifying than good unfrivolous words wedded to a sad whining melody? When Trevor ceased at last everyone knelt and began to pray.

The Brothers Beynon were recognised at once as being of the right stuff, and this first touch-and-go meeting was like a triumphant blast of trumpets.

The hundred chapels of the valley began to hum with activities. There was much competition for the services of the Brothers, which developed into a warfare of quarrelling, spite and jealousy.

124

Rival deacons boasted of the numbers of converts in their different chapels, the gross takings of the collection plates, the length of meetings which often persisted beyond midnight. The native ministers had to lash up their own sermons and exhortations towards the exalted standard set by the Brothers.

Down in the pits men worked to the singing of hymns, and frequently a collier would cease cutting coal in some cramped aggravating corner and go on his knees to call the attention of Heaven to the fact that he had been saved the previous night and had not used bad language that day, so far. There were short, impromptu services, and the singing appeals echoed along the black buried corridors, sped up the pit-shafts and smote softly, as Joshua Beynon said himself, on the vast all-hearing eardrums of God. These underground meetings were approved by the Brothers: they gave an assurance that though held half-a-mile underground, in regions usually associated with the Devil and where bad language and ugly accidents were the rule, the untidy services were probably as sweet to the Divine nose as that great wreath of arum lilies which the colliers sent to the funeral of Ebbie Bowen, one of their number who who had actually been called to the Great Glory above while he was praying down under, a loose stone in the roofing falling on his bent head. To be called while praying! But for the revival Ebbie would not have been busy praying, his eyes shut, and very likely he would have gone with some lewd oath on his lips.

Pubs suffered the most. Barmaids sat on chairs and knitted garments for next winter or spelt out paragraphs in the newspapers. Only the most abandoned drinkers, real soakers, dared to enter the bars. Even those middling drinkers who were of too easy-going mind to be enticed into the revival would not risk the taunts and criticism issuing from the new order of things. More than personal social disgrace, there might arise some ostracism to wife and family, or some pecuniary disadvantage, so powerful was the movement becoming.

As fever-pitch was reached and more and more converts were

gathered into the lusty folds, other tradesmen besides publicans began to mutter. In one or two addresses the Beynons had attacked gluttony, and thereafter the "saved" happily embraced new sacrifices. Butchers' joints swung unsold from the rails, there was no demand for weekday chops, and in the provision shops cheese, bacon, butter and such-like became smellier and smellier. Some wanted to call a meeting of the Chamber of Commerce and draft a demand that the ban be lifted off eatables. One grocer said that some of his customers had ceased buying soap too–why wash flesh that was born a thing of dirt, what did a soiled skin matter, providing the soul was dipped daily in God's lather? The Post Office Savings Bank, however, prospered.

Maldwyn Clarke, a greedy butcher, had been a first-week convert. He was already a big man in a well-to-do chapel and, zealous in Sunday labour, he naturally reaped a good harvest on weekdays among the congregation. The swollen congregations that followed the beginnings of the revival caused him to order extra quantities of beef and mutton, and indeed for the first week or two things went well and he laid his itching fist over a bit of property of this earth that he had long desired, paying a deposit. And then, without warning, the ban fell. The first week he dropped forty pounds, the second sixty, and the third promised hell. Maldwyn, a purple faced man of excitable temper, went about groaning and foaming at the mouth. The strange thing was that no one could tell whether he was still trying to convert others, in the manner of the already saved, or denouncing the foolish turn the revival had taken. His trade sank shockingly, and, being of funny disposition already, he ruptured a blood-vessel one evening while pacing up and down the main street from his shop to the chapel door, back and fore in awful dilemma, unable to stay in his derelict shop, unable to trust himself to enter the packed chapel. He was never the same man again.

Open-air meetings were held on the few fields still left, wedged greyly among the rows, the collieries and the shops. There were festive Saturday afternoon gatherings on these, complete with refreshment tent, so as to attract people from the far-away inner creeks of the mountains. Pedlars would appear with trays of toys, medals and laces for boots and corsets. One set up a plank on two boxes and offered small-beer: it was only made of nettles, but an angry throng chased him away: in the refreshment tent proper, only the weakest tea was sold, half cold, and slices of coarse bread spread with stale butter bought at half-price.

None of the preachers that sprang up everywhere to lead these meetings approached anywhere near the Beynon Brothers in majesty of utterance, in roll of inspiration, in heat of deliverance. None arranged their addresses so cunningly, passing from resplendent imagery to coarse-grained simplicity, from language such as was surely used by angels to phrases of domestic familiarity. In their sermons God entered unrecognised the saloon of a sinful barber and offered the Divine Locks to scissors which, approaching the Silver Curls, turned to lightning in the barber's hand; He played a harp on the green mountain-tops and, walking down into a kitchen in the valley, browned the pie-crust of a converted woman whose pies were always white as marble. He was in everything, but that did not mean He countenanced everything, but only that there was no escape. When pleased He blew His gold voice through the pipes of chapel organs and when displeased caused the rash of measles, the pain of rheumatism. He believed in looking-glasses, so that people could see how their awful faces swelled with gluttony, thinned with wantonness, or just went stupid from vanity.

They would pass arrogantly from abuse to flattery, calling the congregation in one breath a shameful lot of misbegotten baboons that even the fleas scampered from in terror, in the next declaring that the shine of the most precious diamonds came from their eyes and that they were well-dressed in heavenly panoply which nothing they had done had stained or torn.

After the sermons, the reaping began. Grizzled old men stood and, sometimes weeping, sometimes like lions, announced their long lives of evil; young men told of temptations, struggles fought and always lost, a going-down into a hole that led to hell, a wallowing in mud, a delight in burning. Pale, exhausted women, some wrapped in old shawls for many, reaching the core of sacrifice, refused to wear finery in chapel now declared themselves henceforward as brides of Christ only, standing stark in pews. Heads of hair often fell down abandoned in the stress of emotion, and loud sobbing mingled with the gulps and difficult breathing of those who had not the courage to give a grand public release of their load of remorse.

The moans of repentant humanity, used and battered and corrupted and led astray, went through the valley like a great shudder of the long-suffering earth.

II

For long the Terraces remained unconverted. True, work was not attempted on that stronghold of evil until some busybody made count and discovered that out of over a thousand inhabitants only one had been saved, that one being a half-wit. The Brothers Beynon were indignant. Work must begin on the Terraces without delay. This was during the fourth week of the revival.

The first and only attack was a late Saturday night procession through the alleys. The novelty of the time not long before midnight, when the drunkards were about to return to their homes was a clever move. Carrying carriage-lamps, the procession, which prudently consisted of men only, wound through the alleyways, alternating hymns with loud demands to the inhabitants to come forth and wash themselves in a new life. There were pauses and prayers, and for once the Brothers' favourite complaint of stinking places had a basis in reality. They headed the procession and, amid a circle of flickering lamps, threw up their arms towards Heaven to, as they said, pull an unwilling God down to this clogged-up sink.

At first angry mothers ran out of doorways and bitterly

128

exclaimed against the disturbance: children were abed, the sick were starting out of uneasy slumbers. The Brothers were equal to this.

"Bring the little children to us, bring out the sick. There will be no more crying and no more weeping, no more pain. Let us lay hands on them and their sobs will turn to smiles, their aches to bliss."

"What about the poultry?" someone bawled. For all the live-stock seemed to be wakening in the clamour, the voices of geese, ducks, hens and cocks lifted in surprise. Merlin Beynon declared solemnly:

"The noise of poultry is sweet in my ears. Let them, too, wake and peck at the corn of my words. They are waking to a Carnival of God."

Then one of the high windows was opened and a lot of small Sunday-dinner carrots were aimed by a certain woman one by one, at the procession. Each of the three Brothers received one somewhere in his face. But their love remained all-embracing.

"You up there," sang Joshua, "you are throwing vegetables at God Himself. Black my eyes for me and I will caress you, knock out my teeth and I will kiss you with my bleeding lips."

"For a bob she'll give you more than a kiss, Katie will," someone shouted in the mob, amid awful laughter.

And it was then the battle really started. At that shout from someone in the rapidly-swelling crowd, Joshua drew himself up tight: he seemed to stretch like a length of black elastic.

"Ha!" he thundered, "ha, a harlot, eh! A house of harlotry. A den of the biggest damned of all."

He flew like an arrow to the door beneath the windows wherefrom had come the carrots. This was the sin he favoured above all for the most powerful guns of his denunciation. His raised fist struck three resounding blows on the thin door.

"Open," he bellowed, "open. Flames are licking at this house. Its rotten walls totter and the fornicating beasts within will be buried alive."

The door was opened and an elderly man of mild aspect stood in the dim light from within. Behind him, peering out over his shoulders, were two other and younger men. These were the father, husband and uncle of the carrot-thrower. All frowned and all were sober. The elderly man, who looked on the soft side, said quietly:

"Not now. Very late it is. Come to-morrow, after tea-time, shall we say now?"

Joshua did not gather the real import of these words. Instead he answered, his arm raised:

"Now! Tomorrow will be too late. I,"

"Well," interrupted the man mildly, "tonight's too late for us"

One of the younger men pushed past the father. "Lemme get at him," he growled. "One of them revivalists it is, can't you see! Disturbing peaceful folk."

By that time a lot of Joshua's supporters had crowded round the doorway. The lamps shone on faces already alight in righteous wrath. But with a suitable oath the young man swung out his fisted arm from the doorway and caught Joshua in the chest.

"Man," shouted Joshua balefully, "you would smite the thunder and hold the lightning!" And indeed he was terrifying with his own kind of majestic wrath, lifted like a lean black flame, like a spitting serpent.

"Clear off," yelled the young man.

"I have come to clean this house and I will enter!" bellowed Joshua, getting back his wind.

Then the other young man, the uncle, who had a big black moustache and big bare arms, pushed himself out. He spat in his palms.

"Right!" he shouted, "you want a fight then, ah? One two, three!" And he began at once, stampeding into the supporters with great roars.

What followed was an earth victory for the Terraces, but surely a heavenly glory for the revivalists, who here below were greatly outnumbered, being blocked in at both ends of the alley by battle-scenting Terrace people. The fighting spread through the whole length of the particular alley, and presently was not confined only to Revival versus Terraces. Longstanding grievances of neighbours sprang into activity; the drink-inflamed avenged imaginary insults from the nearest man, and a sprinkling of women clawed each other in screaming anger. The carriage-lamps were flung about and smashed. Children's heads popped out of the windows and watched in glee or fear, some egging the fighters raucously. And the live-stock added their nervous cries as rickety coops shook to their foundations: several men crashed into narrow chicken runs and one drunkard was found next morning fast asleep among twenty-six silent hens, having taken early refuge in one of the larger coops.

One by one the revivalists escaped from the alley, fighting or ducking their way through. Merlin Beynon emerged with a cut over his left eyebrow; blood was smudged over his face. Two or three supporters were shot out after him. An onlooker, a stout woman with arms calmly akimbo, said that Doctor Tudor Morris's house was just at the top. Merlin, gasping, was dabbing at his crimson face with a white handkerchief. A supporter exclaimed in wrath at this wounding of the great man. Merlin, however, was not quite subdued.

"What is a thimbleful of my poor blood compared to the sacred gallons that flowed from the Cross! O my poor persons, I am filled with glory at this little loss. I have shed blood on the steps that go down to hell."

The stout woman, a man's cap skewered on the back of her head, was inclined to be sympathetic, declaring:

"A shame it is. Where are the bobbies? Never about when they're wanted. Sergeant Parry now, he ought to be here with his big truncheon.... You go and have your face stitched up, young man, yes indeed, it looks bad. Doctor Morris up there will see to you."

But Doctor Morris was already walking down the slope from his house, coming to see what all the noise was. The single gas-

131

lamp at the alley's end shed a murky light. The stout woman recognised him and called. Roars and screams still issued from the battle area.

Tudor thought it was some family brawl in which all the Terrace people were taking sides, after their fashion.

"Doctor Morris," cried the sympathetic woman, "here's a bloke for you that's had a good clout. Bleeding to death he is."

A supporter cried indignantly, "Merlin Beynon he is, of the Brothers Beynon. His blood is shed! Woe to them that struck him."

"Leave me to bleed," shouted Merlin, swaying. "Rescue thin Joshua and the little Trevor. Their ribs will be broken, and other bones. Not much flesh is on them, but they are sacred meat." He was suddenly fearful as the clamour in the alley rose; it sounded as though someone were being clubbed to death. Shaken now, he sat down heavily on a step; the celestial wrath had gone out of him. He murmured to himself in strange despair:

"What is the world? A patch of turf where the worms crawl and dead leaves rot, after their green season. The stoat chews the throat of the rabbit, and deep down, deep down, is a coffin wherein the hairs of my mother thin off her skull. My nose is stuffed with the odour of blood and earth, my weary jaws are stiff with clay. My poor throat is thick with mud...." He could not swoon without making a fine wordy business of it.

He recovered quickly, however, and without further fuss consented to accompany Tudor to his surgery. The supporters, at his bidding, had gone to rescue the other brothers. With the revival at its height one couldn't afford to lose them.

Merlin Beynon leaned on Tudor's arm and gasped as they climbed to the surgery. But he gasped less from his wound than from the realistic impact of this defence of the Terraces against what was good for them. Obstinacy he had met with before, but never physical assault.

"The persons up here are worth saving?" he demanded wildly of Tudor, peering up into his face.

132

"Is that the only blow you've had?" asked Tudor, looking at the brow-wound as they passed the lamp.

"Or are they as the toads breeding in ditches and bogs?" he went on, raging dramatically now. "Or the wild wolves in foreign heathen countries?"

"Well," Tudor answered soothingly, "there's certainly something untamed in them. They're still pagans in a rough state."

Merlin paused. He had not really expected any reply to his rhetorical questions. He peered anxiously at Tudor, becoming more normal, and asked nervously:

"You are a proper doctor? Not one of these quacks?"

"I'm properly qualified, Mr. Beynon. Are you a qualified minister?"

"Brother Joshua is," Merlin said, proudly. "Stitches there'll have to be?"

"Probably."

Merlin panted. In the consulting-room he sat jerking in the chair. His eyes were neuropathic, sunk deep and heavy with torment. Tudor noticed the rhombic cranium, flattened in the occipital region, and he could see the upheaval that was taking place, under the nervousness. At sight of the needle Merlin cried out.

"Come, come," Tudor protested, "it won't be much."

But with the approach of the needle to the place above his eye he squirmed helplessly in the chair. Tudor drew back and gave him a tonic, sat down for a while and spoke comfortingly of the trivial operation.

"It's the needle," Merlin gasped, "the needle. Like this it is. When I was a boy, before I was converted, very wicked I was. The evil I committed would fill a thick book." Sufferingly he needed to confess. "Once I took my mother's darning needle and pushed it in the eye of a kitten." He moaned. "Lord, Lord, forgive me my sins and I will bring hundreds of thousands to Thy feet!" And he darted out of the chair as though he would recommence his labours there and then.

Tudor led him angrily back to the chair: the blood was streaming again from the wound. Presently the strong tonic, or the assistance of Heaven, worked: the patient submitted, moaning but slightly, to the stitching. When it was over and he was bandaged, he relaxed for a while, but soon started up again violently, greatly vexing Tudor, who had done a neat quick job.

"Keep still," he ordered sharply, and pushed him back in the chair, "or I'll have to use the needle again."

But the feverish energy and the alternating gusts of despair and high-mindedness interested him. He did not want the young man to go yet. He invited him into the sitting-room, and put him in a dimly-lit corner. An oil-lamp with a pale shade burned over some books scattered on the table; there was a low fire in the grate. Tudor had moved into his house, and when the sounds of battle reached him he was deep in a study of the first 1867 volume of *Das Kapital*. At the side of the tattered volume stood a glass of strong whisky.

"You've been working too hard, Mr. Beynon," he said in his best professional manner, the genial one. "Far too hard. Be careful, or you'll soon be having a nervous breakdown."

Merlin was still breathing fretfully. "I cannot stop working until all the people of my land are lifted up."

"To what?" asked Tudor, conversationally calm.

The dark, tormented eyes opened wide. "To the glories of Heaven. A long ladder is placed from earth to Heaven. Poor persons can go up and then with fresh hearts they can come down, having seen the glory for a while. Thus shall they live in patience, knowing the riches that are to come." These were extracts from one of his sermons, and thrown off easily but with inexhaustible gusto.

His nerves were so tense with passionate belief. Did they ever relax? Or would Merlin not dare to let them relax. This high-pitched febrile passion must surely be an escape from some awful anguish of mind. Tudor felt compassionand a faint sense of intimacy for this burning crusader. He suggested quietly:

"But the glories of the earth, my friend why not try to show the people these? Earthly glories, and how to use them, here, now, with their own hands"

Beynon's voice shook with hatred; it seemed impossible for him to simmer down: "Glories of the earth! Where man is, there is corruption. The world is decked with trees and alive with the flowers, but these are not men. Men tear the bellies out of their brothers, and according to their strength steal that which the weaker has gathered with difficult labour. Glories? Excrement."

Tudor felt the sense of intimacy growing. He dare not offer Merlin whisky, for the Brothers denounced drink. If only he would climb down from the exalted throne among the fiercely wheeling clouds....

"But," he coaxed, his fingers unconsciously playing with the pages of *Das Kapital,* "if we teach people to turn their backs on the disgrace of the earth, you're going to make things much easier for the dishonest ones. We've no right to believe *only* that our life here is nothing but preparation: it's such cheating of oneself."

Merlin said with sombre intensity, "While there are children born who suck of the breasts of Satan's wife for wickedness is born out of the womb, it is of the blood the world will be a place of misery. The world is a white rose through which a worm eats its way. White petals, perfume, the dew—but rottenness and decay within." These also from a recent sermon.

"Pluck the slug out, save the young roses," Tudor suggested. But he was beginning to feel rather baffled.

Beynon raised his hand. "The worm never dies!"

"In the case of his human counterpart, he must be taught to keep off doing nothing but feeding on our roses."

So they went together some distance in hatred of the earth. But Merlin wanted Heaven, Tudor the world. The young revivalist, ducking for a while out of the shining clouds, became aware of Tudor as a person. He cooled down for half an hour. In simple phrases he declared his unshakable belief that people's souls badly needed filling and that they could grow stout on nothing in this earth. He defended his extravagant methods of obtaining the heavenly victuals by saying that there was no other successful way: people would not listen to milk-and-water sermons and mild coaxing was no good. The lashes of insult and abuse, God displayed as an easily recognisable figure of mighty limbs, dogmatic announcements of everybody's equal importance in the Divine eye, a passionate fostering of the sense of eternal drama these were the weapons to command obedience.

"You," he addressed Tudor directly almost for the first time, "you, being a doctor, have had so much truck with people's bodies that you've lost sight of their immortal souls."

"Not entirely," Tudor smiled, not disliking this energetic but overheated young man. "I can well see that the particular success of your revival is due to the physical life of the people here."

"Yes?" brooded Merlin, not quite connecting. Industrialism meant nothing to him in the divine scheme of things.

"You *do* lift up people, you *do* make them forget the uglinesses of their lives, the sweat and the worries, the monotony and the fears. But the point is that after making them forget for a while, *they've got to come back*. The nasty world is still here, the valley is still narrow and dark, there is always the fear that next week's pay envelope will be very light in weight, that there is going to be a lock-out, that there is no security."

"Except in heavenly things," Merlin burst in, his head forcefully between the blinkers again.

Tudor sighed. "You," he said regretfully, "you with your magnetic sway over crowds and your picturesque tongue, I hope that if ever you become tired of gazing up so high you'll come and grovel in the dust here. The Miners' Federation badly needs energetic men with vision. But you'll have to keep your eyes strictly on this earth."

"They're on this earth now, and too much they see." But there was a fretful note in his voice now, he looked away from Tudor. His lean face was worn and hollowed. Only the black restless eyes rang with perpetual storm. "The Miners' Federation!" he repeated scornfully, recoiling from the mundane intrusion of the name.

"With your energy," Tudor suggested softly, "you could start many little revolutions in people's lives. Make the workers feel their importance here below, for instance." He was wondering if Merlin, who had such a highly-developed consciousness of the evil of the world, would ever change his conception of that evil. Revivalists usually petered out as such. What became of them? They disappeared like gnats in winter. But surely some of them developed into useful citizens sooner or later.

Merlin came back to Tudor, solemnly, like a young judge. "You are a socialist," he accused.

"I don't know about that. But I'm interested in a few goings on in this place, and in spite of my concern with people's bodies, I'm just as anxious about spiritual constipations.... The real ones, that is, those that when they're cured make things easier and more comfortable in the world."

Pity and compassion were now exuded from Merlin. He treated Tudor as one ill in mind and given to fantastic pranks.

"You are as the dog that goes round and round chasing its tail," he said, "or as the child who wants Father Christmas to come out of the chimney every day.... Always the world will bulge ulcers and boils while it lives, and if you will cure them in one place, then they will break out in another. I tell you, brother," he said solemnly, but beginning to burn yet again, "I tell you that the world will never be a perfect place and that the heart's peace is only gained by the closing of one's eyes and going into God's orchards where the apples shine like gold and the soft music of pianos is heard all day, all day, coming from palaces, where—" The glands of his throat were beginning to swell and work rapidly again.

"Well," interrupted Tudor after a while, "I'm one of those who've *got* to look at the ulcers."

"Do I not look at them too!" declared Merlin, now returned wholly to his pulpit wrath. And his gestures had become dramatic again, so that Tudor warned him about the stitches. "Sores I see everywhere."

"But you don't *touch* them," cried Tudor, becoming irritable.

137

"You leave them to fester, you let the flesh rot." He had become conscious of a peculiar exhaustion and realised that, for all his precautions, the vampiric power of the revivalist had been working, the psychic filching which the Brothers exercised so dramatically in their meetings, sucking power out of the congregations, churning it over, turning it to thunder and masterfully throwing it back in rolling peals over their prostrate victims. "No wonder you want to escape into orchards," he went on exasperatedly, "and listen to pianos all day long. The world is too much for you, and fear is at the bottom of these flights."

The black light of Merlin's eyes, in which all the hypnotic flaming of a powerful neurosis formidably burned, was turned full strength on Tudor. A magician's face leaned towards him, the unquiet flesh tense and drawn. Even the white bandage took on some symbolic quality, the binding of one wounded in some deathly struggle with evil: its whiteness seemed dim, gone into the texture of the flesh. "Brother," whispered a sweet seductive voice, "come with me to Christ. Your soul bleeds, I hear the falling of blood, like the rain falling in a winter wood. The wind wails through the dead trees. Let it be as the fingers of a beloved one on the strings of a harp, calling you to rest—"

Tudor was obliged to make an effort to unhitch his gaze from the magician's face; he swerved it round to the lamp, Karl Marx, the whisky. "Not yet," he said gravely. "Nothing doing just yet in that way." He took a drink of the whisky.

Merlin stood up; he had been about to go on his knees. "Yes, your time is not yet," he announced, closing his face like a book, "and for now I waste my precious seeds on black and bitter ground.... How much is it for the stitching?"

Tudor said he would have to attend him further. Merlin, sombre and a little haughty now, said that he would prefer being attended in future by a chapel-man doctor. Tudor overcame his irritation and shrugged his shoulders. He finished the remainder of his whisky and told Merlin his fee. Then Merlin said that the money would be sent by the treasurer of the chapel to which he was attached that week. It was one of the Brothers' rules never to use money on their travels and activities.

"I'll send the bill to the treasurer," Tudor said. The revivalist was his first paying patient. He felt a little sentimental about it and presented Merlin, as he prepared to go, with a box of pills. "They're always useful," he murmured.

The sitting-room seemed to shrink after the revivalist's departure. Tudor opened the window. Merlin's personality, stoutened to fill big chapels and halls, had filled the room oppressively. That personality could never return to normal stature, it had developed irreparably a kind of spiritual dropsy; its owner could never know again the matter-of-fact size of everyday life. Therein lay the cause of the approaching collapse Tudor thought he detected in him. One couldn't keep one's mind perpetually on the boil without wearing out the pan.

Nevertheless, when Tudor returned to the Marx under the lamp, the revolutionary seemed to be grimly drab, the thesis a Calvary to endure. Workers, workers, workers. Ants, ants, ants: labouring under a colossal stone. He closed the book and began to think of Melville. Surely it was the mischievous Brothers Beynon who ought to be under lock and key, for their sakes as well as others! Melville's clean-minded and delicately ferocious activities had health in them.

And inevitably thought of Melville brought Daisy quickly and vividly to mind. Ah, why was she not there? He would like to take her up to bed now. He needed that good refreshment after this Marxian and theological night.

III

The Terraces yielded a dozen or so converts in the end. But the Brothers earned great credit for themselves by the attack that Saturday night—which was not repeated. That had been real courage, real taking of the light into dark places. Merlin's plastered brow earned him more converts than all his eloquence: the revival increased in splendour.

True, there were one or two peculiar developments. Tudor was called to attend a man who, declaring he had been given power to fly to Heaven, mounted to the top of his garden wall to begin the flight—taking off, he went downwards instead into a bed of young onions, breaking his ankle. A chimney-sweep stole a lamb from the mountain-side and prepared to sacrifice it on a homemade altar, but policemen arrived as the knife was being sharpened and handcuffed him. A woman smashed her husband's violin because it had been bought with money won in gambling; the husband tackled her in an unconverted way and both were taken to hospital.... It was also true, however, that some people took decently and quietly to the business.

Tudor heard that the revival had brought to other doctors a crop of extra cases—chiefly women alarmed at strange palpitations, giddiness and faintings. But his surgery remained peacefully clean: the Terraces were in a state of summer health. Beyond Merlin and the man with the broken ankle, the revival caused only one more case to be brought to him. The surgery bell jangled with impatient hurry one early evening, just as he was deciding to go and visit his father, to suggest that Elwyn should browbeat some of his broader minded patients into shifting their custom to the son. Elwyn had more patients than he could deal with now that he was alone.

Hannah ushered into the waiting-room Mrs. Lettie Phillips, who was panting and accompanied by her thirteen-year-old son Emrys. She was one of the dozen Terrace women who had been saved. When Tudor appeared she burst out:

"Oh, Doctor Morris, this little Satan has swallowed fifteen of his marbles. For a bet in school. Please to get them out as quick as you can, I want to take him to revival meeting tonight to be converted—it's special for boys and girls."

Emrys was making loud protests against the fuss.

"There's nothing a' matter with me at all," he declared violently.

"I swallowed 'em quick and I can't feel 'em nowhere at all." He hung at the back of his mother's skirts. Years ago he had had a tooth pulled out in a surgery without anaesthetic. "They're inside me now," he bellowed truculently, "and no one can't take 'em out!"

"They must be got rid of," Mrs. Phillips panted. She was a tidy but shifty-faced woman of thwarted look. She had always wanted to move from the Terraces, but her husband, a rough, wouldn't go. "You got to come to revival meeting tonight.... Otherwise I wouldn't bother about the marbles at all, you may be sure," she added viciously.

Tudor, winking at Emrys, took the boy's hand and drew him into the consulting-room. Mrs. Phillips trotted after them.

"—yes, swallowing them for a bet. Won a dirty old pet rabbit and come home as if he'd done a good bit of business. Ach, the rapscallion. He got to be saved—"

"I don't want no pincers!" Emrys bellowed when Tudor went to a cupboard. His large observant gaze was missing nothing. "Leave 'em inside me. My marbles they are!"

"I'm not going to touch you at all," Tudor assured him. "All you've got to do is to drink this. Quickly now—"

"—and I've got to take you to see the Beynons tonight," Mrs. Phillips, who had not stopped, sighed, "and a nice thing it would be if the marbles started shooting about in chapel—"

A vicious streak flashed across Emrys's face, his father's Terrace blood spoke up nastily. "I don't want to see the bloody Beynons," he yelled. This surgery put all his nerves on edge. And what was this slippery stuff he was drinking?

"For shame on you, for shame on you," half wept his mother. Nevertheless, she warned sinisterly: "Very well, then. That new suit I'll take back to the shop first thing tomorrow morning, or shall it be tonight—" During this dispute the purge was swallowed, in three angry gulps. "You take my suit back," Emrys stormed, "and I'll swallow ninety marbles, all I've got!"

"Then," Tudor said, "I shall have to use the firetongs. It won't be so easy as this way."

"Oh," moaned Mrs. Phillips, "a handful he's been and a load on my back, a basket of monkeys. I shall be glad to see him down the pit, where nonsense'll be worked out of him—"

"Come on, Emrys," Tudor beckoned, cheerfully.

The boy followed, but suspiciously. His thick sturdy body was hot with resentment at this fuss.... But when he returned he was subdued though panting.

"You're sure there were only fifteen?" Tudor asked, guiding him to a chair.

"Yes, and they was all there," whispered Emrys.

"Were all there," corrected his mother, who could read and write, unlike many of her neighbours.

Oddly, a single tear fell out of Emrys's eye. In his face was a startled look of shame. The treatment had been unexpected and shocking. He would not look at Tudor. But when his mother lifted a hand to caress his hair he turned on her a balefully aggrieved glance that promised dark things.

"There now, there now," she twittered, "you'll sit in comfort tonight. But very early we'll have to be, to get seats. So we'd better be off now, and your new suit you shall put on straight away—"

Emrys disdained a reply: he sat lumped thickly in the chair. But Tudor said firmly:

"You'd better not take him to the meeting. He must lie on the sofa and rest."

Mrs. Phillips jerked and squirmed under her frailty. "But tonight's special for boys and girls!" she cried. "Many's going to be saved, they say."

"Well, you'd better not take Emrys."

Mrs. Phillips cocked a pale stealthy eye at the doctor. Ordinarily a doctor's word was strict law. "Why now, Doctor Morris? Because he'll be wearing his new breeches?"

"Yes, and he's in no fit state to sit in a stuffy chapel for three or four hours."

Mrs. Phillips moaned and sighed. "I want him to be saved

142

tonight. The four of my friend Myfanwy are going to stand up for Jesus, so she says. And only one I've got... a wicked one," she scolded obsessively towards Emrys, "that can do with salvation more than most.... You ugly thing!" she suddenly spat out, squirming.

Emrys repeated, with startling malevolence, "I'll swallow ninety marbles—"

"Not if you was saved, you wouldn't," she breathed. "You wouldn't want marbles even to play with. Bad boys' games and betting.... The nice people everywhere are being saved," she wailed despairingly.

Tudor saw that Emrys would triumph. He gave the boy a handful of sweets out of a bottle he had got in for refractory children and warned him of dire treatment should more marbles be swallowed. But Mrs. Phillips swerved on Tudor angrily. "On his side you are," she squirmed; "you're a sinner, too, as everybody knows. I wouldn't have come here to you except that you were near and the hour of the meeting was drawing close—" She shot again on Emrys: "And if it wasn't for the meeting I wouldn't have took you to a doctor at all, I'd have let you had pains tonight, you ugly frog. Only I was afraid," she cried viciously, "that you'd want to go to the 'w.' in the middle of the meeting." But she collapsed into despair as she went out, calling on God to witness her difficulties.

Beyond Emrys there was no other patient that evening, and there was none to visit. He closed the lobby door, after staring for moments at the outside step, which was always so depressingly clean, scrubbed daily by the energetic Hannah. And in spite of Hannah's whistling of a song in the kitchen—she warbled like a nightingale—the house seemed heavily silent. He paused at the foot of the stairs. There still were various domestic details connected with his settling in which ought to be dealt with; there was a pile of bills in the study waiting to be examined and thought about. But tonight these tasks seemed dreary and obstructive of peace of mind.... He would go up to the villa immediately after eating the cold supper which Hannah had already laid.

And climbing through the valley he decided to get to Bristol soon, to see Daisy. He had written to her once, but she had replied with the briefest of notes—written as if letter-writing were the earth's worst burden—saying she was "all right but didn't know when she would be back. Not until Melville was out, she expected. Her home was sub-let; Melville had about seven months more to do. There was no reason," she said bleakly, "for her to come back."

The old villa was a place of gloom these days. His mother, though better after her attack and capable of moving about, took to her couch with a mysterious obstinacy. It was as though an irreparable blow had been delivered at the spine of her life and she had decided that she owed it to respectable society never to stand straight again. Something had always been missing out of her life, and now there was the opportunity to go into grievance and lamentation silently. Another attack might come—of the paralysis or from the hideous world—if she tempted life by having transactions with it. And so a *malade imaginaire* reigned over her mind, besides the justifiable fear of the paralysis. And nothing she liked better than the visits of the chapel minister, a death-worshipper who had always been her spiritual lover. He would read to her out of the fiery old Welsh sermons for hours, in sing-song style, chantingly.

Tudor she received as though she had borne a Judas whom she was doomed to love. She would whimper very slightly at his entrance into the drawing-room, where she lay on the couch, well dressed and her beautiful white hair coiled statelily as ever; then, as he bent to kiss her, she would stroke his hand forgivingly, bravely. He might have been a convict just released. A black sheep. And her only child.

"Well, Mother, how are you tonight?" he asked. His grandmother was sitting with her. Elwyn was out on a case.

"Better, better." She always replied thus, in a bravely non-complaining way.

144

"Not been up this week?"

"Bronwen took me into the garden on Tuesday to see the sweet-peas."

"For a whole quarter of an hour," murmured Bronwen, who at ninety possessed an odd girlishness compared to her prostrate daughter-in-law. There was a slightly deprecatory note in her voice.

"Bravo. We'll soon have you about again. You're missing all the excitement in the valley, you know.... All this public whipping out of the devil from a place where he's lived so long—"

Bronwen smiled faintly under the square of old lace which she affected on her head. But his mother took no notice. She was determined to worry. Her voice was brave, but one could tell her mind was a mass of anxiety. How handsome she was, Tudor thought, sitting beside her and taking her hand affectionately. Her solid, well-kept face still had something of the publicity look it had developed in the days when she had been a well known vocalist. Even on the couch she was obviously stately, in a short pigeon-like way.

"You are being looked after properly in your house?" she asked. "That housekeeper is a good woman?"

"Splendid."

"As long as she cooks well and sees that your things are aired—" she fretted. "You're not accustomed to a careless house."

She went on making dutiful enquiries, but with foreboding. She was still confused and numbed. If only he had cast himself at her feet and acknowledged his evil behaviour! She could not understand. He was not the traditional black sheep such as many families produced; he had not the manner of one, and he was not a spendthrift or a drunkard. And yet he could do what he had done and he had *got into trouble with the police*. Continually she whimpered when she thought of that half a night spent in a police-cell. And he was behaving as though nothing had happened. Her colourless, rather protuberant eyes slowly searched his face in a vague protest.

"If," he asked, half teasingly, half seriously, "I hire Williams's carriage for an afternoon, you will let me take you for a drive, Mother? You and Bronwen. The days are so warm."

Her lips parted, her eyes became fixed, moved from him. He felt her body stiffen slightly. A curious fear ran across her face.

"I had better not," she said at last. "No, I don't feel equal to it... the... the jolting wouldn't be good for me, I'm sure."

"You know Elwyn said you could go out for a drive," Bronwen put in, a shade sharply. Away in the corner her strong old face was indignant.

"I tell you I don't feel equal to it." An invalid's obstinacy was now roused fully.

Tudor's heart surged with grief for her. He was quite aware of the awful cord that could never be broken, however far he withdrew from his mother. But he would never allow his love to become dangerously submissive. He pressed her fingers.

"You ought to come out with me," he said urgingly.

Something shrank in her face. "Some day I will," she whispered.

Bronwen swished the satin of her great skirts as she moved restlessly. "Take *me* out for an airing, Tudor, goodness me, I need one. They tell me that the new railway station has been opened in Dinas. I'd like to see it." She would be seen with him in public: she also liked to see any new building or development in the valley where she had been a witness of the sinking of the first pit sixty years ago. So Tudor fixed a date with her, patients permitting.

"How's the practice?" his mother asked faintly. "Improving, improving," he grinned. He told them about Emrys and the marbles that afternoon.

"Lettie Phillips," his mother remembered worriedly. "She's been a patient of your father's, she's a bad payer... you ought to ask for cash down, Tudor, up in those Terraces, and only having odds and ends."

"I've got two confinements next week."

"They don't mind you being a bachelor?" she asked. Then he

saw that she was gathering herself to say something of moment to him, and knew what it was going to be.

"Not in the Terraces, Mother."

"Well, Ceridwen," Grannie Bronwen protested, "women are not like that now, dear me. With the twentieth century just coming on us. There's old fashioned you are, really now, Ceridwen." She was still grannily hostile, very pink in her wrinkled cheeks.

"Tudor," his mother said, and, pausing, "Tudor." It sounded like the beginning of a death-bed request.

Bronwen rose, agedly but with the briskness of unaccustomed irritation. "You want to be alone with Tudor, Ceridwen?"

"Yes, Bronwen." She had an invalid's meekness now. Bronwen went out to the dining-room.

"Lately your grandmother has become touchy, Tudor.... I expect I'm becoming a nuisance," she went on in a dulled way.

"Mother," he said suddenly, "I can't help thinking how handsome you look."

"I don't feel handsome," she said pathetically. "But never mind about me." She paused and then the deathbed knell murmured again: "Tudor."

"What is it, Mother?"

"I want you to marry Mildred." She waited and as Tudor said nothing, continued. And gradually pain, pain and a deep gnawing anxiety strengthened her voice. "You have been cruel to her, Tudor. She is a good woman, and I have come to know that even after all that has happened, she wants to marry you. Tudor, she is wasting away, her life is becoming a tragedy—"

He got up abruptly and walked across the room.

"If only I could see you married to her, I believe I could get quite well again.... I don't want to force myself on you, Tudor, but after all, I am your mother, and as I lie here thinking of you—" her voice rose to an entreating cry, painful and aching, "I can't say it, I can't say it," she sobbed. The dumb repressions of her whole life choked her throat.

He could not go near her; he stared out into the dark garden. She controlled herself and continued, almost humbly:

"You need her, Tudor, as she needs you. You need to settle down—I can see it in your face. You... you," she struggled for words, "you seem so *unstable*... drifting. And you used to be so happy together, I used to watch you, there seemed such understanding between you."

"Too much understanding, perhaps Mother."

"What do you mean, dear? You don't know how precious understanding can be, especially later... and it's your later life you must prepare for, Tudor."

He forced himself over to her, sat by her side again. And he was startled at the animal yearning in her pale, baulked eyes; he recoiled inside, afraid.

"You see, Mother, for me there is no excitement in Mildred, no mystery... the future seems altogether too plain with her—" How could he explain to her that the music had fled from the poem, the bloom was off the grape?

"Don't you love her any more?" she asked pathetically. But accusation lay ready in her face.

"I know she would make a first-rate Wife." His voice made the gibing capital obvious.

"What more can a man want?"

He did not answer, but he turned again from the insistent womanliness breathing from her. A harsh voice rang in him: "Woman, what am I to do with thee?" Aloud he said sullenly:

"God knows, I wish I *could* marry her. It would be what is known as being manly, doing the proper thing."

She shrank from the gall in his voice. "Tudor " she breathed, "I wish I could understand you."

"Understand, understand... does one want to understand people one loves or likes? An understanding woman!" He felt himself becoming crude in an effort to subdue his irritation.

"What do you want, then?" she wailed.

"I want to accept people and people to accept me, without

148

straining to understand. To take pleasure in each other without questioning, without interference, without the imposition of *wills*. Trying to understand means either to be nauseatingly submissive or damnably superior, from one's intimates."

She lay stiff then. He felt her go cold.

"You mean," she said, with awful dreariness, "that you want to lead a completely selfish life, that you really want to cut yourself right off from us. That's what I feel in you. Or at least not for us to come too near."

Then he felt exhausted. But he forced his voice into gentleness. "Do you think I'm coming here from a sense of duty, that it means nothing to me to see you lying here like this?" And that cord that could never be severed tugged deeper, with a more bitter pain, into his heart.

She seemed to rouse herself, as though she knew. She became entreating again, with a soft wailing grief. "Tudor, you must marry Mildred and give up all these wild ideas of yours. What are you doing to your life? There is no... no construction in it, and no promise."

"Isn't there, isn't there?" he said between his teeth.

"Living in that gloomy house, among those awful people," she whimpered. "Associating with people who are indecent and criminals." Her face went greyly-blue, her eyes protruded. "Oh, Tudor—that you were my only son!"

He looked at her sharply. "Lie still, be quiet, Mother," he said.

His heart was torn as he listened to her whimpers of interior sobbing. But he could not give way. She was using the power of death; she was exercising the blackmail of illness. Not out of calculated dishonesty, but out of her perverted instinct to preserve him according to her notions. He looked at her from far away, at her body prostrated submissively in the gloom of death, at her head that was now oozing the faint sweat of her effort to preserve him, and though his mind was eternities away, his heart lurched in agony for her.

"Be still, be still," he breathed. Unconsciously he had returned to the couch and was kneeling beside it.

His father arrived soon, to Tudor's relief. Elwyn with his quiet, though unworldly assurance brought an air of mildness to the over-charged room. But his mother was already more subdued, perhaps in a belief that he was coming to heel. He was restless to get away now and said next to nothing to his father. But before leaving the house he went into the dining-room, where Bronwen was peering over some knitting: he could not hurry from the house without a word with her. It was a relief to feel her soft, aged sympathy, dry and unassertive.

"Lying all day on the couch is not good for her," she whispered. "Deliberately putting herself in a position she is, where life can hit at her very well. And a squint-eyed view of things she's beginning to take.... What does she want you to do now?" she asked curiously.

"Marry Mildred," he said in a suffering way.

Bronwen was silent. Then she asked him if he liked the colour of the stockings she was knitting for him, ready for next winter. "Six pairs I'm doing for you, providing I'm spared."

"And there you're with her, aren't you?" he said, still wounded.

"I think Mildred is a very good woman," she said staunchly, "and after a year or two of fighting you'd settle down with her quite neatly, in the manner most people do in this world."

He looked about him restlessly. Was he trying to wrest something remarkable out of the world, something that was granted very seldom... or was he merely a slovenly bungler sullenly refusing to conform? "Do things become so neat?" he asked. "Do people really settle down neatly?"

She was aged and calm and seemed wise; she was beautiful, too, with an unbroken beauty. "They have to," she said.

He fled the house, speeding down into the bed of the valley. There the place smelt of mortared stone, of thickly-sewn humanity, of dusty roads and labour. In the main street men were tramping up to the top pit, for the night-shift. Their nailed boots rang on the pavements rhythmically. In the lamplight their underground-accustomed faces were grey as old rags. Odd how colliers *going* to the shifts looked so diminished and haggard: their clothes hung scarecrow fashion. Coming away, after the shift's hard labour, paradoxically they looked filled-out and stronger, their blackened faces alert. Several greeted him soberly; one stopped and informed him of a meeting in somebody's house a few days hence; there were to be the beginnings of a new grievance.

At a centre place, next to a fried-fish shop flaring with lights but empty of customers, a chapel was occupied to overflowing with a revival meeting. Wild singing came from it and outside were ranged several persons of both sexes ready to pounce on any unwary passer-by. As Tudor approached, a young tipsy man who had been collared by a gaunt woman in mauve was angrily trying to break loose.

"Come inside," she was inviting loudly, "and enjoy yourself truly. Though you smell of the old beer now, soon you'd be sweet as a comb of honey. Glory be."

"Lemme alone," he cried, "lemme alone." And as she persisted, he snarled: "Let go my neck or I'll have you 'rested for accosting me, you old bag."

She dropped him and danced a step or two across to Tudor. "Now then, now then, what about you?" she sang. She was sightless and glorified. "Plenty of young men inside, but room for one more. How now? Good-looking chaps wanted for the steps of Heaven. Would you be a God's doorkeeper, instead of a bad, bad bloke no good to anybody? Come inside then. Glory be."

Tudor dodged her clutch. But she managed to catch his coat-tails. "Let go," he shouted.

"God is pulling you, not me," she declared ringingly. The chapel burst with glorious melody; song was kept up incessantly, for people's deepest feelings are more easily liberated in music. The singing was splendid indeed. It was as if the old mountains had voices which they were now using to entertain the wakened stars.

151

There seemed no doubt that such golden thunders passed even beyond the stars and was listened to by the approving angels. As Tudor freed his coat-tails he was very conscious of that roused human song. He hastened past the accosters and, turning the corner by the undertaker's shop, where a sample coffin lay open behind the glass, entered the Terraces district. But the voices lifted in those yearning peals of wild music followed him implacably.

"Christ," he breathed, "Christ, show them a different way." He leaned against a stone wall. The music sprang past him. He listened, staring at the sky, where the white stars were sprinkled like small wild flowers. "Christ," he repeated to himself, "Christ." He did not know whether he was praying or laughing.

IV

The revival lasted well into July. It died either from the crop of converts failing at last or from a heat-wave. Warmth favours a religious spirit, but boiling heat made the people's spirit wilt. Or perhaps sacrifice of meat, beer, and other vulgar pleasures told at last. Everybody lay low for a week or two, as if their souls had gone to bed of some complaint. There was peace and empty silence in the valley for a short while.

But by the beginning of August, their strength renewed a little, people began to look about them again. This was the month of outings to the seaside, of fairs, of brake-rides to clean country corners just round the ends of the valley mountains. A few well-to-do colliers took a week off, dressed their wives in straw hats and muslin gowns and their children in cotton, and went on visits to those of their agricultural relations who had resisted the temptation to invade the coal places, remaining simple in such shires as Carmarthen, Brecon and Cardigan.

The Beynon Brothers went away quaintly as they had arrived. Though the revival was at its fag-end, they were given a good and affectionate send-off by the valley people, thousands turning out to precede and follow the donkeys down the valley's length, singing and carrying banners. But, what with one thing and another, people were glad to see the Brothers go, as is nearly always the feeling about visitors in the end, however well-liked. A fair had already arrived, and that evening it was a relief to be jogged up and down on a roundabout, or in a peep-show look through magnifying-glasses at views of Niagara Falls and such-like.

The Brothers left behind them, however, a memory of best-class eloquence, sermons that could satisfy the needy human spirit, power that could throw back the doors of the soul and do good to some of the shocking things therein. For years afterwards men talked of the Beynons, comparing them to new revivalists. But the Brothers themselves disappeared entirely from sight after eighteen months or so, though it was said that Joshua had married a tidy woman who kept a private hotel in Llandudno, and that Merlin had had a misfortune come to his mind, and that the vocalist Trevor had gone to America, and was doing well in the theatrical line—this last one the valley people had always suspected of being flighty.

And men began to skulk back to the pubs, women looked once more in drapers' windows and ceased to think of poplin as more suitable to satanic bodies than to saved ones. Those given to it began to chew shag again, spitting on the sawdust of crowded bar floors. Refreshed after a short rest, Sunday-school crowds hired special trains to take them the twenty miles to the coast, the carriages buzzing like hives, thickly packed with adults and children excited in their release from revival sacrifices.

Everybody agreed that the revival had done them good and that life after conversion seemed less of a kick on the rump. There was more meaning to things, they said. But gradually the pleasures of this world came to be used more freely. Magistrates worked harder sorting things out and punishing, and tradesmen won what they had lost. There was a lot of fighting on Saturday nights, a lot of marrying, a lot of moving of buttons on women's aprons, a lot of spending of money put by.

August became a bad month in the pits. By the third week most of them were working only three days a week. There were few orders; once more something had happened to the Continental market, and along the lower sides of the mountains the long lines of empty trucks waited day after day. There were rumours of a big strike. No good striking now, when there would be little loss to the owners. But God knows what was coming in the winter. Those who pretended to smell the real air of things down here below said there was going to be a fine shindy this time. Only a few took notice and put by a sovereign or two in case. The others used up what they had or could get that holiday month. Besides, what was one more strike? They had got through many before, battered and skinny perhaps, but still alive.

CHAPTER V

I

HE found the house at last, a neat square of pale brick down in the docks district, wedged among warehouses. Ship-masts could be seen above the buildings like big cobwebs, and the place, though poor, had the clean, washed look sea air gave. He waited between two slender pillars of a tiny portico, admiring the dainty grace of the house. What was she doing here? Staying with friends, she had said.

Daisy opened the door. He was expected. She complained at once, in a rush of pleasure:

"Why didn't you say the time of the train? I would have come to meet you.... Why, you are looking much older. Come in, come in."

"I had a maternity case due about yesterday and didn't quite know whether I'd be able to get away." He scratched her under the chin, shoved his fist into her midriff. They had stepped into a dignified little room dark with oil portraits and frail lady-like furniture, well bees-waxed. He felt an immediate sense of relief at seeing her. "Am I to sit down on one of these delicate chairs?"

"They've held heavier men than you for many a long year, Tudor." She leaned against a harpsichord, looking at him with a bright pondering. Her rounded cheeks were like young peonies. "Though I don't often sit on them myself, they don't suit me.... How's your new practice going?"

"It's the very devil trying to work it up. Still, things look hopeful-as people's memory gets shorter."

"Poor Tudor. That *was* a bit of bad luck for you that night,

155

wasn't it? I feel wild about it sometimes." She scowled. "Those bobbies, so rude."

"Yes, but what about you?" He had often wondered if she was keeping away from the place because of the scandal and if she was subconsciously blaming him. "Do you feel angry that I should have chosen that night, Daisy?"

"For me, I don't care at all." Under the bright-black swing of her hair her face was staid with composure.

He asked about Melville. She had been allowed one visit at the jail. He had been quite good-humoured, declaring that the isolation and rest were doing him good. Concentration in a cell made his mind very active, he had said, and he had several new schemes and viewpoints ready for use in the battle to which he was dedicated for life. "But," she sighed, "I don't think he'll see what he's after come to pass in his time."

"No, he knows that. Someone's got to do the preliminary dirty work though. What he stands for is not even recognised as being sane yet. More honour to him."

"And you," she said. Her eyes were wide with curiosity. "You've given up a good deal. Comfort and security."

"No, I've given up drabness and dullness." He much wanted to embrace her, as she stood there full of bright vitality. But he was not sure of the house, who might walk in, how she was placed in it. "How long are you going to stay in Bristol?" he asked, glancing round the faded elegance of the room.

"What's the use of coming back to the valley? Except for you and one or two half-friendly women, everybody I really know is in jail."

"All your young men, you mean," he accused, half angrily.

"I wasn't so bad as I was painted, Tudor. I tried to be *nice* to a lot, but I was never free game, as they say…. But I fell a bit in love with *two*," she admitted. Though, with extraordinarily attractive naïvety, she added: "The others I was willing to talk to about women openly and help them to understand things a bit. Which," she said stridently, as if on the defensive, "they badly

156

wanted. Such high and mighty fools most women are—they keep themselves under glass like a bit of wax fruit, and then wonder how it is that men don't know what to do with them." She flashed, lit with something of her brother's high-minded ardour.

"Yes," Tudor agreed, watching her tenderly, "that's quite true."

"Such fuss is made of this business of love," she went on, "such nasty fuss, all whispering and sniggering and underhand behaviour, 'specially among women.... I didn't care what I said, and then people called me a bad woman and a harlot. But I just wanted to be plain and say common-sense things. Why can't people talk about love and what it stands for?" she demanded, with beautiful truculence.

"It seems," he couldn't help laughing at her a little, tenderly, "it seems—oh, Daisy, Daisy, how marvellous you are!—it seems that's going to be one of the teachings of the future. It's difficult now because there's a tradition of terror to be overcome.... But how wonderful to think of you with a school of young men!" He burst again into laughter, and asked if she minded.

"You don't know the questions they used to ask me." She began laughing, too. "So simple, so childish, I used to be shocked. And I used to get angry too, thinking of the wicked waste, and the ugly thinking." She dabbed her eyes, that were the colour of dark violets, but not so meek. "Brought up to believe that we're made of sugar and dust off flowers, the poor chaps. When we want 'em as much as they want us, and more perhaps."

"Well," he said—and her glow had passed to him, he felt roused and quickened, "I for one never believed about these other men—"

"There were two," she reminded him, as if she knew what was coming. "But mistakes, both of them." She sighed.

Then he said, in the same gay mood she had roused: "All the same, I want to ask you to marry me, Daisy."

"Come now, Tudor," she protested, quite scarlet in the cheeks, "come now, that wouldn't be wise."

"Why not?" A cold shiver went through him. He would hate it

if she were going to take into calculation the extraneous world. He wanted, then, to rush this thing through.

She shook her head. Oddly, her expression was cloudy, her eyes indirect. She seemed about to weep.

"You've got your way to make—" she said soberly.

"You don't want to marry me?" he asked in fear.

"If things were different, I would marry you." She would not look at him now. "You've got a long and bitter struggle in front of you, Tudor. I don't want to make it worse for you."

"You'll make it far easier," he said. "But don't think of all that, Daisy, don't. I want us to be together... don't *you* then?" he asked fearfully.

"We must think of those things...' she protested. It seemed she was determined to stand firmly in the earth's dust: "A pretty fine hullabaloo there'd be if you took me home as wife. I, a common woman, and you a doctor that's supposed to be admitted to people's private lives—come now, Tudor my dear, it can't be done."

"Don't you want us to be together?" he repeated.

"I wouldn't mind it," she said, with such queer unnatural shyness that he broke into a cry of relieved laughter. "But—"

"Be quiet, be quiet," he said.

She said no more; though she still looked unyielding. A minute or two afterwards, while, unable to keep away any longer, he was kissing her, there was the tinkle of a bell in the little hallway.

"Tea," she said. "Now you must come and meet my friends, though Melville's they are really."

"You'll marry me?" he demanded.

"Goodness me, anybody would think I got married every Tuesday at tea-time."

"You'll come out with me tonight?"

She promised that. He asked her about her friends. There was the Captain, she said, and the woman he lived with, who wrote books under a man's name. He was a retired sea captain, and she had been the wife of a madhouse superintendent. "Both of 'em," Daisy added, "hot socialists, and she's out for votes for women, too."

They looked trim and placid, seated at the gleaming oval Sheraton table; they had greeted Tudor with fastidious formality. The Captain was old and well-bearded, but in his eyes was a continuous look of bright surprise. The lady, Mrs. Hand, was dressed up to her chin in soft dim laces and she had a smooth middle-aged face with stuck-out cheek-bones dabbed with rouge. A heavy schoolboy tea was packed over the table.

"The comrades making any progress in your part of the coal-fields?" the Captain asked. He had a windy voice, rough and weathered, which boomed a bit and sometimes rose to a hoarse squawk.

Tudor told him how things were at the moment, with the revival at its height. The Captain, eating striped blancmange shape, said it was a pity such vitality couldn't be organised for better use. "I been in these parts myself," he said, "doing a bit of work, and I always said to myself that there's the right guts down there, only they been led astray."

"Melville," said Daisy to Tudor, "hid the Captain up a chimney once when the '89 riots were on and the bobbies were after him."

"Organisation, that's what you've got to learn down there, organisation. There's so many unruly elements and too much mysticism."

"We've got to fight to pluck out a three-hundred-year-old tradition," Tudor said. "Since men were taught that no good could come of this world."

"A slice of this jam-tart, Doctor?" asked Mrs. Hand.

She creaked slightly as she bent. Her greenish hair was pronged with Spanish combs. She looked a strict woman, parsimonious of emotions. But even when she wasn't speaking, her pursed mouth moved perpetually in a circular motion.

"Things have been truly shocking down in your parts," the

Captain went on, "truly shocking—and are." But he was apt now, behind his rich beard and noble brow, to be sighingly reminiscent. "I used to put into Cardiff Docks and take a trip up the valleys, and what was the first sight I saw?—why, hordes of women and bits of children coming out of a pit-shaft after a fourteen-hour day down under. By Christ, and what did they look like? But they wanted to go down under, it seemed, they never questioned it, and not much what they were getting for it."

"They still hang about the tips," Tudor said, "sorting out the coal from the slag."

Mrs. Hand said: "Providing they are paid good money, I don't see why they shouldn't do men's work."

This was a novel point of view to Tudor, who had never devoted any thought to the female aspect of socialism. All he could say was: "They earn a shilling or so selling the coal, which they lug in a hundredweight sack through the place on their shoulders." When he came to think of it, he had to admit they were sturdy wenches; he had attended one for a confinement and she had borne jauntily. Mrs. Hand spoke for a while on the subject dearest to her, the "righting of women in the scale of things", as she said.

"I'm old-fashioned about it," the Captain blew. "I like 'em to have their say, but I can't stomach 'em going down pits and places like that."

"I suppose it's the aesthetic aspect that worries one," Tudor said gallantly. "We want to keep women intact from the squalor and ugliness of the commercial world." But he wondered why Mrs. Hand wrote books under a man's name.

"If you had seen 'em coming out of that black hole, Tom," the Captain said to Mrs. Hand, "you'd have said to yourself: 'Are these my sisters?' No, Tom, I can't have it."

"I don't know about pits," she said, "but I believe that one day they'll be out and about in a lot of men's places."

"I wonder if the British Navy'll ever take 'em," the Captain said, with his look of bright surprise.

160

Daisy said soberly: "God knows, I do feel so unused sometimes, but on the other hand, I think women are best for staying at home. As long as they can manage to keep a shine on their minds—"

After tea, the women clearing away—while Daisy was there they ran the house between them—the Captain settled with a pipe and talked to Tudor. He was garrulous and rather disillusioned now, without much faith in the future of socialism in England—the English mind was too corruptly calm and long-suffering, he said.

It seemed he had not been a sea captain for long—if at all, Tudor thought. But he had knocked round the world, apparently looking for Utopia. ("I lived naked once with South Sea Islanders, and got descendants there now, but that sort of life is a trap for a man with something knocking at his mind–it's a going back.") A follower of Robert Owen in his youth, he had always sought out agitators. He used to drink cups of strong tea with Karl Marx and his daughter Tussy at the house at Maitland Park—"A grand man was Old Nick, as we used to call him, mild as a bluebell sometimes, then roaring to the size of those prophets in the Old Testament, all his mop of hair shooting out of his big head like red-hot wires. But his mind was fixed like an oak to the earth. He knew he had the shape of the future given to him. I felt when I was with him that I was speaking to the next thousand years."

"I've just begun *Das Kapital*," Tudor muttered, wondering when Daisy was going to appear. The evening would soon be drawing in. He couldn't settle to communistic conversation just then. He wanted to get another matter fixed up. The Captain droned on, passing from Marx to Mrs Hand.

Having to visit a relation in the mental institute superintended by her husband, he had rescued her from an unsympathetic clutch, and while he had been away on voyages she had written romances "about women victimised by shallow men." The Captain fondly fetched out of a bookcase a single volume of one of the works, blew on it, and handed it to Tudor. It was called *The Disposition of*

Delia: A Tale of Reward, by Thomas Barnes. "I call her Tom for that reason; we've been with each other for fifteen years now," he said hoarsely. And with a sigh he sat down again and put a gouty foot up on a Chippendale chair. "She sells," he said, with his fixed surprised look, "she sells. Brings in quite a deal."

Tudor kept on looking at the door. How superb Daisy had looked at tea-time, her flesh fluent with health, the bloom of plums on her cheeks! Saying she felt unused. It was a sin that she was unused.

"Then there's this chap Keir Hardie," the Captain continued, "and his Independent Labour Party. I was at his conference in Bradford in '93 He's brought the gangs together sensibly."

"I hear he's standing for Merthyr next year," Tudor said.

"He'll get in down there.... Why don't you set about forming a respectable political party in your district?"

"Respectable!" Tudor repeated, though at the suggestion something jumped clear in his mind.

"Well," said the Captain, "what I mean is that you've got the raw stuff down there all boiling hot. But it wants shaping. The men want ideas put carefully in their heads and not just be let to act with their fists.... You ought to start with a study class, have discussions and lectures."

This had been Tudor's intention directly he had got his practice going to a bread-and-butter degree. He suggested that the Captain came over to give an inaugural address. He felt that the Captain's venerable demeanour, rather suggestive of Mr. Gladstone's, would impress on the workmen a sense of steadfastness and grandeur in the cause.

"That I'll do willingly, my boy." The Captain was pleased. "I'll give 'em a short history of the movement from the Chartist risings and show 'em how they're the spine of the industrial skeleton." He obviously had a load of accumulated stuff which he wanted to dispose of before he quite gave up the ghost. He even offered Tudor some financial support should he get a party going on a studious but active basis.

162

"I've still got some money left, and Tom's books bring in more than she needs.... And, there, coax the women's support, too. Tom would come over and get her suffragette business going—she can honk like a sea-lion if you start her up."

"The women are more difficult," Tudor said doubtfully. "They usually retreat from collective action, though individually they often have a little private revolution inside themselves. But they keep it private; it goes no farther than their domestic life."

"Yes, one of Tom's points is that they want to be taught a more public consciousness." And the Captain also stroked his beard doubtfully, in spite of his suggestion.

"Look how they drape themselves in clothes!" Tudor said. "A manifestation of their need to protect themselves from the draught of the world—some nasty kind of fear."

"Some day they might react and go to the other extreme," the Captain said. "Tom's got the right kind of bee in her bonnet, though for myself I don't like the sound of its buzzing."

Tudor, still waiting for Daisy, began to think how one found active democratic sympathies in the oddest corners and among the most staid-looking of England. When he had been a student in London, he used to sit every other Tuesday in the drawing-room of a lean Countess with a nose as highly curved as the rise and fall of her family history; there were gathered outcasts from the Continent, anarchists mingling quarrelsomely with mild theorists. He remembered a little squat Pole spitting on an oil portrait of an ancestor about whom the Countess had been making dreadful revelations—she, however, scolding him for this gratuitous dirtying of a beautiful painting. The brilliant hospital surgeon who had taken him there alternated bouts of drunkenness with an austere study of the theories of Bakunin. This surgeon it was who told Tudor: "I'm socialist because of what I've seen of the insides of the working-classes, and I'm a drunkard ditto." And there was the nimble and elderly dendrologist he had met in Epping Forest who, a gentlemanly Oxford graduate, had printed seditious handbills and pasted them in pub urinals frequented by farm-labourers, and who, when the police chased him, hid up a chestnut tree for three days. "Drop a seed here," he had said, "and drop one there; they'll sprout in time."

It seemed that right through the latter half of the nineteenth century there were swimming about in the viscid fog of English industrialism strange new fish, spawned out of the unspeakable mud. The flow of English national life was calm, sticky and mud-coloured, but take the fish one by one, and deep quivering torments could be seen behind their cold-filmed eyes, strange, slow, under-sea fire gleaming icily. Tudor, sitting under the venerable grandfatherly spread of the Captain's beard, remembered Shelley.

"You courting Daisy, Doctor?" the Captain asked suddenly.

Tudor nodded. "If it can be called that."

"Then we mustn't waste your time—" Just then Daisy came in, followed by Mrs. Hand. "The doctor wants to read one of your romances, Tom," the Captain blew, to Tudor's surprise.

"Then let him have *Mary's Testimony*," Mrs. Hand said at once. "One of his profession is dealt with in it." Tudor murmured his thanks as the three volumes were placed on a side-table ready for him. Mrs. Hand then began a literary conversation—or monologue—in which she demolished nearly all the writers of the day. She spoke with a stiff heat. But she had ideas and a kind of warped dry personality which compelled attention. Continuing, she implied that she was intellectually liberated now that she was living in sin with her beloved Captain, she was more wholesome of mind now than when she had lived with her deplorable husband, she was able to write healthy books. In them, she said, she tried to draw the attention of modern women to what they could achieve did they but come into the open and boldly announce that they had minds to satisfy as well as bodies. It was seven o'clock when Daisy at last said:

"Would you like to see the old port, Tudor?" And when they had got outside, she sighed: "Mrs. Hand is a good woman, but she's been ruined by brains."

"Perhaps she's more courage than actual brains, Daisy." He

164

was still suffering from the incarceration. But there, there was the depth and richness of Daisy's cheek curved out next to him. "Can we get into the country easily?"

"We can take a tram," she said, brightening. She adored riding on the tops of the new tram-cars.

But he found a hansom, and that she liked still better, clopping through the city, the soft breeze blowing on their chests and heads. It was the first time she had ridden in one, and she preened herself and waved to children in the streets of the suburb. She was wearing a flat white hat, across which a lemon ostrich feather careered in the breeze like a live thing.

"If only Melville wasn't in jail," she sighed, "I'd be quite, quite happy now."

"And I won't be happy until he's my brother-in-law."

"I'm sure he wouldn't approve of your marrying me," she said soberly. "We've done enough to ruin you already."

"Well, we'll risk it and have a new home all ready for him by the time he's out."

"Look here," she said gustily into the breeze, "how would it be if we didn't actually get married?"

"That's so scrappy," he said at once.

"I want to have a baby by you," she said. "I've been thinking about it for a long time. I want a child and I'd like you to be the father." The hansom stopped beside a silver streak of a brook and an apple orchard. The driver opened the trap and called down: "How's that, sir? The country begins here."

"To that wood," shouted Tudor, pointing. The pink glow of sunset ran through the beech-wood. The trap closed. "No wedding, no child," he said firmly.

"I'd prefer *you* to be the father, though, of course—"

"You're a shameless hussy. I suspect Mrs. Hand's romances."

"I've never read them. But, Tudor, it'll be best for us not to marry for some years. I can keep here in Bristol, and you can come and see me. Then when you're established and people have forgotten about me, I can come to you—"

165

He looked at her sharply then. She spoke subduedly, but she seemed serious and unwavering.

"You disappoint me," he said, frowning. "It *can* be done."

"Yes, but it's deliberately making things a hundred times more difficult for you. The world *is* strong," she lamented. "Think of a good man like Melville in jail!"

"The world *can* be strong, but so can we be—together."

"Do you think I don't want to marry you?" she asked, with a strangely moving sadness. "I do." And with quiet modesty she went on: "I want to go to bed with you every night and have a dozen children off you. But though I might appear to be a careless woman, I'm not really. I'm very frightened of certain things—"

"Oh Daisy, I can't understand these excuses."

"I wish you were a common man, working in the colliery."

The driver opened the trap. "Road's too bad to go farther," he called.

Tudor paid off the man, who looked at them disapprovingly out of a father-of-a-family face. He flicked his whip and the equipage prattled away through hedges of dog roses. They walked into the green and pink wood arguing, and they were still arguing when dark fell, sitting in a depth of old leaves. But she would not give way: marriage was too dangerous yet.

He wondered if she sensed in him, not so much a need to establish a place in the world, but a struggling to establish an order in himself, a definite assurance that he had cast off the past finally.

At last she drew him into her arms and mentioned the fact that time was going fast. But he was disturbed, and in his annoyance at her obstinacy and what he considered were trivial ears, some remnant of his upbringing breathed into life again; his mind criticised her harshly. Was she a being of merely sensual activity, after all? That permanency of passionate life that he thought was in her, that abundant awareness of life outside herself—was it merely an idealism in him? Would she become only a cosy slattern?

166

In the dark leaf-wrapped silence the trees were like primitive presences, listening but withdrawn. The wood seemed a vast patch out of some ancient time of the earth. A small animal rustled over the dead leaves near, stood still when it sensed them, then bustled away in terror.

"I like a wood at night-time," Daisy murmured. She breathed, a darkly huddled shape beside him, the faint scent of her flesh mingling with the odour of the wood. "It seems to take one back, to put something back in one's mind," she said.

He was moodily taking up handfuls of the dead, dry leaves and throwing them away. "Stale old bits of the past, dry and rotten," he said vaguely.

"They make comfortable cushions," she said, settling farther into a depth of years. And she passed a finger over his brow down his nose, across the contours of his lips. "Do you know," she said in wonder, "you're losing your name and what you are, in this wood. I can hardly see you, and you're becoming something different. A man without name or a shape that's familiar to me."

"I don't think you've got much feeling for me as a person, wood or no wood," he said. "You're too natural—perhaps too unruined," he conceded.

"You mean I'm too stupid and like an animal?" she laughed. "I wish I was like that Miss Mildred of yours," she added wickedly.

At that name a spasm of pain sprang across his mind. Then her head came subtly out of the darkness, and the soft warm flesh of her face mingled with his. "Let's forget." Her voice was a deep golden whisper, a fragment of some pagan hymn caught out of the dark wood. "Let's forget. No going back or forward, no yesterday or tomorrow. Only now."

Only now it was: and everything was perfect and complete. Her handsome confidence swept him along and there were no concessions. He was certain she had achieved what she wanted, and upon her lips he laughed at last. She smiled too, under his mouth, in sure concurrence.

On the way back he asked her again to marry him. "Perhaps I

will some day, Tudor," she said, gaily absorbed in her own tranquil glow.

He swore, called her selfish. "I don't understand you," he added angrily.

They could not find another hansom and they climbed to the swaying open top of a noisy tram-car. In the murky light of a single electric globe she sat rapt, assured, considerable as some duchess. He noticed for the first time her great air of natural dignity in public. She looked, on top of the tram-car, as though she might own palaces.

"What can one do," he lamented when they had alighted, "instead of clubbing you over the head and carrying you off to some cave?"

"It's still done," she said, "in a different way."

II

And life began to look black in the valley at the beginning of September. The holiday month over and their bits of money gone, the colliers looked askance at the coming winter. Coal prices were still a matter for rue and pay-tickets reflected the mysterious competition on high with mournful faithfulness. Of course, the pitowners suffered too, in the large domain of worldmarkets, but as someone said in one of those black little confabs of the men near the pit offices on Friday evenings, *their* suffering was only a pimple. For in September, after a sinisterly slack month, there was plenty of work, all the pits on full time. Yet pay-tickets had taken on this paltry weight. Coal prices had fallen with a bang, and looked like remaining forcibly in the flattest of conditions.

"Don't blame me," C.P. said in his pit to those of his familiar workmen who made personal complaint to him. "I can't help it. Low prices are due to the operations of middlemen, speculating and juggling. I can't keep our prices up if everybody else is selling low, can I?"

"It's this Sliding Scale, Mr. Meredith," a collier ventured dolefully. "It's a bad old way of paying us. While it's going, the middlemen can feed off us like maggots."

"I've moved for its abolition," C.P. replied testily, "time and again. But what is my one voice?" He spoke as if his was the only owner's voice raised to the Lord in this Gomorrah of a land. Though, of course, there was John Johns, who wouldn't join the local Association of Owners. Johns had pits in one of the off-shoots of the valley, and was in bad odour with his fellowowners.

"Aye, indeed, aye," another collier dared, "there's the whole menagerie of wild animals to tame first, that Sir Rufus Morgan being the nastiest old bear with a sore backside—"

"No need to be personal, Williams," C.P. said peremptorily. "The whole Association has to be convinced."

From the darkest shadow of the stall where this fairly quiet exchange of feeling was taking place, a tight surly voice declared itself:

"Convinced! They've got to be bloody well shoved into chucking away the Sliding Scale. Talk 'on't do it, nor Federation writing fine on paper.... *If* you'll excuse me talking, Mr. Meredith."

Something seemed to break at last in Meredith then. Remarkably he began to swear. "If you men," he roared, "are going to strike again without the agreed six months' notice, I've finished with you, d'you hear? I'll get out a —— black list that'll show you how much I know. I sweat my guts out working for the benefit of you b——s of my pits, and I expect to be treated honestly in return.... Take warning now." He disappeared through the hole, his lamp swinging.

The colliers sat quietly for a minute in surprise, munching their lumps of bread and cheese, taking swigs of cold tea. "They say," said one cautiously, "that he tried to get that twenty per cent for us last strike."

"Aye, and he knew he couldn't make the Company give it," said another. "—but did you hear him swearing?" he remarked subduedly.

Another, hitherto silent, said musingly: "He's two men, is C.P. That's how he comes to look grizzling and bad. Money he wants, and he don't want it. And he's frightened of Jesus Christ. No wonder he puts on clothes like any chap off the tip. He thinks the Lord won't see him if he goes about simple and dirty like everybody else.... But what he want to start cursing for?" he added in a voice of severe criticism.

"Black list!" snapped the surly voice. "Who's frightened of a —— black list? There's not enough chaps in the valleys to go round, and the world's got to making jam of coal now it's so cheap. I can move off in a jiffy to the Swansea valleys and get a job as easy as eating chips."

"If that Regulation of Output comes off, you won't talk so big. There'll be dumps of colliers not wanted then. Seems we're —— up any road we take."

"Aye," said an elderly Irish-blooded collier. He was placing his huge nailed boot delicately on a black-beetle that was circling blindly round a glittering lump of coal. "I've never known anyone at all that wasn't bloody well —— up in this bog of a —— world. Shure I ask meself offtime, where's the man that isn't —— up? Like this little old beetle, that was."

"Well," said someone else temperately, "it's asking that makes us do something about it, Mick."

Meredith made his way through the workings like a fallen angel taking his first angry sniffs of the caves of hell. For some weeks he had foreseen the possibility of a strike. And he was weary to death of them. He was fully aware himself that his weariness came from his divided soul, a filtering away of his energy through two ragged fissures. But now he had made up his mind. No more sentiment. He was Boss. There could not be any mild and religious going back to the men: there could only be a suicidal tumbling down to their levels. Could he throw out a new world from his hand like a God?

And he roared abusively at another stall, where his fuming eyes had detected insufficient timbering. So that the cutters could reach the coal-face easier, they had neglected to prop the sides and roof sufficiently, risking the danger of a fall of stone.

"Fools," he bellowed "idiots. You'll spare the timber here so as you'll have more for your coffins? Would you, would you? O Christ Almighty," he prayed ragingly, "when will men be born with a grain of common sense? Only one little grain!" he pleaded, with dramatic desperation, and swerving again on the men, he let loose in their shocked ears a flow of bad language, thus announcing again the new hard turn his mind had taken. Concluding: "Suppose you're after the compensation we'd have to pay your damn widows, or you want to be abed for the rest of your lives without a bastard of a leg to your name! Get the timber this bloody minute or get out and grow watercress. Call yourselves colliers!"

The news of his fall from grace—for C.P. had hated bad language—spread like wildfire. Yet when he was on top and in the lamp-room he was approached by a wooden-legged man—a one-time cutter put to work with the lamps after having lost his leg of flesh underground—who asked him, first, if he would be chairman at a performance of a "fairy operetta" to be given by some of the Sunday-school children; second, if he knew of a respectable place for daughter Maggie, who wanted to go into service; third, was it costly to apprentice a boy to a London draper?—"my boy, Ivor, who is a proper little dandy, won't come into the pit, Mr. Meredith, so me and my Hilda thought that perhaps you'd give him a character for where he wants to go." C.P. stamped away, but came back in half an hour, accepted the chairmanship, said he'd speak to his wife about Maggie, but could do nothing for Ivor.

"The boy should be in the pit," he said angrily. "You know we're short of boys these days."

"The wife Hilda," lamented the lampman, pointing to his wooden leg, "been encouraging him because of this, saying that one wooden leg is enough for one family.... Now this operetta, Mr. Meredith, *Robin and Snowflake* it's called, and a lot of costumes got to be made for it. Now the committee was thinking if Mrs. Meredith had old bits of her nice clothes that she didn't want—"

Later in the day C.P., riding home on his horse, saw a small meeting of men on a piece of waste land beside the road outside the colliery. His first impulse was to swerve in among them and speak to them out of his bitter wrath. But he rode straight on. And as he proceeded down the long black dale, a sick hate filled him, amorphous and without particular object. Only he knew that the industry had begun to seem to him a creation of the devil, brought to earth to sow disorder, corrupt men's minds, to build these black repellent dwellings and to twist the souls of the people into savage contortions. And the capital of this devil's industry was undoubtedly South Wales: here, under these sombre mountains, was a real parliament of hell. Fairy operettas, by God! Why didn't the men dress up their brats truthfully as little fiends, blacken their faces with coal and make 'em sing about scorched imps that come up balefully out of hell?...

On his way home he thought he'd drop in at a friend's for a drink, and he tied his horse to the railings out side his solicitor's house. A small talk with Richards who was a calm, purring sort of man, would do him good. But Richards was out, said his daughter Mildred, in the drawing-room. She gave him a whisky, however.

He sat looking at her heavily. "You haven't been to see us for a long time, Mildred."

"I don't seem to have been anywhere for a long time," she said, confused a little.

His insomnious face, jowled wearily, was full of commiseration. He knew how that traitorous young doctor had let her down. These things knocked hard at women. She must be about twenty-eight by now. There was a restlessness about her; and she had developed a secret way of looking sideways at one, out of slow, heavy-lidded eyes.

"You've taken your holiday yet?" he asked uneasily, because of a silence.

172

"No. I don't think I'll go away this year." Her voice dragged, as though it longed to recoil into an everlasting silence in her throat.

"I own that little farm in the country," he said, "as you know. Annie is going down there in a week or two. Why don't you go, too? I know she'd be glad to have you with her."

"Is there going to be another strike?" She well remembered the attack on his house during the last one.

"Yes," he said dully.

Over her face passed a curious look of thin, bitter passion. "Then I'd like to be here for it," she said, as though she, too, had need for violence. And as quickly her face lapsed again into its too quiet look of secrecy. "What do they want this time?" she asked drearily.

"Oh, this Regulation of Output. They think it'll cure everything.... But there'll always be a parcel of troubles," he said in released despair, here in a quiet drawing-room with a good-bred woman. "It's a misbegotten industry sent to worry men into their graves."

"What," she asked suddenly, "about this scheme for medical benefits?"

"I hope it will go through, though some of the men are against it." He slewed a dark-ringed eye at her. "The never-ills are against it, but the Federation's favourable, I believe."

"I hope it'll go through," she said then with her thin bitterness.

His mind beat away a little from this atmosphere of female malignity. "Why shouldn't they like it?" he said cautiously; "it comes near socialistic doctrine the fortunate having to help pay for the illnesses of the unfortunate."

"Is it true that you warned Tudor Morris about it?"

"Yes. But the young fool was as obstinate as a mule.... But I had to warn him. He's a local lad, good old family, and his father clean as a whistle." He spoke as though he had no knowledge of her affair with Tudor.

Her closed face dimly flushed, she asked: "He'll lose everything then by being boycotted?"

"Unless he could get the tradespeople and so on," he said warily. "Which I shouldn't think is likely."

"No."

"But what has he got to lose, anyhow, Mildred? A young chap like that can clear out and get taken somewhere as assistant."

"He's bought a house and furnished it and fitted a surgery. And he doesn't want to leave this place." She seemed sunk in hostile pondering, looking at her fingers in her lap. And then she lifted her head, a slight shudder passed across her shoulders, she stiffened her hands, and she looked around the room with unseeing eyes. Her face had deadened.

Meredith rose. There was something like horror in his mind. He could not afford to look upon this new example of stricken humanity. It had nothing to do with him; and he didn't want to be touched any more. Yet he had to say, almost entreatingly, before going out of the door:

"That farm of mine down in Carmarthenshire, Mildred—it's very pretty now. Please to go with Annie down there, if you can. Just had a grand piano put in and one of those phonographs. And very peaceful country down there, as you know, still old-fashioned and clean—aye, clean."

"I know," she faltered, "I know." But she was quite withdrawn, gone far into a secret place. "But I don't think I'll be able to go. Father is not so well as he might be, you see—"

He reached home with a sigh of relief. A one-armed ex-collier hurried from the back to take his horse. Nice house, plain as a box, made of good drab stone. And there was Annie in the hall, plump and placid, but still dressed too dressily for his liking. There was something cheeky in the colours she affected. She screwed up her curly mouth for his kiss.

"Been drinking," she said, wagging her head.

"Aye, aye, one in Richards's. And let's have another 'fore I have a bath." Then he noticed that the expression of her face had an unaccustomed solemnity; it said that something had happened. She stood, poised plumply, obviously waiting with her bad news.

He threw off his boots first and went into carpet slippers. "What now, what now?" he exclaimed. The point of anguish in his voice was as sharp as a needle. He felt he could bear no more just then.

"Bill's dead."

Hard gasps came out of his mouth, his face was puckered up into a thousand wrinkles. The difficult, hard gasps that was his laughter surprised Annie Meredith. She sorrowfully produced a lacquer box and opened the lid under his eyes. On white wadding lay, very yellow, very dead-looking, an old canary.

III

The poky parlour was dark with men. There were not enough chairs for everybody. Bodies blocked out the evening light at the window, sitting on the sill. Beriah Thomas, whose parlour it was, complained when a clumsy young collier knocked a Jubilee mug off the what-not.

"It's only that old Jubilee mug," said the youngster, kicking the pieces out of the way. "Good riddance."

"That's for those who own it to decide," Beriah said mildly. "My daughter thought a lot of that mug.... Well, now then, boys, we've decided on a committee. Who's to be chairman? Who *wants* to be chairman?"

The meeting was an unofficial Federation gathering: it was perhaps the real blood of the Federation, but very far from being its tongue—which was rather a stammering organ as yet.

There were three offers from the fifteen men. The others had no confidence for the responsible honour. Finally, by a show of hands, Doctor Tudor Morris was elected.

"You," said Beriah, who was an elderly collier white and frail-looking as a wind-flower, "you, Doctor Morris, is a responsible chap who knows us, though you've never worked in the pit and got the old black dust down into your belly. Welcome now. We

175

know how it is with you and how you was with us in the last strike. I will say it was Melville we would have had for chairman if he was with us, as is only fair. But you're the next, and you have time to see to things and the method to speak in the mass meetings—"

"I've never addressed one," Tudor said.

"No, but we can tell. Not too much hollering, but a brainy and tidy arranging of what we stand for—same as Melville, who could have the men quiet and obedient with one look and six words."

Tudor felt embarrassed at these compliments thrust upon him. He grinned quietly. Of course, there were to be public manifestations of this "committee", mass meetings called, leaflets printed, a vocal sowing of complaints through the streets. But these were not all the aspects of this nest in Beriah's parlour. It was really a council of action to decide what publicity measures were to be taken during the actual strike. And most of the men in the room had little faith in the persuasions of talk and mass meetings: they would be itching to "do" something. They were quiet enough now. But after two or three weeks of idleness, they would be furtively and calculatingly glancing at the shop windows and the loose stones of the side street roads.

Melville's attitude to the riots of the last strike had been: "Our lot will riot whatever I say to them; I can't control their *blood*, only a part of their mind. So it's better for the riots to have what organisation I can give to them, and try to prevent the *whole* place going up in flames." Tudor knew that he had persuaded a gang against smashing up the engine-house of the colliery.

There seemed no class-conscious distrust of him now in the parlour. He had earned his spurs. Some of the men were from the Terraces, and a grim-jawed lot they were, with black Welsh heads and restlessly gesticulating hands. They looked, too, replenished in some ancient strength of the earth, uncaught and unsubdued.

"Yes, not too much hollering," he said, "and no riots, boys."

"There's nothing like a riot or two to make the world sit up and take notice," a Terrace man said.

176

"We lose the bit of good-will the world has for us," Tudor said. "The pressure of outside opinion has a certain amount of value."

"Can't sit still all those weeks," someone teased, licking lean chops.

"After the last riots the authorities will be better prepared. We'll have troops and mobs of police here in no time. There'll be a lot of jail. Oh, I know," Tudor went on to some of the dubious faces, "a strike is a war and the kings of the world, as our history-books tell us, haven't hesitated to become blackguards and ruffians when they've been dissatisfied. But we'll show we're made of better stuff. Endurance, that's what we've got to learn."

"Endurance don't feed the guts," said one austerely; "it don't make gravy in the pan nor milk in the breast."

"But it'll get you what you're striking for." But he said no more; the question of rioting was almost untouchable. The dark activity, sponsored for so many generations by patriotic wars, glorified in fair poetry, the sword of the gallant and the rewarding smile of queens, was impregnated in the blood. There would have to be long generations of other teaching to eradicate the mischief. Considered psychologically, the men were justified in plundering and rioting. The job was taught them by kings, it was glorified in cathedrals, and death gave it pomp. Perhaps at some future date it would be looked upon as a curiosity of the human race, like cannibalism or crowned heads. Tudor took a sniff of the half-opened rose he had put in his buttonhole before coming out and glanced at the sheet of paper placed before him.

"Now, this medical scheme they're wanting," he said cautiously.

"*We* don't want it," said someone promptly.

"A tanner a week is twenty-six bob a year," another growled. "And I haven't poked my nose inside of a surgery since I married my Bessie in '93 and had to take advice that only cost one-and-six.... Several someones' going to get fat on it, doctors mostly— if you'll excuse me, Doctor Morris—'specially those that's shareholders in the pits."

Tudor explained why he wouldn't benefit, and there were

exclamations of sympathy from those who hadn't known of the threatened boycott. Tudor felt a cluster of warm esteem gather round his head. But he nobly explained at length the advantages of the scheme. Everybody knew of families crippled through illness, physically and financially, in this place where disease and destruction were very active; and who knew what misfortune waited for the healthiest, going down the pit....

Of the men present only Beriah had spent a lot on doctors. He was a white damp-looking man, whose only really steady organ was his socialism. At one time, long ago, he'd had one of the bad jobs in a small pit. Every night, carrying a lighted candle stuck to the end of a stick, he used to crawl on his belly through the deserted underground workings, exploding the gas which had gathered during the day. Though wearing mask and hood and rolled in leather and wool, it was a dangerous job— there would be air he could breathe low down on the ground, under the rising fire-damp, but it wasn't the best kind of air at all, and it was no kind of life for a man to crawl on his belly all night searching for the evil gas that sat up in corners breathing out poison like a witch. As he would say, the explosions weren't really good for the nerves. But the doctor had patched him up one way and another, and for some things he was still sturdy and tough.

However, he too shook his head at the scheme, gazing friendlily at Tudor. "The scheme won't get taken if we can help it. We'll do a bit of work on it."

"What's the talk in the pits about the scheme?" Tudor asked.

"They don't want it," someone said. "They say the women will be running to the doctor every day, enjoying themselves and inventing bad things wrong with them."

"Aye, it'll be like free drink to them," another exclaimed. "There's my Aunt Gwen now—she takes bottles of them bitter tonics regular, says they make her feel happy. She 'on't touch beer, but she goes down to doctor and whines like a sick cat 'bout her low spirits, shamming."

"The local Federation committee is favourable, I hear," Tudor said. "Though, of course, the decision rests with the men."

"We'll preach against it for all we're worth," a Terrace man promised earnestly. "And for your sake special, Doctor Morris."

"The scheme has got its good points," Tudor insisted, "though I think that medical attendance ought to be provided entirely free by the pit companies." He could not help feeling a load lifting off his mind; he was scraping together a few patients, though money was coming in woefully slow, and what was left from Branwen's money was being eaten into fast. But if the scheme were rejected, a couple of years should get him firmly established among the less respectable nonchapel community.

"We don't want it," they said, "we don't want any arranging for us from on high. We don't trust 'em. Too much grabbing there's been in their past history." They had become instinctively suspicious of *any* activity of the Bosses: enmity was rooting more firmly.

The meeting concluded with arrangements for a mass meeting two days hence, to be addressed by Tudor. A big section of the workmen, wearied of the last strike, was wavering from supporting the new one. They must be whipped into fresh realisation. A generations-old heritage of bitterness and resentments was there, but recent defeats had dampened the fire.

Announced by a street crier, but more usefully by word of mouth down in the pits, the meeting, timed conveniently between the day and night shift, was attended by a large curiously interested crowd. It was a shrewd move to announce Doctor Tudor Morris as the speaker. His name had been chucked about in scandal, but for all that, he belonged to the upper hundred of the valley, a "classy bloke". The novelty of one of these descending to sympathy with the miners' cause startled those who only thought of him as an erratic wild young man. The middle-class looked upon it as a public announcement of his final fall from grace. Most of the miners were doubtful and puzzled. One of the traditional enemies walking nakedly into the savage camp! It was queer.

They came out of the dark dwellings spread across the low slopes of the mountains, men grey or swarthy of face, for the most part with hardy shoulders and short muscular legs; they teemed down the dusty bed of the vale, black clots of them moving in one direction—to the sports ground beside the river where recently a revival tent had stood. It was a strong, talkative crowd as it waited, blatantly male and obstreperous; there was a thickly physical atmosphere of unruly humanity. The cocky sing-song voices sounded as though everyone spoke without listening. A rosy sun hesitated above a mountain.

Beriah mounted the rickety back of a brake. His pale used-up appearance evoked respect; he was one of the old colliers with burnt-out insides, and the men saw in him what they all might become. But he had a kind of steadfastness, and his hoarse mild voice had an effective quality, too.

"I'm standing up here to introduce a new leader to you, boys. Doctor Tudor Morris, as has taken our rights to himself as though he was one of us.... And he is one of us too, come of a family that baked their bread here long before them stinking pits was sunk by outsiders and sharp foreign gents from London—"

"Aye," shouted an approving voice, "my grannie knew his grannie when she used to milk the cows that used to stand where the *White Hart* is now."

Beriah made a few more introductory remarks and, with a gentle flourish that would have done credit to an Elizabethan courtier, called upon Tudor, who mounted the brake to good-humoured cheers. But there was still an air of suspicion. The bloke had never worked down the pits. True, he was wearing old clothes like everyone else and his face was familiar to them as the grey-painted window of his father's surgery.

"Men," he began quietly, "this is the first time I have had the honour of addressing you, though I've given many of you another kind of medicine often enough—"

Amid the laughter, someone yelled: "Make it tasty this time, and no old soft soap in the pills."

180

"All the same, I'm not going to suggest this time," resumed Tudor, beginning to speed up his voice determinedly, "that I've got a special poultice for your inflammations or that I can stitch up your wounds successfully.... But I've come up here to tell you that we're approaching a serious crisis in the history of the coal-mining industry—of all industry where men have decided to bind themselves together in trades union." Suddenly very grave, he pointed dramatically at the sun, now half slipped behind the mountain. "Look at that sun!"

The sun had become a savage red, its crimson flowing over the mountain. The men looked; perhaps the ritualistic pointing to it stirred them to atavistic awareness of the opulent fiery orb; they were quite silent.

"Sinking blood-red!" Tudor cried. "Like this century, that's stained bloodier than any other century of military wars and campaigns of the battlefields."

He had obtained attention. The power of the picturesque word, thrown out dramatically. A sigh of satisfaction passed over the crowd; it settled down. The tense young figure standing on the brake made no further gesticulation. Tudor spoke with steady tautness, without any further platform tricks. He was conscious of power flowing up to him from the crowd, entering him like magic, to be cast forth again in alive words.

"You are going to be the important men of the new century, your hands and your brains are going to form the shape of the new years. The old feudal system is dead, and the aristocrats that are left will soon be as quaint as mummies from an Egyptian tomb.... I've come up here to suggest that you have not yet fully realised your strength and your power. The secret of the success which lies within your grasp is solidarity, a binding together of yourselves in a solid lump. You have your Federation, but I'm told that only half of you belong to it. That is why the Federation is weak in the joints and can do as little for you as one of those grey lambs up there on the green. Yet you can make it as hot as a trotting stallion with red fire coming out of his nostrils and a kick like the wrath of God. Men, get a stallion running through these valleys, a red one with a black-as-thunder mane flying in the storm. In other words, begin jogging up your minds, and stop wandering about in different herds, bleating of this and that petty grievance. In still different words, if you're going to strike for the abolition of the Sliding Scale and demand a wage safe from the trickery and cunning of those who juggle with coal prices, then make it a real strike, with every man jack out from every pit of these valleys—and not only out, but determined to keep out until you've obtained the wherewithal not only to spread butter on your bread, but also some best strawberry jam—"

This introduction to the points of his hour and a half speech was received with wondering attention. And throughout the speech Tudor dabbed on colour generously, gradually working in a selection of Biblical texts. The naturally inflammable material beneath him began to burn. He guarded against rousing such febrile shooting of flame as the Brothers Beynon whipped up: he quoted mundane figures of colliery profits and some facts of the internecine competition of prices among the owners. A dark-browed interest was gathered into the faces tilted up to him. He subtly threaded a sincere flattery through the speech. They were the salt of the earth, and it was time they realised it, etc., etc....
Never mind if the salt was grimy and dusty, he thought to himself at the same time: salt they were, after all—

The sun seemed to have gone down quickly, as if glad to disappear, and the shifty grey valley light did not last long. Beriah lit the candles in the two brake lamps. The valley night always tasted of ancient things, the mountains seemed to remember unruly tribes, long-ago battles, druidical circles of brooding men waiting for the moon. Still Tudor, standing between the carriage lamps, went on throwing fiery seed into the dim air, where the grey faces hovered ghostlily. Until the warning nine o'clock night-shift hooter of the Cefn pits hissed forcefully to the sky. There was an abrupt movement through the crowd, mechanical.

"—and the difference of the future will be this: instead of

182

fighting for some sawdust-bellied thing known as Glory or Patriotism, we'll be fighting for recognition of us as human beings with a right to live properly, decently. You have only one enemy; you know what that is; its capitalist voice has just hooted at my speech.... Men, get yourselves into proper union and remember that as our forefathers fought for these valleys against the thieving barons of old, so we've got to fight, but in a different way, for a different reason."

It had been a wild harangue, and Tudor knew it. For this, his maiden speech, he had felt that it would be better to confine himself almost entirely to expression of a creed. He knew the men needed some such crystallisation—and better crudely expressed—of their dumb bowel movements against oppression; he told himself that they hadn't yet realised themselves as the really important props of the modern world. But as he jumped down from the brake, amid applause that had a curiously respectful sound, he wondered if he had been just another fool of a preacher, gluttonous of words and drunk with religious idealism. He wondered—and then told himself proudly: "No, that was a good preliminary speech; they listened carefully; their minds got going on it."

And, except for those who had to hurry for the nightshift the men did not disperse: they stood in groups on the dark field talking in the local shrill thumb-cocking and fisted way. Aye, he was a good chap, this Doctor Morris, and ought to be put on the Federation: let's have him and see what he can do. He don't know anything about down-under though, never touched a pick in his life. Never mind, he's got ideas and bounce and cheek. Look now what he called the Bosses! He's a rum 'un—chucked over his classy people, gone to live 'bove the Terraces, and they say he's after Melville Waiter's sister. Let's have him on the Federation.... A moon began to shine on the field, on the black clots of men.

Beriah shook Tudor's hand. "First class," he said in his primly hoarse way. "Hot and 'portant. It went into their guts and put

183

good food in their minds. You're a new one on 'em, aye, a new one. The chaps say you ought to be on Federation. The old hens there bin sitting too long on their eggs, and nothing coming out."

"If we can only get all he men into the Federation before the strike begins," Tudor said earnestly. "Get them all solid, right through the valley. Have them all in one clean fourteen-mile line." He curbed himself, curious of the dark sinister feeling sense of power growing within him: he must be careful not to be drunk on this. "The strike is coming," he said slowly, "and however untidy it's going to be, we've got to keep the men out this time. Short shrift for scabs and blacklegs, Beriah, but no riots if we can stop them."

Beriah's wrung done-in face was as fragile as the new moonlight. "It's when they get hungry," he said primly, "and see visions of frying bacon."

"We'll have to feed them with other visions," Tudor said wryly, at the same time conscious of the wild disastrous sense of wrong that moved the men.

He was thinking what savage anger prowled about in the world, and how the jungle grew at doorsteps. What tigers slept under chapel seats and how baboons ambled through the back lanes looking for food in the domestic pails. The glimpses of lawlessness he had already seen in the valley were like clairvoyant peeps into the anatomy of the living world, past the decked crust into a dark where an eternal arrangement of rock-like bones held the final mystery of life: a mysterious heart thudding with wild blood.

Beriah accompanied him to the edge of the Terraces. There he stopped and said solemnly: "Very well I know you will keep your head in this business. The men want to see the roads they got to go in the future, but don't you go laying yourself down for 'em to trample over you. I know how it is. A man can't be any little Jesus without going to the Cross. You go home now and chuck off thoughts of the meeting as though it was a lot of dirty old clothes. I been like you in my time, and spent myself like a shilling in a fair. The cause, the men, the bosses, it was all the time. And by and by it comes to seem sometimes nothing but noise and dust and penny shows that's frauds."

"Yet you still go on doing it, Beriah."

"Aye, I still go on," answered Beriah dimly, as if he did not know why.

And back in his house Tudor understood something of what Beriah meant. The house was cold and quiet as a grave, wrapped stonily in the night. Hannah had left on the kitchen table a lonely plate of cold beef and a junket white and still as the face of a corpse. The small fire was silent in the grate. He must get himself a young dog, he thought, as he carried the cold beef into the study, which was more cheerful with the oil-lamp burning under a pale shade and his books scattered about. And even while eating he began a letter to Daisy:

We had a mass meeting tonight, very well attended. Feeling is beginning to run high, and after the recent bout of religion the men are coming back to earth pretty bad-temperedly, beginning once more to ask "Why?" The strike is sure to start during the next few weeks, probably without the proper notice. The danger will be that only the men in the Associated Owners' pits will come out. We're working to get all the men of the valley out; we want the men to feel the strength of unification, the owners, too....

But why are you not here? I wanted you to be in the meeting tonight, to criticise my first speech. You could have put on a pair of trousers, worn a raincoat and shoved your hair up under a miner's cap. (Why do the men look with a hostile eye on their women coming to the meetings, and what would Mrs. Barnes say?) You would have said something to the point, probably—"Awful bad." That apart, why are you not here at this moment, to put my plate of cold beef under my nose, to take it away, to say to me, "we want a spaniel," to rake out the fire, to throw back the coverlet of our bed?

I believe you are placing me on trial because you are uncertain yet of my capability to throw off the associations of the past, my younger life. Aren't you being rather severe about this? Well, I hope that the fact of my first shameless speech to the men in public will help to make you unbend—you royal slut. I understand from Beriah that the men are now quite un-snobbish about me, unlike you.

The practice is getting a little healthier. Some measles this week, a pleurisy and a "nerves". The stench that rises from the Terraces has an autumnal deadness, but the winds of winter will soon rush down from the mountains and so will whisk it up to the face of Heaven. You'll like the house, which is ugly and bare but spacious. Come, and give it a look not of home but of beauty.

Has anything happened yet? Too soon to tell? I forget your date.

Ten days later Daisy replied. Her letter was like a long rambling schoolgirl essay, and he imagined her breathing heavily over the paper while her fist moved in its slow disagreeable labours. She said that she had heard about his speech from one or two friends, and she was very proud. About marrying him, surely there was plenty of time; let's wait until Melville came out of jail. She thought of her sweet Tudor every day and every night, but things hadn't settled down for him yet. Best to be careful and not offend people too much at one go. She described walks she had taken with Mrs. Barnes and what the Captain was talking about. In a postscript she added that she thought she had conceived but wasn't quite sure just yet.

IV

The next few weeks were busy ones for him. Besides the series of mass meetings the Strike Committee had arranged, and at most of which he spoke, his practice suddenly increased at an astonishing rate. The first public announcement of his sympathies had achieved this private fruit. True, most of the patients would be of the ill-paying kind; they vaguely recognised the usual local fees, but when it came to paying, they would lay a solitary half a crown on the table and promise another at some distant date. He might just as well have left a box with a slot in the waiting-room for them to use as they felt moved or could afford.

Oppressed women came to him in droves and the long whine of their troubles became in his ears like some eternal voice of the earth complaining of lives continually hindered. Most of their troubles came from bad feeding, overwork, sexual crudities and endless cups of black tea. He saw how perpetual hard work would keep a neurosis at bay, but took toll by brutal assaults on the flesh. Most of these women who were past fifty continued in the world merely by the will to live: otherwise they were, except for a faculty of tears, occupants of graves. But one woman, refusing an operation, went on her knees and begged him to give her something that would put her away.

"Come now, Mrs. Watts, all this because of an ulcer! It's not serious at all, and that's the real truth. You'll get a good rest in hospital, which you need more than anything. You know you'll never get it at home." She was still grovelling on the floor, sweaty, a collapsed dump. He lifted her gently and laid her on the sofa.

"I want to go," she moaned strickenly, "I want to go. 'Tisn't the operation, 'tisn't the pain. I just want to go."

She had supported a weakly husband who had developed consumption in the pits, she had borne and bred nine subdued-looking children, five of whom had considered it not worth while to reach adolescence. Her arms were amazingly plump, sacks of flesh tied in the middle her hands were big blobs of raw blue. She was odorous as a marsh; she looked like something sagging down to rot at the ends of the world. Suddenly she sat up and a greasy gleam crossed her face.

"Mrs. Roberts number eighteen had a ulcer that burst and kilt her!" she declared triumphantly. And later she backed out of the surgery looking quite refreshed with cunning. She was going to feed that ulcer to perforation point.

Men came with long lists of troubles, nearly all due, they said, to blows sustained in the pits and they having to keep on working because to get compensation out of the owners was like expecting the moon to lay eggs. The tough tenacious appearance of these was only something burnt skin-deep by the colliery-inside they moaned and lamented amid several complaints; everyone thought he was subject to or had the dreaded silicosis. There was one man who, Tudor suspected, had the beginnings of the deathly spirochaetal jaundice, due probably to his working down under in water infected by diseased rats. Many of the colliers worked in foul water up to their knees; this one had fallen into a hole and had been completely immersed, heaving up a bellyful of the liquid as he scrambled out.

Several days there would be at least twenty people in the waiting-room. The smell of ill-humanity overcame at last the bleakly new odour of the drugs. Visits were confined almost entirely to the Terraces, which were slowly becoming wholly his medical kingdom. Probably the other doctors were glad to be rid of the squalid place; in any case, it was no gold-mine. Tudor was especially popular for maternity cases, in spite of his being a young unmarried man—or perhaps because of it—and he was as cheap as a midwife.

In fact, the old habit of having in only a midwife almost died out as Tudor became fashionable. Just the doctor and the woman next door—if friendly—became the habit. The shady Mrs. Violet Fox, who could bring a baby into the world as well as whisk one out, lost job after job. She became viciously angry, but invented a new pill and went round hawking it and belittling Tudor's capabilities. But the women told one another he had lucky hands; one, the hefty Mrs. Rosser, who kept a wet fish shop in her parlour, declaring he had brought out her last as easy as emptying a load of herrings out of a cask.

His firebrand speeches at the meetings were listened to with growing approval. The meetings were always well attended. Nothing was loved more than a speech—providing it was delivered hot and dramatic. There were jeering interruptions, of course, and fun was vigorously poked. Most faithful of the interrupters was the man who cut into the most impassioned flights of oratory with a sudden cry of "Cock-a-doo-dle-doo!" disappearing afterwards. However, it was found that he was only Dannie the Poet, a half-wit who had never done a stroke of work in his life. He had once won the prize in an eisteddfod for a poem on Nebuchadnezzar. Having submitted it under a pseudonym, there was general consternation when Dannie the Daft (as he was known then) walked to the platform on the calling of the winner's name; one of the adjudicators, indeed, wanted to withhold the prize.

But the place was becoming parched in the new bout of poverty, and the meetings all over the valley became like strong drink. His plea for an impregnable union of all the men of all the pits was making a mark. The Federation was raking them in. He was offered the secretaryship of the local lodge, but he declined.

He could not decide that the time had come for him to abandon his practice and plunge full hog into a political career.

"I want to run about the place free for a year or two yet," he told Beriah. "While I'm still more or less an outsider of the pits I feel I can see clearer."

"Aye, and there'd be no part of your soul that'd be *private*," Beriah nodded. "Perhaps you can best serve the place by going into the houses and talking to the chaps and their wives while you're repairing their bodies." He sighed. "Though I'd like to see you made our representative for this new Labour Party that's talked about."

"There's plenty of time, Beriah. I've got a lot to pick up yet round about the gutters of the place."

In quiet remote moments he wondered if he was using the valley as a painter takes a canvas when he is stirred by a landscape and repeats it, charged with the colours of his own temperament, on the cloth. This act of creation was being performed with his own soul for canvas. He was painting there the scarred lineaments of the place and the groups of its oppressed damaged people. And in some way the vision had to be displayed, if only from the back of a rickety brake: he had to bring it forth, else suffer a kind of death, a spiritual suffocation.

But, he thought farther, smiling to himself, he could not tell everlastingly of his vision from the back of a brake. Something more definite had to be achieved. Politics excited one, but after a while he was sure they would seem paltry and dusty, a wandering in windy deserts of words, a going out from oneself and a never coming back. And he did not want to leave himself just yet, he was still uncompleted, he was still intent on painting in those harsh violent colours, those hard contours and those unruly faces, painting them deep into his soul. He saw how every man, for a while, must become the most shuttered of egotists, until he had achieved his vision according to his needs. Afterwards—

A woman, the founding of a family? He wanted them. Particularly, just now, Daisy. But there would have to be something else. And, with a laugh at himself and also a feeling of assurance due, he supposed, to his success at the mass meetings, he thought it would have to be politics. After all, his newspaper often gave him evidence that the slopes of those glorious Alps had been climbed by the clumsiest of fools. And soon there was going to be this new party, founded on the recent better-organised activities of trade unions in England. There'd be opportunities.

These personal moments of brooding were soon forgotten in the rushing of the early autumn weeks. Within a month he had brought to successful birth in the Terraces fourteen babies—two of which were named after him—and addressed a dozen meetings. Those meetings were like the cracks of whips heard up and down the valley: sometimes they broke up into turbulent shoutings among the men, as they expressed their different grievances. The lean faces became lit with that peculiar fire of abuse native to the valleys. There would be small fights, and the police would arrive. Tudor was startled at the ease with which dangerous flame could be evoked.

Then, a sudden clap of thunder, the Association of Owners acted. On a Friday, at the pit-heads of most of the collieries in

190

the valley, notices were displayed announcing a month's notice for the termination of all workmen's contracts. The miners were to be *chucked out*. Most of the men were taken aback at this surprise move, and it was useless for those of shrewder psychological understanding to shout "Silly bluff". And to add to the confusion, the miners' wives began to scream at their men in blame. There was a feeling of alarm in the valley. If all the Owners were *willing* to close their pits, what was going to happen?

Representatives of the Federation waited upon the Association. They were told calmly that the Owners were weary of trouble; and the falling prices of coal, bringing profits down to a few pence per ton, made the working of the pits not worth their while—unless the men were prepared to accept without further question the old Sliding Scale Agreement which, they declared definitely and for the last time, was the only proposition they would recognise. "Blame the world, not us," they implied; "go to the Continent and ask them to stop mining coal there, so that we can have all the markets."

"Yet you have your profits," a representative pointed out.

"Yes, we have our profits," he was told coolly, "such as they are, and we have our shareholders and odd though it may seem, we do expect a little return from our property."

However, they were willing to open negotiations with the men for the continued acceptance of the Sliding Scale. Otherwise, well, to speak plainly—"To hell with the pits."

Sir Rufus Morgan, one of the Associated Owners, was not present during their interview. He still refused any recognition of Federations or Trade Unions: he had bellowed angrily at his fellow-owners for what he considered a weak descent in talking to rascals. Yet he fumed in another room of the offices, the powerful purple-red muscles of his face swollen under bristling brows. An immense emperor of a man, he was so hot-blooded that there was no need for a fire in a room which he occupied. Hearing the miners' representatives come down the passage at last, he could contain himself no longer and with shaking hams he bustled out.

"Huh, what you doing here?" He attempted his celebrated frown, which was indeed a frightening arrangement of his storm-coloured face, with its overhanging brows speared with coarse hairs. "Aren't there enough old rats round the pits already! Phew, get out. I can stand a honest workman or two, but you rats that nibble at their crumbs—no: skedaddle, get out, before I get the hose put on you." And he gave vent to a belch of such deep-bowelled power, it had a grandeur in its own right.

The men walked past him, talking among themselves: they knew all about Sir Rufus. Only J. J. Lewis thought of something and, mustering his faculties until his face went red, broke wind with great triumph right opposite the colossal magnate. It was the sort of language the old bloke understood, he said afterwards.

Sir Rufus was chid afterwards by one of the other owners who had watched the scene from the end of the passage. "That sort of thing won't do now, Sir Rufus. These chaps got affairs at their finger-ends; they've been to school, and they understand figures."

"That's right, that's right," bellowed Sir Rufus; "a bit more scraping to trade unionism and *you'll* be going back to school—to learn a new way of living. Huh, a bitter school it'll be too." He heaved and brought out, the words weighty as flat-irons, his obstinate creed: "You've got to put on knuckle-dusters with the men, Francis; *they* wear them and they'll use them if they get a chance. It's as simple as that. Action and no words. This industry is a war, not a mothers' meeting; it's been chosen by these socialist bastards as their battle-ground and we got to clear them out."

Francis shook his head to himself. He too knew all about Sir Rufus and the elephantine workings of his mind. His bellows were better than his logic. Francis, a younger man, knew that in the future it would be impossible for men like Sir Rufus to attain a similar success in the industry. Sir Rufus was a fearsome symbol of its past.

The valley heard the news with swearing. Eternal continuation of the Sliding Scale: wages everlastingly at the mercy of shifty and crafty speculators. There was an air of consternation everywhere. A strike was a different thing: in a strike one felt strong, at least to begin with. This rearrangement of affairs was confusing. The general attitude was that the owners were performing a dirty trick.

There were few houses where wives did not express despairing wrath. There, look now, what the men had brought on themselves! A strike they more or less accepted in a wild rough way, though protesting; a strike after all was a traditional right of the men. But they were alarmed of this similar activity on high. And, of course, they blamed the men. That first Friday evening the news spread from house to house fast as news of death.

When Tudor heard he rushed up to Beriah's house. Beriah had just arrived from the pit and was sitting at the table in his pit black, eating stew. His wife, Susan, trod about clucking like an angry duck: she had never excused Beriah's activities, but usually she was obliged to keep silent. She looked at Tudor with beady eyes and disappeared into the back, where she held converse with next door's woman over the nasturtium-covered railings.

"A bit unexpected," Beriah said cautiously.

"But a good thing, eh?" Tudor's face was flushed excitedly.

"Maybe. Depends how much of it's bluff."

"Of course it's bluff—all of it. They're frightened, Beriah." Tudor was surprised at Beriah's worried manner. But surely it was only the first numbed shock of the kick.

"I think you're right, Doctor Morris. But the men—you know what they are—most of 'em only see the face of things, and that face looks bad to 'em now."

"And there's our work cut out for us. A meeting tomorrow night. I'll go and get the crier out this evening and tomorrow afternoon."

"Saturday night's a bad time for a meeting—the pubs come first."

"Sunday then."

"The chapels own Sunday," Beriah said doubtfully.

"Doesn't their livelihood come before drink and God?" Tudor exclaimed, still alight in excitement. "Oh, I know, drink and God's a big patch of their life, but Beriah, Beriah, we've got to shout at them now, while they've been made to sit up. A meeting *tonight*. Got some pieces of paper?"

Beriah found an old roll of wallpaper. Tudor began to cut off strips and on the plain backs scrawled with a crayon an announcement of a mass meeting for that night at half-past eight. He asked for a basin of flour and some water. Beriah, becoming roused too now, forgot his stew. He began to mix the paste in the basin. While he was doing so, the wife Susan entered the kitchen. She took in the proceedings with a black glance.

"At it again," she clacked darkly, "at it again!" She could not quite subdue the usual deference towards a doctor, but after a minute she burst. "You men, what d'you. know? Talk to Mrs Clarke next door—five young ones she's got, and one coming. Sowing mischief. Ach, the men ought to be put at the wash-tubs and have truck with the oven for a year. Do they know how to stare at sixpence till you go squint-eyed and make it into a shilling? Ach, do they know how to get meat out of a bone, and a pudding out of dry bread and no butter and currants in the house? They heard babies grizzle 'cos milk's like water and don't feed. No, they go out and sit on their backsides in strikes and *talk*." She breathed heavily and clucked in her rising chest. "God above, why for I didn't stay on the farm and marry Matthew Lark?"

"'Cos he drank and chased after other women, Susan," Beriah said primly. "Get my bath-water, woman, and don't grunt."

"There" she continued, "there, the world was *clean*. In Cardigan where there's trees and birds singing."

"Very glad you were to come here. You said you wanted to live in a row of houses and next door to a pub. Life you wanted to see, you said. What's a tree and a bird to you, you falsehood of a

194

woman. You wanted to go where there was *men*. Get my bath-water at once now."

She tugged in the wooden tub before the fire and emptied into it the pailful of water simmering on the hob. Tudor went on scrawling over the sheets on the table. Beriah quickly threw off his clothes and stepped into the tub, into which Susan, breathing pantingly, had emptied cold water. Blackly naked, he was lean and tough as a whip. She continued to exclaim her own woes and those of Mrs. Clarke next door: she took up a scrubbing brush and began to attack his back with breathless energy.

"Hold off, woman. Am I the kitchen floor or the doorstep?"

"Colliers ought to be born black," she clucked; "it's not right on their wives for them to want a scrubbing every day. Ach, I'd tell all the women of the world, take no carriage or train or footstep to where there's collieries—better marry a real black in a savage land and have done with it."

Beriah put on a purple-striped flannel shirt, green-striped flannel drawers tied at the knees with tape, and he drank a hasty cup of tea while finishing dressing. He found a plaster-brush and took up the basin of paste. Tudor, rolling up the posters, asked Susan to show him her tongue.

"I thought so. What did I tell you last week about drinking that port!" She was in the habit of buying bottles of a cheap concoction called port.

"I got to do something," she sulked. "I don't feel safe to face the day till I've had my half a glass."

"I know, half a glass! Your liver's going to make you face something else soon. I've warned you."

But as he and Beriah marched down the side street, he said: "We'll have to do something about the women soon. They're important. They don't use their minds much, but they've got feelings strong as battleships."

"They've been living so long without minds," Beriah said gloomily. "A thousand-year job it'll be to get 'em into training."

"Oh, they're not so bad as that... I know a woman in Bristol who's got going. She'd come down and start a movement here, I think."

They went into the main street. Wedged between the shops were dwelling-houses. "I know which of them's willing," Beriah said. He hurried before Tudor, knocked at doors, and obtained permission for sticking the posters on the concrete wall beside the door. A policeman had followed them down the street curiously. Tudor cut down a side street and knocked at the crier's door. A little man with a hoarse cracked voice but a brilliantly new bell, he agreed to go out at once, Tudor pushing the fee into his hand.

But that night the valley seemed to growl. The meeting was well attended, but the men at first were surly and distrustful, probably still irritated from domestic scenes. "What," bawled Tudor, "you're not such mugs as to be taken in by that silly notice? Don't you understand what bluff is? That notice is just a sprat to catch the herring. I'll tell you that the owners want to frighten you into accepting the Sliding Scale without question, probably with a percentage off. They care about their pits a hundred times more than they do you, they've got to have their elephant's share while you scramble for a bit of bird-seed. *Are* you going to be frightened, do you *believe* they're willing to scrap their pits—"

"They can fill the pits with scab labour in a month," someone growled.

"Why didn't they do that in the last strike then?" Tudor shouted. "They dare not, they know what would happen, with thousands of starving men prowling about the place. Can't you understand you've got the power, if only you'll unite! You've *got* to get the men of the non-Associated pits out too, from up in Nant Vale. Make it a real strike, ignore that notice—"

"Same thing, one way or the other," someone remarked. "We'll be out."

"It's not the same thing. You've got to believe that *you've* given a kick on the pants to the owners, not they to you. Let them kick at you and frighten you and you'll go under—"

196

"Who's frightened?" several roared at last.

"You are!" dared Tudor. His eyes flashed, he swept his arm dramatically towards the valley's length. "And every woman in all these kitchens up there is frightened. You let them feel the feet of cunning elephants shaking the place. And the elephants *are* shaking the place, you're letting them do it."

The crowd was stirring; it was getting bad-tempered. Hundreds of eyes shone out in the dusk with a cat gleam. A number began to speak and growl among themselves. Tudor, who had learnt to tune himself to the dominant mood of a meeting, raged dramatically. He hammered at the word *bluff*. And finished:

"—strike and get everyone out with you, get at the men of Nant Vale tomorrow night, tonight! Can't you see that you've got to choose this time between slavery and an announcement of yourselves as human beings with a right to live decently? Let your Federation haggle over a Sliding Scale percentage either one way or another and you're lost. Smash the Sliding Scale once and for all or else go back a hundred years to slavery and show the owners that you're a beaten race, beaten, beaten, beaten." He flung himself down from the old brake in wrath.

A youngish collier, alert and muscular—Ieuan Mold, an amateur boxer—immediately jumped on the brake and began hotly: "Our butty, Doctor Morris, is right as a dose of his blooming salts. He knows how it is with them owners. Chaps, we got to stand firm and steady, 'cept for our tails, which mustn't hang like string between our legs, but got to wave as foxy as the way them owners are behaving. We *got* to have that strike we was planning—"

Others followed him on the brake, and soon the field vibrated with an air of entire conversion. Someone broke into song. And song knit them together; they sang hymns and old Welsh war marches. The meeting looked like being a triumph. Beriah told Tudor the next day that he assumed from conversation in the pits that a large proportion of troublesome wives had been clouted or otherwise bullied into submission.

"A pity they get clouted," Tudor said.

During the following week there were mass meetings every evening up and down the valley. The slogan was: "No notices, but a strike." All the speakers shouted particular mockery at the bluff of the Associated Owners; and their energy seemed to have effect. There was extreme anger against the autocratic behaviour of the owners. And bosses were called "owners" merely out of politeness and long habit; the new teaching was rapidly taking grip.

Having started that hare, Tudor and his committee began work on the men of the few pits owned by John Johns, who did not belong to the Association of Owners. These pits had worked full speed during a previous strike in the Associated pits and Johns, as a result, had reaped a fine harvest. Strikers had skulked into his pits and been given work; there had been double shifts, and since Johns's scale of wages was slightly better than other owners', there had, to starving men, appeared to be an abundance of money up in Nant Vale. Up there the smell of beer had still hung round the pubs, joints of red beef and pale pork hung on butchers' rails, children sucked ice-cream cornets out of the Italian sweet shops, and in the chapel eisteddfodau poets and vocalists expressed themselves beautifully on full stomachs and in new clothes. It was bad to see such prosperity next door to one.

This community was up a steep stark cleft in the mountains, the rows of houses pouring like a black waterfall down to the bed of the main valley. It looked a place given over entirely to the stern business of knocking out a living from the grim hostile landscape. Only on Saturday nights there was an air of release and people peered outside their doors, sniffed the air, and scuttled for a while up and down the main road. It was said that there were many wealthy colliers up in Nant Vale; but no one knew what was done with their money; there was certainly nothing to show its existence.

Street-corner meetings it had to be up there; they were poorly attended at first. The most important chapel was holding a Festival of Preaching, well-known ministers coming from afar and giving remarkable sermons; a kind of small intellectual revival, on the stiff side and no rolling about. Tudor and the others made introductory contacts in the few pubs, started arguments, bought drinks, and when a debate was strongly on its feet, suggested a move to the street corner, borrowing a chair out of some house for the speaker.

And here, too, they stoked up the old ancestral fire of battle. The Festival of Preaching turned out to be a useful ally. Crowds coming from the chapel with their minds wakened—not too boilingly, but just nicely simmering—stopped to listen to this extra preaching. Of rhetoric and magic of the word the people could never have enough. Tudor quickly seized his opportunity when a crowd of chapel-dressed people paused curiously at the edge of his audience, caught by the sound of a voice lifted up; he swerved out of the main path of his speech into:

"The Kingdom of Heaven. The Kingdom of Heaven. Where is it? Up there, down here? Up there the perfect one is sure enough, where there's no more day and night shifts, no more tubs of dirty bath water, no more strikes and sliding scales. But down here surely a bit of a heavenly garden is possible too, a little orchard where everyone will have a right to pick a handful of cherries as he wants. Here in Nant Vale it doesn't look as if a fruit tree will ever blossom again, and if a rose blooms the neighbours come and stare at it. Your garden and your orchard will have to be a decent and just wage that will allow you to obtain some of the advantages of the world. Do you know what the profits of your pits were last year? I'll give you some figures—"

And the chapel-simmering minds soon touched boiling-point. The slightly better scale of wages that John Johns shrewdly paid gave the Nant Vale men a feeling of advantage over the men of the Associated pits. This sense of complacence and good fortune had to be dispersed. It was done gradually, by figures and a sentimentally war-like appeal for support of their poverty-stricken brothers. The stark cleft began to glow hot again, a red streak twisted up the mountains.

It was while he was standing on a kitchen chair at one of these street-corner meetings and passionately handling a newly-arrived batch of people that Tudor was interrupted by Beriah plucking at his sleeve.

"Oi," whispered Beriah, "oi, 'portant message for you."

Tudor was so involved in what he was saying that he took no notice, scarcely hearing the whisper. Beriah waited a minute, looking pale and worried. At the back of the chair, shrinking and red-eyed, was a young woman. Beriah made another attempt. Tudor bent down irritably to him.

"What is it?"

"There's your father's servant-gal—" stammered Beriah in distress.

The crowd shuffled a little. It had been usefully silent, with the right sort of silence. Tudor did not look round; he was far gone in this public abstraction. "Tell her to wait," he muttered in vexation. That shuffling of the crowd and the coughing was like a wrong note in a piece of music. He jerked up again. Beriah desperately plucked his sleeve.

"It's about your mother—"

Tudor started. His eyes swept the crowd: he was silent, hesitating. Despairingly Beriah whispered:

"Tudor, Tudor, the gal came to say that your mother is dead."

Tudor shivered. He resumed his speech where he had left off, mechanically at first, so that the crowd began to move shoulders and twist heads; then ardently, amorously, almost sensually:

"—are we living, here in this valley? We are and we are not. We are alive and we are dead. There is flesh that sweats and there is flesh that withers, both of the same body. Your bodies are sacrifices, they are being used not for your benefit and your pleasure. Have you been born, in the real sense of the word, do you *know* what the world is? In one way you are a hundred times more alive than your bosses, in another you are deader than the nails in their boots. They've got you where they want, a pack of slaves chained by habit to a certain system. And you

200

don't want to question the system, you're content to wither away. Ah, I can see in front of me here some fine specimens of humanity, regular young angels become solid with good flesh. A pity they can't keep like that, handsome as they were meant to be when they were put into the world. But as a doctor I know how many shillings some of you are going to put into my pocket, and how soon, how often—"

It was at this juncture that someone interrupted with: "Very gloomy you're talking tonight, Doctor Morris. If I didn't know you, I would have said you was an undertaker trying to sell coffins 'fore they're wanted."

The speaker on the kitchen chair shivered again, as if he had caught cold. But he went on, passing swiftly from his twice-interrupted prelude into a speech that lasted another hour or so. Then up on the chair sprang another speaker, a collier from an Associated pit.

"Boys," he began solemnly, "if you're men with red hearts in you, you got to come out with us—"

Behind the chair, Beriah looked at Tudor with mild astonishment, rather at sea.

"I'd better go now," Tudor whispered. "Not a bad meeting, Beriah. They're listening willingly enough."

"Yes, I can feel they're coming over to us. Slow but sure. That was an extra good speech you made, Tudor—" Beriah shuffled his feet uneasily. "You heard the message that I gave you?"

Tudor nodded. "Yes. I'm off now." He looked white, but returned into himself. "Keep 'em going as long as possible, Beriah."

V

Death had come swiftly, though for days its victim had shrunk farther and farther into some bleak nest of her wilting spirit. Elwyn and Bronwen sat in the drawing-room: Mildred hovered about—he knew how lately she had become like a daughter in the house. His mother had been dead three hours and already the footsteps of the layer-out could be heard upstairs. Bronwen sat very still, agedly statuesque; she peered grievously at him. His father was bowed, scarcely looked up when he entered, remaining for some time in a bitter silence of repudiation.

Tudor had asked how she died. Easily, quickly, with clean obliteration? His heart was plunging in battle. But his mind remained rigid in its refusal to yield to the atmosphere of accusation emanating from his father.

Bronwen gave him the few particulars. He felt her struggle to remove from her voice any comment, any emotional trembling. She sat in an aged acceptance of this death, unnecessary though it was. She had long recognised the hopeless passivity of her daughter-in-law. And Tudor, in the dangerous silence that followed, saw again how his mother had been in love with death, living in a land that gave death the loveliness of a new germination uncorrupted by the horrors of this earth.

"She'll be ready soon for you to see her," Bronwen murmured.

He shook his head. "It's not necessary." She was dead.

Elwyn looked up then, out of his breaking stupor. "She asked for you early this evening!"

"I wish you had found me then," Tudor said miserably.

Elwyn jerked up his head, sternly making the effort, and stared with glaucous eyes at his son. "She wanted to make a last request to you, she wanted to ask you to have done with this evil behaviour of yours—" He controlled himself and added grievously: "I suppose it would have been useless."

"I should like to have seen her alive," Tudor said. Not to listen to death-bed requests or the use of the unholy power of death, but for the sweet company of one's own flesh and blood before the long silence.

Then Elwyn, pitiably astray and disordered, said hardly: "You killed her."

"Elwyn!" cried Bronwen to her son, gently, "Come now, my boy."

Tudor said sharply: "She achieved death herself, she courted death, she wanted to die."

"Because of you!" Elwyn's voice rushed into a small wounded shout, the more awful because of his usual calm demeanour, that spoke of a man who dwelt in a mystical peace outside this world.

Tudor shook his head: his face was white. His hands were gripping the arms of his chair like lead. He forced his voice into steadiness. "Because of herself. She had this fatal weakness, this submission to the world. She deliberately laid herself down, and the wheels went over her." The words were wrenched from him.

"Leave me now," Elwyn said petulantly. "It's no good, no good... Mother, you will pray with me here?" The anguish in his voice whimpered distressingly; he seemed to have shut his son out of his consciousness. Tudor rose and went out of the room. He knew that if he too had stayed to pray he would have been forgiven. He stood in the dim hall with a thudding heart. He could hear his father's voice rising from a broken cry to an impassioned union with the mysteries he invoked:

"Lord, Lord, forgive us our iniquities, cleanse us of our evil ere we approach Thee on behalf of my dear wife—"

And as he went on the horror passed out of Elwyn's voice, he attained triumphantly his vision of bliss; he strode through the land of the dead and reached the verge of Heaven. But the horror had been there; he would come back to it again. All his life he had been the witness of suffering, damnation and death; all his life he had lived among perversions of the human race, paltry, ridiculous and offensive. But there in Heaven was dignity and majesty. Had he not earned his vision? He had been a good man and kind where it was possible in the uncouth earth.... Tudor heard his ecstasy as he looked once more upon Heaven, heard some of the phrases appealing for paradisaical accommodation for his wife. But he did not want to wait for the anticlimax of the return to earth. What more could he do in this house, what use was he here? He stared up the dark staircase. She was there, heavily dead. His heart still thudded and lurched. And he knew that he too had his horror, which was woven inextricably into his sense of life, and that for him there was no escape. He stepped slowly to the staircase. One look perhaps, to seal his long recollection of her. A recollection which, until lately, had been simple and pleasant. Wiping his feet on the mat with the old mechanical habit of boyhood, he became aware of a face watching him out of the dark space at the far end of the hall; it was approaching him.

"Tudor, I want to speak to you, please." It was Mildred; she had been sitting in the dark of his father's study.

He followed her into the study and lit the gas. On his arrival they had sheered off from each other as if in aversion, and he had since forgotten that she was in the house. He looked at her now curiously; he saw that she was darkly stimulated, there was a flush of excited life in her, burning beneath her face, which was heavy with the melancholy occasion. He had noticed that stimulation in others, when on professional visits connected with death. It was probably a secret congratulation of oneself; a deepening awareness of the value of one's own life. Mildred had it in abundance tonight, thick in her maturing body, that sat in a chair with a pliant grace.

"I'm going to insult you," she said. Her greenish-grey eyes gleamed frostily.

He nodded. But he said, from a distance: "I don't see why."

"You're a lout, an oaf—but more than that, you're a ridiculous mass of vanity and a public fool." She spoke in a sudden contemptuous rush.

"Sounds as though you've been learning it off by heart, Mildred."

She seemed to move rapidly about in the chair, shimmering in brownish silk; the lift of her head was full of malice.

"You think you're cutting a fine figure, don't you, prancing about the place like some savage in war-paint, showing off."

"I've never thought of it in that way," he said, with ironical surprise, watching her curiously. "There is possibly some truth in it."

"Well, that's how you seem to most people. And it shocks us, Tudor, it's—gross."

"You're looking very well tonight, my dear," he said with offensive vagueness.

"Do you want me to go on?" And a small sensual grimace twisted her lips.

"If you feel that you're getting rid of something displeasing to you." He still gazed down at her, standing at the mantelshelf. She might be a beautiful-poised serpent, without fangs. But she rose from the chair, realising the subtle disadvantage of being there, and began to move about the room.

"I'm speaking," she said determinedly, "for your dead mother."

"She seems to have given you something of her life—"

"I'm considering if it's my duty to publish through the place the fact that you hurried her to the grave."

He stared at a plaster bust of Socrates over the book-case. The bulldog face looked as though it had just taken the hemlock. "How you must have loved my mother, Mildred."

She stopped directly in front of him: he could feel the heat of her body.

"I loved you much more," she said, writhing. "Do you think I'm enjoying this, do you think I'm just being venomous, the scorned woman?"

"No. Because you're not a scorned woman. You only misplaced your love."

They stared into each other's eyes. Since they had come into the room he had felt they were almost strangers. But now, as she stood close to him, with that dark stimulated life in her and he gazed into her furious eyes, awareness of her trembled through his body. There was no apathy between them now. He felt the burning ferment of her body, roused in a sombre vitality that had only the *expression* of wrath. His gaze was held fascinated in hers.

She said, with slow goading anger: "We, your friends, think you are mad. And I—I can't bear that public cheapening of yourself, I can't bear the futile wasting of yourself.... Why must you do it, why?"

A lock of her hair was loosened. In wonder he took it and caressed its fine shivering threads.

"Why must you grow hair?" he said with a jeer.

She lifted her fist and struck him on the cheek. Twice. Her face was swollen with blood, her eyes spurted rage. He quivered. A quick ugly emotion was loosened in him. She struck him yet again, clenching her teeth. Her fist was ridiculously without power. But at that third blow his arms swung up, unconsciously, and gripped her.

"Mad," he said roughly—"Which of us is mad? What do you want?" She writhed in his arms. And there, agonisingly, was the old worshipped feel of her body, the beautiful slipping grace he had known in his adolescence.

"You'd insult me—" she said through her teeth.

"More than that!" His voice was hard with contempt at her pretence.

And, dragging her in one arm, he crossed to the door and clicked the catch of the lock. Her head thrown back, her throat pulsing, she made show of struggling. He dragged her back into the room. He was about to lift his free arm to the gas bracket, and then he looked down at her. No. Let the light shine on the job. It would be interesting to see her face: he would not allow her any covering of darkness. He struggled against bursting into the insane laughter that shook him.

It was madness and a grotesque abandonment to a calculating move on her part-hurriedly he knew it. But he would show her. She thought he was to be caught that way, did she? He was incensed by the avidity of the move, and at the same time he burned in a new hate of her. There, crushed in his arm, was the old familiar beauty of her body, that at one time had been the ecstasy of life to him, beautiful as spring, a canticle of flowers and buds and morning. She would come to him in this way, would she? Well, he knew a thing or two better than she.

Under the window was a sofa, in which Elwyn of an evening would recline to read his Boethius or other comforters. As he almost threw this new harsh woman on it, the remembrance flashed through his mind that it was on this same sofa, about fifteen years ago, that Mildred had asked him sedately after a birthday tea-party in what way men were different from women.

The pause cleared his mind; the dangerous hatred began to waver out of him; he began to laugh with a soft silent shaking. He remembered that later they had gone over some Wordsworth poems together, after he had said with embarrassment that he didn't know "for sure".

He looked down at the crouched shape waiting beneath him. He dropped on one knee beside the sofa and thrust a hand roughly across her breast, up to her throat, which he wanted to feel throb between his fingers. He could not see her face, she was crouched, as if in protection of herself, as if to hide her head from whatever might shamefully be done.

"So you're ready at last," he whispered. She did not answer, she remained crouched in that huddle of fear, of self-protectiveness. "When it's too late?" he gave her warning, breathing upon her shoulder. "When we've broken apart—?"

She remained silent. But he could feel her throat leaping and pulsing within his hand; it made no effort to escape the clutch. And again, tormentingly, a sense of her beauty, her remembered beauty, furious with chastity and worshipped in the past, long past, years, ached in him. Ah, why had things gone wrong, gone pitiably wrong?... His head slipped on to her shoulder, he breathed in raw and naked pain, as though some delicate nerve beat exposed. "When we've broken apart," he repeated. "Mildred—"

She turned and began to wind her arms about him. But he felt them like strong and destructive bands about him. He thrust them away, at the same time pressing her further into the sofa. He would not have her arms. "Lie still," he said with sudden ruthlessness.

207

Then, the handle of the door was turned, turned again, and there was a light tap. Bronwen's trembling leaf of a voice asked:

"Mildred, are you there?... The lock's caught or something—"

He rolled on to the floor, and strangled awful laughter squirmed in his shoulders, swelled through his neck. His hands beat soundlessly on the carpet. "Oh God, oh God... deliverance... rescued—"

Mildred writhed up. Her face was shattered, contorted. "Open that door," she hissed in a low voice.

He was struggling to his feet. The lock was rattled again. "Mildred, are you there?" Bronwen called softly.

"Yes, Bronwen," Tudor called, in a loud exultant voice. And, ironically, "What's wrong with the door?" He strode over to it. What did it matter?... Bronwen would understand.

By the time he had opened the door Mildred was sitting in a chair looking remarkably a copy of what she had been in the drawing-room—remote, inaccessible, contemptuous of him.

"You're still here, Tudor." Bronwen was startled for a moment, then looked vaguely pleased, glancing at Mildred. "Well, I'm glad you didn't go, Tudor.... You mustn't take notice of what your father said," she murmured with frail sternness. "He doesn't quite understand.... Mildred, it's been nice to have your company today—she's been so good, Tudor." She peered up at him pathetically as she sank on the sofa, his hand tenderly, and gratefully, at her elbow. "So good and helpful."

Mildred sat silent and subdued; only Tudor saw the flickers of half-choked fire pass through her eyes. Gradually life seemed to leave her; she sagged in crude but quiet disorder in the chair. But presently she rose and said with careful evenness that she'd have to be going.

"You'll come again tomorrow, dear, if you can?" Bronwen pleaded.

"Of course... early." She bent and touched Bronwen's cheek. Her face was heavy and blind, like a stony mask. She hesitated.

"You're such a comfort to me," Bronwen whispered. She

glanced pleadingly at Tudor, who had risen and was standing remotely and apparently unseeing at the fireplace. Mildred waited a moment, then went to the hall to put on her hat and coat. Bronwen began a whispered word to Tudor, then subsided helplessly. From the door Mildred called:

"Well, good-bye." After all, she was accustomed to walking in and out like one of the family. The front door closed softly.

"Oughtn't you to have seen her home, Tudor?"

"No."

Bronwen was silent. But her bowed, aged shoulders lamented; she sat in grievous dissent. For the first time he saw her as very weary, very old. He sat beside her.

"Do you know," she said woefully, "you look very shabby, Tudor, and you're thinner…. You're wearing yourself out, and as for your clothes—" She plucked at his sleeve—the edge was frayed; she peered down at his boots, which were falling to pieces. "Your boots, oh dear. I'm ashamed."

"Of my boots or me?" He put his arm about her sadly limp shoulders. "*You're* not going to treat me like a pariah, are you?"

"What is a pariah?" she asked simply. When he told her she shivered, but shook her head. "I take no notice of that," she grieved. "As long as you feel strong, as long as you're faithful to yourself—" But her voice trailed away in strange dispiritedness. He saw that she was still in the shock of the death.

"Don't give way, Bronwen," he begged, "don't give way. We depend on you…. You must keep Father from… from following her, in that way of his, keep him firmly on earth, Bronwen."

"He's become so religious lately," she lamented, in such simple vexation that he wanted to smile. "Even when a dish of cabbage is put on the table, he's got something to say about it from the Bible."

He began to feel a renewal of life in her. She turned to him directly and pleaded: "Oh, Tudor, why don't you take up with Mildred again?—she'll have you, I know. I'm certain of it, in spite of everything that's happened lately."

This was her blind spot, and he could not lose patience. But he had to turn his head away to hide the contortion of ironical laughter, horrible and fearful, that was forced into his face.

"It's not to be," he said. "There's been such alteration in the life that used to hold us together." He paused to control his voice, to keep out of it the harshness and the anger welling up in him. "It would be laying up some pretty treasures for both of us. Treasures of hell."

She said no more. But after a while she implored: "You'll get yourself a good suit of black, won't you, Tudor? You must look decent in the funeral—I mean decent as to mourning," she quavered.

"Of course, Bronwen." He patted her hand.

"Now, let's get a list of people to write to; you must help me there." She began to bustle. "And the notice for the newspaper.... I won't be able to depend on your father," she grieved; "he's so upset."

"Where is he?"

"He's gone up to sit with her."

Tudor stayed with her until midnight, helping her with arrangements for the funeral. He shook off the dreariness and the melancholy of the tasks, carried along in Bronwen's renewed stream of quiet activity—for, beyond her lamentations, she had the native liking for a funeral.

But he could not shake off the bruised consciousness of being a stranger now in this house. Except for Bronwen he felt he could not connect with its life.... And the awful, sickening attempt to reach Mildred. In that had been the true, real horror of death, of damnation and destruction.

CHAPTER VI

I

BY the end of October all the pits in the valley had ceased work; and the usual holiday spirit that reigns during the first week or so of a strike, sprawled lazily over the place. There was whippet-racing on the mountains, there were gardening and poultry activities, there were wrestling meetings and long, long hours of squatting on heels at street corners. The first taste of liberation was sweet, and in the dwellings scraps left over from the working period were bamboozled into fairish meals, helped by those slices of back garden which still yielded autumnal vegetables. A stretch of fine weather aided too; the days were crystal, the evenings soft with red sunsets, no smoke or coal-dust interfering with the windless green heights and the clear-cut stretches of the valley bed. The mountains seemed amiable shapes drowsy as old grandfathers.

"Chaps," said one old squatting collier comfortably, "is wise to stop still for a while. So as to get used to the long stoppage of the grave."

Some of the dawdling younger men took advantage of the offer of that South African war that was going on in the newspapers, and hopped off over the mountains to see the great big world outside. There was an opportunity for you! A real war with guns and charging horses and kill as many blacks as you like. Better than the boredom of a strike and better, too, than going down under to sweat your guts out for a few bob a week.

The Associated pits had, of course, ceased first. The owners' notice to the men had riled, after the first alarm, like an insult:

211

giving good red-blooded workers notice, indeed! And the activities of the Federation had met with rebuff after rebuff. But the first notice posted at the pit-heads was followed the next week by a second, stating the terms under which the owners were prepared, upon the termination of the month's notice, to allow a resumption of work. A howl of dismay went up. The terms were worse than the original ones over which the men had previously contemplated striking. This was a new mailed-fist blow with a vengeance. There was a certain amount of skulking back into fear.

But in the majority the old bitter resentment was throbbing into fresh life; it swelled over the discussion of mere terms obliteratingly. Useless for old sufferers, mild elderly men, worn by past anxieties, to express their hopelessness; useless for wives to show again their provoking weepy wrath. Elementary grievances were expressed healthily. Who were the pits for—six owners or six thousand men? Were they opened to feed six mouths with roast duck and champagne while six thousand had to make do with the plainest of leek broths? The agitators through the valley had less work over this second notice. In a sudden angry burst of temper the Associated pits men downed tools, leaving the mine a fortnight before the owners' month's notice was up. That last Friday evening everyone seemed to be shaking a black fist at the world.

The following week John Johns's men came out, partly in sympathy and support for their fellow-workers, partly in reply to the promptings of old grievances budding again in the fiery warmth coursing through the valley, and partly in warning against the wobbling price of coal, which was showing a nasty tendency to stick its tongue out at hard-working men. And they came out without consulting John Johns; they came out without any notice, flouting an agreement they had made with Johns after a previous strike.

Johns was an independent man, who made no flashy display of character. He was as solid as a bank safe, as impregnable and as full of riches. People never knew whether to admire and like him or to roundly abuse his apparent soullessness. He paid his men a better average than other employers—remaining outside the Association of Owners, whose men he had encouraged to fight for the abolition of the Sliding Scale. In fact, he had inflamed them to a strike once, declaring that the Scale ought to be abolished. When this strike had happened five years ago, his own pits at Nant Vale did very well indeed: a fortune had been made. For this he had been attacked and reviled at the time: he remained unaffected. Besides being an excellent businessman, having several successful irons in the dark fires of commerce elsewhere, he collected Whistler pictures, being, indeed, one of the first admirers of that artist's work.

So, after all, this desertion by his men was Nemesis scowling on Johns. He had had his strikes in the past, but they had been short-lived ones, and after the last one his men had agreed to serve a six months' notice before another. Now he concentrated on this flouting of the agreement and raged grandly for once; he spoke of prosecutions for the illegal action—about two thousand men were implicated. It was said that detectives attended the agitators' meetings: free speech, in a place much given to it, seemed threatened. The men took further umbrage at that, and one evening at a meeting actually attacked a mild-looking stranger listening from under a bowler hat, who turned out to be a journalist.

Johns, simmering down a little, made a "final" declaration to the men, haughty but with a shrewd personal touch that spoke of his wound, the gnash in the rock:

"So be it. You have struck your foul blow. I make no useless complaints, I merely state my attitude. I have got rid of feelings in this struggle, I shall cease to think of you as men in my care and as honest men with a respect for their word. I and my Company are going to stand firm now: we will fight to the bitter end, the last ditch. You need not send your Federation to us with offers. *We* will dictate terms, when *we* think fit. Meanwhile, as in previous strikes, the Company will provide free meals for the children; they must not suffer for the criminal and evil behaviour of their parents. This is my last word; I repeat that I want no offers from your Federation. Signed, John Johns."

This on a large hand-painted bill pasted at the colliery head. The feeling was:

"Let him keep his bloody soup-kitchens. The last time, my Megan came out in rashes from the meat."

"Men in his care! Now then, and isn't his big pocket in *our* careful care?"

"Evil behaviour! 'Ow the devil talks. He's been baptized again then and took back from where he fell?"

The agitators in their meetings jeered at the poster and made mock of its threatening sternness, pointed out its slight under-whine, and declaimed against the offensive charity of the free meals for the children of degraded men. "Remember the pea-soup that they made in '94? The same peas was kept in a bag and dipped in every day for a month: the children used to say they preferred water, it was cleaner: so don't let them soften you with their silly soup-kitchens," etc., etc.

The Associated Owners allowed themselves an icy grin of satisfaction at the action of Johns's men. It would have been maddening if the troublesome old blighter had reaped a second rich harvest out of his fellow-owners' woes. This was the one fragrant bouquet which arrived at their feet among all the rank missiles thrown at them by a valleyful of invigorated men.

Everyone began to prepare for a long struggle: there was unison on both sides. After the second week of the strike the Associated Owners suspended all negotiations with the men's representatives, shutting up shop completely. To all appearances, it looked as though the end of the century was also going to be the end of local industry. Many families began to wonder if they could return to unruined agricultural districts again and wrest a living from the top of the earth instead of far below it: there was always a hankering for this ancient kind of life. One or two of the more weary families actually slunk off, sick of the perpetual local strife and giving up the ghost.

The doctor's house at the top of the Terraces became a meeting-place for rebels. Idle men hung about there all day reading books, raking over the garden, doing odd jobs. Hannah, the housekeeper—she who had been stitched up after partaking of riots in a previous strike-always had something going in the oven, usually a large dish of stewing meat, potatoes and onions; and Beriah or the doctor would read out passages from Karl Marx.

Twice a week there were the arranged Strike Committee meetings; and at these, as a special treat, a box of cigarettes would be placed on the table. Sometimes there was a certain amount of sinister impatience: some of the younger members were itching to cool their blood. These pretended to be law-abiding in the meetings, but they dropped dark hints of their intentions now and again.

"We've got to try and keep the men out of mischief," Tudor declared, and glanced sharply at some of the faces ranged round the room. "I bet there's plans been made already for troops." Extra policemen had already arrived in the valley.

"Chaps get so tired of playing marbles and top after the first month," Ieuan Mold grinned. An amateur boxer, he felt that a strike called for some use of his best-developed talents.

"And if butchers are daft enough to put joints in their windows, just to tease chaps—well," protested Johnnie Davies. "Last Saturday, now, there was a leg of pork mocking at me out of Sam Clarke's window; I was standing on the corner talking about religion with a butty of mine, and there it was hanging fat and pink as I don't know what. Till a young leddy went in and bought it—that young leddy you used to knock about with, Doctor Morris, daughter of the solicitor. Very bad I felt about it," he admitted, "very bad and warm."

"I know," sighed Tudor, "I know. But smashing up the shops is not going to do us any good, I tell you. Violence of that kind loses us public support and sympathy, which are very valuable."

"They ought to see as we're starving and been driven to riots."

"They won't abide violence," Tudor persisted; "they'll begin to

215

think of their own property as being unsafe.... No, we've got to keep on getting across to the public knowledge of your poverty and the evils of the way you're paid. There's enough of us to make the thing a problem of national importance.... I wish we could get hold of a newspaper," he sighed.

"If this Labour Party gets going properly they ought to start a newspaper and put pictures of us white and thin for all the world to see."

Beriah, prim and mild and oddly flower-like, said sedately: "In a war whole towns are wiped out. We steal in riots, though we don't kill. All the same, we got to show we're civilised."

"The bosses don't act civilised with us."

"For that very reason we got to show 'em they're far back in the Dark Ages."

Most of the gathering sat in doubt of this pronouncement. After a while these moved in favour of a demonstration in the form of a definite act of hostility.

"Else," said one, "the strike'll get as sticky as jam, with the men squashed and drownded like blackberries in it."

Tudor realised that this fear of apathy was healthy. But he could not bring himself to countenance rioting. He remembered Melville's hopeless acquiescence in this activity of the men who moved round him—and his grim acceptance of the punishment that followed his recognition of the rioters' primitive sense of justice. But he could not reach so far himself.

"Well, what do you propose doing?" he asked curiously.

They cogitated: their faces became closed and malicious. One suggested firing a colliery office, another a chapel ruled by that minister who always preached against strikes, another merely that new motor-carriage Sir Rufus Morgan had got himself. Another declared venomously:

"Best to catch the old Rufus himself and—roll him about in a lot of tar one dark night. Another motor he could get, but so stuck-up he is that if he was rolled about, his spirit'd never stand up again."

They glinted, full of roused desire. Only Beriah, Tudor and two others were withdrawn from this discussion. Tudor thumped the table.

"No," he said, "none of that here, boys. I don't say it's criminal—there's a special set of laws for the small revolution that a strike such as this is—but it's damned mad. It's bad in theory, and it's worse in practice because ten to one you'd be clapped into jail. Now, none of that nonsense. We'll fix up the speeches for the mass meeting on Tuesday. Beriah, where's your note-book?"

They drew together, apparently accepting the decree. But there was a secret surge of unmollified spirit in the room. Not for the first time Tudor realised how easily the dangerous atavism of these men could be tapped.

There were frequent public meetings. These were mostly opportunities for oratorical displays. Since the suspension of negotiations with the owners, discussion of terms among the men was futile: nothing could be offered one way or the other. Tudor and his followers confined themselves to wordy efforts to keep the men firm, their determination undispersed into fear because of the tomb-like silence of the owners. John Johns was a great help in this work. In spite of the magnate's haughty washing of his hands, as described on that poster, he was obviously worried. His vexation flowed over into articles in a newspaper, the tenor of which was that the men were merely misguided children who needed a good whipping before coming to their senses. He could not keep his mouth locked, like the Associated Owners, whose dreadful silence had a frightening quality. Perhaps he hoped to coax his own men back earlier and thus reap another fortune. Some of his articles wept tears of blood, in spite of the iron look of the phrases. Like C. P. Meredith, he seemed to be harassed by a certain kind of consciousness of the men. But otherwise he was a man of rock, and he could not give way.

At least, he did not give way for a month. Then he offered a five-per-cent advance over the previous scale, promising at the same time to use "all his influence for the abolition of the Sliding Scale". The agitators had to leap into great activity to combat this. They asked what influence he could have with the other owners, who were his enemies? They mocked at the five per cent as a most niggardly piece of cheese put in the mouse-trap. And, of course, the price of coal would be sure to fall again, kicking the five per cent away in its descent. Oh, didn't Johns have a fine opinion of the men's stupidity! Well, make him see straight for once.

But blacklegs began to slink into the Johns pits, mostly to occupy those jobs necessary to keep the pits in good order so that they would be ready for the general return to work. These jobs would be well paid. The agitators watched this slinking anxiously. By the attitude of the men to these blacklegs their temper could be gauged. So it was with relief that the news came of several attacks one night on the houses of the blacklegs.

One of these attacks proclaimed fury loud as a blast of trumpets. It was on the house and person of Will Maddocks, a dour and miserly foreman of No. 1 pit, a shameless creeper to both Johns and God, always slavering in admiration of the former in the pit, and in chapel calling the attention of the latter to his humility and his purified mind. He had a viperish and childless wife, whose only pride was her houseful of fine furniture, which set her above all the women in her street. But she was known also for the fury with which she attacked a fall from grace of any local girl: during the last revival, not having any sins of her own to confess, she had publicly taken advantage of those belonging to other people, naming names and details. He was burly as an oak, but she was only a slip of a woman, though tough as a leather boot-lace. The house was attacked at midnight by about a dozen silent men with blacked faces: they carried axes and hammers.

They worked swiftly, after crashing through the parlour window. Pitilessly an axe cut through Mrs. Maddocks's fine sideboard: ornaments and pictures were demolished. Everything was done in ten minutes, and the rejoicing neighbours only peered discreetly from behind their window-curtains. While two men worked downstairs, the others rushed up to Maddocks's bedroom, pulled him out of bed. His missis they merely tied to the bedpost, stuffing her mouth with a rag soaked in castor-oil: after a gasp or two she submitted with strange meekness to the men's high-handed behaviour. Though she went stiff when one, in the light of a candlestump, began to smash her toilet-set of Swansea china, and her eyes spat rage. Will was bound with some trouble. He was carried down to the passage where a man on guard at the door waited with a can of green paint. A flannel shirt was torn away, and after whipping him the paint was spattered over Will's body and rubbed into his hair. They went through the house smashing everything possible and then scampered quickly as rats.

Other blacklegs' houses escaped with a large tarring of the word "Scab" on door or concrete. This was accepted as a legitimate measure by everybody, but what had been done in Maddocks's house, reminiscent of the fabled activities of the Scotch Cattle earlier in the century, was criticised with the strikers' tongues in their cheeks. The knowledge that a band of lawless men had begun to prowl about at night made it plain that rioting was again not far off.

The police failed to lay hands on the band, though many people were suspected and watched. Doctor Tudor Morris's house was watched continually: the first day after these attacks it was searched from top to bottom while he was out bringing to birth a daughter for single Gracie Vaughan, who had a passion for those same policemen who were now ferreting her doctor's possessions.

The following day a company of infantry—halfbaked recruits from Norfolk, training to go off to South Africa—was drafted into the valley, camping a short way up the mountain-side.

The arrival of the soldiers sobered some strikers. Others it incensed to deeper malignancy. Such invasions provoked an old, old wrath.

Arriving back from the Gracie Vaughan case in the late afternoon, Tudor found a sergeant waiting for him: Sergeant Roberts, who had arrested him that night in Melville's house.

"Well, Tudor, here I am again," he squeaked out of his ginger moustaches.

Hannah, with a face like thunder and fisted hands, was treading the hearth-rug with short, baulked steps.

"They kept me here," she choked, "they—"

"All right, Hannah," Tudor said quietly.

"You can go now," the sergeant added. "And mind we don't have trouble with you this strike," he warned.

But, unlike her acquaintance in the Terraces, Gracie Vaughan, she hated a policeman. "If there's call for my services on the side of right," she declared wildly, going off, "I got two good fists same as before." The door slammed behind her.

Tudor waited, tightly calm inside, for he presumed this was going to be one of the unjust arrests for incitement to disorder. He gazed round at the study.

"We've had to search your place," the sergeant squeaked, looking in despair at this son of an old friend.

"What for?"

"Ah, don't bandy words with me, Tudor," reproached the sergeant. He shook his head. "My boy," he said sorrowfully, "I said to myself, 'it's a good thing his poor mother went'."

But Tudor's calm did not slink away. He felt oddly exhilarated, certain now of a preposterous arrest. "Well, there was nothing for you to find," he said. "A pity your chaps couldn't put things back where they found them."

The sergeant tapped a bundle of books next to him on the table. "There's these," he said, "I shall have to take these away."

Tudor blinked and began to suspect it was not an arrest after all. "What are they?" he asked coolly, and went over to examine the books. There was the Communist Manifesto and *Das Kapital*, and, oddly, a book of Blake's drawings, a de Maupassant in the original and Baudelaire's *Les Epaves* with the Félicien Rops frontispiece.

"But the Blake!" Tudor exclaimed in astonishment. He treasured the book, which had been expensive.

"They look indecent to me," the sergeant's squeak was stern now, "those pictures. Look at the privates! And they're not medical, any fool can see that. There's these French books too, I shall have to see about them. Very sorry, Tudor, but I got my duty."

Tudor struggled between anger and amusement. A sense of futility swamped him: he realised it was useless to try and defend Blake or the others. But he asked, chattily sitting down: "And if you find what you are searching for in those books, what's going to happen?"

The sergeant gloomily shook his head and peeped at Tudor. "Look here, my boy, I'm talking to you as a father would now. Chuck all this business. The authorities got their eye on you."

"For what?" Tudor asked innocently, knowing that by "the authorities" the sergeant meant the pit owners, with himself as their helpless instrument.

"You know what for," the sergeant blinked and pursed his mouth into a little deprecating "O" under his ginger moustaches, nodding his head meaningly.

"I don't, Sergeant." But he knew this old acquaintance of his father was hinting that the "what for" might easily be found. This house-search was, of course, a first warning.

"Don't you get up and preach mutiny to the chaps?" the sergeant demanded.

"Mutiny! Of course not. I only keep on reminding them what they're striking for. Empty stomachs are apt to make them forget."

"Mutiny can be a wide word, Tudor," he warned.

"It can only cover exactly what it means.... I haven't got a whisky to offer you, Sergeant, these are not times for whiskies, are they? Don't take that Blake book," he asked.

"I'm taking these books," the sergeant squeaked obstinately. "You may get them back or—" he goggled again and nodded— "you may hear further." He rose with importance.

Tudor sighed. "There can't possibly be a charge over these books, so I'll be obliged if you'll see they're returned to me in good condition. Two are valuable."

"All I hope is that I shan't have cause to visit you on another errand, my boy." The sergeant strutted through the surgery. "I've had my say, but next time there'll be no chat, Tudor. So now then." He had attended this boy's christening: his wife had played the piano for his mother at charity concerts.

"I know absolutely nothing about the raids the other night," Tudor said sternly, on the doorstep, "and I haven't the least idea who the men were."

"Maybe not, but those men are of the same kidney as these chaps that hang about your house." His voice squeaked with official anger now. "And we're going to get 'em."

He ambled down the garden, the books tight under his arm. Tudor smoked a cigarette in the study before beginning to tidy the disorder. Hannah was at work upstairs. She stamped down presently.

"Ach, a menagerie been let loose in the house. They locked the door," she foamed, "and shut me in the spare room. P.C. Edwards, that one whose ear I bit in the strike before, was with them, and a shove behind he gave me, the fat pig, 'fore I could get at him. Ach, a few things I called them through the keyhole, and I let out who of them had been at Gracie Vaughan. Black boar-pigs that they are," she stamped.

There was little time, though, to brood over the desecration of his home. By the time he had drunk a quick cup of tea and tidied his books and papers somewhat, the evening surgery began. These days he seemed to have no time for any private life at all, any interior marshalling of his affairs. Evening surgery over he would dash out, and be up and down the valley until late. He was one of a score who ran through the valley with fresh loads of

222

fuel for the bonfires. And since there was little for the strikers to do, there were crowded meetings always, with debates, questions, and occasionally free fights.

Worn out, he usually returned about midnight, sometimes with three or four strikers who lived in bad lodgings and hadn't eaten anything all day—these roamed round the kitchen wolfishly, slept anyhow, and next morning teased and played with the exclaiming Hannah, who, though forty, liked being pulled about schoolgirl fashion. Luckily there was seldom a late or night call out to a patient: everybody in the Terraces, once in bed, stayed there; though callers would pant in sometimes quite early in the morning, just after the usual hour of rising for the day shift, with some long vexed tale of disturbances in the night.

The night of the raid on his house he sat down and wrote to Daisy:

—The vermin swept through the house: every corner is contaminated. True, the place of late has been nothing but a lodging-house for hungry and tired young men, but they at least give it a human smell and scrupulously clean up their own disorder. Hannah is marvellously good-tempered and cooks all day long, but she goes at five o'clock. The place needs a real housekeeper that can live in. I don't ask you to come as my wife any more—I have my pride, and I shall not acknowledge my child since you refuse wedlock to its father—but I think you owe it to me to come here as housekeeper. I offer you a salary of thirty pounds per annum, if you'd prefer to come that way, and all found, everything you need. Our standing, of course, will be the usual one held between British gentleman and attractive domestic, and when the child is born I shall pay all expenses like a Christian. Or not, as you please.

I think you're shocking and selfish, enjoying yourself in Bristol while we're all slaving like niggers here for the glory of God's creatures. Besides letting down the Cause, you're depriving one of its hardest workers of his proper sustenance. You have no soul and less shame.

Hannah loyally did her best with the policemen. But what an opportunity you missed as a wife defending the property and privacies of her husband! Come: there'll probably be others. Come: come Saturday. Don't sit down and think. You know behind your breasts you ought to come—

He felt certain that the police-raid would bring her stampeding to offer what she could of defence and succour: she would surely realise at last that her presence could plunge him no farther into disgrace now. And he was right. She telegraphed the next day to say she was coming on the Saturday.... And the same afternoon a policeman delivered the seized books back at the house, with no comment.

Preparing for her arrival, he made a crafty move. He hired a carriage to convey them together from the station to his house: and he prayed for fine weather, which was granted him. The open landau waited outside the station in a clear grey afternoon. When she stepped out of the train he pounced on her as though they had been married a month.

"At last," he sighed, "at last."

She seemed in splendid condition, like a young woman returning from an expensive holiday at a seaside where there were no cares—only blue skies, golden bays, pierrots. Pink of cheek, excited of eye and glowingly pleased to be coming home to her own kitchen. Ignoring the strike, she had obtained a fresh hat like any woman returning to her native place after an absence: it was a mass of flowers.

"Daisy," he said solemnly, "you look beautiful."

"I feel it," she agreed. "But oh, Tudor, not a carriage in these times!" They were outside the station and he was leading her to the open landau.

"I thought you might be feeling tired after the journey—" She hung back for a moment, then clambered in helplessly, pushed by his arm. Her rusty tin trunk followed her. "All right, Dan," Tudor called, and off they trotted.

She endured the journey with a sedate mien, right through the main street, full of the Saturday crowd. But once she whispered in trouble to Tudor: "They will think us shameless, oh, and worse—" She bowed, with the correct dignity suitable in a landau, to an acquaintance who had craned a neck and opened a mouth. "Making a show of ourselves."

"To-morrow," he said, "we'll announce our wedding."

"It's a comfort," she sighed, "that no one can see I'm any bigger just yet."

Strikers idling about the street grinned after the carriage, women hesitated a step on the pavement to stare at the bowling black basin in which sat those two. A policeman narrowed his eyes, a minister of the Gospel ground his umbrella with feeling into the road and looked avoidingly into the sky, stout Doctor Harris, emerging from a saloon bar, stopped rigidly behind the excrescence of his stomach and then spat. Another policeman gazed malevolently and made a remark to a fellow-officer recently drafted into the district. Altogether it was a triumphantly public progress, and Tudor grinned appreciatively at Daisy as the landau turned into a side street to begin the climb to the Terraces.

"Vulgar but necessary," he said.

"Oh, Tudor, I don't know what to think of it," she lamented.

"Now everybody will expect us to get married," he said.

"I don't know that a carriage-ride means a wedding—" she said, darting him a glance.

She was soon exuberant, however. "Well," she smiled, settling back rosily, "I suppose I ought to be proud of myself—me, so common, being proposed to in a landau by a doctor. It's enough to make my poor parents rise up and stare out of their grave. 'Daisy,' my mother used to shout at me, 'you've got no pride in yourself at all, very doubtful I am if you'll ever marry higher than a navvy or a rag-and-bone man.' Very often she beat me," she added in sombre recollection. "She was a heavy one with the stick."

"You know very well you're not common," he teased. "You're

quite aware of your advantages. Think how you've made me run after you," he sighed, "and kept me waiting and worrying all this time."

She said nothing, but looked pensive. He still felt unsure of her. He wondered if she would see the highhanded gesture of the landau as an attempt to oblige her into submission, surrounding her with a public knowledge of their continued association. But there was still that curious tangle of the proprieties in her mind. He felt she would best be caught while in some high rush of indignation against the world. He complained during the rest of the journey of what he had endured from loneliness, police persecution, and ostracism. And, of course, she began to swell indignantly.

"Why can't they see," she exclaimed, "that you're working for peace on earth and good-will towards men?"

"They get so confused if one doesn't do it through religion, and with all the proper conventions.... What a magnificent hat you've got, Daisy."

"Does it suit me?" she beamed, pleased. "There's eighteen roses under the brim alone."

"I like the bunch of forget-me-nots on the top.... But you're altogether grand. I knew I was quite right to get a landau."

She was now quite in amiable mood. "Extravagance is proper sometimes. To remind ourselves of the things in the world. I spent all I had on this get-up. Get rid of all your money," she added pensively, "and it makes you take a new journey into life."

Hannah had left a late tea spread on the study table, but he had to hurry away soon to take the evening surgery. The shuffling noise of talking people in the waiting-lobby excited her. "Patients!" she exclaimed, her nostrils quivering as though she could smell them.

"I hope you'll learn to help me in odd jobs in the dispensary. I can't afford an assistant."

"The patients don't pay anything during the strike, do they?" she asked, troubled.

"I wouldn't say that," he answered lightly. He wasn't going to have any dangerous economic discussions tonight. "Now make the place cheerful by the time I'm done. I'm not going out tonight, of course—" With a rapid secret smile, he waved his hand at her and hurried into the surgery.

From the study Daisy could hear him talking to the first patient about her anaemia—a dispirited woman's voice kept whining that she could "take no interest in things now". After being compelled to hear while, with great appetite after the journey, she finished off a plate of buns, Daisy moved to the kitchen, finishing a cup of tea there. The patient's voice had oppressed her as it went into detail. How some women suffered, poor things. Finishing her tea, she went upstairs and tried on her hat again, before the mirror on Tudor's dressing-table. And at the same time she murmured a prayer:

"Oh God, keep me healthy!"

The cloud did not last long: she became busy examining the house. She exclaimed to herself in affected indignation when she discovered that no bed had been made up for her: in the spare bed the pillows were used ones, and two men's shirts were flung over the bedstead: those strikers slept there, she supposed. What must Hannah have been thinking about?... But Hannah had been her friend for long.

She sighed over the house. She had really not made up her mind about Tudor. But something deep down had forced her to come here. Things were happening to her. One day she felt she wanted comfort and security, the next she would feel she wanted to travel on a camel over the desert and stay for a while with wild Arabs in their tents.... Going again into the study, she heard another woman uttering woe. She hurried out.

She did not want to hear lamentations just then. Standing in the kitchen again, she felt her flesh was a tissue of living moon-like gold about her. All her body was rich and warm and gleaming. And the knowledge of the child was sweet: it seemed to spread colour over her mind, moon-colours, soft and dim and sleek. Her hands gently rubbed her hips: she would be glad when she was larger, the swelling richer and more definite; she would carry the soft weight in front of her as though it were the golden harvest moon in her arms, big and round and heavy with rich light.

And after all, Tudor was the father. He pleased her, his behaviour in the world was clean, and as a lover he had much charm—oh, very much charm. She loved him. But she wished she could live in a desert with him, or in some remote forest, or by some tropical beach. There was all this dirty local world about them, wrangling and petty persecutions and the pointing of sour people, and strikes and what not …. She gazed wistfully at three saucepans hanging over the sink. And she could smell even here the odour of the dispensary; bottles and packages of stuff to cure the sick, the halt, the palsied…. She heaved a great sigh and shook herself. Ah, wasn't Melville in jail, eating dry black bread? And here she was in a beautiful new home, surely as free as anyone could be in this world.

When Tudor appeared at last she had bathed and changed into a soft terra-cotta dress blotched with yellow at the waist and hem. She came downstairs with bare feet. Her feet were well-shaped as lilies. Her handsome mouth glowed red and a thick rope of hair hung black over her shoulder.

"More glory," he laughed. "You blind me."

"I could hear the women complaining of themselves," she murmured…. "Is it very miserable for you every day in there?" she enquired.

"I don't think of it in that way. It's a job to be done." The lamp was lit, the curtains drawn, the fire sparkled. He drew her to the big red sofa slanted across the hearth-rug. "I thought my lodgers had better not come here to-night."

"And you've got no meetings?"

"Of course not. Not until to-morrow night."

"Are the strikers solid this time? Tell me how you managed to get John Johns's men out—"

He stooped and lifted her feet to the sofa. "How lovely are the feet of the king's daughters," he laughed. "I've never seen such perfection in feet, Daisy."

"They are nice, aren't they?" He was stroking them with the delicate touch celebrated in the Terraces. "I read in the paper about the raid on that blackleg's house," she continued. "You didn't have anything to do with that, did you?"

He shook his head, then leaned down and rested under her breasts. "I can't believe you're here in person yet.... For so long I've lain like this against your ghost."

They were silent for a while, her fingers straying over his face. "The Captain and Mrs. Barnes want to come over soon," she murmured. "He wants to know if he can do anything for the strike."

"He can come and speak at the meetings. And, of course, we need funds, if he can afford to give.... Your heart's as substantial as a grandfather clock, Daisy."

"Mrs. Barnes is worrying about the women."

"I'd like to arrange a mass meeting of them for her, later on." He smiled up between her breasts; her face drooped to him. "Gosh, yes, as long as she wouldn't be too flighty with her ideas."

"Do you think the strike will last until Christmas?"

"Lord, I hope we'll get what we want in another fortnight. As long as the owners can see we're keeping solid and Johns's men keep faithful to us... oh hush, Daisy, you're beginning to make me want to rush out to the meeting."

She pressed his head upon her. "You must keep some of you free for other things," she said at last.

"Why did you keep me waiting all this time?" he reproached. "I've felt unequal, unbalanced. Couldn't you make up your mind whether you wanted me or not?" He had felt the yielding of her mind; he felt the repose, the deep golden calm, in her body.

"It wasn't that. I always wanted you, when I thought of you–" she struggled a little to express herself, "—of you separately. I mean away from everything else, with nobody to say anything, or look or interfere."

"I should have thought Melville had taught you to spurn all those fears."

"He taught me a lot, he taught me to live with freedom." She hesitated, caressing him. "I wasn't afraid for myself, I thought I would bring harm to you—"

"You didn't think I'd be strong enough to break out from my–" he was going to say "environment" and said—"my past, and be successful afterwards."

"I wanted to see," she murmured slowly, "if you would break away on your own, without any... any influence from me, for a reason that had nothing to do with me."

"But of course you were mixed up in my reasons—"

"Didn't you break away from your family and from that Miss Mildred because you wanted to be one of the common people and work for them?"

"Oh, Daisy," he laughed tenderly, "you put it romantically.... I saw a job of work at which I might be able to assist, just the same as I would be able to assist at the amputation of a poisoned limb, or a cure for gall-stones. To put it like a book, I felt I could help to improve the lot of the workpeople here."

But she said: "There's more in it than that."

"Your body," he murmured blissfully, "smells like a young tree after rain."

"Something in you had to be satisfied," she said in an odd visionary way, which at the same time suggested strain; "something born in you that came from God knows where. Your heart has... has tenderness for the people."

"Indignation and anger," he said, squirming slightly from the feminity of her estimate. "And, after all, I've got their blood in me. My grandmother was a peasant girl seduced by the son of the squire of these parts, before there were collieries. Just like a drama in a theatre—though she did it deliberately, it seems, and he was in love with her and they would have married if he hadn't died."

"A nice woman your grandmother looks," she said with approval and respect. "I used to see her in the streets."

230

"Come to think of it," he mused, "you and she are rather alike in character and personality. You must meet her soon. She's been very faithful to me," he sighed, "very understanding."

"And the Miss Mildred?" Daisy asked, sounding a little mournful, even slightly ashamed.

His body hardened on her: he was silent for a minute.

"This had to be," he said, sullenly it seemed. He did not see Daisy's face become troubled, uncertain, the gleam of contentment, that covered it like a golden patina, fading.

"But you're still troubled about her," she murmured, "you haven't broken free of her yet."

"Yes, it's all finished now," he said. But gloomily.

"I don't know—"

He jumped up and looked into her face. "*You* don't know, of course. But I know." But he was nervous of the dark uneasiness in her face. "Why did you mention her name at all," he exclaimed—"tonight?" He conveyed that she had been unpleasantly tactless.

"Oh," Daisy said interestedly, watching him, "you're very touchy about her, aren't you?... Do you still really want to go to bed with her, then?" she asked, in a carefully ordinary way, as though enquiring if he wished for pickles with his supper.

He ground his teeth. "No." And at the same time he was resentful at what he considered was a strain of stupidity in her— this too simple and direct explanation of the disorder with Mildred.

"What are you upset about, then?"

"Don't you understand that I can be conscious of her, of what she is suffering, apparently through my behaviour—"

"So you haven't broken out really," she said, almost in triumph. She remembered her doubts.

Exasperated, he cried: "You speak as though it can be done as quickly as jumping off a house-top. It can, of course. But most people would limp about for a while afterwards—"

"Or even break their backs," she said suspiciously.

231

He sat again beside her, gripping her arm. "Well, I've not broken my spine. But I'm left with a few aches and pains. Which you've got to help cure.... No more now, no more looking back."

But she persisted, gently though: "One of the reasons why I kept in Bristol was that I didn't want to stand in your Mildred's way. I thought to myself, well, he might be only attracted to me after... after a fashion, and only *think* it's true love—" She paused, made an effort and then said with modesty, "—mistaking all that fun we had that night, before the policeman came in, mistaking it for true love. So I thought that if I went away your Miss Mildred would stand a chance, and if she had the power over you she ought to have, then she could take advantage of it unmolested by me."

"I kept on writing to you, I came to see you—"

"The fight," she said with sedate and doleful heaviness, "could only be settled by time and separation."

"You asked for a child!" he reminded her suddenly. "Why, when you were suspicious that Mildred still had power and I might marry her?"

"I wanted something to remember you by, in case—"

Delighted laughter broke from him. Caressing her, he laughed into her flesh, mounting to a crescendo of shaken passion. Not quite recovered from her fears that her doubts of him were going to be justified, she remained a little subdued at first. Soon, however, she was replying with her own rich splendour. It occurred to each then that life without the other would be impossible, that life was only to be borne while they could partake of this bliss off the other's presence. And Daisy told him so, convinced now of the truth of this intoxication.

"Though, of course," she added dreamily, "there's much more than this in life.... But it's what one remembers and lives by, even when one is grown old and awful."

"Never awful," he whispered. "Never awful."

She was warm and living and beautiful, lying pensive on the sofa. The whole house was full of her golden light. "We must get married as soon as possible," he said. "I'll go down to the registry office to-morrow."

She nodded, comfortable and coiled into a rich current of life that nothing now could wholly disturb. She dozed for a while before the fire while he went into the kitchen and prepared a supper.

And searching for things, mechanically he began to think of that night's mass meeting. Ieuan Mold, the boxer, was going to be the chief speaker, for the first time. Tudor, placing slices of home-cured ham in the frying-pan, wondered how he had got on. Ieuan remained a bad boxer because, as rounds increased, his vision was apt to be drowned in ill-temper, his mind swamped in personal resentment. He had been cautioned to be careful what he said in his long speech. Breaking eggs into the boiling fat, Tudor repeated to himself that Ieuan had probably been one of the raiders of that blackleg's house: the suspicion had been nagging at his mind for days.

The strike, the strike. The gods grant that it would be successful. He wanted to begin this new life of his with a flourish of complete triumph. There was this excellent handsome woman, and there was this grave passionate battle. His life was compounded of both, and the one had given a portion of triumph.... But he had been aware lately of a spasm of fear about the other, deep in him, and hitherto not admitted into his mind. It had prowled within him when he sat quietly brooding on the strike, and angrily he had refused it entrance.

And there it was now edging the soft golden glow of triumph with a ragged darkness. The strike was doomed to failure, like many another. He struggled against the thought, and in the process his hand became clumsy, so that he broke one of the frying eggs while trying to turn it. Irritated, he frowned into the seething pan.... And what if it failed, after all their efforts, their sweat, their starvation! Surely something would have been expressed, if it was only another clamant statement of the disreputableness of the world.

233

Starvation! he thought, turning out the odorous panful. Well, there wasn't another egg, and these were supposed to be for breakfast. And he hadn't dared to look into his bank balance lately. But Daisy, he knew, wouldn't mind poverty. She would flourish in poverty almost as well as in riches: she had the rare inner wealth that made the possession of cash, or the lack of it, look a mere accident of no consequence to the true business of living.

He took the trayful into the study. Besides the ham and eggs there were bread and cheese and beer: after all, he muttered to himself, knowing what meagre meals were being eaten elsewhere, after all this was a special night of celebrations. But Daisy, drowsy and warm before the fire and rising to the tray with slow animal grace, had no such qualms. She exclaimed in delight over the ham and eggs and took her plate eagerly: she even asked if he had any Worcester sauce.

He shook his head. "I know there's no sauce."

"It's delicious as it is," she said truthfully.

Afterwards she took the tray back and washed up. She sang quietly to herself in a rather musicless voice that seemed to have no consciousness of anything but the contented warmth of the body out of which it came: it was a little hymn of the flesh intended for the vocalist's own ears. But Tudor could hear it, sitting in the study with the door open and idly turning over the pages of Shelley. And a treacherous feeling of resentment visited him. Was she *too* complete, too victorious in herself, too *animal*! That refusal to enter into competition with Mildred, that retirement to Bristol—were they just grand gestures of indifference? Even the need for a child, just the animal promptings of her own flesh without regard to the supplier. There she was, squawking her complacent little song, happy as some gorgeous but mindless bird.

But when she returned, still drowsy-looking and her eyes darkly golden, full of her deep rich power that seemed taken wholly from the earth, he smiled to himself. Of course, she was complete in herself and rightly so. Some soiled grey beam from the shabby past had played into his mind for a moment, shot from the dark corner which had given residence to the sickly expectations of Mildred, the demands, the rigid ritual of worship, the strict adherence to lovers' rules as recognised by old Mother Morality.

This woman would not require a damnable absorption in her, or tributes, or a spreading out of his mind for her inspection. She would not watch and pounce; neither would she hide herself in wounded silences and weep. She required a certain amount out of life, but she would not greedily concentrate on a man and expect him to plunder Heaven for her sake. She would walk in her own sunlight and enjoy the earth from her own awareness of it.

Still smiling secretly to himself, he said: "I have never asked you the usual question."

And she was still absorbed in herself, vaguely tidying the room, yawning, her hair black as sleep about her drowsy face. "What is that, Tudor?"

"Do you love me?"

She laughed, liquidly and opulently, understanding him. "Love seems so silly for grown-ups to talk about."

"Yes, talking about it does make it seem thin and feeble," he laughed with her.

"Worrying about love," she said, looking at the clock, "kills it."

"You'd better go and get ready," he said, waving the Shelley towards the ceiling. "I'll read a few of these poems for a while."

"Is the milk delivered in time for breakfast? I've upset that cupful in the kitchen."

"Yes. . . . Two or three of those boys might come in for breakfast, such as it is."

"It'll be nice," she said, beginning to go, "to talk to some of the boys again." She turned in the doorway. "Every night," she said soberly, "I sit quiet for a while and think of Melville. I send him my thoughts."

"Let's hope he gets them," he said, darkening, "lying on his hard bed." He did not quite like this reminder of prison just then.

After a few minutes he followed her upstairs; Shelley had seemed unexpectedly thin. He caught a glimpse of her before she was conscious of his arrival in the open doorway of the bedroom. She was sitting nude on a stool before the dressing-table, a hand-mirror lifted so that she could obtain a double reflection of herself in the larger oval. Two candles burned on either side of her. She was admiring her body, and he did likewise, in a flash of sweet pain–the pale golden tint of her body, her breasts like crushed bunches of roses, her belly announcing itself like a full rising moon, her legs of the soft radiance of corn. Advancing into the room, he asked, his voice sparkling with pleasure:

"What is truth, Daisy?"

The golden image moved out of the hand-mirror as she put it down. "Ah, that I can't tell you," she said.

"Why?"

III

November cold and rain made the Terraces miserable. Stocks of coal were finishing and what is a collier's kitchen without a fat fire? Pantries were stark as the cemetery chapel, and what is a collier's stomach when it is fed on pap? A place of disorder. There were private squabbles, and there were fights which developed into public battles.

One of these battles was begun by Ellie Hopkins, a strong blonde not long married, who ran out of her house one morning screaming and spitting out teeth. She was pursued by her husband Trevor, muscular and dumpy as a sack of potatoes, but very agile. Outside he caught her a blow which sent her, legs and arms outflung, against the cobbles. It was late morning, just before the children were due from school, and a rough air came down from the mountains in hefty shoves. Trevor's face was a sticky mass of blood; he had been scratched again and again with a metal comb during the struggle inside, which the neighbours had heard but accepted philosophically.

Mrs. Edwards, two doors up, fetching the single paltry egg her three remaining hens had laid between them, let out a savage yell when she saw that blow. So infuriated was she that she threw the egg at Trevor with surprising accuracy, so that the yolk mingled with the blood on his face. He reached her with one jump, his fist landed under her eye and she went over. Ellie, however, was crouching up by this time and she gripped his leg and brought him down smartly on his back.

She stamped her heel into his mouth: there was a click of smashing teeth. Mrs. Edwards had also bounced up, like a ball, and began to aid her neighbour, who had the day before given her a spoonful of tea; she stamped into the hooligan's belly. Strangely, the powerful Trevor did not attempt to rise for a few moments; he only groaned and muttered. Doors were being flung open; people streamed out into the alley between the poultry coops and the long black streak of dwellings. The two women had not ceased to scream, with long high cries that seemed to have something strangely entreating in them. And other women took up the scream; it passed from mouth to mouth and blended in an accumulating shriek that reached beyond the Terrace concerned and was taken up, silently at first, by the women of the other Terraces above and below. There was a rapid rush out of doors, a quick torrent of bodies seethed in the alleys. Men smelt the air as if the scent of blood was already evident.

"Those soldiers it is," someone bellowed, "they've 'tacked someone."

There was a swarming to and fro: the battle began. There were always private grievances to settle; personal disputes, insults and gossip to be avenged at the first opportunity. The shrieks of the women, a barbaric hymn rising vengefully above the grunts and barks of the men, rose to the mountains—and descended to the bed of the valley, where the police station listened. The Terraces were at it again, and this time unfed insides gave the battle a hungry fury.

Brooms were brought into use, scrubbing-brushes and shovels. A man would see a relation by blood or marriage attacked and rush with loud bellows to assistance. Women found active expression for their long haggling with existence. Meg Pratt thrust her wide jaw under a neighbour's nose as it came out, late and nervous, from a door.

"You come out, Sally Morgan," Meg yelled. "Frightened are you—" she thrust back the door with a rude fist. "What's that you said to Mrs. Evans this morning, eh–'bout my washing on the line? *Cat's lick*, was it, eh? Well, how's that for a cat's lick, then? See! And that." She pounded the woman's face with her red fists.

"Ben!" howled Sally Morgan, "Ben!"

There was a sound of thumping feet on the staircase inside. Ben appeared, wearing only a shirt. Of a torpid nature, he had been trying to make up his mind whether to come down from bed to see what all the row was about. His wife's cry had a peculiar effect on him; his body began to move as if alive. He thumped down the stairs, his large fleshy face puce with roused blood.

"What now, what now?" he enquired. When he saw Meg give yet another blow, he heaved to the doorway, took the neighbour by her hair and with a single tug brought her to the floor.

"Tom!" screamed Meg, "Tom!"

And in a moment or two Tom, tall and firm as a lamppost, had dived into the little lobby where his wife had fallen. A swarm of followers, attracted from one dispute to another, became wedged in the doorway. Tom swung his nailed boot into Ben's all but bare backside and sent him flying into the kitchen. He jumped over Sally and was followed by the others. They smashed up the kitchen, tore off Ben's shirt and beat him with a cane, snatched from its place behind a picture of Mr. Gladstone: Ben Morgan

238

wasn't liked on the whole, being bumptious in his inertia and sullen. Moreover, it was said that he was a wife-beater without reason.

"Some of your own medicine," roared Tom, lashing down. "You black-bottomed ape."

"It's blue he is," said an onlooker with interested observation, "blue-bottomed, the tyke."

The fracas had lasted half an hour before the police arrived. One went to the school with an order to hold back the Terrace children until the coast was clear. The police plunged bravely into the alleys with truncheons drawn: their presence gave a fresh impetus to the fighting which was already dying for want of real hatred, nerves and irritability becoming assuaged. The arrival of true enemies was a godsend to those almost professional fighters who gave the Terraces its notoriety. But the majority of the people took fright at the charging policemen and scuttled back into their dwellings, locking and barring doors, so the lawless fighters, to their fury, were left in the lurch.

They did not flinch. Invaders had arrived who had to be met. Harry Bowen, himself a wrestler, tufted with red hair sharp as wire, knocked out four policemen before another sprang from behind a pigeon-coop and split open his head with a truncheon: Harry sank to his knees with a roar and the truncheon thudded on his head again and again, crackingly. Harry's eyes flickered like candle-flames and he went over. He was never the same man again; after coming out of prison he was quite simple and would sit in the back pew of a chapel with tears running over the great yellow pouches of his face.

About a dozen policemen were laid out, silent or moaning, on the cobbles of the alley-ways. But all the fighters were overcome and, to the shrill lamentations of wives, were borne off. Alice Saunders made a hungry attempt to secure her sagging Ernie from the arms of the last P.C.—for they had not long been married—the other policemen being afar at the time.

She received a blow that dashed her against the wall, but

immediately a bunch of watching women darted out and tore with frenzy at the constable. He dropped Ernie and screamed for help; his face was scratched raw of skin; he couldn't get at his whistle. The police at the far end of the alley dashed down, and four faithful women, all connected with Ernie, were taken off.

It was said that no adult person of active age was without some kind of bruise or disfigurement in the Terraces that afternoon. A black eye was a commonplace, doubled in many faces. Many were in various states of coma; there were broken noses, torn ears and bleeding gums. Yet there wasn't a single call for the services of Doctor Tudor Morris: a deep silence lay over the Terraces and there was scarcely a movement in the alleys except from some thin hen or a woman moving quickly from her door to a neighbour's with advice or a tin of ointment.

Tudor had been visiting an odd patient at the far end of the vale at the time of the fracas. When he returned he found Daisy looking irritable and sombre as she stirred a stew for their dinner.

"No patients, Daisy? I ran back when I heard there'd been a row."

"No one's been," she said angrily.

"I heard there was a murder being done." He looked at her with suspicion. "I'll go down after dinner. They're probably too cautious to come out, with the police about…. You didn't go out to it, Daisy?"

"No," she answered, still making efforts at control, "I had to damn well remember I'm a lady now." Like a child suffering, she looked at him sulkily. "I watched from the gate; I saw a policeman hit a woman," she said, with rising passion.

"I don't know what the row was about—" he said doubtfully.

"The police seemed only too glad to show their might, I could tell. One could see they were spiteful."

She went about setting the meal in mortification. "Why can't life have some sort of meaning here?" she exclaimed.

"People are chained together like slaves, they're chucked

together in heaps.... That battle this morning, it was only natural, seems to me."

"Yes. . . . And their resentment's got to come out somehow, even if it's only vented on their own folk." He watched her. "Still, you keep quiet. You can't go running into danger."

"I had to go out and be near them," she said in indignation–"but I stayed at the gate.... Oh, if you had heard the screaming. It—it did something to the blood, Tudor."

"The jungle is at everybody's gate." He sat down to the stew. "You've picked the last of the chrysanthemums," he remarked, looking at the wind-blown claret-and-yellow flowers.

"That's what I was doing when the first yell came."

After dinner he went into the Terraces, calling at the house of Matt Lewis, who was a member of the Strike Committee. Both of Matt's eyes were slunk back amid bluish swellings, but his wife, Nellie, had escaped with minor scratches. Tudor had only been admitted after a long silence, no one answering his knock. All the alleys were empty, the children having been bundled back to school after their cut-short dinner hour. Matt was disposed to blame the presence of the military camped on the hillside.

"It put ideas of fight into people's heads," he said darkly. "They don't like it and you've only got to strike a match for them to go off bang."

Nellie was full of baleful triumph. "A chance I had," she declared, "to get at that Sarah Matthews what insulted me in the train Sunday-school outing in August."

"Hold your mouth, woman," growled Matt, ashamed. "This business is more serious than your silly squabbles." He turned back gloomily to Tudor. "It's the waste it is that's bad. Fighting for nothing, just a fight!"

"Yes," Tudor brooded, "things are getting to a dangerous pitch. We've got to do something, Matt. The mass meetings are not enough now. We've got to give the men something to do."

"Aye, but what? There's this football and the whippet racing—"

Tudor leaned towards Matt, though inside he squirmed from

241

the question he asked: "Do you think the men are weakening about the strike?" He was almost afraid to ask.

Matt's eyes disappeared altogether in the swellings.

"Aye," he muttered shamefacedly, "aye, I do.... It's the way the owners won't say anything that frightens 'em. They're frightened of losing the bloody pits altogether; they don't think how the owners stand to lose much more than themselves."

"We've got to try and get the strike spread all over the county," Tudor exclaimed. "It's a bad influence for the men to feel that collieries over the mountains are working full-speed.... We've got sympathy over in the other valleys, haven't we?"

"Except in the places that we wouldn't sympathise with when *they* had strikes."

"I'll call a committee meeting for tonight." Tudor paced restlessly up and down. The prospect of failure shook his stomach like a nausea. "Hell, we've got to do something more." But he turned with a despairing gesture to Matt. "It's the *clumsiness* of the strike that'll finish us, if we're not careful. Bits of strikes are no good. We've got to have a powerful trade union, every man in. Why hasn't this been done before!" he exclaimed in futile vexation.

"This is a beginning of it," Matt said, his eyes beginning to appear again. "The men are getting better eddicated now, a bit. Before, they couldn't see beyond their own garden wall; they didn't realise there was a world full of workpeople who could help one another."

"What went into this fighting today," Tudor said, "has got to be used properly."

At the meeting that night in his house he suggested that bands of crusaders be formed to journey into the other valleys beyond the mountains. Beriah thought it a good idea. All agreed that feeling locally had become unwieldy and beyond calculation. Something new was needed to direct the men's minds.

"About two hundred men in each band," Tudor added, eagerly; "they can meet the workers at the pit heads as they come out.

There must be two or three good speakers in each band."

"There'll be fights," Ieuan said, pensively. "The owners over there will have their creepers."

A map was drawn. There were about twenty-five districts to be visited; some were ruled out as impossible, owing to bitter enmity arising because of lack of local support during a previous strike.

"But we'll take a smack even at them," Ieuan declared; "I know there's plenty of chaps as will be glad of the chance." Ieuan thought of all crusades in terms of fisticuffs.

Each of the committee of fifteen was by now an experienced speaker in the popular local manner—passionate, obstinate, religious, with words that stampeded like the hooves of bulls: each had plenty of followers. It was decided to hold eight meetings the following evening at various parts of the valley, at which men would be invited to enlist their services.

Tudor knew there would be clashes, not confined to wordy exchanges. He remembered the marauding raids of past ages, tribe fighting against tribe, swooping down from the mountains. But this would be fighting with a difference. They were raiding, not to steal their neighbours' goods, but to oblige them into participation in a common battle against economic injustice. Many could be bullied by words. But others had to be clouted into awareness: the old methods, regretfully, had still to be used.

Daisy brought in cups of tea and pieces of bread and butter. The men treated her with elaborate courtesy now that she was married to the doctor. For them her fame was rapidly establishing itself into a respectable memory of a good-looking woman who tossed her head over petty gossip and stepped with careless dignity into marriage with an independent young man.

Beriah said, delicately sipping the tea out of his saucer: "Well, Mrs. Doctor Morris, your brother Melville will soon be with us again. We must give him a welcome home. A little party or something."

She sank between Ieuan and Noah Daniels on the sofa; they grinned with pleasure at her. "A mass meeting for him to address is what he'd like. I'm praying this strike will be on when he comes out—unless the men win, of course. The last one failing gave him belly-ache for a month and I had to feed him on boiled rice and steamed fish. A fact! The nerves of his stomach break when the men are defeated."

Beriah shook his head with dismal sympathy. "It's the strain. He takes our trouble to heart too much."

"But a good fighter," Ieuan said. "Never giving way."

They ate of the bread and butter with hearty appetite. Afterwards, Noah, who had a prize voice, sang mournful songs in a fierce bass, accompanied by Ieuan, who could play the piano as well as box.

"Twenty-six chaps," Matt said greyly, "was taken up in this morning's fight." By now he was very black about the eyes. "And nothing gained."

Noah sang a hymn. Afterwards Beriah said, "I heard today that the Home Secretary has telegraphed authority for action by the military if it's needed." His frail white face was deprecating.

"Rifles!" jeered Ieuan, looking at his fists, "and bayonets. Well, well."

IV

To go out shopping in the main street could have been a trial for Daisy. She did not allow it to be; she would not be vexed by the hostility and criticism aimed at her. In the shops the middle-class drew away from proximity with her skirts, and the peculiarly powerful talent women can exercise on behalf of their outraged sense of virtue, was directed against her in full strength. Marriage at a register office made no difference; everyone knew she was morally unstable and had helped to degrade a son of one of the best families in the place. Her pregnancy, which was becoming obvious, was dated accurately, too.

At last ostracism reached the point of a woman who owned a

fruit-shop refusing to sell her a pound of **apples**. This shop was favoured by the upper-class of the place and its owner, a spinster called Jane Jenkins, was very active in her chapel. Daisy had entered, wearing the Bristol finery, with which by now the valley people had become very familiar, and, pointing to the basket of apples in the window, asked placidly:

"A pound of those, Miss Jenkins, please."

Miss Jenkins continued to be busy with her daybook: her lips were thrust up under her nostrils. Her face altogether had a punched, flat look, grey and unconnected with life. But she had obstinacy within her own miniature orbit; the foreclosed dun obstinacy of a spinster. Daisy looked thoughtfully at a sack of parsnips in a corner. After a long silence, golden lights beginning to dance in her eyes, she repeated her order. Miss Jenkins closed her ledger with a snap and said:

"They're all sold; all the apples are sold."

"What! You've been busy. And in strike-time, too! Well, those oranges then—"

"They're sold. Everything's sold." Miss Jenkins angrily snatched a pound weight off the scales and banged it on the counter. She was flushingly pondering whether her hint would be broad enough, when Daisy stretched her arm and unhooked a pineapple, one of a fine row marked 2s. 6d. hanging from a shelf. An extravagance for these days, but still....

"Leave my pineapples alone!" breathed Miss Jenkins. But Daisy, opulent and with exaggerated empress gestures, plucked a paper bag off a batch and inserted the pineapple. She opened her purse and laid half a crown on the counter, smiling wickedly.

"You can't be selling many of these pineapples in a strike." She leaned over the counter. She felt that with one sweep of her arm she could annihilate the mousy-grey little woman who was shrinking back now as though from a jungle beast.

"I'll... I'll call policeman," stuttered Miss Jenkins. A sickly flush of fear jumped in her face. She shrank farther back, against some baskets of fruit.

The warm, sparkling woman the other side of the counter leaned farther over, and to Miss Jenkins her smile was full of sensual menace. Was this going to be an assault? The palpitating fruiterer, dimly glaring back with sick hate, felt her knees slink into water. She could not turn and run, she could not scream, she could only pray that a customer would come in and rescue her from those baleful eyes opposite her, that glittering smile.

Daisy drew back, easing her swelling bosom with a laugh. No, the poor little thing was too easy, too defenceless. In a light, gracious way, dropping the pineapple into her basket, she said:

"You mustn't be rude, you know, Miss Jenkins."

Outside, in the idle dismal street, she gave a brief snort. But she was upset too, in an indignant kind of way. Upset not for herself, but for Tudor. That was the kind of malicious resentment he would have to put up with, too. She knew that if she told him of such occurrences he would only laugh. But, because she could not bear the insult to their love thrown by these people, she did not believe in his laugh: it was only a defence. For herself, she felt that personal ostracism did not matter.

She did not tell him of the little affair in the fruitshop, or that she was obliged to buy fruit and vegetables in a distant back-street parlour transformed into an amateur shop. In any case he was very busy, what with Terraces patients and meetings and organising these raids into other valleys over the mountains. She decided that what time they had together was to be devoted to refreshment from the behaviour of the extraneous world, to escape to what she considered women were best fitted for this side of Heaven. So she would chatter about nothing in particular, and flirt with him, and flaunt herself and do what she could to make herself look freshly beautiful, knotting her hair in new ways, painting her face and generally amusing him—as well as herself.

But she was aware of fear. Secretly, she still felt at its mercy. She would never admit the shock she had felt when those policemen tramped into her room and they had all been taken off to cells. The world had such ugly strength, such right to pounce upon one's soul. She had moods of quiet secret terror, alone in the house Tudor out with patients or—worse—at some activity; connected with the strike. Then the child within her seemed to stir in fear too.

Of course that ring of the door-bell was only a professional enquiry for Tudor: it could not be a policeman come to arrest him; why was she breaking into a sweat? And in the street, when a group of respectable middle-class women would stiffen into hostile silence as she passed, why was she so foolish as to think that one of them would strike her with an umbrella or switch a parcel swiftly into her face? She was not aware of the opulence of her own walking of the streets. But she had to force herself protectively to an appearance of flaunting.

Once, at a draper's, she came face to face with Mildred. Coming round a stack of towelling, there was the girl walking into her. For a moment or two the treacherous terror gripped her again; there seemed a dangerous cat-like prowl in Mildred's walk, a focused threat in her greenish eyes. Such women as Mildred had power, the power of law and order and stony morality: if she stood there now and opened her mouth in educated denunciation, the sympathy and support of the women scattered about the shop would be with her. Daisy unconsciously stiffened her shoulders; her face hardened arrogantly. But Mildred swept past her, the prowl a little hastened. All the same, out of her came rays of contempt and hatred; the greenish eyes shot out annihilation. Daisy shivered.

Tudor asked her once anxiously: "Are things comfortable for you when you go out?"

She made a slight grimace of amusement. "Sometimes quite a little adventure it is. The colliers' wives don't mind me much. But the others usually take a step back, for me to go past without touching them."

"You'd carry that off all right, I'm sure." But he looked at her searchingly.

"Well, I try to," she said with a wry smile.

He put an arm about her. "You don't allow them to do anything to you?"

"What could they do?" she asked, restlessly.

"Upset your mind in some way . . . offend you. I thought I've caught you looking worried sometimes."

She sat down, hesitated, rubbing her knee with a new nervous movement. "I'm not worried about them, taken one by one, but–" she struggled "—I don't like a *mass* of feeling against me... us. I expect it's because of the child, a foolish fancy—" He was kneeling beside her, taking her nervous hand from her knee. "But I think sometimes that a mass of nasty feeling has power to do harm, like a lot of witches going round somebody's image in clay and sticking needles into it—"

He caressed her. "Come now, witches. You, so matter of fact as a rule!" But he was troubled: he knew about the occult power of massed hate.

She laughed, twirling a finger in his hair. "I know. When they look at me as if I'm an evil on the face of the earth, I strip 'em naked in my mind and I always find them wanting, and comic, and ugly-ugly, ugly."

"That's the way. Even if it's exaggerated."

She pressed his head into her flesh. "And I get conceited," she went on, "knowing that somehow I've got a bit of the grace of God in me—even if it's a black kind of grace," she added with laughter, "not white and shiny and holy-holy, like women who want to be heaven's angels before the proper time."

He smiled into her body, knowing she was thinking of Mildred.

"Have you run into Mildred yet?" he asked.

She had reached calm now; the deep golden calm that seemed her true country, where, if she were allowed, she might rest for ever. "Yes, we met face to face."

"She was quite stony, I expect."

"She hurried round me like an offended cat...." She moved uneasily again, as her voice became full of oppressed commiseration. "She looks as though she has bad dreams, Tudor.

I hope she finds someone to marry soon," she added heavily. "Some good vicar, I should fancy for her, or some nice home-loving chap that sits about and behaves himself."

"Mildred's more complicated than that," he protested. "At heart she needs someone to do battle with. Only she'd want to be triumphant always: she's a devourer."

Daisy did not follow him now. But she sat in female lamentation for one of her sisters who seemed to have mismanaged her life and looked like being left on the shelf....

"I wish we could all be friendly," she sighed.

"I must take an evening off soon, and we'll go up to see Grannie Bronwen."

"Do you think she'll like me?" she asked anxiously.

"Certain to.... She judges people by the quality within them, not by the stale old bits of the world they bring with them."

"I'd like to go and see her," she said. "I feel I want to know a nice old woman."

Again, in these moments of quiet contact with her, he became aware of her anxiety and fear. He had to leave her so much lately, becoming more and more involved with the strikers and in that dark racial fight in which individuality and personal issues were obliterated. When he returned to the house late at night and walked into the quiet lamp-lit room where Daisy sat waiting, it was as though he came back to himself with a shock, a swimming back into a consciousness which he had left for long. She would ask quietly about the evening's activities, moving about preparing a meal, and gradually he would become very aware of the golden warmth of her movements, her voice—so evenly controlled, but moving with the deep passionate movements of the sea. And her presence would seem to him like a refreshing slumber in which he lay embracing a loved body.

But until lately he had never associated fear with her. She seemed to stand so proudly within her own clear light. Not until tonight, when he had questioned and she had spoken of massed feeling assessed against her, had he imagined her terrorised by loneliness and apprehension of the world. He wondered if her fear was due entirely to the child. Or had his going out from her in this impersonal conflict with the world made him deficient, left *her* deficient, in these first few weeks of their marriage.

"Are you worried at being left alone so much?" he asked.

"No," she said, too easily.

"I've got to go out—be concerned in other things," he said pleadingly. "The strike has reached a dangerous state."

"It mustn't be lost," she said.

He clung to her. "Are you satisfied with me, so far?"

"I try not to be greedy," she said; "not to expect a man to build his world round me."

He kissed her hands in gratitude. "And you don't mind the poverty?"

"That's nothing. I'm well off now, compared to some of the times I've gone through, as you know."

"But this haggling mustn't last for ever," he said desperately. "We've got a right to expect some of the world's treasures. Don't be *too* noble, Daisy, too sacrificial. Demand things of life."

"We've got each other," she said with an odd vague slip into sentimentality.

"That's not enough," he said, restless now. "We've got to connect up with life outside us. We're not born to go grubbing about only in ourselves."

She considered, looking literal. "What do you want me to do? Come fighting with you?"

"Not to be at the mercy of the world by isolating yourself in fear up here," he said with slow pleading. "Don't think of yourself as a woman who has committed a wrong act in marrying me and who must fight inside herself for confidence to make it successful. *Be* a triumph, Daisy, be conceited and vain and flaunt yourself like a peacock out in the world."

"I *do* try and flaunt myself, and it's you sound afraid!" she cried.

"I *am* afraid that they can hurt you."

For a while she was silent. Then she said with slow deep calm: "No, they won't hurt me."

"Sure?"

"Yes." Again the deep calm rested about her.

"And you won't mind me forgetting you, going away with the men?"

"Not if you come back and forget them for a while."

He kissed her and made love to her for the rest of the time that remained before sleep, paying her extravagant high-flown compliments, comparing her to this and that beautiful object of this world. He was amusing and indecent and esoteric, making displays of his particular fetish and generally treating her superb body as though it were put on the earth merely to illustrate technical accomplishments of love. Her laughter rang out, pitched in deep pleasure. A frivolous Daphne, she ran about the house chased by an Apollo in a shirt. She rolled and surged with deep laughter. Her beautiful flesh was radiant in eased pleasure.

"Oh, you're ridiculous, ridiculous," she gasped, rubbing tears away with a rosy fist.

"I know," he said.

A few days later he determinedly took an evening off so that they could visit Bronwen. He had sent a note up to ask if they might come to supper and Bronwen had replied with "Yes", though her note seemed troubled. Daisy, walking up with him to the villa, was subdued and large-eyed with trepidation.

The valley bed was spattered with the dirty yellow light of the street lamps. Odd soldiers were here and there at the corners, looking isolated and alien, for no one would have truck with them. Burly strange policemen in gloomy capes were everywhere. A drizzle was falling and the presences of the damp cold mountains could be felt, looming out of the mist.

"A gang has gone over to Penmawr," Tudor whispered. "I hope they won't lose their way coming back in this mist."

She shivered. Except for the policemen and soldiers there were few people about. Occasionally a collier shuffled past through

251

the drizzle. If three or four happened to meet and stopped to congregate into a bantering group, after their fashion, they were shifted on by a grunting voice and a big black cape bearing down on them. The shops and pubs, though deserted, were for the most part still open: in some murky oillamps and even candles did service for the expensive gas. There was a look of sullen crouching about the place. It was as though some sinister presence waited to pounce, directly a suspicious move was made in those dismal yellow-streaked streets. Two or three women ventured across the gloomy pavements, in shawls or old coats; they peered about suspiciously over wet screwed-up noses.

"One might be down in hell," Tudor murmured.

"Except that it's cold," Daisy shivered, "cold.... Oh, it's no place to sing songs about life, is it?"

"It *was*," sighed Tudor, "it was, according to Grannie Bronwen. God knows if it ever will be again."

"Well," she comforted, "no one can say you're not doing your best to make things a bit more comfortable."

Grannie Bronwen received Daisy as though she had always known her—had even been present at her birth. She fussed over her maternally, enquiring if her feet were dry and insisting that she took the most comfortable chair, close to the sparkling fire. Casually, too casually, she said that Elwyn had been called out to a case and didn't expect to be back to supper. Tudor forbore to ask about the case. He patted Bronwen's fraillooking but sturdy hand.

"Don't you think Daisy handsome?" he enquired, to destroy an awkward pause. And he wanted direct contact established between these two women at once. "She's only three months gone, but it's going to suit her."

"She looks splendid," Bronwen said loyally. "You find it suits you, my dear?" she asked Daisy across the rug, on which Tudor sprawled.

"I like it," Daisy murmured. It was as if a lioness were shy, peeping out from hot golden-black eyes.

"You should see her stripped, Bronwen. She carries the moon under her breasts. A moon under two ruby stars," he laughed shamelessly. "And her long black hair streaming like the night sky!"

Bronwen smiled approvingly: she seemed to understand. Daisy said, sedately, "All I hope is that the moon will carry me safely through the clouds."

"And that it's a moon with a man in it—" Tudor rolled over to her feet in adoration.

"A boy you want, Daisy?" Bronwen asked. Tudor could see she was warming to her.

"I'd like a boy *and* a girl," Daisy said with sudden glowering energy. "To begin with."

"I only had one," Bronwen lamented. "My dear son, Elwyn. And in my day the fashion was for a dozen at least."

"I've told Daisy how you came by my father," Tudor said briskly.

Bronwen, agedly clear-faced, nodded. Her shrewd, quietly examining glances had ceased and she sat in pleasurable approval. She said confidentially to Daisy: "I was nearly as bold as you've been, my dear. But things were easier in my day—not so many people about to fret one, and not all these goings on to frighten a poor girl."

"The Squire's son seduced her," Tudor sang.

"He wanted to marry me," Bronwen said proudly. "Though I was only a poor girl of the village here."

"You must have been its show-piece," Tudor said.

"I had," she agreed, "my charms, I dare say."

"And so respectable now. Such a ruler of the Sunday-schools."

Bronwen rose as the gong sounded. She declared with unashamed gusto: "Where true love is, there are special laws. I would not countenance real bad behaviour." She looked very much the grand old woman of the district who presented prizes at Sunday school sports and glees.

"My sweet Bronwen!" Tudor whispered in her ear, as they went into the dining-room. "Never failing me."

253

Bronwen had provided a flourishing pre-strike kind of supper, even to a bottle of red wine, and the guests ate of it with appreciation they made no attempt to conceal; here were delicacies they had not been able to afford as yet. Bronwen looked a little sad now and again. Elwyn did not put in an appearance; and not a word was said of Tudor's strike activities—each had seemed to decide that this was an evening off, an escape into the calm of a family festivity shuttered away from the scowls of the world. After supper Tudor sat at the piano, at Bronwen's request, and sang in his easy baritone gay old Welsh songs of the pre-nonconformist era: she liked to be reminded now and again of the old bucolic world, when there had not been all this complicated industrial strife.

And Daisy soon sat at ease. Presently, no one could have imagined that fear ever troubled her. She bathed in the good solid comfort of this house appreciatively. Bronwen treated her with a delicate deference. The benign uncorrupted calm of the aged woman spread a peace. They sat talking of children, ovens, bees-wax and antimacassars—Bronwen presenting Daisy with two of the last, which she had recently embroidered with a design of dahlias and cockerels.

"Will you let me come down to see you in your house, my dear?" she asked when it was time for them to go. Elwyn's long absence had begun to tell at last. Tudor had remarked on it pointedly and Daisy had shortly afterwards made the move.

"Why, you know you needn't ask!" Daisy said, in a flush of entreating affection for the beneficent old woman.

Bronwen kissed her. Tudor could see that she wanted, beyond her admiring liking for Daisy, to make up for Elwyn's refusal to meet his daughter-in-law. He was left alone with Bronwen for a minute, and said with a half-playful threat:

"Tell that father of mine I'll be up to see him soon—alone."

She frowned, troubled. "He's become so stern, Tudor, since your mother died. Going into himself. He won't be troubled by... by things of this earth that seem too much alive."

Tudor knew about that retreat into the pleasaunce of death, the agonised longing for a peace that could never be corroded by touch of this world. A sunset anguish covered his father's soul; he was of the earth and not of it, and all mundane transactions were governed by pain.

"What can one do?" he asked helplessly.

"Nothing," Bronwen answered at once. There was a veiled criticism of her son in her voice.

"He wants me to be a stranger now?"

"*All* of us are strangers to him now." She went to Daisy, who had returned dressed to go, and laid her hand on the young woman's arm. "Very nice it's been to have you here," she said. "It's brightened me up." she added, with naïve gratitude.

"I wish you could come and live with us, Grannie," Tudor said.

"I wish that, too," she answered simply. She still burned with a soft radiance of life, enquiring, observant, interested, she was still identified with the grimy, noisy lineaments of a landscape she had seen changed so drastically.

Outside the house Daisy asked eagerly: "She couldn't come to us, I suppose, Tudor?"

He shook his head dismally, oppressed by the thought of Bronwen being left in that silent house. "She'd never leave my father—she couldn't."

"Perhaps he'll marry again," Daisy said hopefully.

"Good Lord, a woman would be much too corporeal a presence to him."

"Well," she murmured, in pensive thoughtfulness, "his son is not like him, anyhow."

"He stayed out tonight purposely," Tudor said, looking at her.

"I thought so," she said tranquilly.

They walked hand in hand down the vale. He was aware with relief of the composed peace of her soul, which contact with Bronwen had given her. He felt that she, too, could go through such a long life and emerge as tranquil as a flower.

255

CHAPTER VII

I

THE fights for the support of other districts beyond the valley were begun lustily. The stagnancy of the strike was being disturbed, there was something definite to do, in which crowds could join.

True, marching over the mountains in cold and wet and on stomachs filled mostly with visionary food, was not inviting. But there was a barbaric promise in the idea, and it was a release from lethargy and an escape from dismal kitchens, cantankerous wives, and children deprived of what gives them pleasure. The pubs were places one entered only in dreams now; chapel was all very fine for Sunday, but in the weekdays the Lord seemed very far away. So the marching gangs did not lack members, particularly at first, while the idea was fresh.

They could be seen wending up the various mountains, swathed in whatever extra garments could be found. The more important processions scraped together a band, and when these reached the tops of the mountains faint scraps of music would be blown down, sometimes with rain or in mist. Others sang their way across the bleak heights, grey choirs wrapped in clouds. Some men caught bad colds and were laid low with bronchial complaints. The mountains were never, as a rule, visited in winter, and their great black shapes looked unused as things of the first seven days.

Up there the days smelled of death and the face of the heavens had a look of anger. Black clouds scuttled down or broke into big rain that spat on the marchers like gouts of mud. Growling with a pre-christian growl, sometimes the sky seemed to speed out of its fastenings and rush down purposely on the shabby intruders of this savage domain. Like elephants the mountains would shake in swellings of black rage.

"Mind," shouted Ieuan, "the cracks. Some places they're big enough to swallow a man whole and for ever."

Owing to these crevices, that jerked about on many of the mountain-tops, the crusaders always had to return before dark. Hollow veins running for distances, it was said they were caused by the subsidence of old pit-workings in the roots of the mountains: it would be easy to break a leg or disappear altogether in them.

A collier, wrapped in canvas sacking, who was marching beside Ieuan, said in happy reminiscence:

"On this mountain it was I courted my Lettie. Only in summer it was then, and there was larks about. We used to pick those whinberries, and once I saw a fox dashing about in the ferns the other side where them rocks are. Aye, red he was, with a tail like fire. He came right up to where I was with Lettie and looked straight at us, aye, mun, so nosy."

"I don't wonder," said Ieuan.

"Lettie went nervous, and shouted it was a wolf left over from bygone days. She wouldn't go up that way no more, such a shock she had."

In broad shallow dents among the arms of the mountains, in low deep valleys, on jutting eminences extended into space like huge hands, there were communities of workpeople, sometimes hiding neat and small, sometimes sprawling in teeming disorder whereever houses could be built without too much climbing to them. Down from the naked heights the gangs descended, entering the first raw streets with songs or musical instruments. They always contrived to arrive when the day-shift would be leaving the pits. On some corner or waste land near the colliery they would accost the workmen in droves and invite them to listen to their tale.

"Oi, look here now, we've come all over the mountains to see you, see! Stop now. We got something to tell you—"

The black faces would look at the grey ones with examining tolerance. The thin brotherhood of the mines, unrealised and created from long periods of stress and danger, was soon established. Few of the districts questioned the right of the invaders to state their case: the ancient and familiar case to be presented yet again.

"You know about our strike over there! Well, you got to come out with us, see? What the hell's the good of us fighting while you b——s next door to us blackleg the cause. You know what we're fighting for, we're all butties in this. Stop now, we got a speaker here that's going to get up in a minute—"

In most of the districts they found a readiness to listen. When sufficient workers had been collected, the speaker would jump on a chair or box borrowed from some nearby dwelling and begin shouting in the popular bristling manner:

"Boys, you know how it is with us. We're starving, we haven't got a fag-end to our name. But we haven't tramped all this way 'cross them nasty mountains to beg brass of you. We've only come to say how surprised, how *very* surprised—" this in imitation of a parson—"we are that you're still working while we—" thundering—"though our guts got nothing but wind in 'em, are out fighting 'gainst one of the biggest frauds ever done against us by them gentlemen that sit in mansions and scheme how best they can squeeze 'nother penny off the pay—"

"Can't remember that you struck for us when we was out in '93," someone objected.

"Ah, that '93 strike of yours!" cried the speaker—this time Matt Lewis. He squeezed up his face in an anguish of recollection. "Was it a proper strike, was it *organised*? You went back 'fore you gave your friends over them mountains time to act. There was blacklegs here thick as rats in a rotten old ship. But this is a strike! There's nine thousand men out already, and it's our third month—" Serious, grave, glittering, the speaker sank to a whisper.

"What are you going to do about it? Don't your bellies tell you it's your job too, and that it's *your* homes, *your* lives we're fighting and starving for? Those big pieces of earth we've just crossed don't stand between us!" He shook his fists. "We're all brothers, sisters, mother-in-laws, grannies and uncles in this. One big black family warmed up in hell!"

But frequently there would be small fights. Insulting remarks were usual in the preliminary greetings exchanged between the visitors and the natives, but as a rule these were treated as belonging to the common language between men. But some jumpy aggressive local chap would occasionally take umbrage, perhaps having called for a pint or two after leaving his pit, and a swelling fight would ensue. Then it was that the watchful policemen interfered and made warning arrests—so sometimes a crusader had to be left behind in a police-station cell, to the horror, or relief, of his wife over the mountains that evening.

The fights, however, were personal and had nothing to do with the large stern issue of their neighbours' strike, towards which the listening men were abstractedly sympathetic. They listened with nodding heads and compressed mouths. All that was needed, after a while, was the magic mob decision that must descend mysteriously, a flame from Heaven. The visitors called also on the local workmen's committees and miners' leaders: these, too, listened and waited for the white flame.

At one place the visitors' meeting at a street corner was attacked by a horde of irritable women with materialistic memories of former strikes. Armed with brooms, pokers, sticks, potatoes and such-like, they swooped down, aprons flying, from a raw-looking street above the corner. Loud war-like cries snapped from between their teeth.

"Out with 'em! No more strikes! What they come here for, where they've no business? Drive 'em out!" They succeeded in breaking up the meeting, swarming into the crowd with that ruthless fury peculiar to fighting women. All the men then struggled with them, and of course could have overcome them:

259

but a meeting swarmed over by hysterical women must be given up as lost. However, good came of this particular attack, for the local men, angry at this interference from a lot of silly wives, took delight in punishing them and putting them back in their proper kitchen places by calling for a strike.

The preaching was for the abolition of the Sliding Scale of payment which was operative nearly everywhere in the county, and for an eight-hour day. There certainly was something to fight for, even in those districts where work was full-time and a slightly better percentage than usual was paid by benevolent owner. Speakers asked of their scowling meetings if men were born for nothing but work. What about pleasure? In London and other civilised places people did not go straight from work to bed, and they yet were paid wages that enabled them to go to operas and entertain their friends to musical evenings and whist parties. Man wasn't born to work so much. The listeners scratched their chins or picked their noses, frowning as the idea sank in. An eight-hour day on bigger pay! These chaps said it could be done. Well, hadn't other advantages been obtained before by fighting for them? Why not?

In one or two districts known to be laggardly in their sympathy, special efforts were made, complicated in the psychological effects aimed at by the organisers. The gangs, swollen for these occasions, marched on to the colliery concerned, in the middle of the shift, and demanded of the manager that the men be brought up at once from a particular pit. Threatening of gesture and menacing of visage, the simmering invaders could be—as every manager knew from bitter past experience—sinisterly dangerous. And all these districts were depleted of policemen who had been transferred to the striking valley. The workers were brought up.

Faced, as they stepped out of the cage, by these hostile visitors crowding over the sooty paths, the men blinked and spat restlessly, at once recognising the sacred cause that had brought these outsiders, half enemies, half comrades, on this accusatory mission. But the bitter flash of recognition would last but a moment.

"Traitors! Blacklegs! Scabs!"

And with roars the strikers stampeded on the muttering workers. The pit cage, clanking again to the surface, brought further loads of interested workers. The fights were just plain bouts of fisticuffs, as indulged in often among the mountains to settle feuds. Straightforward but bloody. Neither side had particular victory. With a common impulse the visitors retreated after a while among the sheds and coal-trucks and, expressing righteous congratulations to each other, marched or staggered away from the colliery top. The manager appeared among the panting workers, observant but aloof.

"You will get back now," he ordered.

Nothing could be learned, however, from the workers' remarks, which were mostly lamentations on their bruises. The attack seemed to be accepted as a proper manifestation of a semi-hostility often directed against this particular colliery by men of other districts.

But the biggest offensive was launched against the hated Abba Vale colliery, where things were always so smugly complacent, its men for some reason or other being seldom sympathetic to any workers' movement: a hard, obstinate lot unaccountably subservient to the pit owners and haughtily enclosed in their own shut-away vale, only coming out on eisteddfod occasions to snatch away first prizes. They seemed immune from the failings common to all other men, no scandal ever penetrating beyond their heavy mountains.

For this attack the best gangs were selected and the heavens favoured the chosen day, withholding rain, though it was icy cold. They started off early in the morning, headed by a band playing stirring marches. A pity a good breakfast hadn't preceded the long, arduous journey! A bowl of "sop"—crusts of bread soaked in weak tea—had been the victuals of the most fortunate: in some pockets further wads of bread and bits of cheese were carried. But the brassy music was triumphant, and a febrile holiday spirit seemed to prevail. A crowd with an objective can

261

feed, it seemed, off the common impulse directing it. Anyhow, when the band was silent the gangs sang as though at some chapel festival in full-pay times.

Behind the band, along with Beriah and two or three other members of their particular strike committee, marched Tudor, looking worried. Just before setting out he had heard from a scout living in the Abba Vale—who had set out in the middle of the night to bring the news—that the Abba colliery owners were fully aware of the attack to be launched that day, and had made their preparations. A large contingent of police had been obtained suddenly and were now barracked in the Company's offices at the colliery. These, however, were not to be used against the strikers unless, by some remote chance, they obtained access to the colliery.

For the Company had decided that the struggle was to be confined to the workers. Let these impudent invaders meet their own fellow-workers and be repulsed by them—that would be a real mind-your-own-business lesson to the bastards: they would see that the Abba workers themselves would not tolerate the interference. And dozens of life-preservers, hurried from Cardiff, had been presented among the faithful Abba men.

The gangs having foregathered for the march, Tudor got up and informed them of the opposition they were likely to meet with.

"—men," he concluded, "it may be a nasty fight. Considering those life-preservers, you had better control yourselves and not start using your fists. And those policemen—believe me, they're not going to remain yawning in the offices while a fight's going on—"

"What are we marching over there for," someone growled, "if it isn't to fight?"

"For mass meetings," Tudor answered calmly—"for an appeal to workers who may not be so stubborn as you imagine—"

"Ah, Abba Vale men!" several jeered. A tribal enmity, longing for opportunity, seemed released in their voices.

"I warn you," Tudor flashed, "that you're not likely to stand a chance in a battle. It'll be better to leave the success of this trip to the speakers." The grey faces beneath him, for all their tensity and gleaming eyes, were obviously under-fed and suggestive of interior hollowness.

But he had shoved away his sick doubt, realising how precious it was to preserve this fighting spirit in a strike that by careful manipulation was emerging from a dangerous period of threatened failure. The bitter ferocity was there, beyond his control, and he had to accept it: the roots of this native life could not be destroyed by a speech or two.... And the big unwieldy procession had begun its march with a loud blare from the band.

The official plans were for several mass meetings to be held in the Abba Vale: in the afternoon, to catch night-shift men; in the early evening for the day men. It was to be expected there would be minor personal fights. And then the gangs were to return late at night by the long main road, since there would be no moon to conduct them over the short-cut across the mountains. "We must get the meetings going as quickly as possible," Tudor said to Beriah as they trudged up a stony path. "All the speakers are here?"

"Six of us," Beriah said. "Bob Richards was sweating all night with a cold and his wife locked the bedroom door on him."

"The five gangs must be made to understand they're with us to support the meetings. No hanging about the colliery." Tudor left his place and began to go down the long straggling procession to find each gang's leader. He told them that on arrival at the bed of the vale the gangs must separate and select their own corners among the streets, to open the day's session of speeches. The leaders agreed.

But as he passed back up the procession Tudor was conscious of the sinister chain of enmity linking the men, a dark flow through the procession. And under all his abstract plans for preaching the Gospel by word of mouth, he had to accept the savage beliefs of the strikers. This was a war. The men had their own understanding of its ritual.

"I feel they're making their own plans," he whispered to Beriah.

"Aye," Beriah said, with hollow deprecation. "I heard behind me that a load of pit timber's just gone to Abba. 'Make a good fire on a cold day,' someone said....I'm feeling they're wanting to burn and smash today."

Tudor looked at the elder collier, who had such a fleshless, saintly appearance: he suspected that Beriah, too, had arrived calmly at the conclusion that only arson and rioting could ease the bitter blood of the men.

But he need not have made worried plans to keep the peace. Warfare was offered the strikers. After five miles of climbing they reached the brow of the mountain blocking the end of the vale, and below them the straggling length of black dwellings looked peaceful enough. Almost under the mountain the colliery sprawled, blackly fat and prosperous-looking. Between it and the base of the mountain a large pond spread, a cold blue patch.

"We'll circle the pond and get on to the main road just past the colliery," Tudor said. He began to lead the way down the steep path.

The procession followed with sundry growls and mutters at this first sight of the abhorred vale. When Tudor and Beriah reached the bed, the tail of the procession was still far away under the sky. The band was assembling beside the blue mountain water, preparing to play *Forth to the Battle* for a coaxing first entry. The first arrivals were waiting on the rough hillocky ground for everyone to get down and form a respectable procession— when, from bushes about the pond and from behind the rocks, Abba men began to appear in sardonic enquiry, growing numbers of them.

Tudor watched their slow approach: there seemed something playful, like the ambling of young bears, in their gait. He saw at once that they concealed weapons. On their arms they wore bands of white linen—so that, presumably, a friend should not be attacked for looking like a foe. A red-headed chap of Herculean build was first.

264

"Come to pay us a visit, have you?" he enquired coyly.

"Now look here," Tudor said abruptly, "don't make a mistake. We don't want trouble. We've come to hold a few meetings."

The man protruded his great heavy eyes. "But *we* don't want no meetings, see?" And around him crowded the usual lickspittles, men of the kind familiar in all large collections of workers. Behind, inscrutable except for an air of surliness about them, waited the true crowd at which the crusade was directed; Tudor felt that the attitude of these was incalculable, and more than ever he burned to get at them.

"Now," he said placatingly, "can't you see we're on your side? What's all the bother about? Do you want to get some fun out of starving fellow-workers?"

Desperately he was aware of the growling and muttering behind him as the procession scrambled down and it was beginning to realise what the halt meant. If he could hold that threatening force behind him in check....

"You got no business here!" snapped the Hercules. And a henchman beside him snarled: "A lot of socialist agitators they are, that's been in jail for rioting—" Beriah's wispy church-window face protested at this: he said respectably: "We are men of peace, but fighting in our own way for a bit of understanding between all us workers. Don't you be cocky now. We got things to chat to you about."

All to no avail. Vehement indignation was being loudly and abusively expressed behind Tudor, who calculated that about a thousand Abba men were now collected about the pond—nearly double the number of visitors.

"Ah, look at 'em—Abba apes! Where they all come from— swung down from trees and out of caves? They got tails back of 'em and came up on all fours.... Abba apes—'ow's the old baboons you've left at home?" And other demands expressive of the general opinion that the Abba Vale was peopled by a race untouched as yet by civilisation and Christianity. Tudor made a last swift effort, turning savagely to the strikers: "Shut up there.

What's the good of all that? Now listen—it seems we've got to have permission to get into the vale—"

"Hell, permission!" someone roared. "We'll get into the old jungle. On 'em, boys." This impudent denial of entry was the last straw.

The wild drunkenness was a revelation to Tudor, for all his knowledge of the uncurbed fighting spirit possessed by the valley men. Why couldn't they see how hopeless was their attack? And, in the moment when the first rushes began, he felt nauseatingly responsible for this unnecessary fighting. He had failed! There was a savage hate in these men that he had failed to control and utilise, that he could not touch.

Here it was. It foamed spittingly about him and Beriah; they alone stood still, on a little hillock above the pond—though not for long. Two yelping men swept up to them; Tudor saw a bludgeon pulled out of an inner pocket. He jumped and leapt neatly into the man's chest; they went over. He scrambled astride the man, sitting on his stomach, and knocked his fist twice into the cursing face; it crumpled up for a moment and then sank into a softly-gasping dreaminess.

Beriah, tough under his frail mien, was dancing about the hillock exchanging smart blows with a short tublike man who was unarmed—Tudor ran up, lifted his boot and disposed of him. At the same time an arm was pinned around his chest and, from behind, a fist crashed under his ear. He sagged a bit and recovered; he felt his mouth become taut in an unfamiliar kind of grin. From then he fought in a strange consciousness, during which the mountain seemed to move like a wave, the pond slide up to his eyes, the bushes dance, the earth shake. But all the time he was carefully on the lookout for bludgeons; in spite of an aching head, a bleeding nose and a half-closed eye, wariness never left him.

Not many, he realised in relief, were stretched on the ground in temporary peace. And he saw with admiration much smart work from the starved but roaring visitors. Screeches and howls ripped the air. He lurched into the pond and brought out a dazedly floundering Abba man left there: there were loud splashes as fighters sprawled blindly into the water. The band instruments were smashed resoundingly to pieces; their owners fought and yelled like demons.

The battle lasted about half an hour. It would have gone on much longer, for the strikers were by no means wholly conquered, if there had not been a sudden swarm of police. These, many and large, approached majestically, truncheons bristling. There was a piercing yell of warning from a striker not yet gone into unseeing fury:

"Look out: police!"

On the low slopes, the tussocks, the pond sides, the small fighting groups paused electrically. Yes, there were police, a shower of menacing black shapes of adequate size. The law, prison! Perhaps rage was already more or less satisfied: there was a wild rush up the slopes, lines of scrambling and running men climbing in all directions. A queer silence fell about the pond; about a score of men were prostrate around its edge.

The policemen strode about with a dignified elegance, putting away their unneeded batons. Abba men sat on the grass panting or nursing their faces: bludgeons were chucked down everywhere. Some stared at the police with obscure hatred, muttering. Others looked vaguely ashamed. The silence was queer and haunting, as though there was mourning about.

Tudor rose slowly to his feet: he had been all but knocked out at last. But with the arrival of the police his mind had thudded back. Aching, he began to examine the prostrate figures, ignoring the police. A sergeant approached and demanded:

"What d'you want?"

"I'm a doctor," Tudor growled. He felt oppressed with a sense of defeat and foreboding. He stared abstractedly at a bloody mouth in the bashed face of a striker vaguely familiar to him; his vision came out of his swollen eye-sockets with difficulty. "I've got some work to do here."

The sergeant said heftily: "You be off. Go on, get back over those mountains. We'll be seeing to these men."

Tudor looked up with caution. He met a pair of conventionally hard and officious eyes. "I want to see to these men—" he began. Vaguely, in far-away anguish, he felt responsible for those prostrate figures.

"Clear out," said the sergeant in warning.

Tudor turned, remembering Melville. Nine wasted months in jail! He jerked away towards the mountain slope. Christ, he couldn't afford to go to jail just yet. And not, anyhow, for a lot of Abba cattle. Heaving up the slope in depression, his damaged gaze saw streaks of men crawling and limping above him.

There was a general rest on the top of the mountain. Most of the men were silent for a while, lying flat or crouching while they nursed various bruises. Several seemed unaffected by the defeat.

"That'll teach the bastards," someone congratulated himself.

"Seems to me we been taught something," a surly voice growled. And that was the general feeling. As the gasps and the pantings died away, an atmosphere of heavy gloom settled. When they got up to begin the long trudge back and someone tried to start a song, his voice remained alone. The former owners of musical instruments scowled and cursed: one owner was also missing.

"What'll I tell my daughter-in-law Lily," an elderly collier asked forlornly, "when she sees I haven't brought Jack back?"

"The cashalties'll get took to hospital and be better off than us.... I wouldn't have minded feeding off meat and rice-pudding in Abba Cottage Hospital, but I got so mad, mun, I lost sense and half kilt everyone that came on me." So spoke a one-time wrestler.

Hungry and dry-mouthed, they trailed back dispiritedly under a sky like heavy grey fur. After a time, with the exchange of anecdotes about the fighting, spirit was revived a little. If only the sky opened and let down barrels of beer or even urns of tea! Things wouldn't be so bad then. Before reaching the descent to the home valley a halt was called, and when the men were assembled Tudor Morris got up on a rock. There was a whinny of tired laughter at sight of his misshapen face: to see a doctor needing treatment seemed funny.

"Sold out of lint and ointment, have you, Tudor?" someone bawled, quite in the old style.

"Boys," he enquired dramatically, "has this been a defeat today?"

The answer came in a quick roar: "NO."

"Some of them will tell us down there we've been fools. Wild fools out to make a row and disturb the peace. They—women especially—can't forgive what looks like defeat. We have *not* been fools, we are not defeated. We've had a clout from traitors, that's all. And we've done something today. We went into an enemy's camp with an offering of brotherhood. Our offer seemed to be chucked back in our faces. But it'll bear fruit. Those Abba men, like all the workers of this country, like all the workers of all the world, are going to learn something soon. They're going to learn the power of federation, of alliance, of union—even though there's going to be a lot of kicks on the backside first—"

"We've had enough of *them* for one day," someone interrupted, with some feeling.

"Aye," another shouted in woe, "I'm gone paralysed there and 'aven't come round yet."

Laughter—though weary-sounding—greeted these sallies. Tudor went on urgently:

"For all our skinny bellies, our rags and our black eyes, this is not a time to weep. It's a time to laugh. We can laugh because we're awake and alive and kicking. We're not members of a dying world, we belong to a new young race. It's a time to dance and laugh!" he continued in admonishing style. "Life's not a funeral, but neither is it a long wedding-day. We're not a good sight to the angels—especially now—but neither are we a lot of burglars of the earth. But don't let's get conceited now. We've got a lot to learn. And one of the things we've got to learn is to laugh at defeat. You go crawling back home now looking gloomy and you're going to pay heavily for all the efforts we've made today, you're going to be a bad influence on the strike. Go down singing, wear your bruises like medals—even if they're on your behinds."

To his own ears this harangue sounded grim. But the words came from an impulse springing like a fountain in his breast: they had no concern with the buried gloom in his bowels. They seemed to have effect. The laughter he invited with his last remark broke out as at a music-hall. They formed into tidy procession and started to march again, with more gusto. Those at the head struck up into song. But what they sang was a chapel hymn, melancholy of tune and earth-denying of words. However, it was music. Hearing and seeing them coming down the black mountain slope, people gathered at corners, mostly women. The long draggled procession approached the bleak rows singing. The waiting wives, shawled and sharp-eyed, refrained from judgment until the men were under their noses: Then angry exclamations burst out at sight of the battered faces and limping legs. Interspersed with jeers.

"Look at them! A lot of rapscallions and rodneys. Been clouted, have they?—serve 'em right."

"Ben!" a young woman shrieked, darting across the road to her husband, who had patches of dried blood about his face. She clung to him in wild passion. "What did I tell you?—oh, you lot of 'ooligans!" she spat venomously on the others.

Ben gave her a push. "Get off, woman." But she clung to him passionately, rowdily, hanging on his neck, shoving her mouth against his blood-caked cheek.

Another woman, discovering the loss of the musical instruments, roundly denounced the procession from beginning to end, her husband especially: it appeared that she had been obliged to forgo a new mattress in order that a cornet could be bought: she did not cease until a policeman strolled across to her. For all the strikers' songs and strutting march, the women seemed to have reached to the bitter heart of the affair.

One by one the strikers fell out as the procession passed the different streets, soldiers watching in idle curiosity, policemen with an appearance of large tolerance; it became a ragged trickle of men at last, shabby and unheroic-looking. The drab, stagnant afternoon, opened for the noisy examination of the returning warriors, closed again on the valley. Like the lid of a coffin.

II

It was her childish habit of eating an orange noisily, with deep mindless sucks out of a ragged hole bitten into the top, that irritated him. He remembered that she was eating one when he arrived home from Abba Vale a few days ago; she ate two a day and said she'd like six if they could have afforded them.

"Daisy, don't you prefer to peel the orange and eat the quarters?" he asked at last.

She jumped a little, looking up from a book. Two or three drops of juice fell on the pages. "I've always eaten them this way—" she began, but quickly received his irritation. "Why, do I make a noise?"

His bruised face reddened in her wide gaze. But he had to say: "Yes. It's an ugly noise."

From being startled she passed into uncomfortable fear.

"You mean it's a common way of eating an orange? A... a lady doesn't do it that way?"

He squirmed then. "I didn't think of it like that—"

She rose, the book falling from her knees heedlessly. Her face had become an offended scarlet. "Oh yes, you did—"

"It's just an unattractive noise, I tell you."

"What else do I do that's common?"

"Now, there's no need to get frantic—"

"Frantic! I'm not frantic. It's you that's frantic." Indignation swelled her throat. "You've been touchy ever since you came back from Abba Vale. It's not my fault if things went wrong." She chucked the half-eaten orange into his waste-paper-basket.

He stiffened. "Were you blamed? Don't be silly."

"—nor if you came back with two black eyes," she surged, "and a missing tooth." Tall, flashing, she was becoming obstreperous. Her pregnancy was gently evident.

"You'd better calm down," he said briefly.

But that infuriated her more. "And can *I* help it if it was too wet for you to have the meeting tonight? You had to stay in with me instead and listen to me eating oranges!" In her anger she lapsed into sing-song "There's a pity, isn't it now? He had to stay in with his wife! Go on out," she stormed, "and shout to the wind on the corner. A lot of time you're wasting here, at home."

But the brilliance of her wrath *looked* beautiful; she stood alert with tall power, starry of eye and ruddy-cheeked. Tudor wanted to smile, and only achieved a wry grimace. "So you *do* think I'm neglecting you," he said.

She shrugged her shoulders dramatically, like a bad actress. "Neglecting me? *I* don't care at all; never have I thought about it."

He turned his face again to his book. Useless to parry with an incensed woman. "Go to bed, girl," he said, "and cool down."

Surprisingly she swept out of the room without further ado. And her steps, mounting the stairs, had a plunging deliberation— he was very aware of them, in his roused sensibility to her.

He laid his head on his arm and listened to the rain beating through the wind. The small careful fire in the grey grate—not black-leaded for some days, he had noticed—had gone out. The room was cold. Under his arm the poems of William Morris slept in their print.

What weather! For two days winter had announced its full presence with icy blasts and torrential rain, using the valley as though it were an attractive abode just discovered from over the mountains. People scrambled through the streets: it was said that the soldiers in their tents on the slopes were all weakened with colds. Outdoor meetings were impossible, and no hall could be obtained.

And what work! Trivial food and the winter were telling at last in the Terraces. He was kept going all day, and often at nights now. Births remained about the same, deaths were more abundant, but bronchitis, pleurisy and pneumonia were very popular: people seemed to take to illnesses with relief, especially men.... But not a penny, of course, was coming into the surgery.

Tudor rose, squirming at the thought of a bill he had received that morning—a third application, with a suave little note attached. That afternoon, having five bleak minutes to himself, he had examined his bank-book. The thirty-pound bill *could* be paid; and he would be left with exactly eight shillings in the world.

But Daisy must have the fruit she craved, he thought, going into the kitchen. He lit the gas—not yet cut off—and found a last orange. After peeling it, he arranged the neat quarters on a pretty blue tea-plate, which he carried upstairs.

He stood beside her bed gazing down at her in the lamplight. Still an awful actress, she was pretending badly to be asleep. At last she uneasily lifted her stiff eyelids.

"An orange," he said. "The last. Enjoy it; you might not get any more for some time."

She sulked for a minute. He sat on the bed and put a quarter to her lips, coaxing it through the pouting scarlet. "You extravagant woman," he scolded, "we can't afford any more oranges, d'you hear? Fruit is not for us." He pushed another quarter into her mouth. "What right have you to expect oranges of the world? You're impudent, woman, buying oranges in these times." He kept on pushing quarters in. "Isn't water good enough?"

"Do you want to choke me?" she mumbled.

"You're idle, luxurious and a spendthrift," he declared, inserting yet another. "A calamity of a woman.... All the same, I'll give you oranges, you shall have all the oranges in the world. You shall have orchards of fruit!"

"We owe Samson the fruiterer twenty-six shillings," she mumbled.

"Oh, God!"

Daisy swallowed the last quarter, skin and all, and looked at him with sober shame. "I've been eating oranges all day," she wailed.

Beginning to undress, he sang hollowly: "Well, eat them until you've got to stop. Order another dozen tomorrow. They may be the last. For a while at least. Until I can get you those orchards.... There's a man calling tomorrow," he added casually, "about a thirty pound bill. If I pay it, we've got eight shillings left."

"Often," she murmured in her sober voice, "Melville and I had no more than eight pennies in the house for weeks on end.... Don't pay that bill yet, Tudor. I'll see the man."

And the following day she met the representative of the nervous Cardiff firm, a grey doubtful-looking little man with a dried-up face. She looked at him on the doorstep with a kind of sensuality, brooding and rapt. "The doctor's out." But she sat him in the waiting-room and stared at him as if he had come from Sodom. "I'm his wife. You've come about that bill. Aren't you ashamed?"

"Ashamed!" he stammered.

"Can't you see that you've come to a place that's living on rain and wind.... Ever heard of Jesus Christ?"

He nodded vaguely, fingering his watch-chain nervously.

"Well, there's thousands of Jesus Christs in this place. We're *all* bleeding on crosses! I wonder you've got the face to bring bills out at such a time."

"Business is business." His gaze was congealed greasily on her heaving breast: he dared not look upon her high-minded face.

"And life is life. My husband works from morning till night. For nothing, just now. Your firm has no right to bother at a time like this."

"Well, you see," he coughed. "Doctor Morris hasn't been long in practice, he's a new client—"

"More reason why you should have patience. Your firm knows him personally. If they had one grain of the love of God in them, they'd see that they're dealing with a genuine article.... Now

274

don't say that business is business. Words like that make my blood curdle."

"Thirty pounds!" he mumbled. "It's a lot of money."

She shook her head, apparently pondering. "If I pick up thirty stones from off the road outside, will that do?"

He got up. "I'm afraid not."

"It's all we've got." She looked now as though the assaults of a depraved world were too much for her. The warped little face under her lamenting gaze was too sinister a menace. "Until the strike is over," she added, peeping at him.

"Will Doctor Morris be back soon?"

"Not until the evening. Besides, what's the good?"

"Very well," he coughed. His face had become filled with a dismal flush. He looked at her suddenly.

"I'll see what I can do.... I can tell that you're a hard-working couple here," he said, with sudden truculence. And, going out, "Things are bad, bad enough to make one weep."

"Oh no," she said, going with him. "Oh no. It's not like that at all. Not enough to make one weep. We're not weeping."

"I hear the men are giving in," he said hoarsely on the doorstep.

"It's a lie," she said. "But even if they are, the strike's not a failure. It's—" she waved her arm dramatically "—it's a sign of life, of wealth! We're bleeding on the cross, but we're alive there, too." And as he was hurrying down the patch of garden through the rain, she shouted after him: "Because we're fighting and what we stand for *can't* die!"

And she briskly slammed the door on the cold wet wind.

The firm lay low for a while. But there were swarms of other small bills. She dealt with them with a great show of assurance, interviewing tradespeople who looked at her with frowning criticism—especially local ones, for gossip still fed off her, and Tudor, of course, was a traitor. Thank God, though, they were nearly always male tradespeople, and these she used with subtle cunning, obtaining butter and meat by artful devices of look, voice and behaviour. But when one, the amorous Samson, greengrocer, suggested a kiss she lifted a swede and hit him on the head: afterwards, being married, he let her have all she wanted, on long credit.

III

Christmas was approaching and the outside world was preparing to enjoy itself. A fortnight before the festive date a determined effort was made by backsliding colliers to unseal the lips of the Associated Owners—they formed a committee on their own and begged for an offer to be made, in this season of peace and goodwill towards men. After a three days' silence they received a curt reply: five per cent *reduction* on the former terms! And the Sliding Scale to stand indisputably for the next five years. Even so weak-kneed colliers were willing to accept and tried to urge the majority to join them. From others a wintry howl went up. There were short tense meetings in the rain and conflicts between the rival factions.

Then C. P. Meredith died. He caught a cold in his new house and, unnursed by his wife, whom he kept safe in the country, he fretted himself into pneumonia. Though attacked—and even stoned—during the high temper of strikes, C.P. was more or less liked by the workers. He was associated with them, he was of their kidney. The rumour got about that he had said on his death-bed that the strike had killed him. Always respecting and emotional about death, the valley population was shocked: it was as though there had been a mass murder by the strikers. They lamented, they truly grieved: it was unwise for anyone to say a word against C.P., now majestic in death.

They attended his funeral in great droves, preceding the coffin in a long ragged cortege, grave with unfed solemnity. They sang all the way to the cemetery. And the mobbed voices were as trees breaking into spring blossom. They became religious again and the seductive promise of death purified the bitter air. Was anything worth fighting for when all ended in death? The world had ever been a despotic place, fixed in the dominion of evil, unfaithful to God; it was under doom. Why try to combat such ancient fast-rooted wickedness? Singing their way to the cemetery the workers ate of this defeatism as though it were a luxurious dish of home-cured ham and eggs.

The blight lasted several dangerous days. And Christmas was approaching, a bespangled mockery: no toys for enquiring children, no order for goose or turkey placed with the butcher, no puddings made. To get back to work now would mean a week's pay and unlimited credit at the shops. The Associated Owners, suddenly magnanimous, withdrew their week-old offer and made a Christmas present: instant return to work on the pre-strike rates. John Johns, up in Nant Vale, went a bit farther, repeating his five-per-cent offer and also promising a twenty-eight-pound bag of potatoes on Christmas Eve to all his workers, from his farms in mid-Wales—it was said by the agitators that owing to a glut on the market he was unable to sell the spuds.

Beriah came up to Tudor's surgery one evening to have an aching tooth out. Even he whined a little and looked dim. After the operation he sat gulping in oppression.

"They're changing," he mumbled.

Tudor gave him a tonic and cleared up the surgery, all the patients gone. Daisy came in to help, moving with soft abundance behind the men, clad in a meek grey.

"What makes you think so?" Tudor asked.

"Ach, I can smell the air."

"I don't believe it," Tudor said, but worried of voice. "There's only a surface tiredness. Thank God the Associated Owners didn't offer a five-per-cent advance—then we would have been done.... And," he said, glancing out at the skulking clouds, "the rain is going to finish. A new lot of meetings, Beriah."

"They're saying things about you," Beriah said abruptly.

"What things?"

"Oh, there's a lot of silly gossip," deprecated Beriah, frailly doleful. "That foreigners are paying you to stoke up trouble, and you're a bad egg—drove your mother to her grave. And that young leddy—what's her name?—"

"Mildred Richards," said Daisy, slamming the lid of a can of salts. "She's been talking."

"I don't know about that. But my Susan says they say you treated her dirty, and she's been took bad with nerves as a result, and all her hair is dropping out—"

"It was always silly hair," Daisy said. "No strength in it."

Tudor had heard about Mildred from his grandmother. She seemed to be going into a kind of vigorous decline, moping but full of baleful obstinacy, refusing to stay in bed, refusing to go for the winter to Torquay. She had gone to a weekday prayer meeting one evening, got up on her feet and delivered a denunciatory address on the criminal elements in the district. She was losing her hair; she had bouts of fury, but also complained weepingly to acquaintances of the treatment she had received at Tudor's hands; to one, a well-known gossip, she had declared that he had thrown her over because she wouldn't allow him to seduce her when he couldn't afford to get married. Her face had developed a wild thin beauty, rasping to behold, unsettling and appealing to one's sympathy. He shrugged his shoulders at the gossip, but what he had heard of her decline made him wince in dread.

The next afternoon, finding himself near her home, he obeyed the impulse that had been lurking at the back of his mind, and knocked at the familiar villa door. Her purring, tiresome father would be at his office. Pally, the servant, opened and dropped her jaw.

"Is Miss Mildred at home, Polly?"

Polly looked severe. "I'll see," she said, closing the door on him abruptly. When she came back she was stiff with disapproval. "Please to come in."

Mildred was sitting at work on some embroidery by the drawing-room fire. Her face was already arranged in malice. But he was shocked at its worn look, showing the bones, the white cheeks hollowed. He approached uneasily and took her hand. She gave him a mocking, but cunning glance, and snatched her hand away.

"What d'you want?" she said in a harsh, jeering way. "Mildred, why must there be all this bad feeling between us?"

"Bad feeling!" she repeated, playing for time. Then with sudden febrile energy: "What d'you expect?"

Unasked, he sat on a footstool beside her. He struggled to keep the compassion out of his voice, as he had swept the horror from his expression when he had come into the room and seen the haggard malice of her face lifted to him. "Why must you deliberately damage yourself?"

She had taken up the embroidery again and was determinedly stitching, with stretched back mouth, like someone condemned to the work in hell. And then she leaned over the silk flowers of the cloth to him, she seemed to spit: "I'm going to finish you in this place," she said.

He felt that he was sitting beside an unknown woman. He was appalled at the gross change in her. A corruption lurked in her sunken eyes. A terrible liberation had come to her, a death in life. He shrank inside, feeling the triumph of that malign death. Had he done this, had *he?* No, no. She had done it to herself, she was another victim, as his mother had been a victim, eaten up in death processes. Why had they to be consumed so, what bestial worm of corruption gnawed at their roots? And suddenly he felt that this coming to her was futile, hopeless. She had her contaminated view of life and she would not, could not, swerve from it.

Yet he had to go on, he had to make the attempt:

"You're going to finish me!" he repeated. "Come, Mildred you're being melodramatic. Besides," he added, "it can't be done any further—I'm ruined already according to all the notions you possess, I've touched bottom."

"The *common* people don't know about you enough," she said

with that brittle mockery. "Bah, you standing up at street corners spouting a lot of uplift, and they listening with open mouths! They want to know—"

He made a gesture of contempt. "Your malice only hurts me in this way, Mildred—I'm angry that you've found malice necessary. I hate it that you've allowed yourself to become like this.... But," he went on urgently, "it's you I've come to see; I haven't come about your activities, this gossip you're spreading about me."

She flashed him a look of scorn. And there was something brisk about her, a polluted briskness, spitting out life from some interior witch-brew. "Well, it's too late," she jeered. "Besides, you ought to be ashamed, you, a married man calling on his former—" She stopped: a cunning little gleam crossed her eyes: she went on stitching, darting him sly watchful sideway glances from under her swollen reddish eyelids. He saw with renewed horror her thinned-out hair, the yellow scalp visible. There had always been a slight suggestion of unhealthiness about her: in her girlhood it had given her a certain poetic charm, precious. It had been kept in check; now it had been given full liberation.

Her threats affected him in no way; he couldn't be hurt *personally* by their trivial efforts, and any mischief they caused in the valley could be fought and, he was confident, destroyed. But that this horror had taken place in her! He made another attempt:

"I tell you, Mildred, it was far better for us to finish. We could never have made a success of life together. It would have been a bitter business, after a while. Can't you see that our problem went beyond love? It became a battle of wills. You couldn't forgo your ideas of what I should be, of what our life together ought to be, and you rather wanted to forget sex—it was an indecent thing to you, you were in love with some sickly angel you managed to perceive in me. And I couldn't submit to you. It's quite simple—"

Her voice came out in a sudden shrill bark: "You took a long enough time to find all that out. And skulking to that woman. Even when you were keeping it up with me.... *You* say I am indecent!" she barked, amid sickening foam at her mouth. "You whoring down in that house the night you were arrested, among a pack of criminals—"

"Not whoring, Mildred. Only trying to get at some reality."

"Bah," she spat madly, "words, words. You're just bad through and through, evil and a rogue."

"Then, surely it's to your advantage that you escaped me?"

Again she leaned towards him, the defiled shine of her sunken eyes turned full on him. "I would have saved you!" she cried. "D'you hear, I would have saved you. Your mother, your father, asked me to save you. Your mother on her death-bed asked me to save you. She said she had failed. And you killed her, d'you hear, you killed her! "

"Nonsense," he said. "Control yourself, you silly woman—" But what was the use of anger?

"And you think you've got your grandmother on your side, don't you? Ah, let me tell you she's only sentimental about you. In her heart of hearts she's troubled and afraid for you, she thinks that woman will finish you—her and the police between them. You'll be in the gutter before many years are out."

"Bronwen must approve of this gossip you're spreading about," he said ironically.

And again the mad jeering malice filled her face. "Bronwen and I have to go different ways now," she said ruthlessly.

Then he leaned to her. Shaken and afraid for her. This horrible rasping venom must not be allowed to go uncurbed, this grotesque futile malice. "Mildred," he urged compassionately, "Mildred, you're ill, you're killing yourself. Listen to me. Let me attend you, let me come to you—"

She sent him one of her cunning side-faced glances. She seemed to be considering his offer, craftily. "What would that wife of yours say?" she demanded.

"Nothing, nothing at all."

"And what's the treatment?" Her hands were clasping rigidly at the embroidery again; she looked as though she would dribble on the silken flowers.

"Talk," he said gently, "talk as in the old days. We'll read poems together again, have some music; we'll try and make some sense of the world."

Her face turned fully to him with a long slow look.

"You mean you want me to be friendly with you and your wife, don't you? Oh yes, you could talk *her* round, I've no doubt—I know her sort. Even to—" She smiled with a thin suggestive wickedness.

"Mildred, don't torment your self so!" he entreated. He was beginning to feel exhausted. But he leaned farther to her, he put his hand on her knee.

With a sudden dart her clawed fingers came down and she plunged her needle into his hand. A low hiss came from between her teeth.

Gasping from the pain, he sprang up. She also darted up, throwing over a small table of work-things beside the chair—it fell with a crash, smashing a saucer of pins. She was writhing with insane delight, her greenish eyes danced.

"You bitch!" Unconsciously, he had gripped her shoulders; he shook her.

She shoved against him, she kicked, she shouted. They struggled and fell, crashing to the carpet together. They rolled over; she was gripping him. When the maidservant flung back the door, Mildred was beating her fists against the floor, Tudor was in the act of getting up.

"Send this ruffian away," she shrieked.

Tudor started; he looked down at his bleeding hand. "You arranged that very well, Mildred," he said contemptuously.

Polly's hips were swaying with a domestic's silent rage as she went to her mistress's assistance. "Send him away." Foam came from Mildred's mouth.

"Polly," Tudor said, achieving calm by an effort, "did you ever stick a needle in anybody's hand?"

"I'd do more if they deserved it," she breathed. But hitherto she had always been friendly with him.

282

He nodded. Mildred had scrambled, with a great air of exhaustion, to her feet. But she dashed across the room, as though in great fear. She was whimpering. And as she ran upstairs she broke into loud sobs, fearful, pitiable, abandoned. Polly hastened after her.

Those broken agonised sobs in his ears, he escaped the house and plunged, almost ran, down into the valley. The horror engulfed him again: he felt he was enclosed in madness, too, that his mind was ripped and split, that chaos threatened him.

He had loved her, ah! how he had loved her, with what a wealth of dreams, a luxuriance of visions. And now she was seething with uncontrolled madness, she was calling with deliberate abandonment on demons, she wanted to squat with the furies in hell. The evils of death were roused in her and she was clinging to them with bitter abandonment.

He pulled up on the bank of the black stream, by a clump of dust-heavy bushes; he fell on the bank and sucked the blood from the wound in his hand. In horror he said to himself that soon she would be a case for a doctor with different qualifications from his.

A scarlet light filled the valley; the sun on the top of the mountains was a piece of red ice. The windows of the grimy rows of houses shone like markings on the backs of long saurian monsters lying in primeval slime. He saw the place as bestial and corrupt, allowed to flourish in unobstructed depravity, meaninglessly foul in the mud, a repulsive life breeding horrors unhindered, encouraged. The whole place was a slimy corruption of underworld life. Beauty became grotesque here, peace a fantasy, tenderness a mockery.

But when he got home he was calmer. And he told himself that according to the laws of the primitive world into which Mildred had now translated herself, she was quite justified in behaving in this menacing way. According to her apprehension of life, he had baulked her of harmony, security of sex, proper flowering.

He would have to let it go at that now, he could do no more

than his offer of that afternoon, which had been spat back at him. Perhaps he had deserved that spitting back. He had no right to breed so much love in his heart. The activities of humanity were not governed by compassion, as he surely should have known by now. Compassion, love, generosity were the luxuries of romantic poets.

But nausea still held him. Cursing over his hand in the surgery—it was wounded badly—he called to Daisy to come and help him bandage it. She moved in; her body seemed to flow softly into the room, drowsy in its maternity: she had been having a little nap.

"I didn't hear you come in," she said.... "You're wanted in number thirty-one: Annie Saunders. She's begun." She spoke in placid approval of life. "Why, what have you been doing to your hand?"

He looked at her sardonically. In a few curt phrases he told her of his visit to Mildred, and the attack. "She got me down on the floor, she screamed for the servant. I suppose she wanted it to look as though I had attacked her... mad, mad."

Daisy listened and began to bridle. But he felt he couldn't bear it if she was going to vent on him a lot of sympathy, abuse of Mildred, and anger. She didn't.

"Serve you right," she said, iron of voice, as, the hand bandaged hastily, he snatched his little bag and began to hurry away. She meant, he supposed, that he needed a final lesson.

IV

The great mass meeting that was held at the entrance to the valley saved the strike for a while. John Carruthers, impressive in his security as one of the first Labour members of parliament, came down and spoke with shrewd intimacy to the unwieldy mob.

They had come from all parts of the county, marchers

284

converging on this central place—the mouth of the stubborn old valley that was always making such unruly assaults on the peace of capitalism. The efforts of the gangs that had visited the different industrial areas with honeyed invitations—and frequently with use of fists—seemed to be bearing fruit: some of the smaller areas, indeed, were already on strike. And there was even a contingent from Abba Vale—obstinate and small, but undoubtedly there. Fortunately, the bad weather had cleared.

Carruthers, clean and stern-looking as a page of the Bible, began by complimenting the men of South Wales on their courage. Purity, he said, and the eternal battling spirit of hope had dwellings among these mountains. He then launched into a passionate plea, weighted by his authority, for a strong union of all the insurgent elements in the different districts. No real good could be achieved while energy was being dissipated in minor strikes and while vale fought against vale in tribal distrust.

With his own particular brand of puritanic emotionalism, he poured fresh strength into the weary, hungry valley strikers. He assured them of outside sympathy in their struggle—all the workers of Britain were watching, perhaps with wonder, the brave struggles down in Wales.... The mob was eased by the flattery of this herald of the new teaching, who was almost respectable, his speeches often importantly in the newspapers. They roared applause at him. Non-strikers began to feel ashamed, and in the collection for the aid of the valley men they gave ungrudgingly.

There were other speakers, among them Tudor Morris. All were listened to attentively: the meeting looked like being a unanimous success. Tudor Morris had been hooted down at a local meeting only the night before, the mob-feeling about him having taken a turn that no one stopped to wonder about: it was as if someone had to be selected for blame at the strike's weary continuance. But today, among this great company, the strikers gave him a cheer.

They marched back up the valley singing. It was believed that there would be important supporting strikes after Christmas, so they'd hold out now. Blast Christmas for themselves—this was

285

six days before the twenty-fifth—they'd make do on the special few bob promised to each, obtained by charity and a contribution from the Miners' Federation of Great Britain.

Tudor marched, as usual, with his committee. But Ieuan, the amateur boxer, by now looking pitiably battered from his many recent political fights, was full of gloomy grunts.

"It's all eye-wash," he kept on saying, "all eye-wash. Jest a spree it was today. Them non-strikers will go home and settle down to Christmas and forget all about us."

Tudor was unsure. But he said: "I don't think they're ready to come out yet. We'll have to start hammering at them again after Christmas.... But we've gained something today. Our men are livelier."

Beriah gazed curiously at Tudor. "You want to go on after Christmas, slogging at the other districts?"

"Why, yes. That's the point of today's meeting."

Another member said: "It would be better if we got up a big eisteddfod and had the men occupied in making poetry and singing and woodwork."

Tudor looked round in alarm, acutely conscious again of the submerged exhaustion in his committee. And he saw at once that it was actually a matter of lack of *food*. Bread, cheese and meat.

"Meetings," grunted Ieuan, "I'm sick of 'em."

"Listen to the chaps singing!" Tudor said indignantly.

"Wait till they get home and the missuses get at 'em again." Black disillusion sprawled on Ieuan's misshapen face. "I 'ad a lot myself this morning."

Through the long winter-cold valley the strikers wound their ragged way, but as they continued the singing became ragged, finally dying out. It was getting near a meal-time. But it was a mock meal-time. What was there to return to? The long roll of cold-coloured rocky mountains gave no answer: the world looked unmovable and unconnected. The faces of the chapels they passed were closed in stony weekday silence, the shops looked hostile, the pubs unused, the assembled policemen stood darkly ironical.

But passing an Associated colliery, some of the strikers raised a faint hoot of derision. At the bridge leading to the pit-heads a dozen policemen stood guard: the long line of strikers passed within a few yards. And suddenly there was an unkempt rush, instinctive as a stampede of animals. It was all over in a minute. But in that minute there were sounds of cracking jaws, savage yells and smashing glass-those who were not bestowing coma on the police had picked up stones from the rough roadside and were throwing them at the colliery offices beside the bridge.

"Christ!" shouted Tudor, turning, "what are they up to?" He and the others were a quarter mile ahead.

"They've got the coppers!" Ieuan bellowed. "Look out!" There was a tense halt of a second, while everyone took in the situation, and then a wild rush across the road to the sanctuary of the dwelling-rows each side, and the mountains. Round corners and through back lanes they ran; almost immediately the road was bare as a knife. At the bridge entrance the police lay tumbled in quiet disorder; one spiked helmet rolled down an incline to the railway below.

Dwellings were invaded by men not belonging to them, who darted in through front doors and back doors. Some hid in the back garden closets; some, without permission from startled but knowing wives, rushed upstairs and dived under beds. Nevertheless, eighteen arrests were made and then, apparently, other police, who had sprinted up quickly, were satisfied.

Tudor and Beriah had dashed into a house together. A stout woman was lifting off the fire a frying-pan containing bread soaked in dripping. Four children sat waiting at the table.

"What the deuce—" she exclaimed.

"There's been a fight," Tudor whispered, laying his finger dramatically over his lips. "Police about. Can we hide?"

Beriah was looking at her keenly. "Minnie Parry, isn't it?" he asked politely. "I know your Dai, in work."

"Ha," she snapped, "ha, is he in it, the rodney? I told him not to go out this morning—"

"Where can we go?" urged Beriah, peering round. A miner's cottage doesn't offer many secret places.

"Come here," she said impatiently. And she placed Beriah in a corner, shifting the sofa against him; Tudor went behind a mangle in the dark box-like scullery. They were preposterous hiding-places, but the chance had to be taken. The children were amused, briskly eating their fried bread. A young policeman actually ran in, truncheon in hand, demanded if any strikers were there, received a surprised "no", darted upstairs, and clattered out busily.

Minnie Parry, still holding the frying-pan like a shield, then shouted to her visitors: "Go out from here; rascals that you are." When they came out, she stamped her foot and writhed with indignation. "Coming into my house as though it was nothing! Go on out. Never has there been a policeman in this house before—" She seemed about to sob at the desecration.

"Your Dai," said Beriah, "will be proud of you."

"Thank you, Mrs. Parry," Tudor said, "for hiding us."

They examined the street before going out. But neighbours were already swarming out: the police had gone with all the arrests they could manage.

But that little fling was the beginning of the Christmas riots; a taste of blood. When it became known that the strike was to be prolonged, various turbulent sections, bored, got busy. In the more solid shops there were collections of Christmas goods, in spite of the strike. Tactless tradesmen had put in their windows fruits, biscuits, pats of butter, cakes, hams, plump geese and turkeys; the middle-class and certain austere mining families who had savings could still buy. The quietness of the strike so far, and the troops in their tents, gave confidence. Pretty garlands of coloured paper were looped across the windows, tinsel glittered, and in one meat shop an enormous rosy pig sprawled across a marble slab, wearing a pair of spectacles and a bowler hat.

It was thought that those eighteen arrests would have been warning. But the looting of the shops occurred the next night and was well planned, hundreds taking part, many of whom got nothing or perhaps a tin of cocoa or a couple of sausages.

They gathered in the black back lanes behind the main streets, the various gangs concentrating on the different groups of shops scattered up and down the valley. It was a surprise move, more or less unprepared for, only the extra police dawdling about and a night quiet beginning to settle; about ten o'clock. The troops, not used yet and torpid in this dismal place, were mostly in bed; those few who had managed to overcome the resistance of the hostile local girls were occupied with them in draughty higher spots; one was found knocked out in a back lane.

The rush of sprinting men into the main street was followed by the quick smashing of the street lamps. At once stones crashed through the windows of the shops, most of which were closed. The streets were filled with jumping, seething black masses.

It was a triumph for the rioters, this first evening, except at one centre, where the police were concentrated and put up a good fight, even so far as to be able to make a few arrests. But at most of the other centres the looting went on undisturbed. Grocers' and butchers' were, of course, the most favoured shops. At Matthews's natty and ambitious provision store a dozen men put shoulder to shoulder and burst open the front door, while others were busy clambering through the windows. So many crowded into this well-stocked shop that they became wedged inside, and quarrelling took place in the dark—the gas had been turned off at the main. Several men tugged together at a fifty-pound slab of butter on the counter, and no one could hold it; it slid to the floor and caused havoc, surging men falling and slipping over it. A satisfied Irishman, with a ham under his coat, tried to push his way out, but the ham was snatched off him and, bellowing, he began a free fight. In the morning splashes of blood had congealed into the stamped-out butter on the floor and twenty-three teeth were found by Matthews.

The uproar in the streets had an abandoned vengeful sound. Those unable to get at the food-stuff shops attacked the drapers' with fury: the screech of falling glass eased and thrilled the nerves. Rolls of cloth were popular, and blankets and overcoats. Having obtained something—anything—the rioters ran or staggered away, climbing and ducking into the secretive back streets. At corners little knots of women watched from shawls, grimly accepting this outburst of the men. One man ran to a group and tossed into his wife's arms a bladder of lard and three twelve-inch bars of soap.

"The turkey!" she exclaimed indignantly. "Where's the turkey? A turkey you said you'd get me."

"Butcher's swept bare 'fore I could get there," he panted. "Some 'asn't 'ad anything, Maggie," he pleaded. "Be satisfied now."

"I want a turkey," she wailed. "First Christmas there's been no turkey in the house!" In her temper she threw the bars of soap on the ground, but not the lard. Her companions tried to comfort her; one picked up a bar and disappeared; another asked anxiously of the husband if he'd seen her Llew—he was going to try to get one of those ready-made Christmas puddings that were in Matthews's window.

"Duw mun," he answered, "Matthews's shop's like an excursion train to Barry, everybody on top of each other and shouting like mad. Can't get in nor out."

"Where's the bobbies?" she asked in fear.

"Those as is not laid out," he said briefly, "have gone 'ome to sit still till we done our shopping…. Hold on now, Maggie girl, I done my best."

"A Christmas with nothing but lard—" she grizzled.

"There's two more days 'fore Christmas," he hinted. Some men were hurrying past loaded with things. Maggie broke out afresh. All the best things would be gone. Her husband, cursing, darted down to the main street again.

The bowler-hatted pig caused some internecine warfare. Dozens of rioters meant to get it. It was first seized by an intrepid young collier heading a certain gang—he smashed a brick through the butcher's window, tore away the jagged segments of plate-glass with his naked hands and snatched out the carcase as if it were a doll. While others helped themselves to the sundry joints and poultry on view, the collier darted through the swarm with a whoop of triumph. But he was followed by jealous men; the pig was in his embrace for about five minutes. According to the tales told afterwards, it was seen in Sychan, three miles down the valley, slung across a red-headed man's shoulders; up in Bryn Hyfryd's windy heights, borne by a staggering woman; across the river in Plas Ddu, its head looking over a bloke's shoulder as he disappeared into a back lane. Actually, it was captured by a gang of four men, who chased after each of its temporary owners until they cornered one in a deserted place. A youth obtained the bowler and took it home with three apples he found in a gutter.

In the morning the tradesmen complained to the police. Why had guard been slackened? And what was the use of the soldiers appearing an hour late? The main streets presented a gaping, shaken appearance. From one street lamp a pink corset still flapped; ground plate-glass glittered frostily over the road. Up in the combs of back streets, a respectable silence reigned; few people came out that day, though there was some creeping through back lanes.

The riots did not end with this pillaging. Blood had been drunk now. There were organised fights with the police the next evening, gang-rushes from street corners. A brew of venom had seethed up suddenly from an old source. The satisfaction of the fight became like a wallowing in a religious orgasm. The place spat with fury, the violence became contagious. More police were hurried in: the troops were assembled at various spots, bayonets fixed.

But the gangs had a gleaming-eyed foxy cunning; they slithered through those useful back lanes, jumped over backyard walls and in a trice were sitting at tables in the dwellings, looking bland. Houses were raided wholesale by damaged police, with little result.

A young man, Dan Roberts, earned notoriety by his leadership of these intractable gangs: unknown before, he sprang yelling from the murky undercurrent now flowing through the valley, as though born of its savage flow. He had a muscular jumping body full of daring, a swarthy gipsy face and a voice that hit like a fist. In broad daylight he would dance out of a back lane to within a few yards of an assembly of policemen and yell, strutting about like an infuriated David before the sacred ark:

"We'll get the whole bloody lot of you yet, we'll put the whole place on fire, we'll roast you all in hell. Ah, we got a thing or two to settle. Call out the whole —— army and navy, bring over wild Indians and blacks from the jungle—we'll strip 'em all of their skins. Hey, there—"

And he would launch into abuse of the owners and the police sergeants, as he jumped and danced near the entrance of the back lane. Sometimes, shouting like this, he would dash out followed by a roaring squad of strikers armed with stones and sticks. The collection of police, bristling out of their inscrutable silence, met them with batons. Skulls were cracked, strikers swayed to the ground; sometimes a shrieking woman, having watched from behind a window curtain, darted into the main road and dragged some dazed relation to safety.

The third night a chapel was set afire—Calfaria chapel, where that minister in some of his sermons left his rightful Bible business and took it upon himself to criticise the strike. The chapel was insured and the walls were ill-built and cracking anyhow: some said the minister had deliberately worked for the arson, wanting to swank in a new chapel. On Christmas Eve one of the managers' houses went up in flames, too, the family having gone away and the couple of police on guard overcome.

A mass meeting was called on Boxing Day, down on the sports field. There were half a dozen speakers, but none was listened to with any prolonged attention. The temper of nearly all the valley had changed. About a hundred constables were ranged round the field, and outside were the soldiers with those long naked bayonets

292

showing. Strangely, there were about fifty hardy women bunched in the mob. Hoots, catcalls and jeers filled the air. What use was someone getting up on his legs and making a speech? What use was *talk?* What was there new to say about the blasted strike, terms, owners? Knock hell out of the owners, get at property and destroy it, *act*. Beriah Evans, of that Tudor Morris gang, was listened to longest, his little white respectable face full of severe deprecation:

"—and I say to you now, solemn and serious, those rioters are behaving foolish, mad. Let them set fire to twenty chapels, loot a thousand shops, and still they're not giving four-pennyworth of help to settle the strike. Stay steady, men, be firm and have a bit of pride—"

"Preaching to the converted you are," someone shouted. "There's no rioters here, Beriah, only a lot of nice bobbies and us, and we're taking out our knitting-needles in a minute." Ironical laughter mocked at the constables' uncommenting faces.

Tudor Morris followed Beriah on the cart. There was a thin wave of handclapping, immediately drowned by a torrent of hoots. The bunch of women—among them Mrs. Violet Fox, herb-dealer—shrieked derision. In a momentary lull, a female voice enquired with harsh venom: "Hey, 'ow many wives you got, you damn Turk. What's these tricks you're up to, hey?" Various comments were heard among the gesticulating female bunch: "A shifty chap. Disgraced his parents, old Doctor Elwyn, and shoved his mother into the grave. Got that slut, Daisy Waiters, up in his house. Ach, abad lot, and him a doctor, too, so he says. Treated Mildred Richards dirty and wants to carry on with her again now! Got no religion too: they say things go on up in that house 'bove the Terraces—" And the men, newly distrustful and for the most part fundamentally puritanic of moral outlook, shouted abuse: what did *he* know about the inside of a pit, why didn't he stick to his own job? A sprinkling of Terrace men, however, took up angry cudgels on behalf of their easy-going doctor. But there were not many Terrace men on the field, where it was expected there would be a lot of police.

Tudor stood looking unmoved, waiting for the clamour to dwindle. But he felt oddly exhilarated by the enmity, and it steadied him. The swaying turbulent mob seemed to him well worth living with. They were superbly *alive;* they moved in the central stream of humanity, shifting with mutinous force to new revelations.... Allowing himself this dreamy vision of them while they clamoured, he took the first opportunity of a lull, coolly beginning:

"Now you've had your fun, I'd like to speak about the support we're going to get from the other valleys, providing we keep our heads and stop this rioting—"

"Ha," a female voice shouted, "you 'couraged the rioting enough with all your bamboozling talk. Didn't he now?"

Companions took her up. "Aye, and he been working for a strike for a year. All right for him, he's never starved, always a bellyful when he wants it."

He flashed into fury: "What the hell are you talking about? This is a strike meeting, not a slanging match—"

"Ha, ha," rocked the women, "that's got him. Get down from there, you dirty old crow, you randy old ——" Someone pushed a fist in her mouth—a Terrace man. And there was an uproar.

Fighting broke out; the jeering anger that had beat through the crowd wholly engulfed it. The meeting broke up, a failure. The strike had got finally out of control.

Tudor walked up to the Terraces with Beriah. He walked with a spring, his face sharpened. Beriah, hurrying along beside him, was inclined to be gloomy.

"It's no good," he lamented, "it's no good. They'll cut their own throats... it's going back," he complained, "to evil times. It don't suit modern times to fight in this way."

"I'm not sure, Beriah—now. They're getting down to natural instinct. After all, highly-educated nations are obliged to have a war now and again—England's got one now.... Personally, I prefer the one we've got down here. It's not so damn futile as the nation against nation kind."

"You've been preaching against the rioting," Beriah pointed out. "And blaming them—"

"Preaching is of the mind, Beriah. They've got their bodies to deal with."

"Well, seems our preaching's got to finish now."

Beriah looked washed-out. "Looks as though those rough 'oomen got you measured for themselves. I been feeling a nasty rising against you for a while now.... That Violet Fox is a dangerous old dame," he hinted.

Tudor shrugged his shoulders. "It'll be years before they accept me. I've got to live down my birth. I smell like a traitor."

Beriah hesitated and then asked: "Why do you do it—I mean come amongst us?... I been wanting to ask you for some time," he stammered.

"Ah, don't ask me that, Beriah—don't disappoint me. Ask me why I breathe or why I've got a nose on my face."

Beriah nodded, smiling dimly. "Yes," he agreed, "yes, I'm sorry now I was so simple as to ask."

He ate bread and cheese with Tudor and Daisy. Daisy was full of cheerful spirits, even after hearing how the meeting had gone; she had been to see Bronwen, who had given her a lot of household linen and an old-fashioned bracelet. Her brother, Melville, was due out in three days and she was planning a New Year's Eve party to give him welcome. A Christmas present of two pounds had arrived from her Bristol friends, the Captain and Mrs. Barnes, and she was going to spend it all on food. "The strike," she said comfortably, "the strike—I'm used to 'em, I've grown on 'em. I was brought up to expect only twenty-six Sunday joints in each year. Other Sundays only sop, with a few currants in it. I asked my father once why strikes weren't talked about in the Bible–for he used to say that the whole of life was in the Bible–and he didn't know what to say for a bit and then all he could think of was Job."

"There was Lucifer," Tudor said.

"Aye," Beriah nodded, "Lucifer was a strike-leader. For in those days God used to be like our Sir Rufus Morgan here, showing off too much in a bossy way."

"Lucifer," said Daisy, carelessly cutting herself still another lump of Caerphilly cheese, "made hell."

"Still," Tudor laughed, "he was an enquiring spirit."

He looked at her with relief, filled with a sense of congratulation at having this woman in the house. Lord, what a dismal and worried evening this might have been had she not been there. Failure and poverty seemed all about the house: but outside, outside. Here, in spite of the meagre table and that drawerful of bills, was a sprouting of luxuriant life. Beriah gone, he leaned to Daisy and gathered the flesh of the back of her neck between his teeth; she uttered squeals of heaving laughter, her swollen body plunging like a ship.

"Haven't you had enough to eat?"

"Never enough of you."

"I wonder will you say that in ten years' time."

"Ah, I don't suppose you'll want me to."

"Well, I like being a married woman, so far." Full-sailed, assured, she swept into the kitchen, carrying the huge loaf she had baked herself. "Be off now and try and get a few bob off some patients—I bet if you tap one or two of them, you'll find they've got a bag of quids put away under the floor-boards."

"Not in the Terraces, Daisy."

"Let me make the round of them, then," she suggested. "I can sniff the kind of women that put money away on the quiet…. If you don't get some new socks soon," she sighed, "you'll have to wear some old woollen stockings of mine."

"Thank God you've got big feet," he laughed, going off.

As it happened he struck lucky on his visits that evening. At a pneumonia case he found an aunt of the patient's wife had arrived from Swansea; a lantern-jawed woman in her best black, who by dint of an unmarried energy had risen from being a little flannel-maker in a cottage to ownership of a shop, to say nothing of a stall in the market. Her flannel was tough and hairy as a terrier's skin and shirted most of the Swansea dock-labourers. She was bristly herself, especially here in this Terrace kitchen, where her little niece Megan lived, married to a good-for-nothing.

"Now, Doctor," she asked, when Tudor had come downstairs, "he is going to die?" Her brief voice spoke business: she had to catch a train back almost at once.

Tudor glanced at Megan, the young squat wife, whose eyes were rolling heavily with grief: he had been having a little conference with her upstairs.

"He's very ill," he said. "Lack of nourishment is at the bottom of his trouble."

"He is going to die?" she repeated.

"Oh, Auntie," cried Megan, burying her face in a towel she was carrying, "I know I'm going to lose him."

"He's very, very ill." Tudor shook his head gloomily.

The flannel merchant turned over the gold watch pinned to her bosom, looked at it with a sharp decisive eye, and then picked up the folds of her skirts. From some interior fastness she produced a small canvas bag.

"You mustn't have a parish funeral, Megan," she said. Out of the bag she took five sovereigns, stiffened herself, and then took another. "Here's six pounds. Funerals are sure to be at low prices in strike times."

"Oh, Auntie!" moaned Megan, still in the towel. "There's good you are!"

"Work it out in wages you can when you come to work for me in my shop.... Now then, Doctor, you been paid?" Her ruthless demeanour suggested that she was determined to clean up any slovenliness due to Megan's foolish marriage. "I don't suppose you have," she sniffed. "How much? I can't abide debts."

"There was my bronchitis in October," Megan prompted. "Doctor Morris been looking after us champion, Auntie."

Tudor made a rough guess and said fifty shillings. The aunt shook up her bag of coins and paid out. "Now then," she said to Megan, "when he's gone, expect you I shall a fortnight after.

Good room for you there is in my shop." She pecked at the girl's wet cheek and hustled out.

Megan excitedly flung her arms round Tudor and then ran screaming upstairs: "Will, Will, she's left six pounds! For your funeral. Get better at once. Oh, Will! We can have a lot to eat. Ducks and tarts and jellies—"

Will would get better. Tudor went home and tossed the gold coins into Daisy's lap. "There, more for the party." They were his first earnings of any consequence.

The day following the meeting on the sports field there was a final concerted attack from the rioters—a furious abandoned attack, for by now the police were everywhere and the troops were ranged for action.

And it was a final day for that riot-leader, Dan Roberts. His despotic mother, the widowed Mrs. Melia Roberts—the only person he was afraid of—intended whisking him off from his hiding-place on the Saturday, to work in her brother's pub in Builth Wells. So Dan was full of a farewell spirit. He got going early with his large gang, making a midday attack on a dozen police who were marching smartly to their beat. By one o'clock they had fired a wooden recreation-hall and stolen most of a bull killed the day before in a slaughter-house on the mountain side. Children were told not to return to school in the afternoon and tradesmen shut their shops. An ominous silence took possession of the valley; the streets were empty of their usual traffic and everyone waited expectantly for night.

What street lamps were left undamaged burned with a stammering light; great lanes of silent darkness were spread through the valley. Now and again the clopping of a police sergeant's horse could be heard. Most of the troops were gathered on the square in the centre of the valley, waiting for orders.

Up in a quarry in the mountains, Dan Roberts was prancing in the middle of a couple of hundred men. His voice sank and rose:

"We got to make ourselves felt, haven't we? What are we—a lot of squashed snails or frightened beetles caught in a pan? Who says woa and stop? Not us! What's a strike for—to sit at home and play ball? Those other chaps, those brainy ones, they tell us to keep on waiting. But we got to warn them owners we can fight in the old-fashioned way, we got to show 'em we own these bloody mountains.... 'Ow's that?" He pranced and struck a warrior pose in the darkness.

"We'd put you up on that Federation when the strike's over," someone said admiringly. "You talk healthy, Dan."

"What do we come into this blooming world for?" he made roaring enquiry.

"Hist," a voice warned, "you don't know what cops are lying about."

"We're not buttercups, are we—" he demanded more softly of the other colliers—"and we're not kids' fairies and we're not pats of butter—nor yet," he added in humility, "are we angels. We just got guts to feed and women to put in clean houses, and children to bring up proper and old grandparents to put out on farms."

"Well, what about it?" someone asked with impatience. "Don't *you* start jawing, Dan."

"I was going to go in for the ministry once," Dan said, momentarily solemn. "But there was no brass to send me to college."

"If your old woman takes you off to Builth on Saturday," a man nearby asked, "who's going to lead us?"

Dan's voice became sulky and ashamed-sounding. "I'm not gone yet.... Perhaps I won't go at all," he scowled.

"Ah, you'll go," an intimate said cynically. "Melia told my Jinny she'd drag you by the hair to the station."

"You go, Dan," another urged. "Working in a country pub now, out of all this botheration—and very good fishing in the brooks up there—a mug you'd be to chuck the chance."

A chorus of impatient voices broke out. "Let's get off, the night's going."

A long stealthy procession, headed by Dan, they filed down

299

the mountain side. On the loose path along the back of the first row of houses they gathered extra stones into their pockets. Several possessed truncheons stolen from constables in previous battles; some had short parlour pokers. The cold rough mountain air blew on their rugged faces, and their short bodies, hard from service in the pits—most of them were young—were hot in determination. They crept past the stony face-frown of Gosen chapel. A lamp gave light here, but they were the only intruders in the valley silence—except for a child, which suddenly began to squeal in a cottage like a hungry puppy.

The offices of the Aber colliery was their objective. And, if possible, the colliery-top itself, where important damage could be done to the engine-house.

They thickened into the back lanes: passing from one to the other through a division in the rows, they huddled close to walls, creeping shadowily along. Once, down in a nearby main road, a file of police passed in business-like formation, going in the opposite direction.

Dan whispered in glee:

"There they go, always the wrong way."

Emerging from the last back lane, to a rough hillock of waste land stumpy with sooted bushes, they could see the colliery below, silent, but hung with a few dingy electric bulbs. Prowling through the bushes they got to the edge of the road, a mass of stooping black shapes. From there they saw, under a high lamp at the colliery entrance, a collection of police and four soldiers. The taut silver tongues of bayonets were distinctly visible. One man whispered:

"Moses, I don't fancy those long knives in my innards."

Dan said, glittering of eye: "They can't use 'em, or the rifles, till the Riot Act's read out. Any rate, there's only four. Soon settle *them*.... Now, boys, ready?" he called hoarsely.

"Aye, all here."

Their footsteps clattered out on the road; their short mountain legs sprang and leapt; they cantered like a herd of wild black cats. Dan's voice burst out in a savage chant.

The soldiers stiffened and clasped their rifles in both hands, but the police surged out in front of them, drawing their batons. A sharp order was cracked out: hordes of police sprang from behind the offices and sprinted over the short bridge.

Sounds of smashing glass testified to the success of some of the rioters in getting through. The first was caught in the act of climbing to a window and knocked out. The four soldiers were ranged at the entrance to the bridge, bayonets pointing outwards. All the police, in those first few moments, were engaged around the offices.

Writhing knots of men sprawled all over the road: the yelling was sub-human, mingled with the sounds of thumping batons. The high lamp swung in the quivering air. Rioters picked themselves up and lurched over to the aid of the less successful, their faces mopped in blood and dust.

A rain of stones fell on the soldiers; two fell, the others charged, their faces roused. But several rioters swung to their backs and neatly kicked them over.

"That'll teach you to open your pen-knives here," one snarled. The four rifles were flung over the bridge.

Dan was well to the fore, yelling directions. He only limped a little, but his face was contorted almost unrecognisably and of a dark yellowish colour.

"Get in the offices and fire 'em! Watkins is out." He threw a bundle of oily rags to some men sprinting up from the battle that was still littering the road behind. "Be quick now and come on to the powerhouse."

About a dozen got on the bridge. They were at the far end when other feet thudded after them. Silver buttons flashed.

"Look out," hissed Dan. "Hide in the sheds."

They sprang into the maze of black pathways cluttered with trucks, dodging among the galleries, most of which were unlit, and through the sheds. One let out a screech as a baton found him; he fell into a heap of coal-dust, thrashing up a black cloud as he whined and beat his arms about; a second blow buried him.

Dan slithered along a line of trucks, his footsteps softened in the layer of dust; he knew the lay-out of this colliery, having worked there as a boy. He stopped, hearing a crisp voice in the distance; he darted to the side of the nearby lamp-room and peered excitedly round its edge. He saw a mass of flames shooting from a window of the offices. His bowels heaved with triumph. When he was fifteen he had stood beside a trestle in those offices, waiting for the ambulance-cart; he had been called up from the pit to go home with his father, who had been working in another part of the pit. The smell of dead blood came out thick from under the blanket on the trestle. Suddenly he had broken out into wild howls. The under-manager, Alec Dunhill, had come bustling from an inner door, papers in his hand. "Ay, there, shut up," he had snapped. "What you howling about? Shut up. Hell, *shut up,* you big baby—what d'you want, a titty-bottle? *Shut up.*" And, maddened at the unceasing howls, he had sworn like a trooper—Dan had been religious in those days—and stamped out of the room.

In his excitement now, he prayed in an audible voice:

"Oh Christ, let the bloody place burn to ashes!" He was still staring, fascinated and abandoned to his ecstasy, at the struggling flames, when he heard soft steps close behind him. He sprang round. A blow from a baton slipped on to his shoulder.

There was a dim light from a dust-caked globe nearby. Dan backed, feeling for a stone in his pocket. The policeman, his bruised face lowered, was staring at him fixedly, with eyes that hung redly out of their sockets. A low hiss came out of the blood-slavered mouth.

"Ah, Dan Roberts, eh!"

Dan whipped out the stone and threw: the policeman dodged and leapt. Dan shuddered against a short loose wall of coal-lumps, swerving. Then he felt something crack inside his head. And yet his hands fumbled for a piece of coal.

"Hell, get out, you."

Dan opened his eyes, snarled at the uplifted arm and flung

302

himself against the dark shape before him. They thudded into the soft dust. Dan was on top. He swung up his arm. His fist seemed to crash through a mass of pulp. He ran.

The colliery-top was sliding about him. He fell over a timber-log. A golden light was plunging everywhere: he realised the offices were well alight. And then lurching into the familiar clearing near the pit shaft, he stopped. Before him a policeman had darted up. He turned: there was another. And another. And another.... Closing in on him. A ring of them. Crouched, stealthy, triumphant.... "There's the bastard!"

"Dan Roberts!"

"Dan Roberts!"

The shouts barked about his ears, thundered in his reeling mind. There were hammer strokes in his head. Defeat, defeat! A cry of agony burst from his lips. His wild swarthy face stared round in horror. The eyes flared with hate. Defeat! To be captured! But there before him was the approach to the pit shaft, a clear golden road. He sprang. At the same time a policeman jumped in his path. He swerved aside and made a little triumphant leap towards the low gate of that half of the pit shaft where the cage was below. Over it. He heard shouts, he hit the black slimy rope that held the cage a quarter of a mile below, he went hurtling down. They said afterwards that he had looked and screamed like a madman. There had always been something wild and untamed about him.

By the time a fresh lot of police and the troops had arrived the attack was over. Only fifteen arrests were made, of unconscious men on the road; all the others got into the mountains and, it was said, stayed there most of the night, nursing each other, but crawling back to their homes before dawn.

The death of Dan Roberts did something; there were no more riots that strike. A consummation had been achieved, an instinct satisfied. A quiet brooded over the valley. People thronged to the chapels that Sunday: a sad tender evening in chapel healed things. Look now how serious life is and how awful! How can things be pleasant here below? Blemish was on the world. What use was it to make a row? Better to sit in quiet society in chapel and listen to good preaching....

And Sir Rufus Morgan rode up the valley on his fine black horse the day after Dan Roberts's last behaviour. To see for himself what damage had been done to his offices. This was a courageous act and he rode without policemen accompanied. And subtle. For unassailable majesty sat the horse, a mass of proud flesh poured into black and white check clothes and baked to a haughty stiffness. His neck burst out of a high collar and held in purple-tinted pride the great red face with the thundering brows and the massive nose that could have given home to a couple of foxes. The pomp of ages sat the horse. It was a picture worth seeing, and indeed, as the word passed up the streets that Sir Rufus was approaching, people clustered out to have a look at the old rascal, the famous nose plunging before him. He gave colour to the drab winter day. Lord of all, sustained by divine right, flesh born to rule. Babies were held up to see the sight— for Sir Rufus did not appear often in the squalid ugly streets. He passed on unseeing, as though nothing were about but the royal mountains, fit background for him, and himself.

V

On New Year's Eve a man emerged from one of the Terrace alleys carrying a live goose in his arms. He spoke soothingly to the bird, gradually calming its agitation at the journey, and by the time they had reached Doctor Morris's house the goose had settled obediently. There was an affection between the two. He called her The Princess.

The door was opened by Mrs. Doctor Morris, dressed in red, with paper roses in her hair. Sounds of enjoyment came from behind her. She peered at the goose, which partly hid the man's face.

304

"Who is it, what d'you want?"

"It's me, Matt Lewis. I been invited."

"Oh, Matt! Come in, come in." She ushered him into the hall-way, where a gas-jet burned. The goose gave another nervous squawk. "Tudor invited the fowl, too?" she enquired. "Or is it ill?"

Matt stood the goose on a chair and stroked its trembling neck. "Because of the wife, Nellie, I brought her," he explained. "Please to find a little corner for her to lay safe. Nellie been mad to kill her since Christmas and I can't abear the thought of it. A bad row I had today with her and she was swearing she'd break into her coop tonight and do the job.... Come now, The Princess," he cooed, "don't you be frightened. Safe you are now."

Daisy was disposed to be sympathetic towards Nellie, considering the times. "A goose still alive doesn't seem right at this time of the year, Matt. But bring her in, bring her in. Put your cap up there."

"She's my pet," he said, carrying her into the sitting-room. "And a very 'telligent bird she is, with a taste for music."

"But you can't take her about everywhere, Matt," Daisy protested. "Will you take her down the pit with you when the strike's over?"

"When strike's over I'll be able to leave her safe—Nellie can buy proper red meat in a shop then." To his relief everybody in the sitting-room welcomed the goose, which, after some fussy observation of her new quarters, settled down watchfully on the coal-box. He felt easier with her under his eye; Nellie was quite capable of prowling round the house, though she had refused to come to the party.

Doctor Morris handed him a glass of beer. "Lord," he whispered, shy in the assembly, "only night 'fore last I was dreaming I was having a glass of beer again.... 'Ello, Melville, nice to see you back again... aye, a first-class New Year present for us all."

Losing his shyness, he slapped the just released prisoner on the back affectionately. "Pity you been missing our big strike, you'd have enjoyed the ructions."

Melville had become a little leaner. But prison seemed to have developed his spiritual look. And his thin, hollowed face, under its shoved-out mat of black hair, still suggested that his mind was in a perpetual Gethsemane. But it was obvious that he would be able to chuck away from himself any squalid influence of prison: he looked as if he had, in still greater measure his own kind of lean force, single and not to be deviated.

"I hear there's been better unison among the men this strike, Matt.... You been preaching too, I've been told." Matt had often been down in the house by the stream, trying to learn things.

"Oh," Matt said gloomily, "I got up once or twice and spoke as solemn as I could." He looked ashamed. "Seems as if," he growled, "we'll all be back in the pits next week. For all my preaching!" he winked.

"Never mind, Matt," comforted Melville, "we've got to work sometimes, to know what we're striking for. Let the God-damn wages sink lower still. As long as the men get into training as human beings asking things. That's *our* work."

"Sometimes," Matt sighed, "I look at my goose The Princess there, and I wish I had feathers and wings like her. I'd be off; I wouldn't stay. I'd be off over the sea! But there's no wings on me—no, and even on my feet four toes are missing from when I was under that fall in the pit...'Where are them old toes now?' I shout to myself sometimes, Nellie says, when I have my nightmares, and then I feel I got to stay in this place till my toes are found again, and I go searching all over the pit, in the dark." He shook his head. "Nightmares, nightmares, that's what I have."

"Matt," urged Melville, "you mustn't let yourself go thinking too much of that goose. She's getting to mean to you what death is to a lot of the religious people here. You *can't* fly away, Matt. You got to stay with us here and help do the job we've set ourselves. That'll help to cure you of the nightmares—"

Daisy thrust between them her head with its chaplet of red, white and blue paper roses. "Now, you two! Leave the strike alone. Come on, Matt, come over here—" She pulled him away.

306

The room was filling up. It was cheerful-looking. Paper streamers hung their rainbow tints from wall to wall, bunches of berried holly were stuck on top of pictures and in vases. Over Bronwen's chair was suspended a huge green bell of honeycombed paper. People talked in that brisk bustling manner common in their social meetings. At the piano a member of the strike committee was sitting singing a ballad about the lord of a Glamorgan castle, his wife, and another man whose head was chopped off long ago. A big white iced cake, brought by Bronwen, rested on top of the piano: it was for midnight, together with the six bottles of champagne she had wickedly brought, in spite of the strike.

Very grand in a billowy purple and grey satin gown, Bronwen sat in a high chair facing the room, beside the hearth. Her abundant hair was piled up in silver glory, real pink smudged her cheeks—for she was beginning to enjoy this party, in spite of her son Elwyn's silent disapproval as she set out in the hired carriage, which was collecting her again at twelve-thirty. And though still in mourning for her daughter-in-law, she had told herself stoutly that Tudor needed her presence at the party; she compromised by wearing dark purple and grey. She also liked a party.

Daisy had presented Matt to her. "I remember you," he stammered. "You was giving the prizes in Gosen festival in '89. The flute solo I was."

"And I can remember," she smiled, "not only you, but your grandfather, Obediah Lewis. He had his leg broken in two places in the floods of '74. My son set it for him.... Do you still play the flute?"

"Aye, and I brought it with me," he said, feeling an inner pocket. "I thought that if The Princess sitting there got cantankerous, I would play her a tune. A good ear she has for music—though where she hides it I don't know."

Daisy went to greet a new arrival, her friend Maud Powell, elocutionist—a gold-medalled one. Daisy's arms swarmed round her in affectionate gusto, though often enough she had quarrelled

307

with her poetry-reciting friend. She was alarmed that Maud would remain single to the end of her days.

Several men had tried to court her, but her habit of trying to improve them by reciting long passages of Welsh poetry had put them off and it looked as though she would remain for ever married only to her muse. This offended Daisy's sense of the fitness of things. Useless for Maud to declare grievously: "Men don't interest me, they leave me cold, I can't get warmed up about them—" Daisy was always trying to put men in her way. She looked round the room now calculatingly: there were a few single young colliers in the room.

"Here," Maud said hurriedly, "I've brought a box of mixed sweets." Unable to earn her living by reciting, she had opened a little sweet-shop. "Oh, the lovely goose!" she exclaimed. "Is it alive?"

Tudor was receiving two more guests: Beriah and his wife Susan. Beriah wore his black and a very high stiff collar usually reserved for funerals. Susan was beadily observant, not sure whether she ought to have come to this house about which things were said. Bronwen's presence, however, eased her; it was obvious that nothing shifty could flourish where she was. So Susan consented to remove her bonnet, though she sat in her gloves of black lace and kept as near Bronwen as possible.

Daisy was full of happy spirit. Let worries and problems and strikes be forgotten tonight. And her brother there too, safe out at last! She offered a sweet to the goose. "She likes it, she's eaten the jujube—" Her voice, palpitating with pleasure, cried through the room. She crouched blissfully before the snowy bird, caressing it. In her scarlet dress, well filled, she looked gay and resplendent. It was the same dress that she had worn at the police-court some months ago, though she had let out the seams.

Susan leaned over and said, her face dour with criticism: "A cold it has that you are keeping it indoors?"

"No," Daisy laughed. "She is Matt Lewis's pet."

"Oh. I thought a jujube you was giving it for a sore throat. Well, well." Susan struggled to suppress her outraged domestic sensibilities. Her glance grubbed about the coal-box, her nostrils trembled expectantly. "Awful to have a sore throat in a neck as long as this—" Daisy stroked the length of pulsing plumage. The goose was full of a current of white placidity now, accepting with unruffled boot-button eyes the festive room and the crooning caresses of the woman in red.

"Play your flute to her, Matt," someone called.

Matt took out his flute and, sitting in front of the bird, played very well a beautiful melody. And the goose bestirred herself, the squat white body quivering; she lifted her neck and lunged her head here and there, as if seeking to pluck the notes like corn out of the air. Her body shivered with chilly, gristly ecstasy, its sinews wheeling with strange down-dragging heaviness, while the long throat lifted itself and the head searched upwards. Then, as Matt continued, the snowy wings opened and beat, the black eyes glittered: she looked as though she would fly off, neck in tense search of some paradise of plumage and reedy pools, up beyond the paper streamers. Matt stopped in time. And the goose, slowly and with heavy dignity, lapsed back on to the coal-box, slackening her neck, folding her wings.

Tudor was sitting watching with Melville in the bay window. He was not sure that he liked the performance of the goose. It had a chilly deathly quality; the fowl had looked like some unhappy white ghost fastened into plumage and gristle. And out in the room a little quiet had fallen, broken soon by Daisy taking the box of sweets round. But the melody had been beautiful. "Do you know what that tune was?" he asked Melville.

"Wasn't it Gluck's 'Song of the Blessed Spirits in the Elysian Fields'? God knows where Matt picked it up.... The goose looked as though it was straining to get on those fields."

Tudor watched Daisy's scarlet progress about the room. "How well pleased with herself Daisy looks.... I've been waiting for you to tell me that your sister has married successfully, Melville."

Melville grinned. "She always had a physical calm. Now she positively shouts of ease. I hope she won't become smug."

"She was alarmed at first, thinking everybody's hand against her. She *could* have gone under. But after floundering about a bit, she breasted the little uproars as playfully as a dolphin." Tudor watched her taking a shy young committee-man in hand. "She's got no prejudices, she's had a wonderfully natural education."

"I could never get her to despise even the bourgeoisie," Melville sighed. "I had to give her up politically."

"She's no more political than a plum-tree, thank God. Look at her! She's bringing Hugh Watts into new life—he told me once he 'didn't hold with women', he looks on them as snares and dangers."

Melville watched his sister flooding the flushed, smiling Hugh with her resplendent glow, thrusting her arm under his, asking him flattering questions. "She was very useful as a decoy in my various campaigns, roping in young men and making them want to fight. She could make some stubborn ones sit up and want to do something about life." There was a slightly mocking sound in his voice, an obscure comment. Somewhere, deep in his soul, disillusion sat. And was kept buried.

"Sorry to have made her domestic, taken her out of your shocking clutches."

"You're entitled to her. And you'll make good use of her.... Some day when we've got things going on a prosperous basis, you'll be full of speeches in Westminster and she'll be at the end of your dinner-table with a swarm of the Party around her."

"More likely she'll be helping me to kick out the duns from this house. Hell," he exclaimed softly, suddenly serious, "it gives me gripe sometimes to think of the mess we're in here. In evil moments I even long traitorously for the strike to end, on any basis, so that some money will come in."

"Such people as us," Melville said, with unmoved calm, "are always in these disorders. We've got nothing and we've got to make something. In the other way of living they've got their easy age-long habits of achieving success—that ritual they call grit and brains, and so forth. We've chucked the ritual away and we're naked. We're bound to feel icy cold sometimes."

"Let's hope," Tudor said broodingly, "that we earn ourselves one decent garment before we're dead.... What we've got to guard ourselves against," he went on, pulling himself up, "is a feeling of frustration, of thwarted ambition. We can't afford to go inside ourselves and feel either triumph or disaster, we've just got to go on plunging about in the disorder of the world—large words, Melville, aren't they, for our little socialistic bouts in this valley? But—"

"What's going on in this valley," interrupted Melville, "is a fine early example of the struggle that's going to batter the whole world soon—next century perhaps, tomorrow!... Ah, bigger words, my boy!" He lifted his narrow hand, his voice was a mock preacher's. But his visionary eyes flashed the authentic fire.

They grinned at each other. But each knew that already they had achieved something concrete, out on that dark scowling valley beneath the house....

"Anyhow, we're starting the new century without any encumbrances. Quite naked," Tudor said. "Absolutely stark." He wondered how much longer he'd be able to keep the piano.

"*We* are. But not the country. A marvellous century the last has been. It's going out gasping with over-fed luxuriance.... But can't you hear some rumbles in the organs, slight little thunders of protest from below?"

"More than slight in this district. Menacing growls."

"Light will come!" And again Melville's voice mocked a preacher's, again he lifted a John the Baptist hand. "Murky and spluttering at first, then a sun, a sun!"

"Someone is giving a sermon in the bay-window," Daisy said out in the room, which buzzed with voices. She spoke jokingly, but a slight frown hovered about her nose. She wanted her brother to take a long rest, she wouldn't have him burning himself up in the manner of his former conferences with strikers and revolutionaries down in the house beside the stream. She wouldn't believe that he had got all the rest he wanted in jail. She thought he looked worn and ill. Actually he was in better physical condition than before.

Complaining that this was no time for private little confabs, she pulled him out into the room and sat him with Bronwen. Beriah's wife looked shiftily uncomfortable; this was the first time she had had contact with a man from prison. She behaved as though she expected vermin to swarm from him still. Bronwen was saying: "Daisy tells me you're very fond of ginger-nuts."

"She greeted me with a bag of them on the station yesterday." He glanced with uncertainty at the calm pink and silver face beside him. He half suspected that this fine-looking old lady concealed little nerve-shocks at her grandson's mingling with these rootless and disreputable people. That fondness for him triumphed, however. And that a sentimental rescue-impulse was at work behind these maternal conversational flourishes to himself, a bruised and suffering jail-bird. "She had made them, poor girl," he added in a harsh unyielding voice he often used on platforms. "But prison had either taken my taste away or Daisy had mixed them with sawdust—they had no more bite in them than a curate's prayer."

"I'm going to make you some, if you'll let me. No one in this place can make ginger-nuts to equal mine." Beriah's wife, in a hostile effort to be magnanimous said: "Yes, indeed. I remember you made them for our Sunday-school tea once, and the children fought very rough for them....Pale you're looking, Melville Walters. They treated you bad where you was?" she enquired roughly.

"I go pale on occasions." He turned yieldingly to Bronwen. "Put plenty of ginger in them," he whispered. "And a drop of brandy, if you've got it to spare."

"Indeed, yes. More than a drop. Even my Sunday-school ones had brandy. I was never one for teetotal ginger-nuts."

Ieuan Mold arrived, late. He grinned sheepishly in the doorway. His boxer's face, previously battered, was now entirely incoherent with fresh bruises and pushed-about bones. Tudor and Beriah glanced at each other when Daisy brought him in; they had been told he had been arrested in that Dan Roberts affair at the Aber

312

colliery. But triumph glistened over Ieuan's green and purple complexion, over his livid eyes and the squashed tomato colour of his lips. All the same, he sidled into the room along the wall and swung a difficult glance at the curtained window.

The room settling down after the apparition, Tudor took him aside with a glass of beer, which was drunk at one swig, and asked if anyone had seen him approach the house.

"I came down from the mountain at the back ," Ieuan answered, beginning to beam, greenishly, in the festive room. "I been hiding in a bloke's house over in the Garw Vale. Hello, Melville, how was quod? They got new feather beds in Cardiff jail yet? They used to be lousy."

"Hish," warned Daisy, who had come over with a plate of cake, "hish, Ieuan, there's ladies here." Presently she took him over to Bronwen, who was being continually used as a beneficent influence. Beriah's wife at last got up and went over to sit by Maud Powell, the next most respectable-seeming person in the room. The elocutionist looked as though she were reserving judgment on the party.

Bronwen was startled and compassionate at the squashed face presented to her. She wasn't told of its connection with the dreadful Dan Roberts tragedy. "Hadn't Tudor better dress it for you?" she asked in grandmotherly distress.

"It's had wuss in its time," Ieuan assured her. "And it always comes back dainty as a rose. Don't you worry 'bout it. There's no pain now. What's that goose doing 'ere?"

And after a minute she was laughing at his jokes.

Soon, however, the front-door bell clanged loudly. Everyone stopped talking and glanced hurriedly at Ieuan. The black-gloved hands of Beriah's wife beat agitatedly. A man with a face like Ieuan's and with his manner of entering a room, must surely have the police in pursuit. Then Daisy's cool deep voice said:

"That must be Hannah. She said she'd be late."

But Ieuan as a precaution went to the back door, while Hannah was admitted. She strode into the room like a wind, swishing her skirts. Bronwen knew her history, though they had never met. An old-timer of the strikes, she had plunged into a dangerous riot once to try and rescue her brother whom she had seen from an upper window dropping under truncheon blows: she had been in hospital three months as a result. When she wanted to earn some extra money she would join the sturdy bunch of women who comb the tips of the collieries for odd pieces of coal—having collected a hundredweight, slinging the sack across her shoulders and offering it for sale in the streets. She wore tonight a blatantly new white silk shawl, grandly holding a bunch of it at her bosom while she swept in.

"People beginning to sing and dance in the Terraces," she said, "though everybody is sober. New century's going to come in bone-dry here. Hope it won't keep like that."

Daisy looked at the shawl, Hannah looked at Daisy. Daisy had seen it in the draper's Christmas window, before the riots. She couldn't help looking shocked; for once she was at a loss. Neither Hannah nor anyone known to her could possibly afford a shawl like that in these times.

Hannah did not seem disposed to remove the shawl in the warm room. After shrieking with laughter at the goose, she sat preening herself in the lacy silk folds and chatted with Bronwen.

"Oh God," Daisy prayed, nervously shaking up the box of sweets—there seemed only aniseed-balls left for Hannah—"don't let the police come here tonight."

Hannah loudly declared: "A disgrace it is. Pitowners ought to let bygones be bygones and have barrels of beer set up at corner of every street. No sense they have. Strike would be over tomorrow then. Everybody starving and in rags."

"Nice shawl you got there, Hannah," Ieuan, who had slithered back into the room, observed. And he managed a horrible wink.

"Oh, Ieuan, your face!" Hannah rubbed her stomach as if in pain. "Take it away and lay it in a bread poultice for a month.... Daisy, haven't you got a bit of old veil he can put over it for tonight?"

Ieuan, who had gusts of passion for Hannah, began to bait her.

Soon they were insulting each other. So Daisy coaxed Maud Powell to recite some poetry.

Maud stood in the middle of the room, right under the yellow gas-light, and, striking a fierce pose, broke into a craggy piece of Welsh poetry. About old kings and things: Cadwaladr and oaks, Lud of the Silver Hand, flowers and Merlin, wild Lear and gay King Cole. And she recited as though these long-ago persons were still just outside in the streets that very moment. She sat by Savaddan lake, among the gloomy Beacons, and once more invited the faithful birds to open their singing throats and proclaim the rightful ruler of the scarred lands. Her voice was on the mournful side, but it could call up pictures.

The room listened respectfully. But the worst of Maud was that once well started she was apt to go on for ever. Yet she was modest about her gift; and though many people said she made up the poetry as she went along, she denied this—her own reply was that she was only a spout through which poetry comes. Daisy had been friendly with her since they were babies, so she could take advantage of Maud's gaze sweeping near her now and make a sign, bringing a detailed description of an Arthurian banquet to an early close.

Everybody, except Beriah's wife, then accepted refreshment, congratulating Maud on her gift. Maud went back into her puffy appearance of a gold-medalled celebrity, sitting by Bronwen, who asked her if she knew the poems of Howel ap Gethin, an eighteenth-century bard:

"—in my father's house in Pembroke shire we had an old harp that had belonged to him. He wrote a lot of songs about fish. There was one about a salmon—how does it go—" She searched in her remote childhood but could not remember the words.

Maud shook her head. "I don't know any poems about fish." She dealt mostly with warriors, big happenings, great ladies watching from castle towers. "I've never heard of Howel ap Gethin."

But Bronwen was now brooding over the peaceful country of

her childhood, with its ancient farms, its drowsy landscapes ever covered in unsullied silver dew for her. She had seen a long lifetime of industrial troubles since then, the growth of a great clanging industry, the spitting up of the earth into stormy upheavals, a race of dispossessed people scrambling for new understanding of the world. The romantic poetry she had just heard made her sigh, though she had always said that it was no good crying for the past. She pulled herself up with a jerk and said to Maud: "Howel ap Gethin ran off with a great-aunt of mine. She could play his harp and they wandered over Wales earning a few pence and a meal by giving recitals in farm-houses. I used to think that must have been a pleasant life. But Howel used to beat her and get drunk and she came back alone with her feet ruined, half her teeth gone and thin as a rake. She died in consumption."

"Perhaps she had been in love with him," Maud said sentimentally.

"Perhaps." Bronwen was gazing dreamily on an agate ring on her right hand. "She taught Howel's songs to my mother and asked for the harp she had stolen off him to be buried with her. But it wasn't. My mother thought it ought not to be wasted in the earth." Out in the room Hannah was flinging her arms round Melville's neck, enveloping him in shawl: she had been helping herself rapidly to the beer. "Oh, Melville, *cariad*," she sang, "nice it is to see your serious old face again. Was it awful in jail? A pity you been missing this strike. And now the rodneys are going back again with their tails under their legs—" She kissed with gusto his austere lips. "I wish you'd marry me, Melville, a first-class wife I'd make you. The bobbies would never cop you again."

"I couldn't keep you, Hannah," he laughed. "You're too fond of the bottle."

"I can go collecting coal on the tips, I can take in washing like Daisy used to before she married so grand; I can have lodgers and make rag mats, and in the summer I can brew small beer out of nettles. Marry me, Melville!" She hung to his shoulders, amorous and rolling seductive eyes.

Ieuan cried from his squashed lips: "Ach, the woman's awful and awful! Leave the man be, gel. Can't you see Melville's suffered enough just now in quod."

"Ieuan," Hannah called, "what your mother done with all those baby's napkins she used to have? Surely she got one to spare to put your horrible face in."

"Ah," she snapped in contempt, "ah. Her in her shawl!"

Beriah's wife went to her husband and privately plucked his sleeve. "Surely time to go it is now?" she whispered.

Beriah had been telling Tudor of the rumour he had heard on the way up, that the Associated Owners were going to make a new offer the next day. Five per cent increase. But that treacherous Sliding Scale rate to stand. And at the mass meetings to be held on New Year's Day, he added bitterly, the first day of the new century, he was sure there would be almost unanimous acceptance of the bastard terms. "Susan," he said testily, "what's the matter with you? Go and sit with the ladies."

"Susan," Tudor said, "I've just remembered I've kept some port for you. But let me see your tongue first."

Sulkily she put out her tongue. "Better, better," he nodded. "The strike's done one good thing. Now you shall have some real port.... Never mind Beriah" he grunted darkly—"we've only just begun, after all. The new century's not going to lie flat."

As midnight approached there was a clamour outside the house. A contingent of Terrace folk, hearing a party was in progress in the doctor's house, had clustered round. Everybody knew he was dirt-poor, but still there was a party, and no doubt a doctor could get credit in the shops.... So children began to sing under the windows and their elders swooped across the garden.

"Oi, open the doors and the windows. Doctor Morris, Doctor Morris! Let's hear the music and see the fun."

Daisy stood in the middle of the room her head lifted, her full figure swaying, but caught in lamentation. "I wish I had tons of food," she burst out, "tons of food and shovelfuls of sovereigns! They're hungry, they're cold, they've got nothing."

"They're singing!" Bronwen murmured. Older voices had joined the children's. They sang a Christmas carol.

Ieuan croaked, shaking his battered head: "No Christmas they had, poor dabs."

"Whose fault is that?" Susan mumbled, half to herself and flashing a disagreeable look at several people in the room.

"Shall I recite to them?" Maud suggested to Daisy.

It was all she could offer. "From the window."

"The children will be knocking soon," Bronwen said. "Give me my purse, Daisy—it's with my bonnet. There's some shillings in it."

"They sing like angels," Tudor said.

"There's courage in their voices," Melville said. "Trumpets and morning."

"I hope my Nellie isn't with them," Matt muttered, "after The Princess." He had gone to the drowsy bird.

It wanted a few minutes to midnight. Tudor had brought out the champagne and the glasses and cups. Daisy threw up the window and leaned out. The gaslight streamed on about fifty people. From the Terraces below came the noise of singing voices, dancing, shouts. But of the sober kind. They were doing what they could on bread and dripping, a few bones and weak tea. Coaxing voices shouted hints from the garden.

"Now then, Mrs. Morris, a happy New Year..."

"Play the piano to us—"

"Tap the barrel—"

"Throw out the meat patties—"

It was the custom for roving bands of children to go round on New Year's Day seeking gifts of the bigger houses and the shops. This time they were early and accompanied by their elders. They were out there in the dark bleak night, determined to extract something out of the festival, however lean. The children were knocking at the door now.

"Come in," Daisy cried in an exultant voice, "all of you! Come in and have what we've got. Come in, come in."

Melville gazed ironically at Tudor, who grinned back. The

318

presence of champagne would give some pretty ideas of non-existent riches. And with all that money owing to him in the Terraces. But he did not try to intercept Daisy in her grand red-billowing sweep to the front door.

The children came in first. Their faces glistened as though with frost, their clear mountain eyes, set roundly among lithe bones, stared hesitatingly over the festive room. The sight of the goose eased them. And, yes, one girl was carrying a Rhodd Calennig, sacrificing a valuable apple. It was stuck properly with oats and a sprig of evergreen.

"Oh, my dear!" Bronwen called, moved to a flush of happy pleasure. "Come here." She knew about the old custom. "Who made you that?"

The child went hesitatingly to Bronwen, holding out the apple. As she expected, Bronwen found that the Rhodd Calennig had been made by a country-sick Terrace woman, the girl's mother, who had wandered from Pembrokeshire to these hard, fighting valleys. "Will you give me the Rhodd Calennig?" she asked the child.

The little girl, who had a thin chilly face, looked at her carefully: she was not going to hand over the precious apple too imprudently. And then she saw that the old lady was holding a purse; she was opening it. "You must give it to me and it will bring me good fortune."

Clutching the apple hard, the girl waited while the old lady peered into her purse. She did not intend letting it go under sixpence: she was dazzled when a halfcrown shone under her eyes. Her hand trembled as she snatched the coin. And immediately, after pushing the apple into Bronwen's hand, she darted away into the crowd that swarmed into the room, her cold face tense with fear that the old lady would discover her mistake of giving a half-crown for a penny.

The room was filled with clamouring voices: the elders had followed the children in. Most of them had been patients with Tudor. All were stone sober and looked bleakly baulked of something. But they kept up a shrill patter of festival exclamations. Known to most of them as one of their fighters, Melville was lionised, everybody shaking his hand and welcoming him back.

"Oh, a nice warm room, and bottles, and cake. Doctor Morris, Doctor Morris, you been left money!"

"They're all gifts," he shouted, laughing. "But help yourselves."

Daisy staggered in from the kitchen carrying a tray covered with more cakes, fruit, large loaves of white bread, a dish of butter and a pot of jam.

"Corn in Egypt!" bellowed a young Terrace man for whom Tudor had recently got a free truss.

A woman lowered her patched baby-smelling shawl off her bony head and sang: "We was all saying to go and wish New Year to Doctor and Mrs. Morris. Well, well, our noses knew where to turn. What's that there in the bottles, Mrs. Morris, under those gold corks?"

The bells of St. John's began to clatter. But no colliery hooters shrieked in the New Year, even though it was the first of a new century. The room became packed, the passage outside was full. They roared. "Happy New Year! Happy New Century!" Around the table there was good-humoured struggling for the cups and glasses, filled by Tudor and Melville. None of the proper guests got champagne. At the piano Eli Bowen was playing the one tune he had taught himself: *Jerusalem the Golden*.

"—With mi-ilk and hon-ney blest—" a crystal soprano voice sang happily.

"Something more cheerful, Eli," a woman protested. "Ach, not a funeral we are, surely?"

In a corner Matt Lewis was squatting on the floor with the goose on his lap, even though a neighbour assured him that Nellie was not in the crowd. Bronwen, who had distributed all her cash, sat guarding a fragile-looking little girl on her lap. She was thinking, in relief, that her grandson would be sure to get some sort of living out of these friendly Terrace people—when the pits were working: they would remain loyal, give him a living.

320

They had cleared all the victuals: the children quarrelled over the aniseed-balls. Tudor locked the surgery door. For they were clamouring:

"Now what about some pills, Doctor Morris, and a drop of tonic. Come now, New Year gifts !"

"Yes, pills, pills—"

"That peppermint medicine—"

"Bandage for my leg!"

"Sulphur tablets."

But Daisy was calling with determined authority: "This way out. Time to close. New Year's in. This way out."

They began to go. A few women surged round Daisy and began to tell her a long list of troubles. She beckoned them into the kitchen. And she distributed to them rashers of bacon, a few eggs, potatoes, a packet of tea: one, catching sight of a bottle of sauce, begged it for her gammy-legged husband Emrys, who hadn't done a stroke of work for three years. Receiving it, the woman laid her hand on Daisy's body:

"A good woman you are, Daisy Morris. Bless what's here, as I can see. May him be as strong as a mountain if a boy, handsome as yourself if a girl." And she grizzled a little, wiping a few tears away with a grimy hand: she went out with the last of the Terrace crowd.

At the door Bronwen's hired carriage was waiting. She appeared muffled and bonneted, Tudor's arm about her shoulder, Daisy's round her waist. "It was beautiful, beautiful," she was whispering. "I'm glad I came, I enjoyed myself much more than I would have done at the minister's"—where Tudor's father was unrelentingly spending New Year's Eve. She peered into the valley night, at the mountain shapes. "Oh, look, a bonfire!"

Far away on the mountain-top at the head of the valley big flames leapt, golden and red. They lit up the green earth, they licked the stars. Small figures, aboriginal-looking, could be seen leaping about in its glow. There was wild singing down in the valley.

"Some young people dancing about on the mountains," Bronwen murmured, "surely?...Well, heartening it is to see them like that."

"A time to dance!" Tudor shouted, now between Bronwen and Daisy, arms about them. "And a time to laugh!" All night he had been staving away thoughts of the strike's failure.

"Let's hope it will never be one to weep," sighed Daisy, with prompt sententiousness. "The sun rises and it sets," she added, with solemnity. The mysterious valley night, the mountain fire, the wild singing, the crackling stars, seemed to invite the utterance of such thoughts.

Bronwen moved to the carriage; the driver was waiting at the door. She felt divided. She did not want to go, she wanted to remain in Daisy's warmth, in Tudor's young urgent regard and with his planning for the future. And she wanted to go: far back in her mind she felt cold and a little frightened. While they tucked her into the rugs, she said:

"Well, it's been a full century for me. I've seen such a lot of things come to pass. I'm ready to go any time. My eyes have had their full share. Railways and collieries and strikes and riots; people going hungry, people disbelieving in God; Queen Victoria; balloons taking men to the sky, people saying we are little better than apes; and all this socialism—oh dear, what's this century going to bring to *you*?"

Tudor pushed her hands into the astrakhan muff.

"We're hoping men will become much better than apes," he said.

She shook her head a trifle gloomily. The driver settled himself on his seat and took up his long whip. Then she beamed out on them. "Well, you're two healthy children, anyhow. Happy New Century!"

"Happy New Century, Bronwen."

The carriage creaked out on to the bumpy road skirting the ends of the Terraces. Daisy, who had come out without a coat, had begun to shiver and ran back into the house. Someone was playing the piano, thumping it truculently: probably Ieuan Mold. She would have to beg forgiveness that none of the invited guests had been able to get any of that precious champagne. Ah well, a pot of good tea—

The fire on the far mountain-top still burned in red brilliance, the golden figures still danced. He stood leaning against the porch, watching them, breathing the cold mountain-smelling air. They were dancing on the green heights, abandoned to the ancient magic of the night, obeying some wild liberated impulse of their ancient blood, up there under the clear untarnished stars. They were dancing in a bubble of brilliant light, in a fragile golden globe magically released in space, floating in free boundless heights. They were calling on the ancient powers of ecstasy, of freedom, of fiery light, of untrammelled movement.... He stood watching them and saw them as abstractions of the tenacious beauty that still clung to their world. And at the same time, smiling to and at himself, he thought that if it wasn't for the strike those dancers would probably be down in the valley dead drunk on beer and stuffed with a celebrating feast of onioned cold poultry and cake.... But something had to be done about the death of the old century, the birth of the new: better than nothing a bonfire and a dance, in spite of empty stomachs.

Below, the raw grimy habitations were flung down in corrupt disorder, rotting husks, ugly and mean. But they seethed and sprouted with life, a confusion of fertility, rank and vigorous, evil and beautiful. Waste, stupidity and brutality ran in disorder through the place. But also there was a music, a magic, a calling forth of old deep powers, a leaping out of stagnation, a sharp clean thrusting of green leaves from grimy trees, from bulbs half rotted in the winter cold earth....

And he saw that the women did not lean exhausted breasts against dead mountains, that the men had within them the power of enquiry. Yet... could they, did they *want* to walk on the mountain-tops and look down on the world, not as a hovel where they were obliged to live a life of anxious battling with poverty, but as a country they might alter to their desires? Yes, he murmured to himself, yes... in their way, in their disorderly half-blind way. And they would listen. Gloomy from old repression they would listen, laughing from still older mirth, they would listen. For long they had been trying to tear open the heavens and peer therein for the perfection denied them in the acrid earth. Let them return to the earth and see that there lay their strength and their faith.

The old, old anguish beat up in him as he stood there breathing into his living lungs the cold sharp mountain air. What was it, what was it! A longing for lost beauty, an ache for a loveliness beyond mortal possibility, a bitter, bitter torment of despair that life would never yield the richness demanded by the soul?... He lifted his clenched hand in a sudden unconscious gesture and beat his breast in a movement of wild baffled agony. Would that anguish ever be stilled!

Tumult and disorder, frustration, wages, strikes, riots debts— were these to be his world? The architecture of his earth was a muddle of low squat evil dwellings in which lived an aboriginal race dispossessed of any original dignity it may have held. What right had he to extravagant flights of idealism about these people? Matt's chilly deathly-looking goose was their symbol, all they had of yearning for beauty. For them no elegant swans basking on lilied lakes. A domestic alleyway goose dragging grimy feet over rank earth—that was their emblem. Ugliness, squalor and meanness was their portion.

And yet, and yet.... He would stay, struggle, go among them with an intent watching. They were the world with its beauty, mystery and pain; they fought and yielded, they were garlanded and they were battered. They had the full tarnished brilliance of life in them... . And he began to laugh, with a soft low sound half caught in his throat. He was laughing at himself, and at the people who were about him. Oh, life... rich, yes, it had all the soul demanded.

Luxuriously, preposterously, abandonedly rich. And always a new earth and a new heaven to discover.

Daisy came out, searching for him. "When are you coming in, Tudor? Why are you staying here all this time?" She peered up at him. His head was half hidden in his arm, which leant against a post of the porch. She lifted her hand and laid it gently on his chest. "My love, my love—" she whispered.

And she clung to him in a quiet passion of awareness, of soft gentle abandonment to his silence, his dark, half-hidden face. She laid her head on his shoulder and tears began to roll out of her eyes. Then he turned and, glancing up in her anguish of obscure grieving, she saw that he was smiling. He was laughing, he was shivering with laughter.

"Why," she whispered, "I thought you were grieving about something... worrying about us."

"Grieving, no! Why should I grieve?" His hand tightened about her, he began to move with her into the house. "With all this wealth."

"Well, it's a kind of wealth," she said. Her warm strong hand was within his. "And it's enough for me."

"Life's not going to fail us, I promise," he said urgently. "We've got too good a hold on it. I'm afraid there'll never be much money, but we've got healthy minds, Daisy, we're not greedy. Laugh, for God's sake, laugh."

"Why, I am!" she said. And she smiled, going into the sitting-room, where the others were sitting quietly talking, the goose being fast asleep.

Chris Williams is Professor of History and Head of the School of History, Archaeology and Religion at Cardiff University. He has written extensively on the history of the South Wales coalfield, including *Democratic Rhondda: Politics and Society, 1885-1951* (1996) and *Capitalism, Community and Conflict: The South Wales coalfield, 1898-1947* (1998). He edited *The Richard Burton Diaries* (2012) and currently leads the Heritage Lottery Fund supported project Cartooning the First World War in Wales: www.cartoonww1.org.

LIBRARY OF WALES

The Library of Wales is a Welsh Government project designed to ensure that all of the rich and extensive literature of Wales which has been written in English will now be made available to readers in and beyond Wales. Sustaining this wider literary heritage is understood by the Welsh Government to be a key component in creating and disseminating an ongoing sense of modern Welsh culture and history for the future Wales which is now emerging from contemporary society. Through these texts, until now unavailable or out-of-print or merely forgotten, the Library of Wales will bring back into play the voices and actions of the human experience that has made us, in all our complexity, a Welsh people.

The Library of Wales will include prose as well as poetry, essays as well as fiction, anthologies as well as memoirs, drama as well as journalism. It will complement the names and texts that are already in the public domain and seek to include the best of Welsh writing in English, as well as to showcase what has been unjustly neglected. No boundaries will limit the ambition of the Library of Wales to open up the borders that have denied some of our best writers a presence in a future Wales. The Library of Wales has been created with that Wales in mind: a young country not afraid to remember what it might yet become.

Dai Smith

LIBRARY OF WALES
FUNDED BY

Noddir gan
Lywodraeth Cymru

Sponsored by
Welsh Government

CYNGOR LLYFRAU CYMRU
WELSH BOOKS COUNCIL

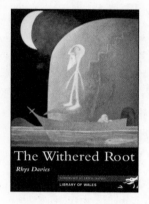

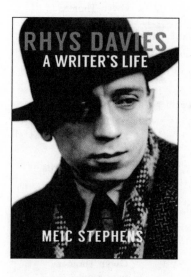

"[Meic] has done more than justice...to the black humour of Davies' writing and that of his life. This is a delightful book, which is itself a social history in its own right, and funny."
The Spectator

"In writing this informative, intriguing biography, Meic Stephens has done the reading public a great service."
Wales Arts Review

The first full biography of the important Welsh writer and a milestone in Welsh biographical writing.

Protecting his privacy and fearing intrusion into his inner life, such a man presents challenges for the biographer which Meic Stephens accepts with alacrity. Drawing on hitherto unavailable sources, including many conversations with the writer's brother, he describes the early years of the Blaenclydach grocer's son, his bohemian years in Fitzrovia and visit to the Lawrences in the south of France, his love-hate relationship with the Rhondda, and above all, the dissembling that went into *Print of a Hare's Foot* (1969), 'an autobiographical beginning', which he shows to be a most unreliable book from start to finish...

BIOGRAPHY

www.parthianbooks.com

28·11·14

ROGERSTONE